INVESTIGATION INTO AN IMPOSSIBILITY

"What about symptoms, Mrs. Yablonski?" Hammond asked. "Anything physical—?"

"Oh, God—I've seen him wake up in a cold sweat, shaking, even babbling. Sometimes, just for the first few seconds, I could swear he's trying to get it out, to tell me, but he just can't! Then he lapses into this utterly awful state. He's . . . so helpless . . ." She covered her eyes for a moment. . . .

"There is something else," she said. "Several times I woke up and found him out of bed, across the room at the window, or on the floor, or holding onto a chair. . . . Once I woke up before he started screaming. . . . I saw him at the wall . . ." She stopped, shivering at the memory. "I saw him at the wall. He . . . he was stepping *through it.*" She looked up at Hammond, frightened. *"From the next room."*

Other books by George E. Simpson
and Neal R. Burger

GHOSTBOAT

THIN AIR

GEORGE E. SIMPSON
and
NEAL R. BURGER

A DELL BOOK

Published by
Dell Publishing Co., Inc.
1 Dag Hammarskjold Plaza
New York, New York 10017

ISBN: 0-440-18709-5

Printed in the United States of America
First printing—January 1978
Second printing—April 1978
Third printing—May 1978

For Jean and Maureen

ACKNOWLEDGMENTS

Our deepest thanks to Jeanne F. Bernkopf, manuscript editor, whose ideas were as sharp as her pencil; to William R. Grose, Editor-in-Chief, Dell Publishing Company, Inc., for support and deadlines and good sense; and to Stuart M. Miller, our far-seeing literary agent and good friend.

In gratitude for help and assistance: Donald E. Baruch, Chief, Audio-Visual Production Branch, Department of Defense; Kenneth Dorward, friend and consultant; Lieutenant Kathy Gray, USNR, Navy Office of Information, Los Angeles Branch, California; Daryl Henry, friend and consultant; Chief William A. Liedtke, USN; James Mallison, Manager, Quality Engineering Laboratories, Douglas Aircraft, Long Beach, California; Petty Officer First Class Frank E. Presby, USN.

1

Four cranes loomed like sentinels in the fog—steel frameworks dulled by the mists swirling over the Navy Yard.

There was the clanking sound of the anchor chain running, then a splash. The shudder of the deck beneath his feet as the engines stopped.

His footsteps echoed loud on the wooden deck as he turned to the others.

Fletch, old buddy! We gonna do it today?

Looks that way, he answered—as he always did.

He saw the ripple of apprehension, and felt it, too. Always the same every time.

The captain jumped down to the forward deck and droned orders at them. *Form up—everybody in a circle—maintain hand contact—*

He stiffened when the alarm sounded. In reflex, his arms shot out, grabbing the two outstretched hands on either side.

The humming tone started low and distant, from behind the bridge and below. He felt the vibration building up through his shoes.

Then the deck started to go.

The dark caulking strips lost color, then definition. The wood faded.

The circle moved, each man trying to draw closer to his neighbor.

He shifted, adjusted his position, and stared aft, locking onto the bridge.

The deck! Look at the deck! someone yelled.

He swung his eyes down, then sucked air.

The deck had vanished.

Beneath his feet, he saw the vague outline of what must have been the chain locker. And below that—nothing.

Nothing except the dark waters of the river.

The humming tone climbed the scale, piercing through his body. A force gathered and swelled with the rush of noise.

The circle of men writhed, contracting like a mindless animal in pain. He watched a man's features contort with fear, the mouth moving, trying to form words that never came. The man's face vanished. All that remained was his right leg.

He watched the dismembered limb jerk back and forth in empty space, riding the roll of the invisible deck.

Harold Fletcher sat bolt upright in bed—screaming.

His terrified wife switched on a bedside lamp.

She ripped a hand free from his iron grip and cradled her husband's head against her breast. An hour later his heaving sobs finally subsided.

2

Hammond bit at his toast and leaned back in the chair to read the telegram once again. An autumn breeze stirred the curtains and he glanced up at them. They were hers. She had bought them and put them up herself—the girl in the telegram. Girl, hell. Woman.

He reached into his shirt and scratched his chest, looking out the window and down at the still green waters of the C&O. The Chesapeake and Ohio Canal ran right through Hammond's front yard. The locks were only two blocks away, the barge landing even closer than that.

They used to walk together—he and this woman—down the cobblestone bike path that had once been the old canal towing road, and they had picnicked together on the grass fronting the canal.

Jan Hoyle . . . she had long brown hair, huge green eyes, a pillowy body, and tanned skin. After their last fight she had walked out on him, left Georgetown forever, and he hadn't heard from her since. Almost two years ago, this coming Christmas.

Now, out of the blue, he'd received a telegram:

> ARRIVING WASHINGTON SEVENTEENTH. URGENT MUST SEE YOU. SAVE LUNCH MONDAY. LOVE JAN.

Today was Monday. Hammond pushed his toast aside and got up with the wire. He had read it four times since getting home Friday. It had haunted him all weekend. All the feelings he had worked so hard to bury had come rushing back to the surface: how much he had loved her once, how furious he had been when she'd left him.

About two a.m. last night he'd been unable to sleep. He had gotten up, had taken a long slug of brandy, and then had come to a smug conclusion: she wanted him back.

He had gone back to sleep feeling satisfied, but this morning the doubts were stronger than ever.

Damn the woman. And damn Western Union.

He glanced at his watch. She would probably call him at work. He thought about making a reservation at one of the Pentagon restaurants and the glorious folly of staging a *scene* for the benefit of tired generals and admirals.

Hammond was feeling nasty and self-righteous. He imagined all sorts of entrances, greetings, thrusts, and ripostes . . . but in the back of his head nagged the thought that revenge wasn't justified. Yes, *she* had left *him*, but after three years of living together the subject of marriage had finally come up and he had said no. She had been shocked and hurt and had demanded to know why. He couldn't bring himself to tell her about his divorce: *that* he'd never told anyone.

At twenty-two, he had married a high school cheerleader just turned eighteen. The marriage lasted two months, just long enough for him to get his first sailing orders and for her to find a sugar-daddy.

The experience had even soured him on being at sea. Never again did he want to be caught in that position. So he finished his tour, then had gone back to get his pilot's wings and served a hitch in Naval Air. Today he was a "zoomie," attached to Naval intelligence, a land-locked career man from a family of sailors. And he'd never remarried. The reason why was a secret even to him, because he tried never to think about it.

So he had given Jan his customary line of poop about marriage: that it wasn't for him, it was too demanding, and these days nobody had to anyway. She had listened with the hurt building to tears, then she had taken a swing at him and called him names. She called him "liar" so many times he began to believe it.

In the two years since she had left, he had somehow managed to convince himself that it was all her fault, that they could have lived quite comfortably without the little ties that bind if she hadn't been so old-fashioned. Now, here she was on his doorstep again, and he was totally unprepared. What could she possibly want from him?

He glanced at his face reflected in the toaster and wondered what the attraction was. She wouldn't come back to him just for sex, would she? He felt a tingling of interest.

He finished his coffee quickly and pushed his cup and plate into the sink. He lived in a four-hundred-dollar one-bedroom apartment in an old two-story Dutch townhouse. He had a kitchen, a living room, and a small den which he had converted to an office after Jan had moved out.

He loaded his briefcase and stood for a moment, taking stock of himself again. I'm thirty-eight, he thought, unmarried. No immediate prospects, but no anxieties about it either. I've got a flat, a car, a job, and plenty of accrued leave. I can have any woman I want, within reason, and with no strings attached . . . so why am I alone?

He scowled at himself and cursed Jan again. He reached for his uniform blouse and cap. He was out the door and walking over to Thomas Jefferson Street a moment later.

In Washington, no one paid attention to the tall figure in uniform. Navy commanders were a dime a dozen in the nation's capital. Hammond jumped into his Ford Maverick and drove up to M Street, joining the flow of traffic headed west across the Key Bridge.

He parked in the north lot and walked across the grass to the Mall Entrance of the Pentagon. He cleared past the guard and went up the escalators to the third floor where he entered a door marked Naval Investigative Service, Pentagon Branch, Room C-630.

Hammond stopped at the receptionist's desk and gave her the required morning smile. She smiled back, pulled her blouse straight, and reached around for a stack of memos and TWX's. She handed them over ceremoniously and announced, "The director will be around to see you in twenty minutes, sir."

"Thanks." Hammond walked into the Pit, a long room with glassed-in cubicles on either side of a wide aisle. Most of his co-workers were already in: he could hear chairs creaking, typewriters clacking, and voices droning on telephones. The daily drudge for the ten to twenty Navy officers on duty at this branch of the NIS. Yet they were supposed to be an elite task force, answerable only to the director. Some elite. Their operations were an unending exercise of clearing through red tape, bureaucratic hierarchies, and their own internal filing procedures. Much the same as any other government institution.

Hammond entered his cubicle in the center of the aisle, the only one big enough to hold a second desk.

"Coffee, sir?"

He glanced at Ensign Just-Ducky: gorgeous, but a walking block of ice, except for the amenities.

"Black or brown?" she inquired with a stewardess' smile.

"One of each," Hammond smiled back. She ducked out, taking orders down the aisle. Hammond dropped the papers onto his desk and took Jan's telegram out of his pocket, slipping it under the phone so he wouldn't forget lunch. Already he found himself torn between hope and dread for her call.

He flipped quickly through the memos and tossed them into action slots. Most went under FILE, but three crept into SOON, and one into HOT.

Ensign Just-Ducky returned with his coffee. He started sipping the black and then the phone rang.

"A Mrs. Fletcher for you, Commander. She says you probably remember her as a Miss Hoyle."

He was very still for a moment. *Mrs. Fletcher.* So she was married. He punched into the line and said softly, "Hello, Jan."

"Nicky."

There was an embarrassed silence at both ends. "I got your wire," he said. "Where are you calling from?"

"The Watergate. Harold's firm keeps a company apartment here."

"You're married," he said flatly.

"Yes."

"Is . . . is he with you?"

"Not now. He's at a meeting. Nicky, would you have lunch with us?"

Us, he thought. All his fantasies that she might be after him again were dispelled.

"You want me to meet him?" God, I must sound slow, he thought.

"Yes."

"Why?"

"It's very involved, Nicky. And unfair, I know. . . . After all this time . . ."

"You better explain."

"Just a second—"

He heard the phone rattle as she put it down and moved away. He waited patiently, hearing something rustle, then a sharp intake of breath—a sob?

"I'm really scared, Nick . . ."

"Of what?"

"Harold."

Hammond choked back a laugh. He had visions of the man she had married: some hulking Boris Karloff slinking through the corridors of a ritzy hotel, hand outstretched for a quick strangle. . . .

"Not the way you think," she was saying. "He's been very good to me . . . but he's got this problem . . . and I'm at my wit's end trying to cope with it. . . . So is he."

Hammond felt something tighten across his chest. He had a sudden desire not to hear any more. He didn't even want to imagine Harold's problem and he felt certain she was going to tell him over the phone.

He drained his black coffee. For a moment, all he could think about was the objective reality: old girl friend calls up because her marriage is rocky. If he had ever wanted revenge, this was perfect, although distasteful.

"Jan, I'd like to help you, but I don't know what you're getting at."

"Nicky, please. I can't take much more. He gets depressed and irritable—he even cries. Last week was the worst yet. And he's convinced it's real, that these things happened to him—"

"What things?"

She stopped, recovering her reticence. "Nick . . . it's taken me months just to get him to agree to approach the Navy. He's so scared of what he's going to find. It's got to be someone he can trust—"

"Wait a minute. What has this got to do with the Navy?"

She was silent a moment then said quietly, "He has nightmares. He dreams about some sort of awful experiment they're putting him through . . ."

"What experiment?"

This time her silence was so long he thought he'd been cut off. "He's on a ship . . ." she began. "He's on a ship. . . . It disappears . . . and people . . . people disintegrate. . . . I don't understand any of it, I'm sorry."

She paused again, finding it hard to relate this. "You're

the only one I know in a position to help," she went on. "Harold doesn't know anybody: he's forgotten the men he served with. Please—you've got to talk to him!"

Hammond sat back for a long moment, frowning to himself. He was growing angry with her for dragging him into this domestic quagmire. And one question was plaguing him: "What have you told him about us?"

"Just that we . . . dated."

"I hope so, because if he believes it was anything more than that, this unstable husband of yours, I might not survive lunch. When do you want me?"

They made an appointment for noon at the Watergate Terrace. Relieved, Jan opened up and started to tell him about Harold's good qualities: his job as a vice-president of the Tri-State Insurance Company, with offices in New York, Washington, and Los Angeles; their California ranch home in Brentwood; their sedate life together. Hammond got the impression Jan had just what she'd always wanted, and what he'd never offered: a loving husband and a happy, uncomplicated, if somewhat dull, existence.

Except for Harold's "problem," which was taking on a magnitude in his mind that it probably didn't deserve. He was both curious and repelled.

But as he thought about it more, paying scant attention to her chatter, he was relieved in a sense. She wasn't after him at all. The hell with his ego. He'd always preferred his women playful and deceptive, with flaws you could count on two hands. He liked the games they played, the lies. . . . He enjoyed feeling superior. And safe.

As long as he didn't have to become the Fletchers' bosom buddy, a lunch wouldn't do any harm.

She was being grateful when he stopped her and said he had work to do. She thanked him warmly but reminded him not to forget the lunch. He promised to be there and hung up.

He was just reaching for the brown coffee when Admiral Gault strode in flashing a taut smile. Hammond rose. Gault was in a grouchy mood.

"I've got Wharton breathing down my neck about everything. He's not content to be Commander of Naval Intelligence. Wants to be Traffic Commissioner of Washington, D.C., as well. Gets himself a parking ticket going to some third-rate massage parlor, so now he wants NIS.

to investigate the meter maids. If I were him, I'd keep my mouth shut."

Hammond grinned as Gault dropped his tall frame into the other chair. Rear Admiral Robert Henry Gault, Director of the Naval Investigative Service, was in his early fifties, handsome and brisk, and new to flag rank. He had been a rear admiral for a mere twenty-nine days and was having trouble losing his familiarity with old buddies and cohorts, Hammond prime among them. They were tennis partners, and they used to spend every Sunday on the Naval Rec courts until Gault's work began to interfere. Now there was no such thing as spare time. Gault had a twenty-four-hour job and was starting to show the strain.

He opened his briefcase and drew out some papers. "All admirals are entitled to aides, but mine is so busy they should make him an admiral too. Okay, here we are."

He tossed a pile of papers at Hammond, who pulled the clip and glanced through them.

"First this business," said Gault. "Large scale pilferage at Pearl Harbor. CINCPAC is royally pissed and wants it cleared up right away. Can you dispatch one of your boys to help the regional office?"

"Don't want to step on toes, sir."

"Step away. They're snails out there."

"I've got one bloodhound in Tahiti . . ."

"Send him."

"He's on leave."

"Revoke it. Give him another ten days when he's finished."

"Yes, sir."

"Now, here we've got something on a black-market ring at the Yokosuka Naval Base in Japan," Gault mumbled, shuffling a few papers aside.

"Drugs?" asked Hammond.

"Meat. The price of meat in Japan is off the wall. Some of our boys are pushing fresh meat liberated from the mess supply. The base C.O. wants us to come down hard."

"Hard it is."

"Finally, Okinawa. Someone sabotaged the propulsion system on a missile cruiser. Someone on our side."

Hammond whistled.

"Mundane, huh?" snickered Gault.

"Not as mundane as something I just heard."

Gault glanced up, still shuffling through papers.

"You remember Jan Hoyle?"

"Sure. Nice girl."

"She's married to some guy now. And he's got *a problem.*" He put sarcastic emphasis on the words and looked at Gault for reaction.

"What's she looking for—a pinch hitter?"

"No." Hammond paused, carefully choosing his words. "Have you ever heard about a Naval experiment to make a ship disappear?"

Gault stared at him suspiciously, expecting a punch line.

"Her husband has bad dreams about it."

"You're serious."

"She is. I'm meeting them both for lunch—a threesome."

"When?"

"Today."

Gault nodded and threw the papers back into his briefcase. "Okinawa is urgent, Hammond. Make it a short lunch—and no matinee."

Once he got used to the dark, Hammond was impressed with the Watergate Terrace. He glanced around the room. Nicely done up in brick, wrought-iron grillwork, and dark paneling, with carriage-house lanterns set into the walls, it was warm and cozy.

He followed the maître d' past a wine barrel at the entrance to a small bar, past a fountain in the middle of the room to a row of canopied booths, separated from each other by glassed-in sides.

Then he saw Jan.

Her hair was cut shorter than he remembered, softly framing her face. She must have seen him at the same time because she took a healthy swallow from her drink before she smiled at him.

"Nice to see you, Jan," Hammond heard himself say. He was shocked at the slight puffiness of her face and the red-tinged eyes that looked up at him. Lack of sleep or crying, he figured. The man sitting next to her struggled to his feet.

"Thanks for coming, Nicky," she said. "I want you to meet my husband, Harold Fletcher."

Hammond extended a hand. "How do you do?"

Fletcher nodded curtly. "Commander."

Hammond slid into the booth and studied him. Fletcher's face was flushed, the color extending to his balding head. Large eyes, slightly protruding, gazed back at him with the barest hint of hostility. His blue suit was well-cut, but Hammond could see a bulge in the mid-section, the beginnings of a pot.

"Join us for a drink?" Fletcher asked.

"No, thanks," Hammond said, watching Fletcher grind out a cigarette.

"S'matter—don't they let you drink on duty?"

"Depends on my work load," said Hammond, ignoring the dig.

"Very commendable." He flagged a waiter. "Two more martinis—gin with a twist—and bring me another pack of cigarettes."

They lapsed into a strained silence. Fletcher drained the rest of his drink and fixed Hammond with a measured scowl. "Is that your real rank?" he asked.

Hammond was taken by surprise. "Yes. Why?"

Fletcher smiled thinly. "Jan told me you're with Naval Intelligence. I thought you people always wore civvies. You know, not so conspicuous."

Hammond wasn't sure whether it was the liquor talking or Fletcher just going out of his way to be nasty. "I can use any rank I choose," he replied. "Any rank, any insignia, any uniform. But then, uniforms aren't conspicuous in Washington, or haven't you noticed?"

Fletcher indicated Hammond's wings. "You really a pilot?"

Hammond forced a smile. "Yeah. Really."

The drinks arrived. Jan pushed hers to one side and watched with dismay as Fletcher started to work on his. Jan turned away, then glanced at Hammond.

"You're looking well, Nicky," she said. "Are they keeping you busy?"

"Very," Hammond answered, aware she was trying to change the course of conversation. Pointedly, he added, "I've got enough to keep me going the rest of next year."

"Is that good or bad?" She was looking right at him, silently pleading with him to be patient.

"Good," said Hammond lightly. "It keeps my mind occupied."

Fletcher fumbled a cigarette out of his fresh pack and worked his lighter several times before he got it lit. "Jan tells me you don't live far from here. Near the canal, isn't it?"

Hammond picked up the undertone of bitterness and stiffened. If this clown wanted to get into a what-were-you-doing-with-my-wife-before-I-met-her routine, it was going to be a very short lunch.

"That's right," he answered evenly. "Do you know Georgetown?"

Jan jumped in before Fletcher could answer. "Darling," she said smoothly, "Commander Hammond just told us how busy he is. Why don't you put down your drink . . . and we can talk . . ."

"I told you I didn't want to go into this with anybody," Fletcher said sharply. "All I want are my records. If he can help me get them, fine." He looked right at Hammond. "I don't want to waste his time . . . or mine."

Hammond rose, his anger barely in check. "The only reason I'm here is out of friendship for your wife. If you've got nothing else to say, I'll be going."

Jan reached over suddenly and touched his hand. "Please, Nick," she begged. "Harold and I both need your help. I don't know how much more I can stand." She swung her head sharply at Fletcher. "Stop acting like a child. Nick *can* help you."

Fletcher's face tightened for a second, then relaxed. He lit another cigarette, ignoring the one still burning in the ashtray. "I'm sorry."

Hammond eased back into his seat.

"She's right, you know," Fletcher mumbled. "This thing has got us both crazy."

Hammond's emotions subsided. "Why don't you start at the beginning?" he said. "Let's see if we can sort this out."

Fletcher pushed his martini aside and fixed Hammond with a steady gaze. "I might as well tell you up front—I've been seeing a psychiatrist for over twenty years." He paused. "A Navy psychiatrist."

Hammond betrayed nothing. "Did you have some sort of breakdown while you were in service?"

"No. After I was discharged. But don't get the idea

I'm a nut case. To quote Dr. McCarthy, it's always been just a matter of keeping things under control."

"McCarthy is your Navy psychiatrist?"

Fletcher nodded and took a long pull on his cigarette. He made an impatient face at the waiter who came back to take their lunch order.

Strange, Hammond reflected, the Navy never provided psychiatric care unless it was service-related, and up to twenty years after service? Hardly.

After the waiter left, Fletcher had difficulty starting again. He couldn't seem to put the words together. Jan reached out and twined her fingers in his for reassurance. Her small hands were covered by his large, carefully manicured fingers. Hammond watched quietly. He had the feeling Fletcher's hands didn't go with the rest of him. Big and blunt, they looked like they belonged to a laborer or a mechanic—not to the vice-president of an insurance company.

Fletcher finally composed himself. He pulled his hand away from Jan's and took an envelope from his inside coat pocket. "Look at this," he said.

Hammond opened the envelope and removed a set of neatly folded forms. Fletcher's discharge papers. He glanced over them, then looked up and saw tension on both their faces.

"I enlisted in '51," said Fletcher. "It says there I was stationed the whole time, four years, at Newport News."

Hammond checked the papers. Fletcher's rating had been Machinist's Mate First Class. Hammond felt a twinge of satisfaction: Fletcher *had* worked with his hands at one time.

"Have you ever been to the Navy Yard at Philadelphia, Hammond?"

"Yes."

"So have I. But only once that I can be sure of. The Korean War ended in July of 1953. I recall we took a destroyer up from Newport News the year before to mount new guns. We didn't berth until noon, and our whole crew left the same night, back to Virginia by train. And the day was sunny and clear." He looked right at Hammond as if that had great import.

"I don't follow what you're trying to tell me, Mr. Fletcher. Can you be more specific?"

Fletcher exhaled and brushed away ashes he'd spilled

on the tablecloth. His eyes bored into Hammond. "If you believe my discharge papers, Commander, I was never stationed in Philadelphia."

"Certainly if you were there only one day, it wouldn't show up here." He tapped the forms.

"I was there for more than a day," Fletcher said slowly. "I was there over two years! Those papers are not right!"

Hammond swallowed and checked the forms again. He threw a glance at Jan: she had shrunk back into her seat, listening but staring at the table.

Fletcher licked his lips. "Look," he continued, "I can remember a few things about Newport News, but why should I get these flashes about a long tour of duty in Philadelphia? I'm positive I served there!"

"When?"

"Right around the time of the Korean Armistice. And I stayed there until my discharge. I never went back to Newport News!"

Hammond glanced again at Jan. Tears welled up in her eyes. She brushed them away quickly, her face a frozen mask.

"What reason would the Navy have for falsifying your discharge, Mr. Fletcher?" he asked with incredible patience.

"I don't know. That's what I'd like you to find out."

Fletcher paused while the waiter served lunch. Jan picked at her salad, her face still drawn but the tears under control. Fletcher dove into his sandwich while Hammond watched. How could the man eat with all this torment boiling inside him? Hammond couldn't.

"What does your doctor think of this Philadelphia business?"

"He says I'm wrong."

"I see."

"Do you, Hammond?" He smiled coldly.

"Tell him the rest, darling," Jan said.

Fletcher finished the sandwich. He wouldn't look at Hammond. "I don't see any purpose, honey. He wouldn't believe it."

"Try me," said Hammond, pushing away his untouched plate.

Fletcher stared at the table a long time, and then said flatly, "It's a dream."

"Jan told me that this morning."

Fletcher nodded, then continued. "Usually I can't remember it when I'm awake." He stared at his hands.

"Just a minute," said Hammond. "You think your records are false because all this business about Philadelphia happens in a dream?"

"A nightmare," insisted Fletcher. "You ever have any?"

"Once in a great while."

"How fortunate. I've lived with mine since 1955."

This was getting sillier by the second. "Is that why you see this Dr. McCarthy?" Hammond asked.

Fletcher took a deep breath. "Yes. I started having problems as soon as I got out of service. I'd have one bad night and that would start a whole series of them. I'd wake up knowing I'd had a nightmare, but I wouldn't remember any of the details. I thought I was heading for a crack-up. Then all of a sudden I got a call asking me to come in for a routine post-separation checkup."

"Routine?" Hammond said. There was no such thing, unless . . . "Were you in the Reserves?"

"No. Full and complete discharge."

Hammond let it go by. "What did they do with you?"

"Introduced me to Dr. McCarthy. He put me on the couch and talked to me for a long time . . . then I went home. He told me the nightmares might recur, and if they did to get in touch with him as soon as possible. And that's how it went from then on. All I ever had to do was call him and he'd see me, usually within a day. He took care of everything, and I learned to live with my problem. Twenty-three years . . . My first wife passed away some time ago. . . . Six years ago my company sent me to Los Angeles. I panicked. . . . I was going to lose McCarthy. I suffered some bad nights without calling him, just to see if I could do it. I couldn't. . . . I flew back to see him."

It must have been a great moment of weakness for him: Fletcher sagged in shame.

"That was the last time you saw him?" asked Hammond.

"No." Fletcher looked up as if Hammond had missed the point.

"McCarthy got a transfer," said Jan. "To Long Beach."

"California?" said Hammond. "How obliging of the Navy."

"He got caught in a big cutback," said Fletcher. "They closed a bunch of hospitals and moved around a lot of staff. It was pure coincidence."

Hammond found that hard to believe, but he kept his skepticism to himself.

"I was getting along fine. I met Jan last year and we got married and she . . . she started questioning what was wrong with me."

"Did you meet with McCarthy?" Hammond asked her.

"He refused to see me."

"A psychiatrist refused to see his patient's wife?"

She nodded, unable to conceal bitterness.

"I've stopped going to him," said Fletcher.

Jan started to cry. "It's my fault, Nicky. I made him stop. And it's just gotten worse."

Fletcher put his arm around her for comfort. She cried silently, cupping a hand to her face. "Let's go back to the apartment, honey," Fletcher murmured.

For the first time since sitting down, Hammond sensed love between these two, and it depressed him. Clearly, Fletcher without his "problem" would be without his hostility as well, and was probably a warm, affectionate husband.

"Come on, Jan." He was trying to get her to her feet. She shook her head, took the handkerchief he offered, and dabbed at her eyes.

"Not until you tell him the rest," she said. "You've got to tell him the rest!"

Fletcher released her and lit another cigarette. My God, thought Hammond, the man's a human smokestack.

"How good are you at remembering people? Or places you've been to?" Fletcher asked.

"As good as the next person, I guess. Why?"

"Because when I'm awake, there's a two-year chunk missing out of my life. I can remember it only during the nightmare. I see faces I recognize . . . I hear names. They call out to me, talk to me, then . . . then I go through hell with them."

"Mr. Fletcher, didn't you say you weren't able to recall details?"

Jan responded. "Since he stopped seeing McCarthy, a lot of it stays with him."

Hammond nodded. "What kind of hell?" he asked.

Fletcher's breathing became shallow. "It always starts with us in a circle . . . on the forward deck."

"Aboard a ship?"

"Yes. A destroyer . . . no, a destroyer escort, an old DE."

"What's the name?"

"I can't remember. . . ." He looked dejected.

"Go on," said Hammond, preparing to ride this out.

"We have to hold hands. The skipper's very firm on that."

"Is this part of a drill?"

Fletcher nodded. "It must be. We've done it before, but this time it's for real . . . and it's early morning . . . heavy fog. I can just make out some people standing on the dock. I don't know them as well as the men I'm with . . . but they're watching us. We move away from them. . . ." He went pale and his eyes closed intermittently. "Tugs are pulling us out into the river."

"If it's foggy," said Hammond, "how can you be sure you're in Philadelphia?"

Fletcher's eyes popped open. "Because I know what the yard looks like—in fog, in rain, in sunshine. I recognize these giant cranes . . . and I know these men. I've worked with them. None of us are part of the crew. We're volunteers. We've trained for this for six months, drilled every day, taken every precaution they could think of . . . but the way it *worked* was so frightening. . . . We're moving out to the middle of the river. We stop . . . then the humming starts. And the vibrating. First through the feet, then my whole body."

Fletcher's hands were half-raised over the table, his fingers gripping imaginary somethings. "It was an experiment. More than that—a big Navy project. In those days, if the Navy said squat, all you could ask was how long. If the Navy brass said, 'We're gonna run an experiment on you and you're gonna come out of it okay,' we figured they were telling the truth. We all wondered what they were using us for, but we knew why they couldn't tell us.

"So we're told we're going to feel disoriented. That's all they say. But it's worse than that. The deck goes away . . . dissolves . . . disappears. We're still standing there. . . . I can feel it under my feet, but I can see through it, right down to the water. . . . The man across from me is gone. All that's left is his leg—"

He made a jerking motion with his arm, then shivered at the memory. He sucked in another breath. "I watch them disintegrate with the ship. We all go with it. It's like falling into a dark hole, then it gets light again. It's sunny, the fog is gone. We're not on the river anymore—a bay. Someone breaks the circle. He's shouting for us to look. . . . Then the vibrations start again. We try to get back into the circle, but the blackness is all around. . . . The man who's shouting the loudest tries to jump overboard. He . . . he's *blown apart. . . .*"

He stopped and shook his head, forcing away the image. "We come back to the fog, and . . . that's all I can remember."

He reached for his drink. Hammond stared at him. Even for a nightmare, the story was wild, and it made no sense. It was a full minute before he realized how anxiously Jan was looking at him.

Tentatively, he asked Fletcher, "You think some of that actually happened to you?"

"Oh, God," moaned Fletcher. "I don't know what to think!" He was shaken by a burst of sobbing. Jan calmed him, caressing his face and whispering in his ear.

Hammond felt another wave of depression. He couldn't take much more. "If I get your personnel records and see if they correspond with your discharge papers, you think maybe that will put this to rest?"

"I don't know." Fletcher pulled himself together. "It's all so damned *real!* I could see their faces in the dream, but for years I would wake up unable to recall anything about them! It was like they'd been wiped out of my head."

Or were never there, thought Hammond. He looked at Jan and sighed. "Okay," he said, "I'll run the files down for you." He waved the discharge papers. "Mind if I keep these?"

Whatever strain the Fletchers were under began to dissipate. It was as if their lives hung on Hammond's willingness to help.

"Thank you, Commander," Fletcher finally said. "I really appreciate this."

"Wait a minute," Hammond cautioned. "I don't know what I'm going to find or how long it will take. Will you be in Washington a while?"

"Jan is leaving for New York tonight to visit her mother, but I'll be here three more days. If you can't reach me at the apartment, just leave word with the Tri-State office."

Hammond took the card, glanced at the number, and put it in the envelope with Fletcher's discharge papers. He stood up, smiled at Jan, and had his hand gratefully pumped by Fletcher.

"Thanks for letting me bend your ear, Hammond."

Hammond regarded him quizzically. The man was as changeable as a chameleon. Jan's eyes gleamed with gratitude.

He left them still sitting in the booth, his head spinning from the emotions they had let loose.

It seemed an easy matter to clarify: he would make a comparison of the discharge records in Fletcher's possession to the ones in his permanent file. From his office, Hammond used the WATS line to St. Louis, Missouri, contacting the National Personnel Records Center maintained by General Services Administration. The 601 files on all retired or discharged personnel were kept there. He gave Fletcher's name, serial number, and date of discharge. They promised to call back within half an hour.

While he waited, Hammond studied Fletcher's discharge. It consisted of two papers: DD Form 214, Report of Separation from Active Duty, and his "Page 5," a History of Assignments. There was nothing out of the ordinary in either of them. Fletcher had been a run-of-the-mill enlistee, his duty assignment limited almost exclusively to service at Newport News. There was no mention of an assignment to Philadelphia.

The Center returned his call. They had no records on any Harold Fletcher of that serial number. Hammond hesitated. "I have the man's discharge right in front of me," he said.

"Yes, sir. All I can think of, sir, is that certain records were destroyed in a big fire we had here a few years back and his may have been among them. Lost a lot of microfilm then, sir."

A fire. Hammond vaguely recalled it. A lot of valuable records gone forever. "What about the originals?"

"Well, sir, you can try BUPERS or the Manpower Center at Braintree, Maryland. But don't hold your breath."

Hammond thanked the clerk and hung up. BUPERS was right over at the Arlington Navy Annex. He decided to walk.

He cleared through the guardpost and went up to the enormous wing occupied by the Bureau of Naval Personnel. He asked for Retired Records and was directed to the inactive section.

The reception room had a counter, a Wave secretary busy at a typewriter, and a Chief Petty Officer acting as clerk.

Hammond asked the chief for the service records on Harold Fletcher.

"Can't help you, sir," drawled the chief. "All personnel records are private and restricted to . . ." He stopped as Hammond produced his NIS identification card.

"I'm here on a matter of Naval Intelligence and this request is pursuant to my duties." The phrase was stock answer number five and it deflated the chief.

"You'll have to fill out these forms, sir." The chief produced something in triplicate and a hard white card. Hammond quickly entered the information, pausing over the card, which requested his name, Social Security or serial number, Navy classification rating, and assignment—and the same information on the person he was inquiring about. He pulled out Fletcher's discharge and completed the card.

The chief asked him to wait and then leisurely walked through a pair of swinging doors. Hammond caught a glimpse of filing cabinets stacked ten feet high. The inner vault went on forever.

The doors banged open and the chief returned with a thin old manila folder. He pulled a red card from it and shoved it into a pneumatic tube along with the white card Hammond had filled out, then shot them away somewhere into the building. In a smooth, practiced movement, the chief spread the folder out on the counter and slowly, deliberately, counted the papers before releasing them to Hammond.

"What was that red card?" Hammond asked.

"Just a follow-up on certain requests, sir. Nothing but routine. Here they are all in order. But you'll have to check 'em here. Can't let records out—NIS or no NIS, sir."

Hammond ignored him and slowly examined the papers with the chief leaning over the counter, impatiently knocking his knuckles. Hammond reached out and clasped the chief's hands tightly together, looked into his startled eyes and said, "Listen, sweetie, you'll get them back when I'm ready to give them back. So relax."

The chief blinked, pulled his hands away, and retreated to his desk, his dignity shattered.

Hammond bypassed Fletcher's discharge and looked at his "Page 5." He checked the entries made by several commanding officers. Nothing indicated that Fletcher had ever served anyplace but Newport News. No mention of duty aboard any destroyer escort nor time spent at the Philadelphia Navy Yard.

It wasn't until he turned back to Fletcher's discharge that things started to look funny. Under Terminal Date of Reserve Obligation, Fletcher's copy showed the same date as his discharge. But the original gave no date at all.

Under Remarks, on Fletcher's copy there were none. But on the original, a single addendum was typed in: "Placed on Inactive Reserve, 4 Feb 1955."

There was nothing to indicate he had ever been removed from that status. That meant he was still in the Reserves today.

No wonder his records couldn't be found in St. Louis. But what were they doing in the inactive section at BUPERS? And why didn't Fletcher know about this? Hadn't he distinctly said he'd never been in the Reserves? He'd been discharged, period.

He was mistaken. But why? And why didn't his copy match the original? Hammond thumbed through the rest of the papers, looking for the Reserve Enlistment Contract Fletcher would have to have signed. . . .

There it was. He checked to see if the signatures matched. They did.

Fletcher knew. He had to know. But why didn't he remember?

Hammond felt a crawling sensation up his back. This was more real to him than Fletcher's dream. It was a clear contradiction of facts, not some outlandish nightmare.

Fletcher could be recalled to active duty at any time. Although unlikely, it was an open-ended obligation. And Fletcher was unaware of it. Who had put him in this vulnerable position? And why did it only appear on one set of records?

Hammond looked up at the chief, who was studiously doodling on a pad. He tossed the folder back to him and said, "Copy everything in there and send it to me, pronto."

The chief nodded and put the folder on the Wave's desk.

"No, *you* do it!" barked Hammond. "It'll save you having to count them again."

Hammond returned to the Pentagon, wondering if he should speak to Fletcher right away and have him take up the matter with the Board of Correction of Naval Records. He decided to find out first which destroyer escorts were stationed at Philadelphia in 1953, get a list, and present it to Fletcher. He might recognize a name or number.

He called NAVSEACOM, the Naval Sea Assistance Command, and requested fleet disposition on all DEs assigned to Philadelphia between 1953 and 1955.

"I'll check it for you, sir," said the clerk, "but it may take a few days."

Hammond didn't want to stall Fletcher that long. He dialed the Watergate. Nobody answered at the apartment. He fished Fletcher's business card out of the envelope and dialed Tri-State.

A secretary answered. "Mr. Fletcher's office."

"Commander Nick Hammond. May I speak to Mr. Fletcher?"

"I'm sorry, Commander. He's left for the day. May I take a message?"

"Have him call me when he returns." Hammond left his number, then hung up, realizing he was spending too much time on a personal matter. Besides, if it weren't for Jan, he wouldn't give Harold Fletcher the time of day.

The next two days were hectic. The matters Gault had turned over to him had become pressing problems in need of constant monitoring.

Fortunately, the pilferage at Pearl Harbor had turned out to be a false alarm. The "stolen equipment" had been misrouted to a base in Alaska. NAVINTCOM had assigned Hammond three men to investigate the Yokosuka black-market ring, so Hammond had turned his own efforts toward the missile cruiser sabotage at Okinawa. CINCPAC had stepped in and demanded jurisdiction, but Gault had fixed that: "Piss on them. I'm not going to be told what I can investigate and what I can't," he told Hammond, and proved it by calling the admiral himself.

CINCPAC agreed. A team would leave for Okinawa within seventy-two hours. And Gault wanted Hammond leading it: "Just to get the ball rolling, Nick. And to make sure we're calling the shots."

Hammond had given up on hearing from either Fletcher or Jan, so he had no complaints. He was even looking forward to spending some time out of the country.

The rest of the day he concentrated on the sabotage case. He made notes for the team briefing he was to conduct the following morning, then cleared his desk to go home. He came across Fletcher's envelope and wrote a note for himself to get someone else to follow up on it.

Just as he was about to leave, the phone rang. It was Harold Fletcher.

"Uh . . . Commander Hammond?"

"Mr. Fletcher?"

"Yes . . . uh, Commander Nicholas Hammond?"

Fletcher sounded as if he were speaking to someone he had never met. "I'm returning your call, Commander."

"Well, thank you, sir. . . . I've run the background check you asked for. . . ." He paused, waiting for a question. Instead, there was silence until Fletcher cleared his throat nervously.

"You have?"

"Yes, sir. Excuse me, but you do recall our lunch the other day? You and your wife and I?"

"Lunch . . . ?"

Hammond was still for a moment. The lights went out in the Pit. It was quitting time. Maybe there was someone in Fletcher's office, someone who shouldn't hear this conversation. That's why he was acting so funny—

"Look," said Hammond, "I have the information you wanted. Can I give it to you over the phone?"

There was a hesitant "Please do."

"Okay . . . I couldn't find anything to verify your story about being stationed in Philadelphia, or assigned to any DE."

"Yes?" Fletcher sounded confused.

Hammond tried a stab in the dark. "Any more problems with those nightmares?"

There was a sharp intake of breath, then a long pause. Then Fletcher said hoarsely, "What nightmares? Who am I speaking to?"

"Commander Nick Hammond of NIS, sir. We had lunch thc other day. Don't you remember?"

"No, I don't—!"

Hammond stayed calm. "Look," he said, "I did meet with you and Jan whether you care to admit it or not. And I did some work at your specific request. Now, there was one discrepancy in your record—"

"I don't know what you—" Fletcher started, then paused. "Discrepancy?"

"Did you know you're still in the Reserves?"

"I'm *what?*"

"I didn't think so. If you'd care to talk about it—"

"Commander Hammond"—his voice sounded barely controlled—"I don't know what you're up to, but I think you better stop. Unless you're conducting an official investigation, don't go any further. I won't have my privacy invaded! Is that clear?"

"Whatever you say, sir."

Hammond put down the phone and sat in silence, wondering who was actually having the nightmares. He got up, turned out his light, and went home, completely baffled.

3

Hammond picked up a quiche from Publick House on M street and drove home. He ate in darkness by the kitchen window, watching the barge creep by, her lights illuminating the grass and trees as she passed. He finished the quiche and downed a bottle of beer, then leaned back in the dark and stared at the blank screen of his TV. He wanted to turn it on and become oblivious, a mindless zombie staring at flickering colors, but he couldn't push Harold Fletcher's tense features out of his head.

The man was definitely a mental case. But something apart from Fletcher's antics nagged at him, something that had happened in the course of his brief investigation. He remembered stubbing his proverbial toe on it at the time, but now he could not recall precisely what it was.

Something at the Watergate? Something on the phone? At BUPERS? What?

Everything became jumbled in Hammond's mind, so finally he succumbed to the lure of his TV and turned it on. He blinked and flinched as the shark loomed up out of the sea and Roy Scheider leaped backward in the boat. *Jaws* had finally made it to television. Hammond melted into his sofa and watched the rest of the movie. But his mind was somewhere else.

He woke up in the morning remembering exactly what it was. He'd had a nightmare of his own, a cross between Fletcher's crazy dream and the movie he'd seen on TV last night—Fletcher being gobbled by a hungry shark, blood spurting all over an invisible deck like red paint smearing unseen planking . . .

Red.

The color had caused him to remember the card that idiot chief had pulled from Fletcher's personnel file. The card had been *red*.

* * *

He was standing in the hallway outside the Inactive Personnel Records Section when the chief came to work. He didn't even give the man time to get his coffee.

"A few days ago you pulled a file for me on a man named Fletcher. There was a red card in it which you sent somewhere in the pneumatic chute. You said it was routine. I'd like to hear more about that."

The chief stared at him, this time careful not to betray his feelings. "It's called a flag," he said. "Very common in personnel files. They come in all colors." He paused, but Hammond held him with a look. "They use 'em to call attention to a special routing," he continued. "It means there's somebody who has to be notified when the file is pulled."

"What does the color red signify?"

The chief shook his head. "I just shoot 'em up the tube, sir."

"Is anything printed on the card?"

"Sure. Information for the computer. The red card and the white card you filled out both go to one place, a computer on the fourth floor."

Hammond thought a moment, then came around the counter. "Let's go back in the vault and have another look at Fletcher's file."

"Sorry, sir. Can't allow that."

"No? Well, I suppose I could take it up with Captain Haglan. . . ."

Hammond saw right away it had been worth it: taking the trouble to look up the name of the chief's immediate superior. The chief moved without a word to the double doors, then paused for a last try: "Of course, you'll have to fill out another white card," he said.

"Put it on my tab."

They walked back into the vault and Hammond had a better look at the aisles filled with filing cabinets and rolling ladders. Dust was conspicuous by its absence. "Went on a clean-up campaign after that St. Louis fire," said the chief. "These are the only remaining files on umpteen-zillion inactive personnel. Costs too much to convert to microfilm, so we're pretty careful about . . ." He trailed off as they reached the *F* files. The chief climbed one of the ladders, opened a drawer, thumbed through the folders, and pulled one out.

He came down the ladder in a jump. It was Fletcher's

file again, but when he opened it there was no red flag. "Guess it hasn't come back from upstairs yet," ventured the chief. "Wanna check back tomorrow?"

"No." He stared at Fletcher's file a moment and then asked, "You wouldn't remember seeing another flag like that on someone else's file recently, would you?"

The chief closed his eyes tolerantly, then asked, "Do you know how many files we've got in this place, sir?"

"Yes. Umpteen-zillion." Hammond paused. "Just answer the question."

"Yes . . . and no. I've seen flags, yes, but on whose file, sorry."

"Red flags?"

"Sure. There was one last week—"

Hammond's eyes flashed and brought the chief up short. "Those other papers I filled out," said Hammond. "You keep them here?"

"One set."

"Well?"

The chief grunted angrily and led him back to the reception room. He yanked open one of his own files and started thumbing through papers. Hammond waited patiently. The chief pulled out a form copy and held it up.

"Yup. This's the one. I remember the name. Yablonski."

Hammond took the form and read it quickly. "This was three weeks ago. Your memory's better than you think, Chief. C.L. Yablonski, Seaman First Class, USN, Retired. Requested to see his records on twenty-seven September."

"He was worried about something," added the chief. "That's how come I remember him so well."

Hammond eyed him dryly. "I want to see his file."

They went back to the *Y*'s and the chief found it without any trouble. He popped it open and inside was a four-by-five red card: a flag. Hammond drew it out and looked at the lines typed on one side:

9805CGN-166
YABLONSKI, C.L.
2194557

Yablonski's name and serial number. The top line Hammond couldn't figure out. That had to be the routing code. "Any idea what these numbers are?" he asked the chief.

"No, sir. But that was on the other guy's card, too. Now that I think about it, the same stuff appears on a lot of those red flags."

"Why did Mr. Yablonski want to see his file?"

The chief shrugged. "Don't have to give a reason. Any man who wants to see his own records just has to ask."

Hammond nodded and looked through Yablonski's file. Immediately, he noticed a similarity to Fletcher's. Entry into service in 1951, separation in 1955. The actual dates were different but close enough. Yablonski's four years were spent piloting heavy cruisers out of the Boston Naval Base. According to these records, he had never been at Philadelphia either. Hammond wondered what had prompted Yablonski to check into his service record at this time.

Was it possible there were two men running around suffering from Naval nightmares? And how had Yablonski reacted on seeing the entry under Remarks on his Page-5 document: "Transferred to Inactive Reserve 11 May 1955"?

"I want copies of all this." Hammond returned the folder along with the form Yablonski had filled out to examine it. The chief never saw Hammond remove the red flag and pocket it.

"Where do I find this computer we've been talking about?" Hammond asked. "The one that gets all the flags."

"Fourth floor. This wing. Room B-418. Central Personnel Assistance."

"Thanks, Chief. You've been a peach. I'll send over a purple heart."

The chief grunted, past caring.

Hammond took the elevator up to four and located Room B-418. He was passed through a lobby into a temperature-controlled computer complex, a long room with rows of programming decks and memory retrieval banks. The guard delivered him to a young lieutenant. Hammond showed him the confiscated red flag.

"Lieutenant, if this came through the pneumatic chute—"

"The Hoover, sir." The lieutenant grinned helpfully.

Hammond smiled back. "Where would it come out? Who would get it?"

"Ensign Cokeland, sir, right over there." He pointed

to a flatbed programming desk. Sitting in front of it was a little brunette given to a degree of plumpness, all of it pleasing. She smiled as Hammond introduced himself and became terribly bright and alert when he produced the red card.

"Oh, yes, sir. We get a few of those now and then. I feed the information right into this computer."

"What information?"

"Everything that's on the red card and some items from the white card that has to accompany it." Hammond nodded. He produced a blank white card, which he had liberated from the chief's supply, and filled it out for her, using Yablonski's name as the subject of his inquiry and his own as the inquirer.

"Now, show me exactly what you do with all this."

She examined the two cards, poised herself over the computer teletype, then asked, "You don't want me to send it through, do you?"

"No. Just write it out exactly the way it would go in."

She copied down names and numbers and, when she was through, showed him a card:

9805CGN-166
YABLONSKI, C.L. 2194557 USNR
HAMMOND, N. 573-58-6641 USN NIS

"The first line is the routing," she said. "The second is the subject, and the third is the person making the inquiry."

"Where does the information go?"

"I'm sorry, sir. I just don't know."

"Oh, come on." He smiled. He tried charm, but she really had no idea who was on the other end of that routing.

"The computer does it all," she said. "All I ever get is an acknowledgment of the message."

"Look, would you demonstrate for me? But let's use another name." He gave her Harold Fletcher's data and she punched through:

9805CGN-166
FLETCHER, H.B. 2193209 USNR
HAMMOND, N. 573-58-6641 USN NIS

He waited patiently with her until a few moments later the screen printed out:

9805CGN
STANDBY

"Looks like we touched a nerve," he said.

Ensign Cokeland was perplexed. "Usually it comes back with just that number and the word 'received,' then signs off. I think there's going to be someone up here in a minute."

She sat back and stared at her machine, two fingers pursing her lips.

"Look," said Hammond, "I'm going over there to talk to someone else. Let me get a look at whoever's coming in before you point the finger. Okay?"

She looked at him as if he were about to leave her to the wolves. Bravely, she nodded. Hammond strode over to another computer and struck up a conversation with another operator. Two minutes later, the doors opened and a female lieutenant came in and went straight to Ensign Cokeland.

Hammond watched the supervisor give the ensign the business. Cokeland put up a front of ignorance until she saw Hammond coming over.

He looked at the lieutenant's nameplate and smiled pleasantly. "Lieutenant Frankel, my name is Hammond. I'm from NIS, doing a little research, and I think you can help."

Lieutenant Frankel eyed him suspiciously. "In what way?"

"Well, it appears my request set off a little burglar alarm. Would you care to fill me in?"

She hesitated, then spoke defiantly. "There must have been something *irregular* . . ."

"Irregular to whom?"

"The people receiving your request called for a spot check."

"Who called?"

"The computer."

Hammond blinked. "No telephone?"

"The computer," she repeated, enunciating firmly. "They wish to remain anonymous."

"Then who do you report back to?"

"The computer."

Hammond almost laughed out loud. "Let me get this straight," he said. "Details of my inquiry go through your computer to notify someone unknown to you. And if the party doesn't like what he gets, he buzzes you and asks for a check. And you go through a whole security rigmarole without ever knowing who you're doing it for?"

Lieutenant Frankel sighed with annoyance. "That's it, yes."

"What the hell is this?" Hammond barked. "You're like Pavlov's dog! They ring a bell and you salivate on cue!"

She got defensive. "That's the procedure," she said, then went into a lengthy explanation of how the Navy computers have routings that crisscross the country, how computerization has become the most secure method of setting up notification procedures. Hammond ignored her: he was trying to figure out what had happened. He had sent through the same request on Fletcher as before, only this time, the second time, it hadn't gone through smoothly.

Maybe because it *was* the second time.

He interrupted Lieutenant Frankel, thanked her for the information, thanked Ensign Cokeland, and left. Stepping into the elevator, he was conscious of the most obvious fact of all:

Somebody had to have programmed the damned thing.

Hammond was back in his office before 0930, checking with Ensign Just-Ducky to see if the admiral had been through yet. "No, sir," she said, "but he wants to meet with you and your special team at lunch today."

A voice sang out from the aisles, "Okinawa is calling me-hee-hee-hee! I hear Okinawa calling meeeee!"

Lee Miller posed in Hammond's doorway. "Never been there, Nicky. Is it anything like Fire Island?"

"I don't remember requesting you," growled Hammond.

"Good Lord, you mean I don't have to go?" Miller dropped his pose and looked relieved.

"Well, we shouldn't let your enthusiasm go to waste—"

"Let it! Let it, my boy. I would rather push my pencil."

"Where are the other guys?"

"Waiting for you to call a meeting."

"Tell them lunch with the admiral. And listen, Miller—I would appreciate it if you would take over filing the usual papers with NAVINTCOM."

"Sure—"

"And hold mine aside. Write them up, but don't send them through."

"You're not going?"

"I'm not sure." Hammond picked up the phone and gave him a steady look. Miller took the hint and left. Hammond called Admiral Gault and waited patiently until the secretary got him to the phone.

"Hullo, Nick. Got your boys together?"

"Yes, sir, but I have a problem."

"Don't we all. Make it swift."

"Sir, do you recall I spoke to you about a man who was having a problem with his service records—?"

"Jan Hoyle's husband."

"Yes, sir. Well, I met with them and he gave me a wild story about some nightmare he's been having for twenty years in which he—well, some of the details are a bit much—but it's led him to believe there are discrepancies in his Naval records. So I did some checking and I've uncovered a few irregularities." Gault was silent, so Hammond continued: "He believes he was discharged in 1955, but the record shows he's still on inactive reserve. The forms he's carrying differ from the forms on file. I think there's been some altering. And in the file I came across this flag . . . a red card bearing a code of some sort. Maybe you'll recognize it, sir. Nine-eight-zero-five-C-G-N-dash-one-six-six."

"No. Means nothing to me."

"Yes, sir. Well, I thought maybe it was just a single isolated incident, but then I stumbled over another file with the same card in it—"

"All right, Hammond—"

"And the second man has a *similar* military record. Same years of service, and he's also carried on inactive reserve."

Gault made some inarticulate remark, then was silent a long moment. "Well, it does sound strange. A lot of cloak-and-dagger shit. The Navy doesn't usually operate that way. But, Nicky, why are you spending NIS time on this? It's not really our business."

Hammond was taken aback. "I think it has far-reaching implications."

"Maybe it does and maybe it doesn't. So far, it involves two men who have been out of the Navy for more than twenty years. If they're in the Reserves and don't know it, I think there's little chance they'll ever be called up. To get the Correction Board involved would only release a steamroller that could bury these guys."

Hammond wilted. The admiral was right. Sticking his nose into this was a mistake. It would be better to close the book and forget it, Jan's feelings notwithstanding. He was tempted.

"Excuse me, Nicky, for getting personal, but this whole thing is kind of funny."

"How so, sir?"

"Your ex-girl friend's husband—and you're going out of your way to help him? That's what I call *chivalry*."

"Would you mind, sir, if I spend some time on it?"

"And what am I supposed to do with Okinawa? Certainly not!"

"Spare time, sir."

"You have spare time?" Gault chuckled in his throat.

"I'll give up going to the can." Hammond hated having to resort to jokes, but Gault wouldn't take this seriously.

"Exactly what do you want to do?"

"Run down that code number."

Gault grunted. There was a silence as he covered the mouthpiece, then Hammond heard him come back. "You leave for Okinawa in forty-eight hours. What you do until then is your business, but if it doesn't turn out to be NIS business, drop it."

Hammond hung up, unnerved, and turned his attention back to the code number. He studied it for a few minutes, trying to shake Gault's warning from his mind, then called the Office of Naval Research and asked for the Code Division. A young civilian bureaucrat politely informed him, "Sorry, sir, that doesn't come under ONR jurisdiction. Better check with NAVINTCOM."

Hammond groaned and hung up, then ripped through the directory. Under NAVINTCOM there were two possibilities: Intelligence Research Department and Internal Cryptography. He mumbled to himself about the idiotic proliferation of bureaus within bureaus, then tried Internal Cryptography. Dead end. They turned out to be a merry little band whose job it was to create codes for Naval Intelligence use only, not for the Navy at large.

A lieutenant in the Intelligence Research Department listened to him describe the code, then said in hushed tones, "Can't handle that over the phone, Commander."

"For Christ's sake," yelled Hammond, "this is the fucking Pentagon!"

"Sorry, sir. You'll have to appear in person."

Hammond stormed down one floor to the offices occupied by Naval Intelligence Command. He found the Research Department and confronted the lieutenant, who looked to be a recent college graduate. Fresh-faced, crew-cut, crisply uniformed, Lieutenant Armbruster completely disregarded Hammond's demands and asked why he wanted to have the information.

Hammond restrained himself and said calmly, "Before you decide that it's classified, why don't we find out what it is?"

With Hammond breathing over his shoulder, Lieutenant Armbruster researched the code-number digits and came up empty-handed, *and* deeply concerned.

"This is a special setup," he admitted. "Obviously designed to be closed to scrutiny."

"That's what a code usually is," cracked Hammond.

"Well, I've never come across a designation quite like it."

What? In all your years? Hammond was tempted to ask. Instead he said, "Then how was it set up in the Navy computers?"

Armbruster was upset. He had no idea.

"Sorry I ruined your day," said Hammond. "If you do come up with the answer, let me know. And, Armbruster, keep it at your level. Don't let it get any higher."

"Yes, sir. I'll track it down if it takes me a week."

A week, thought Hammond. The guy could be on this job till he retires.

Hammond was in a dark mood as he returned to the NIS complex. The receptionist held up several sheets of Xerox paper. "Someone from NAVSEACOM dropped these off for you," she said.

Hammond examined them as he walked back to his cubicle, his stomach growling for lunch. Now he had the list of ships he had requested, the names and numbers of every destroyer escort stationed at the Philadelphia Navy Yard between 1951 and 1953. He sat at his desk and pored through them, looking for something even vaguely familiar. It seemed hopeless.

He was staring at the last group of numbers on page four:

DE 162	Levy
DE 163	McConnell
DE 164	Osterhaus
DE 165	Parks
DE 166	Sturman
DE 167	Acree

Something seemed to jump right out at him. At first he wasn't sure, then he was excited. He whipped out the red card he had liberated from BUPERS and looked at the code number again.

9805CGN-166.

166. Could the last three digits refer to DE-166, the USS *Sturman*, stationed in Philadelphia in—he checked the date—1953?

He felt adrenaline pumping as he frantically called the chief he had spoken to at NAVSEACOM. "DE-166, USS *Sturman*," he said. "Can you tell me where she is now?"

"The last page in that group I sent you shows current disposition on all those numbers—"

Hammond threw the other sheets aside and ran a finger down the last page, stopping at DE-166 and moving across. "Struck from the registry as of 1957," he said.

"Then that's where she is."

"Well, yeah, but was she sunk, scrapped, sold—what?"

"Don't know, sir. It's likely she was sunk for target practice."

"Okay . . . thanks."

He didn't need the *Sturman* anyway. He just needed the name and number. He hung up and stared at the scant information on the *Sturman*. She was an escort ship of the "Cannon" class, constructed at Federal Shipbuilding and Drydock Company, Kearny, New Jersey, contract awarded 18 January 1942. She was commissioned on July 4th of the following year.

Could she be the ship Fletcher was dreaming about?

If so, the connection was held together by the flimsiest

of threads—from the man's dream to his contradictory files to the code number on the red flag to a destroyer escort built over thirty years ago.

Hammond was just about to reach for the phone again to dial the Watergate when it rang. He blinked in surprise, picking it up, half-expecting to hear Fletcher's voice on the other end.

It wasn't Fletcher. It was Jan.

She was hysterical. Hammond was immediately exasperated. Now what? Then, in the jumble of words mixed with sobs, he managed to comprehend that she had just received a call from the Washington office of Tri-State Insurance. Hammond's eyes widened as the rest of what she was saying registered.

Harold Fletcher was dead.

4

"He missed a meeting this morning. Tri-State couldn't reach him by phone, so they sent someone over to the Watergate. He was already . . ." She stumbled over the words. "It was a heart attack."

"Jan . . . I'm sorry . . ."

"I can't believe it!" She covered the phone and he heard a muffled sob. He waited patiently until she came back, breathing hard, barely able to speak. "He wasn't . . . wasn't that old. . . ."

"Where are you calling from?"

"My mother's house in New York."

"Is there anything I can do?" He heard her cover the phone again. "Jan?" he repeated.

"Yes . . ." she finally replied. "Would you go to the Watergate . . . and take care of . . . ?" She broke off in a choke and he heard another muffled outburst of crying. This was getting impossible. He swore under his breath. He was jealous; she had never shown him this kind of emotion.

"Nicky?" She was back on the line.

"Yes, I'll go over there, if that's what you want. But shouldn't Tri-State handle it? They know him a lot better."

"Nicky," she said haltingly, "if you could just *be* there . . ."

"I'll do what I can," he found himself saying. "Are you coming back to Washington?"

"Yes. The company is making arrangements . . ."

"What flight? I can meet you."

"I don't know yet. Not even sure . . . where I'll be staying." Her voice quavered. "If I can't reach you at your office . . . is your home number still the same?"

"Everything's the same," he said. He was immediately sorry—she might take that the wrong way. Everything is different, he wanted to say. Don't come! For God's sake, don't come. "Try the office first. There's always someone on duty."

There was a long silence, then, "Thank you, Nicky."

The connection was broken before Hammond could answer. He returned the receiver to its cradle and sat there, stunned. It's too pat, he thought. Too goddamned neat. He dialed Fletcher's apartment at the Watergate.

It was picked up after the third ring. "Medacre," rumbled a disembodied voice.

Hammond used his most authoritative tone: "This is Commander Hammond of the Naval Investigative Service." He waited in vain for an acknowledgment. "I'm calling about Harold Fletcher. Who am I speaking to?"

The man grunted. "Detective Lieutenant Medacre, Metropolitan PD. What can I do for you?"

Hammond shot back, "Would you confirm a report we just got that Harold Fletcher is deceased?"

"Very deceased. Was he one of yours?"

"No, but we had an interest in him. Lieutenant, I would appreciate it if you would leave everything as is until I've had a chance to look it over. Tell Watergate Security to expect me. I'll be there in twenty minutes."

If Medacre was impressed, his voice didn't show it. "Hammond, right? I'll leave your name, but make it snappy."

Hammond tried to reach Gault by phone, but the admiral was already on his way to the lunch meeting. He grabbed Lee Miller in the hallway and gave him a message for Gault: "Tell him a friend has died and I've been called away."

"He's not gonna believe it," Miller smirked.

On his way out the door, Hammond shot back, "Miller, you better *make* him believe it."

Hammond hit traffic once he crossed the Potomac and felt impatience rising again, his instinctive reaction to pressure situations. He parked his car with a slam of brakes and a squeal of tires, then hurried across the little shopping mall.

The security desk was expecting him. He was whisked up to a cop on the eleventh floor. Medacre met him in a small anteroom just inside the door at the end of the hall. He was big, with a plain, open face, but his eyes had the weary look that comes from seeing too much death in all its forms. His handshake was firm and strong, blunt fingers wrapping around Hammond's outstretched hand. "He's in the living room, Commander. We'll hold off until you're finished. "

"I shouldn't be too long. Is the coroner here?"

Medacre nodded. "Yeah, inside with the deceased."

There were six other men in the living room. Two of them were unfolding a body bag; another was on his knees drawing a chalk circle around an ashtray that lay on the carpet, while a fat little man sat in an armchair busily working a toothpick in and out of his mouth. He was watching a photographer taking pictures of the corpse.

Fletcher's body was knee-down on the carpet in front of the couch. The torso was slumped over a low, glass-topped coffee table. His head, framed by an outstretched left arm, rested across a pile of scattered playing cards. His face was turned sideways, features contorted, a blue tinge to the slack skin. One bulging eye stared dully into unseeing space.

Hammond winced. He'd seen his share of bodies, but that terrible lack of dignity always bothered him.

Idly he wondered if Jan had bought the blue silk robe that Fletcher was wearing. His eyes picked up the dry, rust-colored line that ran from the one nostril that he could see, staining a card resting under the dead man's nose.

Hammond stepped carefully around the overturned ashtray. It was in direct line with Fletcher's out-thrust arm. "Why the blood?" he asked.

Medacre shrugged. "Hey, Brody! Get over here!"

Hammond watched the fat man ease himself out of the armchair and waddle over. "You ready for me?"

"Not yet. Commander Hammond, meet Doctor Brody."

Brody waved a chubby hand. "What can I do for you?"

"The commander would like to know about the bleeding."

Bored, piglike little eyes glanced down at the body, then up at Hammond. "With a heart attack, you never know. Some are quiet, others messy. This one convulsed, slid off the couch, had a strong spasm, jackknifed forward, and bingo! Hit the table with his nose. If it means anything to you, it must have been pretty quick."

"You're sure it was a heart attack?" Hammond asked.

"Classic."

Hammond's eyes fell on the overturned ashtray. He knelt down, slid a finger under, and flipped it over. It was spotless.

Medacre caught the startled look on Hammond's face. "Something wrong?"

Hammond's brow furrowed. "I'm not sure. Doctor Brody, how long do you think Fletcher's been dead?"

Reworking the toothpick in his mouth, Brody looked at Hammond, slightly annoyed. "Can't tell for sure, but I'll give you an educated guess. Condition of the body—say maybe ten, twelve hours. I'll know more after the autopsy."

Hammond was still looking at the ashtray. "Medacre, what about his movements yesterday? When did he come back to the apartment?"

The detective pulled out a notebook, flipped some pages. "That's locked in. Fletcher spent all of yesterday in business meetings at the Tri-State office. He had dinner last night at Billy Martin's in Georgetown with, among others, a Mr. Charles Rankin, a close associate of his. Afterwards, the two of them returned here for a nightcap. Rankin left shortly after nine p.m. Security desk confirms their arrival and Rankin's departure." Medacre closed the notebook. "Took that statement from Rankin. He's the one Tri-State sent over. . . . Found the body. . . . Claims Fletcher was fine last night."

Hammond was trying to assemble his thoughts. He stared at the ashtray and then at the coffee table. The cards were arranged in columns, in sequence, and by suit. Fletcher had been having a game of solitaire. He died twelve hours ago; that would have been around two a.m. His friend had left at nine p.m. There were five hours when Fletcher had been totally alone. And he hadn't smoked a single cigarette?

A chain-smoker?

There wasn't even a half-empty drink on the table. Nothing to indicate that poor, nervous, distraught Harold Fletcher had actually spent five hours alone in this room. Hammond thought back to that last peculiar phone call he'd had with the man, when he'd seemed so different, so changed. Was this part of the change? Had he suddenly given up drink and smoke? If so, why?

Had Fletcher met with his psychiatrist? Doctor what's-his-name? *McCarthy*. Could McCarthy have influenced him, caused this improvement in behavior? Hammond didn't know *any* psychiatrist that good.

"All done, Lieutenant," said the photographer as he returned from the bedroom, packing his gear.

"Terrific," drawled Medacre. "Make me some nice blowups. Brody, it's your party."

Brody nodded and his pudgy fingers reached for the phone. He ordered the security desk to send up his ambulance attendants with the stretcher.

"Will you consider the possibility of suicide, Lieutenant?" Hammond asked.

Medacre's eyes narrowed. "Why?"

"Mr. Fletcher had emotional problems. He was under the care of a Navy psychiatrist."

Medacre opened his coat and thrust his hands on his hips. He looked squarely at Hammond. "What the hell is your interest in this?"

"I'm a friend."

"You said before it was Navy business."

"It's that, too."

"You're playing close to the vest, Commander. How about turning up a card?"

"I'm only asking one thing. Don't treat this as an open-and-shut case."

"I'd need *cause* to treat it otherwise. Have you spoken to the man's shrink?"

"No."

"Why not?"

"Haven't located him—yet."

A faint smile creased Medacre's ample jaw. "You're with NIS and you can't find a Navy psychiatrist? Isn't that a little strange?"

"I'll handle that end of it, Lieutenant. Just send me the autopsy report."

Medacre turned away, indicating he was through being polite, then turned back suddenly. "Twenty years I've been on the force and I've never heard of anyone committing suicide by heart attack!"

Hammond was expressionless as he pulled a card and gave it to Medacre. "Thanks for your time, Lieutenant."

By the time Hammond returned to the Pentagon, his anger had subsided. He expected little from Medacre and his coroner, but he still sensed something out of kilter.

Maybe it was inside him—an overworked imagination. What he had come to know about Harold Fletcher's life was so odd that his death couldn't possibly be normal. Yet it probably was. Best for everyone if he consigned Harold Fletcher's case to oblivion. With the subject deceased, there was no purpose in continuing. He could investigate that code and the red cards in his spare time. It wouldn't make any difference to Jan now. He tried not to think about her. In one sense, her problems were over. In another, they were just beginning. He didn't want to become the center of them. Get on a plane to Okinawa and get away from her, he told himself.

He checked his watch. Gault would still be at lunch with Miller and the team. He wondered if he had shoved himself into the doghouse over nothing. Certainly, Gault wouldn't let it pass without a royal chewing-out.

He had hardly stepped into his cubicle when the phone buzzed. "Chief Levering to see you, sir."

"Send him in."

The maintenance chief bustled into the room, a toolbox practically chained to his wrist. "Christ Almighty, Commander. I wish you'd tell me when your equipment goes on the fritz."

"What?"

"Your phone." Hammond looked at it. "Oh, it's all fixed now. They left about ten minutes ago. And I only find out about it by stumbling in here. I'm supposed to be *running* maintenance— What's the matter?"

Hammond was staring at the phone.

"Didn't they get it ri—" Hammond cut him off with a signal. He closed the door to his office and motioned the chief down the hall ahead of him. He crossed to the receptionist and said, "Get Internal Security up here on the double." He ignored the startled expression on the girl's face. "I want a full electronic sweep of my office."

He turned to Levering and saw him blanch.

It took less than fifteen minutes to find the three bugs. One had been placed in his phone, one under the corner of his desk, and the third behind a file cabinet. Hammond watched the four-man security team make one last check. Their little black sensing boxes remained silent.

Ensign Collins, the team leader, nodded to Hammond.

"You're clean now, Commander." He held up a metal chip no bigger than the head of a match. "Pretty sophisticated stuff, sir," he said. "I've never even seen this last little gadget before. And whoever planted them was good, too."

Hammond didn't appreciate the assessment. "Send them over to the Naval Research Lab and get a receipt," he ordered. "Tell them I want the name of the manufacturer."

"What about fingerprints?" asked Collins, tossing the bugs in his bare hands. Hammond gave him a dark look. Collins caught the bugs in his palm and gazed sheepishly at Hammond. "Sorry, sir," he said.

"You wouldn't have found anything anyway."

Hammond watched the four men file out. They stood aside in the doorway to let Admiral Gault charge through under a full head of steam, with Lee Miller and the Okinawa team in tow. Gault listened patiently while Hammond filled him in, then snarled, "What the fuck is going on around here? Who the hell would bug you?"

"Don't know, sir," said Hammond. "But there are some other funny things going on right now." Gault looked at him, barely tolerant. "You recall that business with the altered files?"

Gault sighed. "How could I forget what's-his-name?"

"Harold Fletcher, sir. The *late* Harold Fletcher. He died last night."

Gault regarded Hammond keenly. "Killed?"

"Don't know that either, sir. Everything points to heart attack, but . . ." He fell silent.

Gault knew right away what he was suggesting. "What's the connection?" he asked.

"I'm not sure if there is one. But I've got the feeling . . ." He shrugged.

"*That* feeling, huh?" It was something between them, something they had shared back in the days when they had worked closely together. The feeling was a hunch, an uninformed certainty of intangible foulness. Gault was quiet for a moment, his face impassive except for a small muscle that throbbed in his cheek. When he finally spoke, it was in a low voice with a thin, biting edge to it. He turned to Miller. "Lee, you'll take over the Okinawa investigation. Nick will give you all the background."

Miller nodded. "Yes, sir."

"And you," Gault continued, looking at Hammond, "you'll drop everything and get to the bottom of this bugging crap."

"Can I follow up Fletcher, sir?"

"Yes, but first find the man who did *this!* Because when you do, I am personally going to shove a listening device up his ass and monitor his intestines!" Gault glared at the gaping onlookers, then opened the door and left.

Miller whistled. "Cheese und crackers, Hambone! What have you been up to? How come you rate?"

Hammond felt the tension draining. He waved Miller into his cubicle and spent the next hour briefing him, turning over all the information on the Okinawa case. He had sandwiches sent up and grabbed mouthfuls while they talked. Then he met with Pentagon Security, all of whom were quick to pin the bugging job on outside agents. But Gault had shaken enough trees to make them amenable to Hammond's suggestions. He requested them to button everything up and de-louse the entire building. Access would be tightened, spot checks made, routines reinforced. Even with all that, Hammond did not expect them to get answers.

When he was alone, Hammond closed the door to his office, sat back in his chair, shut his eyes, and tried to sort everything out. He couldn't be sure the bugging was connected to the Fletcher case, but it was the only thing he was working on at the moment. And what about that computer business at BUPERS? Had he really set off an alarm somewhere? Person or persons unknown at the other end of that red flag had discovered Hammond's interest in Harold Fletcher. And now Fletcher was dead, victim of a heart attack—or murder? Hammond shook his head to clear the cobwebs. The implications seemed to grow but lead nowhere.

And Harold Fletcher wanting to check into his records because of some recurring nightmares. Hammond kept coming back to that. He couldn't make sense of it. Then he remembered the other man with the flag in his file. He too had gone to BUPERS to check on himself.

Hammond rummaged in his briefcase for the copies BUPERS had sent over. There it was: 601 File, C.L. Yablonski, USNR. Hammond pulled out a Xerox of the form Yablonski had filled out, and checked his address. He lived in Cotuit, on Cape Cod. Phone number . . . it was all there. Cotuit was near Otis Air Force Base. He could be over and back in an afternoon.

He reached for the phone and dialed long distance. A woman answered and gave him a soft, questioning "Hello?"

"Uh, hello. May I speak with Mr. Yablonski, please?"

"He's not here right now."

"Is this Mrs. Yablonski?"

"Yes?"

"My name is Nick Hammond, ma'am. I'm with Naval Intelligence. I'd like to speak with your husband."

She hesitated. "He's out on his boat. I don't expect him before tonight. May I help you?"

Hammond frowned, then decided to proceed. "Yes, ma'am, you can. A routine paper came to my desk. . . . It's a request your husband filled out at BUPERS here in Washington, to see his old Navy files. I'd just like to know if he got everything he wanted."

"I . . . I'm not sure."

"He was in Washington about three weeks ago and he made a personal visit to the records center. If it's important and there's anything I can do to help . . ."

"I . . . frankly, Mr. Hammond, I don't know if he found what he was looking for. We haven't really discussed it."

"I see. Tell me, Mrs. Yablonski, does your husband know anyone named Harold Fletcher?"

"No."

"You're very sure of that."

"We don't have a lot of friends, Mr. Hammond, just the people we know on the Cape."

"Yes, but it's possible your husband might have known this man during his service."

"My husband doesn't keep in touch with *anyone* from the Navy. His service was not very pleasant. He still suffers nightmares because of it. . . ."

Hammond sat up straight. He couldn't believe it. "Nightmares?" he repeated.

Mrs. Yablonski hesitated. "Yes."

"Excuse me, ma'am, but would they have anything to do with a ship . . . in the Philadelphia Navy Yard?" He heard a sharp intake of breath and knew he had hit the jackpot. "Is he seeing a psychiatrist about this, Mrs. Yablonski?"

"Yes . . ."

"A Navy psychiatrist?"

"Doctor McCarthy, yes."

Hammond felt something curl up in his stomach and flutter around. "How often?"

"Whenever he has to. Mr. Hammond, why are we discussing this? I don't see how my husband's records have anything to do with his . . ." She broke off.

"Mrs. Yablonski, I think your husband could be of help to me in an investigation. And I would like to come up to Cotuit tonight to see him. It's very important."

There was another pause and Hammond sensed fear. "Is something wrong?" she asked.

"No, ma'am. Nothing at all. I don't want to upset anyone. I just need to talk to him about something. Would it be all right if I came this evening?"

"I suppose so."

"Thank you, Mrs. Yablonski." He hung up quickly so she wouldn't have time to reconsider. He could hardly contain his excitement as he placed a call to the NIS Data Center at the Hoffman Building in Alexandria. He got hold of a girl in the personnel division and asked her to track down the names and locations of every Navy psychiatrist named McCarthy and to send him a list as fast as possible.

His second line rang. It was Lieutenant Armbruster, almost violent about 9805CGN-166.

"You mean you can't crack it?" Hammond asked, trying to sound surprised.

"Crack it? Sir, I can't even find it! There's nothing remotely resembling the motherfu—" Armbruster restrained himself. "No source, no originating authority. As far as the Navy's concerned, that code doesn't exist. I'll keep trying, but I don't know where it will get me."

One more strange piece of non-information, Hammond thought. He thanked the unhappy lieutenant, made a quick call to the MATS facility at Washington National Airport and ordered them to ready an F4 jet.

Then he called Security. Things were moving along: the building was being de-loused with negative results, and a lot of negative uproar from brass who didn't want their offices turned upside down. So far, Hammond's was the only office to turn up bugged.

He decided it was time to lock his desk and go home. Halfway there, he realized he had heard nothing further from Jan Fletcher. It was too late to call the Tri-State office; he would have to get in touch with her tomorrow. He had just enough time for an early dinner before heading to the airport for the flight to Cape Cod. He was conscious of a growling in his stomach. He had wolfed down the sandwiches and they were churning unpleasantly down there.

As he unlocked the door, he was debating what to do first, eat or shower. He never made the decision.

His hand froze reaching for the light switch. A faint scent filled the room, an all-too-familiar fragrance. He stared into the dark.

"Jan?" he called.

She rose from the couch and turned on a side lamp. She smiled wanly, her pale, tear-streaked face illuminated by the soft glow.

"I couldn't face a hotel room," she said quietly.

"How'd you get in?"

She held up a key. "I still had this."

5

Hammond closed the door and gave in to a surge of anger. How could she intrude on his privacy like that? What if there had been another woman living here? He was tempted to let her have it, tell her how far she had overstepped the bounds. But she took another step forward into the light and he saw the black circles under her eyes. She looked tired, frightened, as if all the stuffing had been knocked out. She was shapeless in the beige wool suit. Even the expensive pearls around her throat had no luster. She was anything but appealing.

Despite himself, Hammond softened. "Little girl lost," he said. She took that as a cue and stumbled into his arms, nestling her forehead in his shoulder and releasing her weight.

There was nothing he could do but hold her as deep sobs wracked her body. The anger fled and he found himself flattered that she still needed him. It was a small triumph.

"Jan," he said softly. Her only response was to pull him closer.

"Sorry . . ." she finally mumbled. "I can't help it."

He led her to the couch and made her sit down. "Do you want a drink?" She shook her head. He decided to mix one anyway. He made a vodka and tonic, just the way she used to like it. "Best cure in the world for grief," he said. "Get blind drunk and stay that way for a week."

She took it, hardly noticing what it was, and drank it down. Then she slumped back on the cushions. "God, Nicky, how could it happen?"

"The coroner says heart attack, pure and simple," he said. Why complicate the situation?

"But he never had a history of heart trouble," she protested.

"He never *told* you he had a history," said Hammond.

"He had insurance checkups just recently. He was healthy."

"Maybe—" Hammond stopped himself. What was the use of speculating? It would only get him into things he couldn't talk about yet.

"He was a sweet man, Nicky. He married me on an impulse. There was no soul-searching, no hesitation. . . . He simply wanted to marry me."

It could have been you, you bumbling idiot, he told himself. He got up and refilled her drink. She was already starting to slur.

"He'd been married before," she went on. "She divorced him fifteen years ago and then died suddenly. . . . They had a son who's grown up now and lives in Virginia." Jan paused. Her voice trembled. "We don't get along." She took another healthy swallow of the liquor and her head lolled back.

"I was good for him, Nicky. He needed me. There was no competition in our relationship. He worked and I . . ." She stopped and looked blearily at Hammond, perched on the chair in what she took to be a disapproving pose.

"I didn't marry him for his money," she said sharply.

"You don't have to tell me any of this, Jan."

Her eyes searched his and then looked away. He wondered what she saw. She looked around the room. "You haven't changed things much. You never got that sofa re-covered." Absently, she fondled a small jade elephant on the side table. "Haven't you found anyone, Nicky?"

To take your place? he thought. Sure, baby, hundreds of them. One a night. "I never did find it easy getting involved."

"No," she agreed. She looked at him a long time, took some more liquor, then leaned forward, supporting herself on one arm. "You don't hate me, do you, Nick?"

"No." He laughed hollowly.

"Tell me the truth."

"Water under the bridge, Jan."

She looked at the floor. "Could I stay here—just for tonight?"

He hesitated, then spread his hands. "Stay if you want. But I won't be with you." He got up. "I have to pack."

"You don't have to move out," she said. "I won't get in your way."

"I've got business," he said with a reassuring smile. "Maybe your mother could—"

"We fight. We had a big battle this morning. She decided now was the time to tell me what she thought of Harold."

Hammond whistled. "How about a friend? Call anybody you like. Have them stay here."

Jan shrugged.

"Look, I'll be back as soon as I can. There's enough food in the refrigerator so you won't have to go out."

She stood up suddenly, her eyes searching his again, terrified. "Don't leave," she begged.

He surveyed her darkly. This time his arms moved first and they stood quietly together, leaning on each other.

He made her another drink, intent on deadening her anguish. She fell asleep in a chair. He carried her to the bedroom, took off her suit, and tucked her under the covers. He was almost out the door when she woke up and pleaded with him to stay. He dropped into the chair by the bed and, in the dusk, watched her soft form rustle under the bedclothes.

He sat there longer than necessary—long after she was asleep—thinking about her. Three years she had spent with him—in this very apartment. And they had been good together until she'd ruined it all by demanding marriage.

He had told himself that her leaving was all for the good. She didn't know him at all, what made him tick. She had even poked fun at his work, his involvement in "national security." She had found things funny that he didn't and she'd never understood the things he had laughed at. What did she expect of a man who had been raised and suckled by the service? He thought he had more of a sense of humor about it than most.

And her husband? Harold Fletcher, insurance agent. What was so distinguished about that? Sure, he probably made more money, kept her happy and secure, but what did they ever *talk* about? Did they go for walks, visit the museums she had always loved, go to the same movies three and four times? Or had they spent their evenings lounging around Harold's country club, boozing it up with Beverly Hills doctors and dentists?

What had she lost that was worth crying about? What

was there about Fletcher that Hammond had lacked?

He glanced at the clock. It was almost six p.m. He had to get going or it would be too late to visit Yablonski. He went to his closet to fill a flight bag with a change of clothing. On the way out of the bedroom, he paused for another look at Jan. She was sleeping soundly now, her head buried in the pillow, her arms embracing it.

He closed the bedroom door behind him.

The dispatcher at Base Operations confirmed that an F4 Phantom was waiting for him. He could take off in twenty minutes. That didn't even leave him enough time to get sandwiches.

Hunger pangs growing, Hammond put on a G-suit and walked out to board the aircraft.

As the F4 roared down the runway, the enormous pressure pushed him back into his seat. With a slight touch on the control stick, he lifted the sleek jet up and into the evening sky.

At Otis Air Force Base, he requisitioned a car and a thermos of soup. It was pitch dark by the time he reached the outskirts of Cotuit, a small summer resort town in Barnstable County on Nantucket Sound, noted for its oyster beds. He stopped at a beachside trailer advertising "Oysters by the Dozen," bought a bagful, and asked for directions to Yablonski's home. He drove through the town, then inland a half-mile or so until he saw a fresh-water pond gleaming through the trees. Old New England frame houses ringed the pond at obscenely spacious intervals. He rattled carefully around the shore on a dirt road until he saw a two-story yellow clapboard house with bright red shutters.

Hammond parked across the slope of the embankment and got out, looking around the yard. Grass grew in ragged patches, but there were two fenced-in gardens—one for flowers, another for vegetables. A sagging pier thrust into the water at an odd angle. A rowboat up on the dirt was tied to a stake. The air buzzed with insects. He walked up to the verandah and stared at the old porch swing and the lazy retriever lying on it with one eye on him. Hammond winked at the dog and called, "Hello the house! Anybody home?"

The kitchen light was on, but he didn't see anyone moving behind the screen door. He waited a moment before calling again, reflecting on this throwback. He remembered homes like this from his boyhood.

"Yes? Who is it?"

A woman appeared at the door. The light was too dim for a clear view, but she must have recognized his uniform.

"Oh, hello." She pushed open the screen door and came out wiping her hands on an apron. Mrs. Yablonski was in her early fifties, with a great motherly bosom and a ruddy New England complexion. Her hair was done up in a bun; the blonde in it reflected the porch light.

"Mrs. Yablonski, I'm Hammond." He presented her with the oysters and her eyes lit up.

"You must be a New Englander," she said.

"I was once—and I've never lost the taste for those."

She laughed and led him into the house. They cracked a couple of oysters and ate them, then she gave him coffee and pumpkin pie. They were friends within moments. Hammond listened to her chatter on about the house, the years they had lived here, and the gardens she worked so hard to keep. She had a genuine love for the Cape and it was hard for him to change the subject.

"What made you pick Cotuit?" he asked.

"Oh . . . Cas wanted to be away from the cities. Doesn't function well in crowds. He's always loved the sea."

"Your husband is a professional fisherman?"

Mrs. Yablonski nodded. "He's quite successful. Runs charters to Martha's Vineyard and Nantucket. Berths at Hyannis Port. He's very well known . . . and respected," she added.

"How long has he been doing that?"

"Fifteen years." Mrs. Yablonski smiled proudly.

Hammond smiled and glanced at the clock. "Does he always stay out this late?"

"Usually calls as soon as he puts into port. I did radio him a message that you were coming up tonight."

"Maybe I could drive down and meet him."

"I'll go with you." She rose and bustled into the hall to get a heavy sweater from the closet. "Do you like deep-sea fishing, Commander?" she called back.

"I've only been out once, ma'am."

"Someday you'll have to go out with Cas. You'd have

a wonderful time." She led him outside, closing the door behind them. The dog looked up.

"Does he sail alone?" Hammond asked.

"He's got two permanent crewmen. Lovely boys—Greg and Paul McKay."

Hammond heard a wheezy whine behind them and looked back. The retriever was standing on the porch, looking forlorn and deserted. "If you want to bring the dog, ma'am, it's okay."

"Oh, he's not ours. Go home, Georgie, go home!" The dog shuffled off the porch and strolled into the woods. "He sort of belongs to everyone around the pond."

As Hammond opened the door for her, she climbed in and smiled up at him. "It's a very warm, safe community, Commander. We never have the kind of trouble you see on TV these days. Thank God for that."

It was ten miles across the Cape to Hyannis Port. Hammond chose his questions carefully.

"What's Dr. McCarthy like?" Getting no reply, he looked at her in the near darkness. She was gazing intently ahead. "Is he tall and thin, short and fat, what?"

"I don't really know, Commander. I've never met the man."

"Not once in all these years?" She shook her head. "Didn't you want to? Weren't you curious?"

"Yes," she said with hesitation. She added nothing.

"How often do they have their sessions?"

"They don't meet regularly. Only when Cas needs help."

"How often is that?"

Mrs. Yablonski fell silent.

"I'm sure it sounds as if I'm prying, ma'am, but you must believe me—I'm very concerned about your husband's welfare."

She looked at him with surprise. "Why?"

He found himself reluctant at first to tell her the truth. He wanted to make up some story about re-evaluating the psychiatric program for veterans, but somehow he didn't think she would fall for it.

"I have some doubts about Dr. McCarthy's abilities," he said finally, then glanced at her expression. She considered his statement carefully.

"McCarthy's been a godsend," she said, and he sensed

she was trying to convince herself. "He'll see Cas any day of the week on twenty-four hours' notice. We couldn't ask for better treatment than that."

"Are you sure?"

She glanced at him uncertainly.

"What about the nightmares?" he asked. "What are they like?"

"Awful."

"Is it one nightmare, Mrs. Yablonski? Always the same?"

She watched the road ahead for a long moment, then said, "It has something to do with a disappearing ship."

Hammond held back a reckless urge to describe Fletcher's dream: it would only succeed in shocking her.

"He's never been more specific than that about it," Mrs. Yablonski continued.

"How does he go about getting treated?"

"He calls McCarthy on a WATS line, then drives up to the Naval Hospital in Boston. They meet for several hours."

"Several?"

"As long as it takes." Her voice shook.

"What about symptoms?" Hammond asked. "Anything physical—?"

"Oh, God—I've seen him wake up in a cold sweat, shaking, even babbling. Sometimes, just for the first few seconds, I could swear he's trying to get it out, to tell me, but he just can't! Then he lapses into this terrible state. He's . . . so helpless . . ." She covered her eyes for a moment.

She regained control as they drew abreast of the Hyannis Port docks. She directed Hammond to her husband's pier, then waited while he shut off the engine.

"There is something else," she said. "Several times I woke up and found him out of bed, across the room at the window, or on the floor, or holding onto a chair. . . . Once I woke up before he started screaming. . . . I saw him at the wall . . ." She stopped, shivering at the memory. "I saw him at the wall. He . . . he was stepping *through it.*" She looked up at Hammond, frightened. *"From the next room."*

Hammond was very still. "Through it?" he repeated. "You *saw* him do this?"

She nodded. "I screamed and I don't know what happened next because I shut my eyes tight. When I opened them, Cas was shaking me and he'd put the light on. He was frightened and demanded to know what I'd seen. When I told him, he flung himself away from me. He insisted *I* was the one who was dreaming. . . ." She stopped and rubbed her eyes. "I've always hoped so."

"Did he make an appointment with McCarthy?"

"Oh, yes. He was gone for three days. He came home and it was like it never-happened. Even now, I don't dare mention it."

She looked at him anxiously and her voice quavered. "It's getting so I'm almost afraid to sleep with him."

Hammond shuddered.

Cas Yablonski and Harold Fletcher were as inexorably linked as Siamese twins.

A thirty-five-foot Bertram Sportfisherman chugged toward the dock, the harbor lights showing off her glassy white hull, varnished woodwork, and the handsome flying bridge.

Mrs. Yablonski pointed out the tall sea dog at the helm. "That's Cas," she said. He was wearing a white shirt open at the collar, a blue pea-coat, and a yachting cap. His face was darkly tanned, tough and lined, his hair iron-gray.

As soon as the boat was tied, Mrs. Yablonski waved to her husband and came down the pier followed by Hammond.

"Had a great day, Momma!" Cas called, in a voice that boomed across the dockside. His client, a cigar-smoking yachtsman of diminishing years, hoisted himself out of his deck chair and stumbled uncertainly to the side.

"Look what Mr. Carey bagged!" Yablonski yelled, and as Mr. Carey proudly displayed a huge fish, Yablonski held up a plastic bag containing empty beer cans, pointed at Carey, and made a drunk-out-of-his-mind face.

"Come ashore," called Mrs. Yablonski. "There's someone here to meet you."

Yablonski smiled and waved again but took a good look at Hammond's uniform. He left the boat to be secured by the McKay brothers, then paused to shake Mr. Carey's hand.

"Send me a bill!" slurred Mr. Carey. Yablonski helped him ashore, handed him his fish wrapped in plastic, and wished him goodbye. "An' I wanna go again next week!" Mr. Carey insisted as he stumbled off into the night.

Yablonski came up to Hammond and stuck out a hand, regarding him warily. "Casimir Yablonski," he said.

"Nick Hammond, sir. Pleasure to meet you."

"Likewise. Care for a beer?"

"Sure."

"Hey, Paul!" he yelled. "Get that other six-pack up here."

"Righto, C.L."

Hammond studied Yablonski. Weatherbeaten skin, wide shoulders, powerful muscles, enormous hands—Yablonski didn't seem the sort to suffer from nightmares. He had none of Harold Fletcher's jackrabbit furtiveness.

Yablonski put his arm around his wife and hugged her. He smoothed her hair and pulled her sweater tight. "Cold tonight, Momma."

"Why don't you invite the boys home for the weekend, Cas?" she asked.

"They're planning on it." Yablonski took the six-pack from Paul McKay and motioned for Hammond to pull himself a can. They cracked beers and stood on the pier, drinking.

"So what does Naval Intelligence want with me, Hammond?"

"Well, I . . ." Hammond was reluctant to discuss this in front of the McKay brothers.

Yablonski persisted. "I'm just an old sailor, Commander. You know, catch-a da fish?" He glanced at Paul McKay and saw him smiling. "I take my boat out, I mind my own business, and I appreciate other people who feel the same way."

"Cas . . ." Mrs. Yablonski was looking at him oddly.

"It's okay, ma'am," said Hammond. "Mr. Yablonski, would you have any reason to fear an investigation?"

Yablonski expelled his breath. "No . . . of course not."

"Then let's be friends. I'm here to *help* you."

"How?"

"On the seventeenth of September you went to BUPERS in Washington to examine your 601 file. Did you find what you were looking for?"

Yablonski stared at him a moment, then smiled for Paul McKay's benefit. Casually, he sauntered along the dock, nodding for Hammond to follow. As soon as they were out of earshot, he asked, "What's it to you?"

"I think you found some discrepancy that you can't account for."

Yablonski stiffened slightly but continued walking. He drained his beer and crushed the can. "You tell me," he said.

"You thought you were discharged from service in 1955. You found out you're still carried on the Inactive Reserve list."

"Very good. Why?"

"I don't know."

Yablonski stopped and turned, his face flushed with anger. "Does anybody know? Does the Navy know?" he asked with an edge of sarcasm.

Hammond retorted, "Does McCarthy know?"

Yablonski eyed him darkly. "He says it's a mistake."

"When did you ask him?"

"When I came back from Washington."

"You saw him after that?"

"Of course I saw him! He's my doctor!"

"Well, I think he's wrong. It's not a mistake. There's a reason why those records are different." Hammond paused. "And yours are not the only ones."

Yablonski glanced at him sharply, then looked away.

"Why did you go to Washington, Mr. Yablonski? What prompted you?"

"The same reason you're here. Curiosity."

"Was it the dream? The disappearing ship?"

Hammond was watching his back and caught a slight twitch of the jaw. "How did you know that?" Yablonski asked.

"Your wife." Yablonski flashed his wife an angry look. "But eventually I could have guessed. I told you, sir, you're not the only one."

Yablonski turned back, his face flooded with terror. He stared at Hammond, searching his eyes, then looked off into space and seemed to be deciding something for himself. "McCarthy said I should forget my preoccupation with the dream . . . I was being self-destructive . . ." He looked at Hammond for understanding. Clearly, he didn't understand it himself.

Hammond grunted. "Then he's the first psychiatrist I've ever heard of who's not interested in dreams."

Yablonski got defensive. "Look, he does his job. I get these horrible nightmares, I go chasing off to him, and he makes me forget about them. *He's* helping me!"

"Then after twenty-odd years, why aren't you cured?"

"There's no cure . . ."

"McCarthy said so?"

Yablonski moved sullenly to the edge of the dock and stared down into the water.

"Tell me about the dream," Hammond said softly.

Yablonski laughed. "Tell *you?* Where's your couch, Hammond? Did you leave it in the car?"

Hammond regarded him seriously until he stopped laughing.

"I don't need this," Yablonski said through his teeth. "I don't belong to the Navy anymore—I don't care what it says on my records!"

"Wouldn't you like to get it straightened out?"

Yablonski sighed. "You guys. You're like crocodiles with lockjaw! You grab pieces and pull until they come off! I've known people from NIS, Hammond. When you decide to pin something on a guy, you find a way to do it! *I don't like what you do!"*

Hammond smiled. "I keep telling you I only want to help."

"You want to help yourself." Yablonski smiled back at him knowingly.

They stared at each other, measuring determination. They didn't even hear Mrs. Yablonski pad softly up the dock. She crept to Cas's side and touched his arm. Then she smiled nervously at Hammond.

"Come back to the house, Commander. You can fight better sitting down."

Hammond drove back alone. The Yablonskis took the McKay brothers and went in Cas's jeep. It was nearly midnight when the party tramped back into the house by the pond. The McKays excused themselves and went to the spare room to bunk down.

"We can put you up on our living room couch," offered Mrs. Yablonski. Hammond cast a quick look at Cas and saw abject disapproval.

"Thanks very much. I just have a few more questions," he said.

She made tea and they sat down at the breakfast table.

Yablonski leaned back in his chair, arms folded across his chest, regarding Hammond darkly. Physically, he was telegraphing "The hell with you." Hammond didn't need a course in body language to read that message.

"What's McCarthy's first name?" he asked.

"Lester," Yablonski snapped back.

"Could you describe him?"

Yablonski opened his mouth, then froze. His expression switched to astonishment as he searched his mind, then came up with blank fear. Why should such a request frighten him? Hammond wondered.

Unless he couldn't describe the man.

"What the hell is this?" barked Yablonski. "Goddamned third degree?"

"No, sir . . ." Hammond decided to go easy on him. Stick to facts. "Do you know a man named Harold Fletcher?"

Yablonski shook his head. "No."

Hammond quietly gauged the answer. It was the first question he had thrown that hadn't unnerved the man. He seemed sure. Yet . . .

"You and Harold Fletcher have the same doctor," he said. "And I think the same dream."

Yablonski didn't move. "What are you talking about?" he said hoarsely.

"Two men who have much the same service record, the same Navy psychiatrist, the same neurosis. . . . The only difference is that you're still *alive*."

There was a long silence, then Mrs. Yablonski leaned forward, her lower jaw quivering. "Would you please explain?" she asked.

Briefly, Hammond told them about Fletcher and Jan and Fletcher's problem. "I don't want to tell you any details of his nightmare because it's more important for me to hear yours, uninfluenced. When you're ready, of course."

"What happened to this Fletcher?" Yablonski asked. All the antagonism had fled, replaced by pure need-to-know.

"Found dead in his Washington apartment. Apparent heart attack." Hammond refrained from expressing any suspicions about Fletcher's death. He left the intimation that somehow Fletcher's problem and his demise were related.

Yablonski got up and walked to the sink, ran himself a tall glass of water, and drank it down. When he turned back, he seemed fraught with anxiety. "I trust McCarthy. Don't you see . . . ?" He choked off. His wife rose and reached for him. He pulled her close and looked at Hammond in silent appeal.

"Do *you* trust him, Mrs. Yablonski?" Hammond asked.

Cas looked down at her. After a long moment, she shook her head. "No . . . not now . . . oh, I'm not sure."

Yablonski pulled away, staring at her, then around the room in confusion. He moved to the hallway, then glanced back. "I'm going up to bed."

"Mr. Yablonski." Hammond stopped him. "The next time you get these dreams, don't call McCarthy. Call me." He reached into his trouser pocket and pulled out his wallet. He left a card on the table.

Yablonski stared at it from the doorway, then his eyes met Hammond's and seemed to reflect a great sadness, as if he knew the worst was only beginning.

He left the room and Hammond heard Mrs. Yablonski stifle a sob. He turned to her—she was rubbing her eyes. "I'm sorry," she said.

"Mrs. Yablonski, I'll have to depend on you. It's imperative he doesn't see McCarthy next time it happens."

Mrs. Yablonski looked at him with alarm and stood clutching the sweater about her shoulders. Finally, she nodded. "He's difficult," she said. "He's always been."

"With reason, I think," Hammond said and smiled in reassurance.

He left quickly, driving back to Otis over unlighted roads, intending to bed down at the Transient Officers' Quarters. A problem took root in his overworked mind. Somehow, Dr. McCarthy had already lost one patient that Hammond knew of.

How many others?

6

Hammond's footsteps echoed hollowly down an empty corridor of the Boston Naval Hospital in Chelsea. He passed two deserted nurses' stations, their desks covered, strands of wire hanging from open telephone junction boxes on the walls. Heavy steel fire doors blocked connecting corridors, locks securing them to clasps on the wall.

He had flown up to Boston from Otis, borrowed another car, and driven out to this ancient facility in Chelsea—all before eight a.m. Curiosity had defeated sleep and hunger. As he walked through the deserted wing to get to the Psychiatric Center, Hammond got the impression that this was a terribly unsavory place to conduct therapy. For Yablonski, in an awful mental state, walking these halls must have increased his fears a hundredfold and made him desperate to see the doctor.

And how did McCarthy work it? On twenty-four-hour call to Yablonski here in Boston and Fletcher in Los Angeles and to who knows how many others in different parts of the country. The nation's only interstate shrink. Did he keep a private jet in the basement?

He hoped McCarthy would be here, but he found himself doubting it. Certainly it was too early even for a resident.

A young officer sat with his back to the door of the admittance office.

"Where can I find the duty officer?" Hammond asked.

"That's me, sir. Lieutenant Spaulding. Can I help you?"

"I'm from NIS headquarters in Washington." Hammond flashed his ID and Spaulding checked it casually. "Can you tell me where I might find Dr. Lester McCarthy?" Spaulding looked blank. "I believe he's a member of your psychiatric staff."

"Sorry—never heard of him, sir."

"Are you sure?"

Spaulding nodded.

"Do you know every doctor on staff?"

"Hope so, sir. I've been here two years."

"Could he be a consulting associate or something like that?"

Spaulding shook his head. "I'd know the name, sir. And there aren't that many. I guess you noticed the sealed-off corridors. We're being phased out. Caught in the fiscal meat-grinder. Of six men originally on the psychiatric team, only two are left: Dr. Kaplan and Dr. Brown. The other four have been reassigned. And none of them is named McCarthy."

"Could he have been handling out-patients?"

"This is a Navy hospital, sir, not a private clinic. He'd never get authorization."

Hammond glanced down one of the empty corridors and frowned. Two men with the same insane dream, the same doctor. Now McCarthy was beginning to sound as unreal as the nightmares.

"I'd like to check on a patient, Lieutenant. Would you mind showing me the medical files?"

Spaulding hesitated, not sure whether this was in order.

"Official business." Hammond smiled.

Spaulding took him to the file room and waited while Hammond searched through the *Y*'s. He found no records on Yablonski. No file, no card, no chart. He slammed the drawer shut. What kind of crazy game was this?

"Anything else, sir?"

Hammond rubbed his chin and tried to think. No doctor, no records—he'd gone down a blind alley. But at least he could check out McCarthy's purported base of operations.

"I'd like to see the psychiatric wing," he said.

Spaulding led him down another corridor. A burly Navy Corpsman unlocked the security door and looked Hammond up and down. They were in a large room opening into a labyrinth of corridors. The lady or the tiger, thought Hammond. He heard low animal moans coming from the hallway on his left, and he checked the sign that read "Permanent Ward." Permanent, indeed. Whoever was making those noises would be there till the building came down. And from the looks of it, that would be soon.

"You want to see the ward, sir?" Spaulding asked furtively.

"What else have you got up here?"

"Just the consultation rooms, sir." The Corpsman pointed down to the end of a sealed-off corridor. "Beyond the fire door. I'll have to open it up for you."

He fished out a key ring and the three men walked down the hallway. Hammond and Spaulding waited while the Corpsman opened the lock and rolled back the heavy door. "Light switch on the wall, sir. Consultation rooms start after the first right turn."

"We'll lock up when we leave."

"Thanks, Lieutenant." The Corpsman hurried back to his post.

The sealed-off section smelled musty from long disuse. Hammond and Spaulding made the right turn and stopped before a large wooden door. Hammond's eyes took in the rest of the corridor. At its far end was an exit which presumably led out of the building.

Hammond wrinkled his nose. Could Yablonski have been mistaken about the hospital?

Spaulding opened the door to the consultation room and stepped aside. "They're all pretty much the same," he said.

It was bare with the exception of two chairs and a table up against a mirror that ran almost the length of one side of the room.

"That's a two-way mirror, sir. Observation from the other side. Access through one door in the back of this room and another out in the hallway."

Hammond peered at the back wall. "I don't see it."

Spaulding smiled, walked to the paneling, and ran his finger down a seam next to the end of the mirror. There was no knob. The door fit flush against the corner. "Want to see the observation room, sir?"

"No thanks." Hammond stepped out to the hall and waited for Spaulding. "What about the exit?" he asked.

"Secured. Along with the rest of this section."

"Mind if I check it?"

Spaulding glanced down the hall, but Hammond didn't wait for his answer. He walked to the door, depressed the bar lock, and pushed out. The door opened and a breath of cold damp air rushed in. It wasn't locked at all.

Hammond began to see the picture. With that kind of

access, and with a proper uniform and ID, McCarthy could have the run of the hospital. Who would question him?

The lieutenant kept up a steady stream of apologies all the way back to his office. "Damn, that's careless, sir. I'll see that door is secured right away—"

"The hell you will." Hammond cut him off. "You won't mention this to anybody. Understood?"

Surprised, Spaulding just nodded his head. "Whatever you say, sir," he answered weakly.

One hour and forty minutes later, Hammond was back in his Pentagon office. The receptionist handed him an envelope, telling him it had come over by police messenger.

"Anything else?"

"Three phone calls from a Mrs. Fletcher. She'd like you to contact her. She said you have the number."

Hammond dialed his apartment. While the phone was ringing, he tore open the envelope. It was from the coroner's office. He scanned the Xerox copy of Harold Fletcher's autopsy report and found what he was looking for on the second page.

Cause of death: *cardiac arrest.*

Someone, probably Detective Lieutenant Medacre, had underlined the two words with a felt-tipped pen. What a nice touch, thought Hammond.

The phone kept ringing. Obviously, Jan was not at the apartment. He hung up, stuffed the report back into the envelope, and popped it into his desk. Jan would have to wait. He buzzed Ensign Just-Ducky and asked her to contact two men at the Naval Research Laboratory, Intelligence Division.

"Cohen and Slater," he said. "Tell them I want to see them in my office at eleven-thirty."

His eleven a.m. meeting with Security was a complete waste. They had come up with no clues, no leads, and no motives. The lab had identified two of the bugs—they were a standard make in the bugging fraternity. But the third one, the little chip that Collins had handled, had them stumped. They wanted more time, so Hammond gave it to them.

After they left, Hammond grabbed a note pad and

started jotting down everything pertaining to the case. A knock at the door broke his concentration.

"How's your hammer hanging, Nick?"

Hammond looked up at the two men standing in the doorway. "Well, if it isn't the Gold-dust Twins," he said.

Larry Cohen and Tom Slater slouched in. Cohen was the taller of the two, with a pleasant, open face and a pair of light blue eyes that looked out on the world with blank innocence. Slater was shorter by a head, with shoulder-length, sun-bleached hair. A neatly trimmed black beard framed his round face.

Hammond waved them into chairs and said, "It's unbelievable. How can we all be in the same Navy? When did you grow that foliage?"

"When he realized how many nickels he could save on razor blades," Cohen said dryly.

"Ignore him, Nick. He's jealous."

Hammond was looking at two of the best-trained specialists in their field. Mind-benders. They could take apart a subject's mental blocks, with or without drugs, uncover his darkest secrets and either cure him or restore the safeguards—as required.

"So, Nicky," said Cohen. "What's cooking?"

Hammond told them everything: his meeting with Fletcher and the man's appeal for help; his subsequent denial; the irregularities in the service records; Fletcher's mysterious death; the elusive Dr. McCarthy; and Hammond's first meeting with Yablonski. He held back telling them anything about the bugging of his office or his involvement with Jan.

"Let me get this straight," said Cohen. "Two men from separate parts of the country, with completely different backgrounds, have service-related nightmares. A Navy psychiatrist treats both of them. This treatment has been going on over an extended period of time. He's on twenty-four-hour call, sees them, then disappears until the next time he's needed, just like Batman, right?"

Hammond nodded. "What do you think?"

"I think you've been smoking funny cigarettes."

Hammond didn't even smile. "I have my own ideas," he said, "but you're the experts. You tell me what's going on."

Cohen nodded. "Okay. What you've described sounds like a classic example of post-hypnotic trance coupled with an autosuggestion override designed to lock up both ends."

Hammond looked from one to the other. "Plain language?"

"It's quite simple," said Slater. "These nightmares are held in check by inducing a post-hypnotic state that dims the memory—"

Cohen interrupted: "But if you can't get deep enough into the conscious or subconscious mind to erase that memory, it resurfaces."

"You're assuming the nightmare is rooted in a memory," said Hammond.

"Well, it comes from somewhere," barked Slater.

"Where does the autosuggestion come in?"

Slater leaned forward. "Conditioned reflex. Push a button, get a banana. Have a nightmare, call the shrink."

"McCarthy's your key," said Cohen. "Their key, really. He's the control. And he's built a nasty little package."

"Suppose we wanted to unravel it. How would you guys go about it?"

Cohen eyed Hammond carefully. "You mean with your man Yablonski? Using a great deal of caution, Nick."

"Risky?"

"Oh, ever so. You told us yourself. When you met with Yablonski, you asked him what McCarthy looked like and he couldn't remember. If somebody sees you on a regular basis for twenty years, you should be able to describe him—unless, of course, there was something planted in your mind to prevent that."

"A deep block?"

"Exactly. Built in. And who knows what else friend McCarthy is dabbling with? Yablonski could be a mental land mine. Step down too hard and *boom!* He comes off the wall with his brains in little pieces."

"You fellows have anything to counteract that?"

Cohen jerked a finger toward Slater. "Tom is the nuts-and-bolts man. I deal in technique."

"As a matter of fact, there is something," said Slater. "It's pretty new, so nobody's too sure of all the side effects." He fell silent and looked straight at Hammond with the tiniest of smiles. Hammond could tell he was just itching to get the chance to use it.

"You two get your magic act together," he said finally. "You're on the case as of now. Keep the office posted on your location because when we hear from Yablonski we're going to have to move fast."

Cohen and Slater stood up. There was an awkward silence, then Cohen grinned. "Do we shake hands and call a lawyer—?"

Even Hammond smiled. The phone rang. He picked it up, listened, then signaled them to wait. He switched on the desk speaker. "Okay, go ahead."

It was the clerk at the NIS Data Center at Hoffman. Her voice came back through the speaker: "There are eight McCarthys presently on duty with the Navy Medical Corps, sir. None of them listed as psychiatrists, and none with the first name of Lester. Would you like me to read them to you, sir?"

"Please. And where they're stationed."

Dutifully, she read off the eight names. Not one of them was stationed anywhere near Los Angeles or Boston. It was a total dead end. Hammond thanked her and switched off. He faced Cohen and Slater. "As far as the Navy's concerned, Dr. Lester McCarthy doesn't exist."

Cohen snickered. "I could've told you that. The Navy doesn't maintain any such psychiatric program, especially for *ex-servicemen*. No program, no McCarthy. Doesn't take a genius to figure that out."

"Uh-huh," said Hammond. "Except, then, who is he?" They shrugged. "Thanks. Keep yourselves available."

He opened the door for them just as Admiral Gault walked up. Gault stared after the departing Gold-dust Twins. "Some company you keep," he said, and flopped into a chair in Hammond's office. "Know where I've just come from?"

"No, sir."

"Brief meeting with John Allen Smith. He doesn't appreciate yesterday's bugging. Do you want his official reaction?"

"Gutter language will be fine, sir."

Gault sighed. "The Director of Naval Intelligence was so mad he didn't know whether to shit or go blind. Because of our security crackdown, he's got every hunk of brass in the building down on his neck. They want us out of here. They're saying our operations jeopardize the security of the Pentagon—we've got our own building, why don't we stick the rest of our people in it!"

Hammond stared at him. "It's only one incident, sir."

"That's all it takes, Nicky. Now, I like this little setup. I like coming over to the Pentagon for lunch and seeing my friends. But more important, the integrity of our bureau is at stake. After a mere thirty-odd days as an admiral, I don't intend to get booted out of the Pentagon!" His face was red. He took a couple of deep breaths and sat back. "Anyway . . . Smitty wants to be kept posted on nailing the buggers. You follow me?"

"Does he want it daily, sir?"

"I was hoping you'd say it'll be wrapped up by tonight. No, Hammond, call him when you have something." Gault heaved himself out of the chair. "And that better be soon," he added as he left.

Hammond closed the door and grunted to himself. He didn't care what building they occupied. Brass politics, what a pain. He sat down and pushed it all out of his mind. Jan—where the hell was Jan? He picked up the phone again.

She answered on the third ring—with new problems. Fletcher's son in Virginia was causing trouble. Paul Mallory, the president of Tri-State, had helped her make arrangements with the funeral home and was acting as a buffer between Jan and the son.

She was silent for a moment and Hammond sensed something coming. "Paul asked me something this morning . . . and it has me quite upset."

"What was that?"

"He was curious as to why the Navy was setting out to smear Harold's memory."

Her tone was icy. Hammond was silent a moment, taken by surprise. Then he snapped back, "That's ridiculous. I'll straighten him out." He reassured her as much as he could and promised to join her for dinner. As soon as he hung up, Hammond dialed the Tri-State office and made an appointment to meet with Paul Mallory.

The Tri-State offices were at 1839 M Street. As Hammond threaded through Washington traffic, he thought about what Jan had said. Smear Fletcher's memory, indeed. Where had that come from? He ruled out Medacre and the coroner's office; there was no reason for them to interfere. It had to be someone familiar with Hammond's interest in Fletcher, but who?

9805CGN-166?

Five minutes later, he was ushered into Paul Mallory's office. Paul Mallory stood a few inches over Hammond, six-foot-two and well-built. Hammond guessed his age at roughly forty-five. His thinning hair was neatly barbered, sideburns bracketing a pleasant, well-tanned face. He fit snugly into the mold of the successful executive. He radiated a smooth confidence Hammond could never hope to have.

Hammond's eyes flicked over several photos displayed on one wall: three pretty girls and a good-looking young man, all bearing the stamp of family resemblance. Another showed Mallory standing next to his radiant bride. On the right was his best man, looking stiff and proud in a tux: it was Harold Fletcher, younger, thinner, handsomer.

Mallory was toying with a small white envelope on his desk as he asked, "What can I do for you, Commander?" The tone was proper, but there was a distinct coolness to it.

"I imagine Mrs. Fletcher has told you all about me."

Mallory shook his head. "No, Jan hasn't mentioned you at all." He tossed over the envelope. "This arrived in the morning mail."

Hammond drew out a single sheet of notepaper and quickly read it:

13 OCT 1977

Mr. Paul Mallory
President
Tri-State Insurance Co., Ltd.
1839 M Street, N.W.
Washington, D.C.

Dear Mr. Mallory,

Please be advised that the U.S. Navy is looking into the background of your late associate Harold Fletcher. This investigation is being conducted by CMDR Nicholas Hammond of the Naval Investigate Service.

It would be in the best interests of your company to discourage this investigation as soon as possible. It can lead to harm not only for Tri-State but to the memory of a man no longer able to defend himself.

A friend

Hammond noted the military dating and the identification of himself as "CMDR." Only someone familiar with the recent changes in Naval abbreviations would have used "CMDR" in capital letters. The postmark on the envelope was from Washington, dated the same day. Either McCarthy had moved around or he had "a friend."

"That's a pretty strong letter, Mr. Mallory," Hammond said. "Inaccurate as hell, but strong."

"Then there's no truth to it?"

"None whatsoever. At the request of Fletcher's wife, I helped him check on his service record when he came to Washington. That's the extent of my involvement with him. Nobody in the Navy has been trying to besmirch Mr. Fletcher's good name. And no one will. Do you mind if I keep this?"

Mallory regarded the letter with distaste. "Not at all. Frankly, I despise anonymous tips. And I've always prided myself on my judgment of men. Harold Fletcher worked for this company for many years. In all that time, he was never once involved in anything shady. He was a vice-president and a fr—" He choked. "My closest friend."

"I understand," said Hammond. "His wife is an old friend of mine." Images of their "friendship" shot through his mind in the brief silence. Then he asked, "Mr. Mallory, how would an investigation of Harold Fletcher be harmful to Tri-State?"

Mallory grunted. "It would and it wouldn't. Probably depends on our poison pen pal there." He sat up and sighed. "We suffer from gossip and rumor as much as any other industry. I suppose if one of our top men was under investigation by any legitimate authority, and word of it leaked out, we could lose a number of sensitive clients."

"Could you give me an example?"

"We underwrite government vendors, companies that do business on a large scale with institutions like your Navy. They're some of our biggest accounts. Any hint of scandal and they would drop us like a hot rock. With what's been going on in Washington these last few years, I could hardly blame them."

"Mr. Mallory, could you get me a list of those companies?"

Mallory regarded Hammond with hesitation. "Why?"

Hammond waved the letter. "Just a stab in the dark. Wouldn't you like to know who wrote this?"

Mallory relaxed and pressed his intercom button. "Claire, would you make up a list of all the government vendors we insure and send it to Commander Hammond's office? He'll give you the address."

"Yes, sir."

He clicked off and managed a businesslike smile. "You'll have it in a day or so."

Back in his own office, Hammond slid open his bottom desk drawer and pulled out his Jolly Roger skull-and-crossbones flag, his not-too-subtle signal for everyone to stay clear. He dropped it on the hooks outside his door, closed it, and sat down alone.

He examined the letter Mallory had given him. It was the first hard evidence that someone didn't want him looking into Fletcher's past and that same someone was going to a lot of trouble trying to shut doors before Hammond could open them. Although the letter probably established a clear connection between the Fletcher case and the bugging incident, it wasn't proof enough to send up to Smitty.

He put it aside for the time being and began instead to prepare his assault on Yablonski's mind. He jotted down a list of questions, then tried to shift them into the proper order.

After an hour, he was dead-tired. He stuffed the Jolly Roger back in his drawer and left the office, taking the work home with him.

He stopped off to pick up steaks for dinner. When he entered his flat, only the kitchen light was burning. He put the meat out on the counter and went looking for Jan. He found her asleep on the couch. Gently, he woke her up. Through half-closed eyes she smiled at him—a warm bedroom smile that belonged somewhere in their past. It faded after a moment.

She went to wash her face while he prepared the steaks. He shoved them under the broiler and remembered that Jan liked hers medium-well. She came into the kitchen and wordlessly threw together a salad.

Dinner was quiet. Hammond was preoccupied, anxious to go to work on the Yablonski list.

Toying with her food, Jan broke the silence to tell him that arrangements had been made for Harold's funeral. She waited for a response. Hammond only grunted. "I was right about the family," she said. "Especially the son. This is turning into a convention for vultures."

Reluctantly, Hammond gave her his full attention.

"They insist on burial in Virginia," she said. "In the family plot. And I know Harold didn't want that. Oh God, Nicky, I have to go down there tomorrow. It's going to be an ordeal. Will you come with me?"

Hammond stared at her.

"Please come with me," she pleaded.

He regarded his dinner in silence, wary about where this was leading. "I know this is the worst time to ask the question," he said finally, "but did you really *love* Harold Fletcher?"

She looked at him a long time before answering: "Not as much as I loved you."

She got up to clear the dishes and wouldn't even look at him. He followed her into the kitchen and leaned on the counter watching her wash. "You can stay as long as you like," he said.

"Thanks, but I'll look for a hotel tomorrow."

He was stunned at a feeling of imminent loss. He reached for her shoulder and gripped it. She looked up and he said, "No. Stay. Please."

Hammond felt warmth flood through Jan again. She smiled at him.

"How did it go with Paul Mallory?" she asked.

"Fine."

"You will . . . stop looking into Harold's past if that's what Paul wants . . . won't you?"

"There's nothing left to look into," he lied.

He helped her dry the dishes, then she went off to soak in a hot tub. Hammond closed the door of his office and sat down with the notepad in front of him, but he couldn't work. He sank his head down on his arms and tried to clear his mind. He hated this situation. Sooner or later, Jan would have to know what was going on and how it involved her late husband. How would she handle it? And what would her reaction mean to *him* . . . ?

The knock on the door woke him up. It was Jan, wrapped in a huge towel and drying her hair. "I didn't mean to disturb you, but . . ."

"It's all right. I must have dozed off."

Jan studied him. "You look terrible," she said. "I'm out

of the bathroom. Why don't I make up the couch so you can get some decent sleep?"

Hammond offered no resistance. He couldn't think anymore. Fifteen minutes later, he slid between the sheets, closed his eyes, listened to Jan moving quietly in the bedroom, and drifted off. . . .

He picked up the phone on the second ring, rolling off the couch in the darkened living room. It was the night receptionist at NIS headquarters in Alexandria.

"I'm holding a call for you, sir—a Mrs. Yablonski."

"Tell her I'll call right back."

Hammond slammed the phone down and ran into his office. He rummaged for Yablonski's number, glancing at the clock as he dialed. It was just after four a.m.

"Hello?"

"This is Hammond, Mrs. Yablonski. What's the trouble?"

Her voice choked with relief. "Commander, I'm sorry —I know it's late but I just didn't know what to do—"

"It's all right, ma'am. What's happened?"

She sobbed into the phone. "It's Cas . . . just terrible . . . since midnight—"

"Why didn't you get in touch with me then?"

"I couldn't," she said. "He wanted to call Dr. McCarthy —I wouldn't let him."

"You handled it fine, Mrs. Yablonski. Where is he now?"

"Taking a walk—around the pond. Sometimes that helps. But I don't know how long it will last. Please! He needs somebody right away!"

"Now listen. I'm coming up to see him. I'll leave as soon as I finish speaking to you. I'll be bringing two Navy doctors with me. We should be there in four hours, maybe less. Don't worry about anything. Just trust me. The most important thing you can do now is keep your husband quiet. And *keep him away from Dr. McCarthy*. Understand?"

"I-I'll try."

"You've got to do better than that, Mrs. Yablonski. I'll see you in four hours."

He hung up and called the headquarters receptionist back. "I need several things. Get hold of Larry Cohen and Tom Slater. Tell them to be at the MATS terminal at

Washington National in forty minutes. Call operations. Have them fuel and warm up a Lockheed Jet-Star on my authorization. Then call Otis Air Force Base and make sure they have a car standing by for me. Got all that?"

Hammond made her repeat the instructions, then hung up. He moved to the bedroom door, careful not to wake Jan. He went to his closet and pulled out a uniform, planning to dress in the kitchen. Then he noticed her sitting up in bed.

"Sorry, didn't mean to wake you." He grabbed his shoes and headed for the door.

"Christ, Hammond. The middle of the night," she said. "You haven't changed."

Hammond froze in the doorway. Their former life together had been filled with moments like this—with him creeping out in the dead of night to accomplish she knew not what. And how she had hated it. But how could he possibly explain to her what was going on tonight? He fought down a quick surge of anger and answered her quietly.

"One thing's changed. I don't apologize for it anymore." He closed the bedroom door quickly.

7

Slater whistled at his first sight of the storybook cottage set in front of huge willow trees only forty yards from the water. Cohen got out of the car and assessed the surroundings.

"This is a guy who likes to retreat from society," he announced to Hammond.

"I could have told you that," Hammond said.

"Yeah, but I've got the degree, so it means more."

Hammond smiled as Mrs. Yablonski banged through the front screen door and waved anxiously at them. "Hello!" she hollered, and hurried down to meet them. "I'm so glad you came, Commander, I can't tell you . . ."

Hammond introduced Cohen and Slater as doctors and Naval colleagues. She glanced uncertainly at their white t-shirts and slacks. But they put on the charm and in a moment she was convinced.

"How's your husband this morning, ma'am?" asked Cohen.

Her smile fell away. "Not good," she said, glancing at Hammond. "He had a terrible night. You should have heard the things he's been saying about you. I've been pumping him full of coffee since six this morning. He hasn't called Dr. McCarthy, but if you're unsuccessful, he won't hesitate."

She took them inside and gave them coffee and homemade doughnuts. She urged them to make themselves at home, then went upstairs to get Cas. Slater worked on the doughnuts while Cohen roamed through the house, inspecting paintings, trophies, bric-a-brac—trying to get a clue to the tastes of his subject-to-be. He moved from one thing to another like he was touring a museum. Hammond followed, aware more of the overall impression—smallish rooms with old-fashioned furniture. The living-room sofa sagged with age and had a musty smell he remembered from childhood, sort of a doggy odor. The retriever probably slept here on occasion. The den and living room were filled with deep-sea mementos: a swordfish mounted on a wood plaque in the den and a small shark mounted in the living room.

"He takes a certain pride in defeating dangerous game," Cohen analyzed. "Probably has the killer instinct himself."

Hammond wanted to laugh. Yablonski a killer?

"Look at this," said Cohen, bending down to inspect a collection of fishing trophies shoved haphazardly into a bookcase at floor level in the den. "Obviously, he doesn't care much for medals and awards. A real sport-fisherman would have these up here—" He indicated the mantelpiece.

Slater appeared in the den, downing his second or third doughnut. "Okay, Sherlocks," he said, "I'm going to get my gimmicks from the car." He went out the front door.

"There are only two things in his life," Cohen continued. "Deep-sea fishing and running his excursion boat. Look at this den. There's only one chart on the wall: Cape Cod to Martha's Vineyard and Nantucket. Mr. Yablonski lives in a very small world. I'm willing to bet Mrs. Yablonski manages the business as well as the household. And all her husband knows is fish."

Hammond smiled. "What if this is her den?"

"Then I'll go back to college."

Cohen gave Hammond a smug look and returned to the kitchen to wait for the Yablonskis. Hammond remained in the den for a moment. Through the window, he watched Slater trudge back to the house carrying his recording equipment and a black medical bag.

Hammond sat down at Yablonski's desk and admired it. It was the kind he'd always wanted for himself, with cubbyholes and little drawers and the varnished rolltop. The façade was beautiful: hand-carved antique cedar with triangular notches at the joins. He couldn't help himself; his fingers automatically explored the cubbyholes. He thumbed bits of paper and postcards Yablonski had tucked away. Then his eye caught the open book in the corner, a personal phone directory, open to the letter *M*.

McCarthy, L. And after it, a WATS number: 800-676-0999.

Hammond picked up a pad from the desk and wrote the number down. He wondered anxiously if Yablonski had called the doctor after all. And what if McCarthy decided to respond with a house call? Hammond fully intended a confrontation, but he didn't want to make Yablonski the battlefield.

"Commander?" He heard Mrs. Yablonski calling and hurriedly shut the directory, put the paper in his pocket, and went to join the others in the kitchen.

She was introducing her husband. Hammond was shocked at the way Cas looked. What an incredible change! Dressed in an old bathrobe and pajamas, he looked deathly ill. There was a line of perspiration on his upper lip; his hair was askew; his eyes seemed sunken into their sockets and frightened; his face was pale and haggard.

Yablonski gazed balefully at the three men. He had caught Slater with another doughnut half-eaten. Cohen was coldly assessing him just as he had the man's home.

Yablonski's eyes narrowed as he stared at Cohen. "You're not a doctor," he said suspiciously, and took a step backwards.

Slater had the presence of mind to display the black bag. Yablonski eyed them all warily once more, then relaxed and sank into a kitchen chair.

"Some more coffee, Momma," he said, and held up a cup.

"Sorry," said Cohen, taking the cup away, "but we can't allow any more of that."

Yablonski looked surprised. "McCarthy even pours it for me!"

"Uh-huh," said Cohen, "and what do you suppose he puts in it first?"

Yablonski blinked. "He wouldn't!"

"We'll find out, Mr. Yablonski. Now, I'd like to brief you on what we'll be doing. We're going to give you Zethacide-B. Do you know what that is?"

"No."

"It's like Sodium Pentothal—truth serum. It's going to have something of an opposite effect to what your Dr. McCarthy has been doing. Instead of closing the mental wound, so to speak, we'll be opening it up, exposing it and probing it, and we hope the end result will be *elimination.*" He paused and gave Hammond a here-goes glance. "If you have any doubts or questions, feel free to express them now."

Yablonski met his gaze. "Is this really going to help me?" he asked.

"Positively," Cohen hoped.

Yablonski grunted and got up. "Where do we do it?"

"Your bedroom, I think, since that seems to be the scene of the recurring crime."

Slater went first with his equipment and Yablonski followed him. Cohen paused for a whisper with Hammond: "Give us fifteen minutes to get him under, then come on up. And get Momma out of the house."

Hammond watched the parade file up the stairs, then moved to take charge of Mrs. Yablonski. He went straight for the coffee and gave her a reassuring smile. She smiled back shakily, then asked, "Is he going to be all right?"

"Yes, ma'am. He's in better hands now than he's ever been."

"Are you sure?"

"Yes, ma'am." Hammond went to the kitchen door, sipping his coffee. "Mrs. Yablonski, why don't you take a walk around the pond. A long, slow walk. There's nothing you can do here right now."

"You're probably right," she sighed after a moment. She hesitated, looking upstairs, then she turned and went out the door.

Hammond waited until he could see her starting around the pond, hands thrust into the pockets of her sweater, eyes glued to the ground ahead, then he relaxed and finished his coffee.

Fifteen minutes later, he went upstairs.

The curtains were drawn and Yablonski was stretched out on the bed, his right pajama sleeve rolled up. They had removed the bathrobe. Cohen sat beside him on a chair, taking his pulse and watching his eyes, now and then rolling back the lids to check his submission to the drug. Slater was in another chair where he had set up his portable recording studio: a collapsing table and a Uher CR-134 cassette deck. He had positioned an omni-directional microphone on a stand over the bed. He was wearing headphones and he nodded as Hammond came over.

After a moment, Cohen whispered, "He's under."

Hammond removed his uniform coat and pulled three sheets of paper from the inside pocket. He gave them to Cohen. "You handle the first page," he said, and tossed his coat on a rocking chair.

Cohen studied the questions. "Have to wing it a bit," he

said softly. He bent over Yablonski and quietly said, "Cas . . . can you hear me?"

Yablonski's head rolled barely an inch and his mouth opened.

". . . Yes . . ."

"I'm your friend, Cas. I'm Cohen."

". . . Friend . . ."

"That's right. And there are other friends here. Everyone in this room is a friend. Am I your friend?"

". . . Yes . . . friend . . ."

"And you can tell a friend anything, can't you, Cas?"

". . . Yes . . ."

"Are you comfortable, Cas? Just nod."

Yablonski nodded.

"Do you feel sleepy?" Yablonski nodded again. "Do you like being asleep?"

Yablonski hesitated. His nod was not convincing.

"You're not sure about that, are you, Cas?"

". . . No."

"Do you have trouble sleeping?"

". . . Yes."

Yablonski shifted his lower body, as if he were trying to get comfortable.

"You don't like going to sleep, do you?" Yablonski nodded. "You go to bed late?"

". . . Yes."

"How late? Later than your wife?" Yablonski nodded. He was tossing and turning. "You like to put it off as long as possible?"

"Yes."

"There's something about sleep that bothers you, isn't there?"

"Yes."

"What bothers you, Cas?"

There was no reply. Yablonski lay there, his eyes barely parted, milky and lost. He had stopped tossing.

"Dreams bother you?"

". . . Yes."

"The same dream?" Cohen was consulting Hammond's prepared questions now, planning ahead.

". . . Same dream."

Yablonski's huge hands fluttered as he answered. Cohen watched them for reactions.

"It's not a very nice dream, is it?"

"No."

"In fact, it's damned unpleasant, isn't it?"

"Yes!" Yablonski was getting excited.

Cohen paused, then took another tack. "You were in the Navy, weren't you, Cas?"

Yablonski nodded again.

"From 1951 through 1955, correct?"

"Yes."

"Did you like the Navy?"

". . . Yes."

"Are you sure about that?"

"Yes."

"What did you like about it?"

"My job."

"And what was that?"

"Pilot. Harbor pilot."

"That sounds like a good job. What exactly did you do?"

Yablonski's reply came out like rote: "I was a harbor pilot in the Boston Navy Yard. It was my job to guide heavy cruisers out of the harbor into the bay."

Cohen stared at him, then got up, motioned to Hammond and drew him across the room to the window. "He's been told how to answer that question."

"Autosuggestion?" asked Hammond.

"Yes."

Cohen returned to Yablonski. Hammond looked out the window and saw Mrs. Yablonski standing down by the shore, looking up at him. He turned away quickly.

"How long were you a harbor pilot?"

"My whole tour. I was a pilot for four years."

"Without a break? You served no other duty?"

"I served no other duty."

"What about training? Where did you train?"

". . . Boston."

Cohen was quiet for a moment, then he blurted out: "Philadelphia Navy Yard."

Yablonski's hands fluttered, but that was all. He said nothing. "1953," Cohen said, again prompting. Yablonski's eyes rolled back as if he were trying to force himself out of this.

"Harold Fletcher?" asked Cohen, reading from Hammond's sheet. Yablonski seemed to freeze. Cohen said it louder: *"Harold Fletcher?"*

Suddenly, Yablonski let out an animal groan—his hand snaked out and clutched Cohen's shoulder.

"Fletch!" yelled Yablonski. *"Fletch!"*

Cohen stared at the big fingers splayed across his back. He had to pry them off.

Yablonski looked around in surprise, then his head dropped on the pillow.

"Slater, give him ten more cc's," Cohen said.

Slater went to the bathroom and returned with his horse needle. He gave Yablonski another dose of the drug. Hammond took Cohen aside and advised him that it was time to press into the dream. "Make him relive it," he said. "I want him to face it and remember it."

"We'll see," said Cohen. "I don't want to hurt the man. There is the chance that McCarthy has been right all these years in suppressing this thing."

"It's also possible he planted it," Hammond replied.

Cohen grunted. In a few moments, the drug took effect and he was able to resume.

"Cas, do you know a man named Dr. McCarthy?"

". . . Yes."

"Who is he?"

"My psychiatrist."

"Can you describe him?"

"I . . ." Yablonski hesitated, struggling with that. Finally, he exhaled and lapsed into silence. Cohen exchanged a look with Hammond. Hammond motioned for him to continue.

"When you see Dr. McCarthy, what does he do with you?"

"Talk."

"He talks or you talk?"

"He does."

"Don't you do any of the talking?"

Yablonski squirmed. He was having trouble with probing questions; he seemed unable to linger on a subject. ". . . Not much," he finally said.

"Don't you tell him your dream?"

". . . No."

Cohen looked at Hammond again. "Cas . . . What does Dr. McCarthy say to you?"

". . . Don't know."

"You don't know or don't remember? Think."

Yablonski screwed up his eyes with the effort. He sagged after a moment, his mouth opening and closing involuntarily.

"Does McCarthy use any devices in his treatment?" Yablonski looked puzzled. "Any gadgets, electronics, pieces of jewelry, any objects . . . ?"

". . . Tape recorder."

"He uses a tape recorder?"

Yablonski nodded.

Hammond came around the bed and whispered to Cohen, "What the hell would he record if he's doing all the talking?"

Cohen ignored him. "Cas, what makes you sure that the doctor actually treats you?"

"I feel better."

"You mean he makes the dream go away and your anxiety with it? He gets rid of your fear?"

". . . Yes."

"But he doesn't do anything to you that you can remember other than talk and record himself?"

". . . Right."

Cohen sat back a moment, then leaned closer and spoke softly into Yablonski's ear. "I want you to relax now, Cas, just loosen up. You're at home, in your own bed, and no harm can come to you here. You're feeling sleepy, just as you feel every night, and you want to drop off; you want to relax and forget everything. . . ."

He watched Yablonski's chin drop to his chest and his mouth close, then he said in a clear voice, "Is anything stopping you?"

For a moment there was nothing, then Yablonski's hand fluttered. His lip curled in what might have been distress.

"Is anything wrong, Cas?" asked Cohen.

Yablonski shook his head slowly.

"Anything bothering you?"

". . . Don't want to . . ."

"Don't want to what?"

". . . Sleep . . . afraid . . ."

"Of what?"

". . . Dreaming."

"Dreaming what?"

". . . No!"

"Cas, you *are* asleep. You *are* relaxed. You're lying in your own bed and you're sleeping."

Yablonski relaxed again.

"Now . . . you're beginning to dream."

Cohen checked the list of questions. "You're dreaming about the sea. . . . You can smell the sea . . . damp air. . . . You're on a ship . . ."

He paused. Nothing was happening. Yablonski wasn't responding. Cohen rose and huddled with Hammond. "It's not working," he said.

"Is he fighting it?"

"I think so. He doesn't want to remember. We've got to do something to make him *feel* he's at sea."

"What you want is sort of a psychodrama?" asked Hammond.

"Exactly."

Hammond looked around the room, but there wasn't anything that could help simulate the sea, except . . .

"The bed!"

Cohen stared at him. Hammond moved to Yablonski and motioned for Cohen to help him. Together they raised Yablonski to a sitting position.

"You're standing, Cas," said Cohen. "Standing on a ship's deck . . ." Cohen prompted him until he rose of his own volition and stood upright on the bed.

It was a very soft old mattress and Hammond was grateful for that. It made what he was about to do much easier. He put both hands on it and shoved downward. The bed undulated, causing a slight rocking motion.

Yablonski grunted.

"You're standing on the deck, Cas. Can you feel it?" said Cohen. "Feel the rocking motion? It's the sea, Cas. You're at sea."

Hammond continued pushing against the mattress while Yablonski waved his arms a bit to steady himself. "At sea . . ." he finally said.

Cohen said nothing for a long moment, allowing Yablonski to convince himself.

"Now, Cas . . . you're on a ship . . . in your dream. . . . What do you see?"

". . . Fog."

"You see fog." Cohen smiled triumphantly at Hammond. "What else?"

" . . . Cranes."

"What cranes? Where are they?"

". . . Shore."

"You're on the shore?"

"No . . . see them . . . from the ship . . . moving away. . . . They . . . they're gone . . . in the fog . . ." He seemed actually to see something fade from view, then he looked down.

"You're moving away from the dock," said Cohen. "What do you see on board?"

Yablonski's eyes searched the imaginary deck, his lids barely open. "The deck . . ." he said, ". . . the men."

"Other men? The crew?"

". . . Yes."

"Who are they, Cas?" asked Cohen. "Names."

". . . Terkel . . . Olively . . ." He looked around, as if peering through the fog, trying to make out figures. ". . . Martin," he added, squinting in Cohen's direction.

Then he reacted to something; he seemed to be listening. Suddenly, he shouted: "Fletch! Get your hands up! Didn't you hear the horn?"

He raised both hands from his sides and motioned for imaginary crewmen to join him. "Come on!" he said.

Cohen looked at him questioningly. Hammond climbed up on the bed and hissed at Cohen to do likewise. Hammond raised a hand and Yablonski grabbed it.

"That's it!" he said, then looked right at Cohen. "Martin! Come on!"

Cohen climbed up and linked hands with Yablonski. Their movements rocked the bed and made him tighten his grip. He began to glance around furtively, waiting for something, listening.

Hammond kept up the rocking motion by flexing his knees every few seconds.

"Those bastards . . ." Yablonski was looking over his shoulder at something behind Hammond. Instinctively, Hammond followed his gaze and immediately felt foolish. "You wouldn't catch *them* standing here . . ." he continued, and smiled as the imaginary man to his left laughed.

"Fog's lifting," he said a moment later, then cast an apprehensive look backwards. From then on, he kept looking back, waiting for something to happen, except for a moment when something to his right irritated him.

"Martin, will ya can the whistling?!"

Cohen flinched, then said, "Anything you say . . . Cas."

Hammond had the feeling this wasn't going anywhere.

Whatever Yablonski was waiting for had to be prompted. He wondered what it would take. Then suddenly, he hit on it.

"Holy shit, Cas, here we go!" he called out.

Yablonski stiffened. His grip on their hands tightened. His face contorted in fear and apprehension. "Hang on!" he yelled.

Hammond glanced at Slater—he was staring up at them in total disbelief. What a picture they must have made.

"Oh, God . . ." moaned Yablonski. "Here it comes."

Then Hammond had the strangest feeling, a sensation crawling up his body from below and behind. It was a moment before he realized it was Yablonski quivering next to him—no, vibrating like a tuning fork—and his vibrations were spreading through his outstretched hands and into Hammond and Cohen. Hammond's mouth opened in disbelief—

"The deck! Look at the deck!" Yablonski yelled. He was staring down at the bed. Hammond and Cohen looked.

"It's going!" Yablonski shrieked.

"What is it, Cas? I can't see!" Cohen said.

"The deck! It's not there! It's gone!" He stared, his leathery skin shaking. "I can see the river!"

The vibrations coursing through him began to shake Yablonski around, and he pulled the other two men with him, contracting and advancing. His head snapped up and he looked at Cohen with terror. "It's okay, Martin, it's okay—!"

Cohen felt the grip tighten into a viselike crush as Yablonski clenched his teeth and closed his eyes. Hammond heard something clicking and realized it was his own teeth. The vibrations from Yablonski were tearing through him. The bed rocked and squealed from their movements.

Yablonski abruptly threw his body into an upward strain and tightened every muscle into a knot. Then he came down in a powerful bounce that set the bed to rocking violently. Hammond almost lost his balance.

When he looked up again, Yablonski was staring around, then squinting up at something to his right. It took a moment for Hammond to realize he was looking into the sun. . . .

"The sun?" said Hammond.

"It's bright," Yablonski replied. "Where the hell did it

come— Jesus, look out!" He ducked and pulled Hammond and Cohen with him. The bed rocked again and Yablonski followed something with his eyes.
"What was it?" asked Cohen.
"That little boat just missed us!"
Hammond studied Yablonski's face: he was looking around with real interest, putting a hand up to shield his eyes from the sun and staring off into the distance.
"What's happened?" asked Hammond. "Where are we, Cas?"
"I don't know. Terkel—?" Yablonski dropped their hands and motioned to one of the other men. He seemed to follow where "Terkel" was pointing. After a moment, he glanced sharply away, then blinked in surprise.
"Norfolk!" he said.
He turned back to Hammond. "Fletch! We're in Norfolk!"
Hammond gaped at him, but didn't have time for another question. Yablonski glanced sharply up at the wall behind them, reacting to something, then leaped back into place. The bed shook as he grabbed Hammond's hand and fished for Cohen's, but it was as if he didn't even see Cohen—he kept missing the outstretched fingers.
"Martin," he snapped. "Martin, come back!"
Hammond nodded to Cohen to get to the edge of the bed, to follow Yablonski's lead. Cohen stepped as close to the edge as possible. Yablonski looked right through him.
"Martin, it's starting again! Come back!" He wiggled anxious fingers at him, then his hand seemed to be snatched from the right as the next man closed the circle.
The vibrations started through Yablonski again. He watched "Martin," terrified, following him with his eyes as he seemed to move further away. "Martin!" he called again.
The quivering got violent and Hammond felt Yablonski's body tense under it. "What's happening with Martin?" asked Hammond.
Yablonski's eyes flicked open. "Get away from the bow—!" he yelled, then lunged forward but was "held back" by the circle.
"What's he doing?!" yelled Hammond.
"Don't jump—!" Yablonski ripped his hand free of Hammond's and the movement pitched Hammond off the

bed to the floor. Yablonski was still "held back" by the man on his right. He lurched forward again and shrieked once more, "MARTIN!"

Then a shiver of horror shot through him. He screamed and threw up a hand to shield his eyes from something. His body jerked and then was viciously whipped about by an unseen force. His screams mounted—

The bedroom door was thrown open and Mrs. Yablonski stumbled in, staring wildly at her husband and sobbing, while Cas stood cowering and whimpering on the bed until he sank to his knees. . . .

"That's not a nightmare," said Cohen. "That's a fucking pageant."

They were holding a conference in the bathroom. Slater was still in the bedroom, watching Mrs. Yablonski tend to her husband. They had got him quieted down without giving him another shot, and he was resting now, stretched out on the bed. Mrs. Yablonski was bathing the sweat from his face and whispering in his ear to soothe him.

"His dream sounds the same as Fletcher's," said Hammond quietly. "How could two men, living completely separate lives, have the same outlandish nightmare?"

"You're still assuming it *is* a nightmare," said Cohen.

Hammond eyed him uncomfortably. "Or something induced under hypnosis," he said.

"Or maybe they both lived it."

Hammond regarded him grimly, then closed the door and sat down on the john. "Impossible," he said.

"Well, that may very well be," Cohen retorted, "but I wouldn't be quick to rule it out."

"Are you willing to believe it?"

"It's not a question of what you're willing to believe. That's the way it appears. You have to prove it one way or the other."

"Please don't tell me my job," said Hammond. "I can't even figure out what we're being asked to consider. What happened? Disappearing decks, the guy quivering like a piano string, and what's all this stuff about Norfolk?"

Hammond jumped up and paced. "If this really was Navy, who in hell was behind it? And what's the big secret that for all these years had to be locked up inside that man's head? And Fletcher's!"

"I don't know, Hammond," said Cohen, "but if someone was willing to go to these lengths to bury it, then maybe it did happen!"

It made a crazy kind of sense. A group of men involved in a secret project many years ago, brainwashed to wipe the event from their minds—only it resurfaces in the form of nightmares, requiring frequent relaundering. Enter Dr. McCarthy. But who was he working for? The Navy itself?

Hammond opened the door and looked out at Yablonski again. Researching a man's records, digging facts, finding the men who had bugged his office, putting the collar on Dr. McCarthy—these were things he could deal with. But disappearing ships, psychological tampering, people with the same nightmares—he was in over his head.

Cohen handed him the list of questions and said, "I believe it's your turn now. We've unlocked the door. You push it open."

"DE-166."

Yablonski's head rolled over slowly and one milky eyeball fixed itself on a point somewhere over Hammond's head.

"DE-166," Hammond repeated. He was in Cohen's seat now. Slater was still manning the recorder. Cohen was leaning against the wall, prepared to grab Yablonski if he showed signs of excitement. Mrs. Yablonski had been prevailed upon to leave. She was downstairs in the kitchen.

"DE-166, USS *Sturman.*"

A long silence with Yablonski licking dry lips. Then he croaked, ". . . The ship . . ."

"The ship? What ship?"

"*Sturman* . . . Philadelphia . . ."

"The Navy Yard?"

"Yes . . ."

"When, Yablonski?"

". . . 1953."

"You were assigned to the *Sturman,* DE-166?"

Yablonski nodded.

"At the Philadelphia Navy Yard in 1953?"

"Yes."

"But that's not the truth, Cas. You told us you spent that time in Boston, didn't you?"

"I . . ." Yablonski's brow furrowed in confusion.

"Which is it, Cas?"

He licked his lips again and moved his head.

"Can't you get your story straight? Come on, which is it?"

Cohen made a motion for him to go easy; Hammond ignored him.

"I . . . was a harbor pilot in the Boston Navy Yard—"

"Oh, come on, Yablonski! That's bullshit! That's what he *told* you to say. You *were* in Boston, but you were in Philadelphia, too—isn't that true?"

"I . . . yes."

Hammond glanced at Cohen and saw him relax.

Success was short-lived. He could not coax a description of McCarthy out of him. The doctor had walled that up too well. But Yablonski was able to describe Harold Fletcher, right down to the man's vanity about his hands.

"He used to manicure them all the time. He was even dating this little manicurist in Philly . . ."

Yablonski was able to remember other names, too. Olively and Terkel surfaced again, and Martin. . . . At the mention of Martin, Yablonski quivered on the bed.

"What's the matter, Cas?" asked Hammond. "What about Martin? What happened to him?"

Yablonski's head rolled; his eyes went back into his head. His hands tensed, clutching the sheets. Cohen stood up straight, ready . . .

"Martin, Cas. Tell me what happened. Why does he scare you? Did he hurt you? Come on. . . ."

". . . Martin . . ."

"That's right. Let's have it. Tell me and it won't hurt anymore."

"Won't hurt. . . . Martin . . . he was the only one. . . ."

"Only one what, Cas?"

His head rolled faster now and he was starting to get the shakes. He broke out in a cold sweat, then groaned, loud and long. Cohen dropped a hand, ready to grab Yablonski's arm.

"The only one *what?*" presssed Hammond.

"Went zero . . . *ZERO!*" The scream started low in his throat, reaching out, trying to escape—

Cohen was on him first, but he thrashed around so violently that it took both of them to hold him down. The scream broke off and he was yelling at the top of his voice. Hammond was electrified listening to a broken jumble of barely comprehensible phrases—

"Zero . . . Gone! . . . Rinehart warned us . . . don't get locked out! . . . Terkel suicide . . . Olively and Butler . . . walking through walls . . . Rinehart . . . those bastards! . . . They knew! . . . The project . . ."

Yablonski grabbed Hammond and pulled his face close and Hammond could smell the bile in his breath. His eyes were wide and his nostrils flaring as he screamed, "What happened to me? What happened to me—?"

He fell back on the bed, laughing hysterically. He was too weak to thrash about anymore, so Hammond and Cohen let him go. He laughed himself into helplessness while Hammond stood up to regain his composure. Then he leaned directly over Yablonski and said, "Who was Rinehart?"

"He . . . ran the project . . ."

"What project, Yablonski?"

Yablonski's helplessness vanished so suddenly that Hammond barely had time to jump out of the way. Yablonski leapt off the bed and flung himself against the wall, screaming, "THIN AIR! MARTIN JUST VANISHED! STEPPED OFF THE DECK AND WENT ZERO—!"

Yablonski went rigid. His screams broke off, and finally he slumped to the floor, unconscious.

They stood there in silence, all three of them staring at the rag doll on the floor as they became aware of their own breathing. Cohen was first to draw himself up and move to Yablonski. "Christ, Hammond, you don't leave me much to work with. . . ."

He and Slater pulled Yablonski up and dragged him back to the bed. He looked harmless now, a tired, middle-aged man who'd reached inside himself and found hell.

"What are you going to do with him?" asked Hammond.

"Rebuild the brick wall around that . . . *experience.*" Cohen spat out the word distastefully. "Have to plant the suggestion that it's real, that he lived it, and that it can't hurt him anymore. It'll take time before he's willing to unlock those doors himself, but we'll give him all the keys."

Slater fumbled in the black bag and produced a small, battery-powered light device. Cohen settled it into his palm and flipped it on. The light spun around on a cycle, appearing to go on and off at a constant rate. He switched it off and looked up at Hammond.

"It's all real, Hammond. I don't know how, but he lived through all that."

Hammond was almost ready to admit it to himself, but he asked, "What makes you sure?"

"He gave only one answer by rote, the one about his duty in the Navy. That's the only thing that was actually planted. He retold the dream in his own words: *his* images colored by *his* language. But there's something else I should have caught even earlier: there would be no point in implanting a nightmare and then working so hard to make him forget it."

Hammond stared at Yablonski's quiet form as Cohen continued, "However, someone who suffers from a bad experience can be induced to forget it—for his own well-being. That's what your Dr. McCarthy has done, drawn a screen over something in this man's life that he would be better off forgetting."

"Probably right," said Hammond, "except I don't think it was done for Yablonski's well-being, but for someone else's."

Cohen did not reply. He shook Yablonski awake and held him so he could see the milky eyes, then aimed the cycling light at them.

Hammond backed out of the room and left them alone.

In the early afternoon, Hammond walked Cohen and Slater back to the car, asking them to analyze the tapes of their session and break down Yablonski's comments into topics.

"I want every name he mentioned on a separate list. I want locations cross-referenced with dates. I want questionable statements broken out but in context, and then I want a complete transcript in order. Send the names over to our Data Center in the Hoffman Building with a request to check them through BUPERS. I want a follow-through on each one from 1953 up through today."

"Okay, boss," said Slater. "And if the patient has a relapse, give him these." He gave Hammond a bottle of pills. "One at a time and four hours apart."

"Thanks, fellas. For everything."

They shook hands, started the car, and drove away. It had been agreed that Hammond would stay behind to give Yablonski moral support.

He turned from the disappearing car and looked back at the house. It was quiet now; there was no indication of the drama that had unfolded only a few hours ago.

Yablonski and his wife were downstairs in the den, listening to music. Cohen had sedated him enough to keep him relaxed and had forced him to take his mind away from what he'd been through.

Hammond gazed out at the pond and wondered about the facts in Yablonski's dream. What in the world had he been involved in back in 1953? Why the incredible secrecy? Why had there been only one doctor on his case over twenty years? Was the Navy trying to cover up a terrible mistake in its past?

Was it the Navy at all?

He sat down in the den with the Yablonskis. They were on the sofa. Cas had an arm around his wife and she was resting against his chest. He watched Hammond, waiting for the next move.

"I would like to set up a meeting with your Dr. McCarthy," said Hammond.

"Why?"

"The man is a phony. His credentials don't show up anywhere at BUPERS. Nobody I've talked to has ever heard of him. And for more than twenty years, he's caused you and your wife unnecessary grief. I want to put a stop to it."

Yablonski eyed him narrowly. "What's all this got to do with Naval Intelligence?"

"Somebody's been tampering with Naval records. And lives. Your old mate Fletcher is dead. And I believe McCarthy's responsible."

Yablonski scowled at Hammond, but it was his wife who got up and faced him, quivering with emotion. "You can't . . ." She choked on the words. "You can't put him through any more. I won't allow it!"

"I'm sorry," said Hammond, rising and facing her. "But your husband may be in danger, Mrs. Yablonski. Fletcher died shortly after he talked to me. Your husband has made inquiries at BUPERS that touched off an alarm. They know their hold on him is weakening—they're waiting to see what he does."

Yablonski got up, face flushed with anger. "Who is *they*, Hammond?"

"Other than McCarthy, I don't know. But it has to be more than a one-man operation."

"If they're going around killing people, why have they waited twenty years?"

Hammond thought for a moment, then realized the answer was logical: "Fletcher was no longer a safe risk. And now, neither are you."

"But why?" Mrs. Yablonski asked. "Why would they do this?"

"To conceal whatever it was that happened back in 1953."

Yablonski gave him another one of those blank stares, then looked at his wife. She went to the window and folded her arms across her chest. She wouldn't let them see her face. Yablonski seemed to give it some thought, then faced Hammond again.

"No."

"Look," Hammond said, controlling his exasperation. "You were treated by the man for twenty years. You can't even tell me what he looks like! Where do you meet him?"

"At the hospital—"

"Where at the hospital? How? You just walk in and ask for Dr. McCarthy? I tried it. He doesn't exist!"

"The back door," Yablonski mumbled.

"The back door." Hammond repeated it for effect. "You meet with a legitimate psychiatrist by going through the back door? Doesn't that seem odd to you?"

Yablonski sagged. He glanced at his wife again, torn between her feelings and necessity.

"What do you want me to do?"

"Get in touch with McCarthy. Set up a meeting for today. I'll go with you." Yablonski looked hesitant. "We have to get our hands on him, Mr. Yablonski, and fast."

Mrs. Yablonski whirled. There were tears running down her cheeks and her voice shook as she advanced on Hammond. "If anything happens to make my husband worse—"

She broke off. Yablonski stared at her, surprised.

"I'm going with you!" she added, glaring at them both in defiance. She stalked out of the room.

Hammond stared after her, conscious of an inner excitement at her protective strength. Just the sort of woman he should have had, he thought. But it wasn't going to be easy to convince her to stay in the hotel during the session.

Yablonski turned back to him. "If you're wrong," he

said, "if you've been wrong down the line, then I'll be losing the only man who has ever helped me."

"Call him," said Hammond. "And let's find out."

8

The atmosphere in the narrow observation room was oppressive. The walls, thickly padded to deaden sound, retained heat as well. The musty smell of old insulation hung heavily, discouraging conversation among the four NIS agents who watched Yablonski through the two-way glass. He paced the consultation room restlessly.

Jack Keyes, the electronics man, finished plugging in wire leads that ran from the junction box on the shelf between two small consoles. He wiped the perspiration from his forehead and looked at Hammond. "That's it," he said. "We're in business."

Hammond grunted. Through the glass, he saw that Yablonski had finally stopped pacing. He stood by the table, fingers splayed out, his right hand running along the edge, as if trying to get reassurance from the solidity of the wood.

For a fleeting second, Hammond thought about Mrs. Yablonski. Maybe he should have permitted her to be there, if only to see McCarthy in action. He dismissed the idea immediately. It was bad enough she had insisted on coming to Boston with them. But if she were here now, instead of stuck in a hotel room, would she be able to control herself? And wouldn't their attention be on her?

Keyes flipped a switch on the console. Yablonski's heavy breathing whumped through the speaker, picked up by the sensitive button mike under his shirt.

Andrews glanced up at the speaker, then at Hammond. "Your man sure is jumpy, Nick. Who are we expecting —Dracula?"

Hammond smiled and eased past Michaelson, heading for the connecting door.

He stepped into the consultation room, loosened his tie, and tugged at the top button of his shirt. The movement jiggled the headset of the two-way radio attached to his belt.

Yablonski watched him readjust it. "Is he here?" he muttered.

Hammond gave him his most confident smile. "Soon. Why don't you relax? You're not alone, you know."

"I hope he doesn't show," Yablonski said bitterly.

"Has he ever missed an appointment?"

"No . . ."

McCarthy's instructions over the phone had been very definite, directing Yablonski to Consultation Room 12 at the Boston Naval Hospital. "Just take it easy," he had told Cas, "and we'll have you as good as new."

Keyes' voice came over the speaker. "Mr. Yablonski, would you mind saying something? I need a level."

Yablonski whirled around and stared into the mirror. "A wh-what?" he stammered.

"A voice level. Count to ten and speak normally, if you would, sir."

Yablonski started counting, his eyes darting, trying to penetrate the mirror. Keyes made him do it twice before he was satisfied.

Yablonski's stiffness subsided. He pushed off from the table and shuffled over to one of the two chairs in the otherwise bare room. He sat down and stared at Hammond.

"I'll be all right," he said after a long silence.

Hammond nodded and left the room.

Michaelson helped Keyes into a metal harness that fit over his shoulders. Keyes pulled the chest strap tight and grabbed a small video camera. He screwed it into the mounting plate, adjusted the height, then plugged it into the recording console. "It's not the best light for this," he said, "but I'll get it all."

"Everything else check out?"

Keyes ran a hand over the console. "Channel two is Boston PD, three is for video, four is for us."

Hammond looked at his watch. McCarthy was five minutes late.

Hammond's headset clicked. It was Hernandez, hidden behind the pumping station with a clear view of the unlocked back door. "Got a car," he said. "Navy staff. Making a second pass."

"Occupants?" asked Hammond.

"Driver only. Couldn't get the plates. He's turning the corner. Maybe Oviott can pick him up—"

From the far end of the building, Oviott cut in: "Got 'em first time around."

"Hold everything," said Hernandez. "He must have made a U-turn behind the building. Coming your way, Nick."

Michaelson and Andrews moved to the two doors of the observation room and watched Hammond for a cue.

"Oviott," said Hammond, "you'll be patched into Boston PD. Have them run the plates. Everyone else stay put until I give the word."

While Keyes made the connection, Hammond bolted for the connecting door. He stepped into the consultation room, fighting back a surge of excitement. "Cas," he said quietly, "looks like he's on his way in."

Yablonski half-rose out of his chair with a stricken look. Hammond waved him down. "Just trust me," he said. He closed the door and stepped back into the observation room before Yablonski could reply. He pressed the headset to his ear.

Hernandez came back on the line. "He's parking it . . . coming out of the car . . . Jesus—he's a big one, Nick. Light Commander, carrying a briefcase. . . . Oh-oh, isn't that cute? He's squatting down by the rear tire, like he's checking it . . . taking a good look around. . . . Now he's heading toward you. . . ."

Damnit, thought Hammond, getting nervous. Does McCarthy know he's walking into a trap? Impossible. Yablonski hadn't tipped him off. . . . He decided the man must be taking normal precautions.

"He's inside," said Hernandez.

Hammond took short breaths, straining to listen. He heard the muffled sound of a door closing in the corridor outside. Andrews checked the cylinder of his .38 snubnose.

"I want this to go down smoothly," Hammond warned. "No guns unless we have to."

Andrews shrugged and stuffed the pistol back into his hip holster. Keyes raised his video camera and aimed it through the glass at the door of the consultation room. As it opened, Hammond whispered into the mike, "Got him."

Then he took a good look at the uniformed man who stepped briskly into the room and greeted Yablonski.

McCarthy *was* big. Hammond pegged him at six-four, 230 pounds. A shock of red hair, graying at the temples, a large meaty face with a prominent "drinker's nose." Tiny red veins tracked out from the nostrils and colored his cheeks. Hammond watched and listened with fascination as McCarthy put Yablonski at ease.

He had a surprisingly soft voice. As he chatted, he removed a portable tape recorder from his briefcase and unraveled a microphone. All the while he was studying Yablonski.

"You sounded pretty bad over the phone, Cas. How do you feel now?"

Yablonski mumbled, "Glad to see you."

McCarthy pulled a looseleaf notebook from the briefcase and flipped pages, a reassuring smile creasing his red face. He studied the notebook, grunted to himself, then placed it on the table. He plugged the mike into the recorder.

"All set, Cas. Now just relax. You'll be feeling better in no time."

Hammond caught the slight movement as McCarthy switched on the tape recorder. He heard a low hum coming through the speaker in the observation room but couldn't identify it. McCarthy began waving the microphone in front of Yablonski's face.

The effect was amazing. Yablonski went glassy-eyed. He slumped in his chair; his head lolled to one side; his jaw went slack—

"Now, Cas, you're feeling better, aren't you? You always feel better when you see Dr. McCarthy. Dr. McCarthy cares about you. He knows how to make you feel better, doesn't he—?" McCarthy kept up a singsong commentary as he waved the mike and examined Yablonski's face. "You won't be having any more dreams for a while, will you, Cas? Will you? Come on now, nod your head and repeat after me: no more dreams for a while—"

"No more . . . dreams . . . for a while . . ." Cas nodded, almost in rhythm with the moving microphone.

"That's right, Cas. No more for a while. But you'll have them again, won't you?"

Hammond's mouth opened, appalled.

Yablonski was nodding.

"Sure you'll have them again," said McCarthy, "but things have been getting a little out of hand, haven't they? Maybe we shouldn't let so much time go by before we see each other again. You've been worried, haven't you, Cas? Worried about your dreams. You've been doing some checking up on your own, haven't you?"

Yablonski nodded. "Checking up . . ." he repeated.

"That's not good, Cas. You're supposed to come right to me when you have problems. Don't go to the Navy. Don't go to BUPERS, Cas. They can't help you. *Can't help you*, Cas."

"Can't . . . help . . ."

"*Never go there again.*"

Hammond swore to himself. Yablonski was nodding. This was just like pressing buttons. The man was a monkey in an electronic cage.

"You know what'll happen, Cas? If you go there again? Your nightmares will just get worse. Worse, you hear me? And we don't want that, do we? We want to keep them under control. That's our job. We've tried forgetting them, haven't we? But that just doesn't work. They keep coming back, so we fight them, you and I together. You can't fight them without me, Cas—"

Hammond had heard enough. He nodded to the agents. Michaelson slipped out to the corridor, leaving the observation room door open so he could hear Hammond's signal. Andrews stood by the connecting door.

"Now!" Hammond barked.

Both doors flew open at once. McCarthy spun around, his face instantly flushed with surprise. For a moment, it was a frozen tableau, then he recovered and bellowed, "What the hell do you think you're doing? Can't you see I'm treating a patient?!"

Hammond raised the speaker mike. "Please stand perfectly still, Doctor, and turn off that machine. Then put your hands at your sides."

McCarthy was slow responding, but did as he was told. Michaelson and Andrews blocked the doors, their hands inside their coats. McCarthy looked around furtively. His gaze settled on the two-way glass with sudden comprehension.

Hammond entered from the corridor. McCarthy studied

his uniform. "You better have a damned good reason for this, Commander," he snarled. "You've got no right barging in on me like this!"

Hammond ignored him. He was staring at Yablonski in the chair, his head at an awkward angle, slumped over the table, as if waiting for the ax.

"Andrews," said Hammond, "see if you can bring him around."

"Don't touch him!" yelled McCarthy. "That man is under *my* care!"

"And I'm sure he's grateful," said Hammond.

Andrews broke an ammonia ampule under Yablonski's nose. A pungent aroma filled the room. Yablonski moaned, jerked his head back, then staggered to his feet. His eyes focused on McCarthy and instinctively he backed away.

McCarthy exploded. "Idiots! Do you know what you're doing?!"

Overplaying your hand, chum, Hammond thought. "I think we do," he answered coolly.

"Then let's hear what the hospital administration has to say about it!"

"Fine. But first I'd like to see some identification, if you don't mind."

McCarthy didn't flinch. "So would I."

Hammond flashed his NIS card. There was a flicker of recognition but McCarthy disguised it well.

"This is an outrage," he snarled. "Who do you think you are?"

"I've just shown you," Hammond said quietly. "Now cut the crap and identify yourself."

McCarthy glared at him, then pulled a wallet from his inside coat pocket, slowly—so the agents wouldn't get upset. He passed a laminated card to Hammond. "Will this do?"

Hammond scrutinized it: an officer's ID card, and it looked authentic. It had McCarthy's picture above his Social Security number.

"You won't mind if I run a check on this, will you, Doctor?"

"From here?"

"We have two direct lines to Washington."

McCarthy stiffened. His bluster vanished. "I don't see any reason for that, Commander. There must be some misunderstanding." He slid a baleful glance at Yablonski.

"I don't see why Mr. Yablonski should have lost confidence in me, if indeed he has, but this melodrama is ridiculous!" He laughed, then got friendly. "Let me do this," he offered. "Let me get someone else to take over his case. I can arrange for a replacement almost immediately."

"I'll bet you can," Hammond said flatly.

McCarthy shook his head and sighed. "At least let's stop this foolishness."

It was a masterful performance. Yablonski went weak with confusion.

"That's very thoughtful of you, Doctor," said Hammond. "But I can't believe you'd relinquish a patient just like *that* after twenty-some years. Now suppose you stay put while we get this sorted out."

Yablonski stood in the observation room with Keyes, watching him patch in the direct line, but deliberately avoiding the view through the two-way mirror.

"All set, Nick," said Keyes.

"Give him the extra headset, Jack. I want him to hear this."

Keyes handed a set to Yablonski, who fitted them to his head.

Hammond picked up a phone receiver from Keyes' equipment and read into it from the ID card: "McCarthy, Lester J., Lieutenant Commander, USNR, Social Security number one-two-zero, two-four, seven-nine-zero-three."

BUPERS came back first. "No record of that name, rank, or number on our rolls, sir."

The Social Security Administration took longer. "We show that number, Commander, but not in the active file."

"Which means?"

"That the Lester J. McCarthy with that number is listed as deceased, as of January 3, 1955. Place of death, Brooklyn, New York. The number has never been reassigned."

Yablonski swore.

"Are you positive?" asked Hammond.

"No doubt about it," explained the clerk. "The name and number match."

Hammond asked for a copy of the file to be sent to his office, then hung up. He turned back to the glass and studied the bogus doctor in the other room, anticipating denials. "What have we got on the car?" he asked.

"Oviott's standing by," said Keyes, flipping a switch.

"It's hot, Nick," Oviott reported. "Boston didn't show anything, but NCIC did. The car was stolen from Moffett Field near San Francisco. It's been on the list since the tenth of March."

Moffett Field, Hammond thought to himself. What the hell was a Navy staff car stolen from northern California, doing in Boston?

Hammond ordered Oviott to stay with the car. He had Keyes call the Boston PD again, to get some lab people around to dust for prints.

Yablonski lowered the headset, a look of grim comprehension in his eyes.

"Any more doubts?" asked Hammond.

Yablonski shook his head.

McCarthy watched them re-enter. He looked detached, but Hammond felt the danger lurking behind that changeable façade. "We know your name isn't McCarthy," he said. "What shall we put on the arrest report?"

McCarthy was silent.

"Have it your way. We'll find out."

"What are you charging me with?"

"Impersonating an officer, trespassing on a military reservation, possession of stolen government property, and false identification. Andrews, pat him down."

Andrews led McCarthy to the wall and frisked him. They stripped off his coat, turned his pockets inside out, and placed everything on the table: wallet, key case, and a cigarette lighter. Andrews also took his watch and the single ring he was wearing, then scooped everything into a plastic bag.

"When do I speak to a lawyer?"

"After you're booked—in Washington."

"You can't take me there."

"The hell I can't. And after the government gets through with you, Mr. Yablonski can file a whopping civil suit. Practicing medicine without a license is strictly illegal. I don't think room and board will be any problem for you for the next twenty years."

Yablonski crossed the room, hands held at his sides. "What in God's name made you do this?" he said. "Why? I never harmed you."

A thin smile curled McCarthy's mouth. "What have I done to you, Cas? Other than help you."

"And the others?" Yablonski demanded. "Did you help them too? Fletch . . . Fletcher and—?"

"Fletcher who?" McCarthy smiled quizzically.

"Liar!" Yablonski yelled, lunging for him. Michaelson pulled him away. Andrews covered McCarthy. The two antagonists glared at each other.

"Too bad your friend couldn't leave well enough alone," McCarthy said. "You've started something, but I'll finish it! I've got a long reach."

The threat was chilling, and for some reason Hammond believed him, probably because of the man's unflappable arrogance. "Get him out of here," Hammond said.

Andrews manacled the pseudo-doctor's wrists and pushed him toward the door.

"Put him in a padded cell in the psycho wing," Hammond added. "He might as well get used to it."

Michaelson released Yablonski and followed the others out.

"Bastard," muttered Yablonski.

"He just threatened you."

"So what? If there's enough to hold him for trial, what can he do?"

"He's not working alone. There may be others who can make good on it. I'd like to place you and your wife under protective custody, put you into what we call a 'safe house' for as long as it takes to wrap up the case."

"That's ridiculous," said Yablonski. "He's nailed and he's blowing hot air. There's nothing he can do. Christ, he's done his worst." He looked right at Hammond, then laughed bitterly. "You know what's so crazy about all this? That guy *did* help me. He hurt me and helped me at the same time. I'd like to know why."

It wasn't until the Boston PD showed up to tow away the car that the ideas buzzing around in Hammond's head struck with full force. *The date*. The date Social Security had given for the death of the real Lester J. McCarthy—January 3, 1955—was just prior to Fletcher's discharge from the Navy. Fletcher had been separated in February, Yablonski in May. And "Dr. McCarthy" had come into existence around the same time.

A mental laundry had been founded in the spring of 1955, and had been operating smoothly ever since, apparently with only one "physician" in attendance, able to commute cross-country at a moment's notice. If it was all a sham, then why was it so elaborate? There had to be something enormous they were trying to hide. And who *was* Dr. McCarthy? Who did he work for?

Hammond watched them tow the car out of the lot and realized his nervousness had returned. Something else wasn't right. Why was McCarthy using a car stolen three thousand miles away? And how did it get here?

Hammond had a sudden feeling he shouldn't have let McCarthy out of his sight. The man was just too sure of himself.

The restraint rooms were off to one side of the main ward. Heavy steel doors with small barred openings were built into the walls along the corridor. A single bulb glowed weakly from a ceiling fixture, casting elongated shadows. Streaks of cracked green paint hung soddenly where dampness had undermined the many coats.

Michaelson and Andrews were sitting on broken-down chairs outside a bolted door. They got up when Hammond and Yablonski approached.

"Ready to go?" asked Andrews.

"Yeah," said Hammond. "How's our guest?"

"Quiet. We took off the cuffs before we put him in the rubber room. Said something about a bad shoulder."

Hammond's eyebrow shot up. "Put them back on."

Andrews shrugged and pulled out the cuffs. Michaelson moved to the door and tugged on the bolt. It shot back with a loud clang. The heavy door creaked open.

Andrews passed inside, then stopped, frozen in his tracks.

"Holy shit," he said, looking around in confusion.

Hammond moved past him. His eyes circled the cell, taking in the heavy padding, the built-in bunk and toilet attached to one wall. He scanned the ceiling and the corners. . . .

The room was empty.

There wasn't a sign that McCarthy had ever even been there.

"Wrong cell?" he asked.

"Not a chance!"

Andrews jumped to the door and looked down the hall both ways. Michaelson stepped in further, touched a wall, then began to search for seams in the padding.

Hammond stared around in disbelief. McCarthy had been locked in here and there was no way out but the one door. There were no windows. Not even a vent wide enough to crawl through. No way in the world for McCarthy to get out unless he'd been *let* out. Michaelson and Andrews would never . . .

What if McCarthy had hypnotic abilities they hadn't seen yet? Hammond laughed involuntarily. Was the guy actually Mandrake the Magician, able to cloud men's minds—?

Hammond's gaze swung around to Yablonski: *his* incredulity was giving way to stark fear. Then Hammond jumped at a sharp sound.

Andrews was pounding on the walls, raising clouds of dust. Then he began ripping away the padding, exposing solid wall beneath. The other three stood motionless, watching his frantic efforts. After five minutes he stopped, leaning against the one intact wall, knowing it was useless to go any farther.

Their gazes met and they all knew the same thing.

Michaelson said hoarsely, "There's no way he could have done it, Nick."

"Then where is he?" Hammond asked.

No one answered. Hammond turned slowly and his gaze again fell on Yablonski, white-faced and grim, standing in the doorway.

"About that safe house," Yablonski said.

9

When they walked into the hotel room in Boston, Mrs. Yablonski jumped off the sofa and went right to her husband. He hugged her and smoothed her hair, whispering in her ear that everything was going to be all right. She looked at Hammond then, trying to read his mind.

Hammond spoke quickly. "Mrs. Yablonski, this is Michaelson. He's going to drive you back to Cotuit. I want you to pack clothes for a vacation. We're going to take you and your husband somewhere where Dr. McCarthy can't find you for a while—"

"What happened?" she interrupted.

"Michaelson will explain in the car."

"No! I want to know *now*!"

Yablonski wrapped an arm around her shoulder. "Momma, I'm okay. Really. We've got to trust them . . . for a while." The last he said with a dark glance at Hammond.

"Mrs. Yablonski," said Hammond, "I wish I knew enough to tell you exactly what's going on, but I don't yet. Until then, you and your husband will be somewhere safe, and if he needs medical care, he'll have it."

She frowned at him in mistrust, then caved in. She went to get her purse and Hammond gave out instructions. Andrews and Keyes would personally deliver the videotape and sound master to Cohen and Slater at the Naval Research Lab in Washington. Hammond himself would send all of McCarthy's effects over by special car when he got back to the Pentagon. He and Yablonski would fly back to Washington aboard the Jet-Star and meet Mrs. Yablonski at Hammond's apartment.

He didn't remember about Jan until the moment his key entered the lock. He opened the door and switched on a light. She wasn't there. Leaving Yablonski in the living room, he ducked into the bedroom. She wasn't there, either. Her clothes and luggage were gone. He stood trying to figure where she might have gone. He looked around for a note, but there was nothing. At least he wouldn't have to explain her to Yablonski. He went to the kitchen to get some beer.

NIS headquarters was still open, so Hammond called Jack Pohl, Assistant Director for Operations, and pressed him for a safe house.

"The one in Herndon sounds fine. Is it available?" he asked. "Well then, how soon? I got a guy sitting here with no place to stay."

He winked reassuringly at Yablonski, who was slumped in a chair, his legs up on the driftwood coffee table, one hand methodically sifting his thinning hair. Hammond checked his watch. Mrs. Yablonski would be arriving in another hour. He wanted everything set up so he could leave them alone overnight. He definitely did not want them here in his apartment.

"Yes, Jack, I'm still here," Hammond sighed into the phone. "Yes, Admiral Gault is well aware of what I'm doing. Uh-huh. That's fine. What day can we have it?" Hammond listened, then swore under his breath. "Let me know when I can return the favor." He hung up and turned to Yablonski. "There's a house in Herndon, Virginia, out near Dulles Airport, code name MAGIC. We can have it in a couple of days. Meanwhile, there's a beautiful little inn right up the street. I suggest we stash you there. Security will be a little tough, but we'll make every effort."

Yablonski was angry. "What makes you think anyplace is safe from that Irish Houdini? You saw how he got out of that cell. He can probably get in just as easily!"

"I didn't see *how* he got out. I would very much have liked to. And as for getting in, first he's got to know where you are. The Herndon house is very safe: it's unknown outside of NIS operations."

"I don't know, Hammond. . . . I'm not too happy about subjecting my wife to any of this."

Hammond cracked a beer and handed it to Yablonski. "The more I think about it," he said, "the more I'm positive there was a secret exit in that detention cell. McCarthy *knew* the building."

"Oh, come on, Hammond. How did the guy know you were going to put him in *that* room? How could he have made preparations for being caught and jailed in the same place?"

Hammond sipped his beer and tried not to think of the answer, but it was right there in front of them: somehow, Dr. McCarthy had *dematerialized.* Hammond shook his head and was about to make another idiotic guess when the phone rang. It was Jack Pohl. He had secured penthouse number nine at the Georgetown Dutch Inn, a two-story apartment with a kitchen and two baths.

Hammond relayed the information to Yablonski, who grunted in grudging approval. Then Hammond added: "I'm giving you an agent. He'll sleep on your couch."

"My wife'll probably cook for him."

"Then I'll get you one who's undernourished."

After arranging for Mrs. Yablonski to be met and brought to the inn, Hammond threw on plain clothes and walked Yablonski up Thomas Jefferson Street. Yablonski glanced over his shoulder at the C&O.

"Got a great view of the canal from that penthouse," said Hammond.

"I don't give a shit about canals. Just get my wife here."

"Shortly."

The penthouse suite started on the sixth floor. Hammond looked it over carefully, checking closets and rooms while Yablonski watched him. The security agent arrived. Ike Menninger was a tall kid with a perpetually open mouth, and he certainly looked undernourished. Hammond left them alone, admonishing Yablonski to send out for food as needed or to let Menninger go get it. "I'll pick you up at nine a.m.," he said, and left.

Back home, Hammond tumbled into his own bed for the first time in days and reflected briefly on Jan Fletcher's whereabouts before falling into a dead sleep.

Hammond picked up Yablonski promptly at nine, pausing only long enough to be certain Mrs. Yablonski was comfortable and to reassure her that everything was going to be all right. He left Menninger with her and drove to the Pentagon with her husband.

"How long do you think this will take?" asked Yablonski. "Catching McCarthy."

"Not long," Hammond said hopefully.

"I'm liable to lose a lot of business while you're playing

Kojak. Maybe I should give you a week and then go home and take my chances."

"Fine," said Hammond. He could negotiate for more time later.

He stashed Yablonski in his office and let him use the phone to call the McKay brothers and arrange to turn his boat over to them until further notice.

Hammond ducked into another cubicle for privacy, and made the obligatory call to Admiral Gault.

"I suppose you're going to want expenses for all this" was Gault's first comment after ten minutes of listening. "I'd like to see that videotape," he added.

"I sent it over to Slater for copying. I can have him run it for you later."

"Why didn't you tell me about these, uh, dreams before?"

"Honestly, sir, I didn't put much credence in them, but now since there are two men with the same—"

"You better write it all down, Hammond. You know, the way we usually do things around here."

"Yes, sir—"

"I suspect you're trying to tell me this McCarthy bugged your office?"

"I think he knows who did, sir."

"And you want to press on even if it turns out he didn't. Right?"

"On the nose, sir."

"Well, where is McCarthy? I'd like to have a word with him."

Hammond closed his eyes and struggled to describe how he and Yablonski had entered the detention room where McCarthy had been locked up and found him missing.

"Whaddaya mean, *missing*?"

"Gone. Vanished. He slipped out. I have no idea how."

There was silence for a long, agonizing moment, then Gault came back. "If you didn't have that videotape, you'd be picking up your discharge right now."

"Yes, sir."

"I can't go to Smitty with a fruitcake story like that, Nick!"

"Maybe on paper—"

"Put it there fast! Because you're still leaving me wide

open to two questions: who bugged your office and what's being done about it?"

"Yes, sir . . ." Hammond replied meekly.

He finished the conversation and got up, depressed that Gault's major concern was still the goddamned bugging incident. Hammond opened the door and looked down the hall. His eyes fell on Ensign Just-Ducky, wearing a plaid sweater and skirt and looking good enough to eat. What he wouldn't give right now for two weeks on a beach with her.

He straightened as Cohen and Slater entered the Pit and came toward his office. Slater was lugging a heavy suitcase. They convened in Hammond's office and he closed the door.

Yablonski was slouched in a chair. He met the boys' cheerful smiles with a blank stare. Slater dropped the suitcase on Hammond's desk with a resounding thud. "Greetings," he said.

"What've you got in there?" asked Hammond. "Dr. McCarthy?"

"Wouldn't that be cozy?" said Cohen as Slater popped the lid and exposed the innards stuffed with tapes and graph paper and bound reports and McCarthy's personal gear. Cohen turned to Yablonski and told him, "We put your Zethacide session through the voice-print analyzer, and it's taken the position that your dream experience was real—at least to you."

"Didn't fare quite so well with McCarthy," added Slater. "We put the tape of your Boston Tea Party through the analyzer, too. And just look at the pretty pattern." He held up a print-out that looked like the cardiogram of a patient badly in need of heart surgery. "Here, see this spot? The bozo lied right off the page!"

Slater put a report on Hammond's desk and announced, "Transcript of our session with Yablonski, more copies available as needed—" Then he shoved a handful of rough-typed copy under a paperweight. "Transcript of your meeting with McCarthy, typed by two left-handed monkeys. Here's the original software and two copies."

Slater turned over the videotape and sound master and the copies they had made. Hammond's desk was nearly covered.

"We culled out all the names mentioned in the session with Yablonski, and your Data Center is running checks on them through BUPERS. We instructed them to pinpoint the ones marked with red flags but ignore the code follow-through."

Slater moved the suitcase to the extra desk and hauled out McCarthy's gear, including the cassette recorder, a big envelope containing his personal effects, and the file notebook on Yablonski.

Cohen opened the envelope and dumped McCarthy's effects on the desk. He picked up a gold ring with a red stone set in the center. "High school ring. Black-Foxe Military Institute, Los Angeles, California, 1962."

Hammond looked puzzled. "McCarthy's a lot older than that."

"It's not his ring. Probably picked it up in a pawn shop somewhere. Thought it would give him the image of a regular guy. School doesn't even exist anymore. However, Slater located a former graduate from two years later who checked his old yearbooks. No McCarthy at all."

Cohen picked up McCarthy's wallet. "Every scrap of ID in here is phony, but none of it is stolen, and it's all been carefully pieced together to give no indication whatsoever of the man's true identity."

"Too bad you didn't get his clothes," said Slater. "We could have traced the labels."

"Government issue?" Hammond snorted.

Slater shrugged. Cohen held up the cassette deck. "A standard Sony TC-66 Auto Shutoff Cassettecorder, several years old, serial number expertly burned off, probably with a soldering gun. It's like every other model of its kind except for one thing: it *doesn't record.* Instead, it throws out a low impedance oscillation, which, in combination with a rhythmic motion of the microphone, can induce a state of hypnosis. I put Slater under in five minutes."

"It's really not very sophisticated," Slater commented, "just insidious—and effective."

"We thought perhaps we could work on Mr. Yablonski with this for a while—" Cohen glanced at Yablonski, whose eyes were shut, hands pyramided before his mouth and nose. "See if we can't peel him back any further. Using McCarthy's gear, we might be able to reverse the process."

Yablonski's eyes opened and he stared uneasily at the small black instrument.

"Not just yet," said Hammond. "Carry on."

Cohen flipped open McCarthy's notebook. "Basically, this book is a record of McCarthy's treatment for Yablonski, complete with update notations and separate status reports. There are progressive instructions on how to deal with him: some typed, some written in several different hands. The progressive comments lead us to believe they were perfecting their technique over a period of years. New ways to keep the patient under control, tailored to the man's current psychological profile and taking into account changes in his personal life."

Cohen walked behind Yablonski. "They watched him; they judged him; they even molded him a little bit."

He threw a cautionary glance at Hammond, who looked to Yablonski. The older man was staring at the floor but well aware of Cohen standing behind him. "Don't hold back on my account," Yablonski said.

Cohen turned pages in the notebook. "It's right here in black and white: clear instructions on how to get the patient to do whatever they wanted. Mr. Yablonski, do you own a Bertram Sportfisherman?"

"Yes."

"When did you buy it?"

"Three years ago."

"August, three years ago?"

"Yes."

"Here's a report dated the previous April, in which McCarthy has located three boats to choose from and he recommends the Bertram Sportfisherman." Yablonski looked up. "There's an entry in early June," Cohen went on, reading: " 'Bertram Sportfisherman, first suggestion to patient.' " Cohen faced Yablonski. "He *made* you buy that boat, Mr. Yablonski."

"I *wanted* to buy it!" Cas bellowed.

"He made you *want* to buy it. He guided you. He led you by the nose."

Yablonski stared up at him, angry, tensing to spring.

"That's enough," Hammond said softly. "We get the idea."

Cohen shrugged, unflappable. He flipped a couple of pages and resumed. "Phone calls—Yablonski's requests for help—all logged in here along with date and place of treatment. They've been using the Boston Naval Hospital for better than fifteen years. During that period, the spread between time of call and time of treatment has been substantially shortened. In 1964, Yablonski called on a Tuesday and met with the doctor on Thursday. Last year, he was able to call on a Monday morning and be treated that same night."

"And yesterday, the spread was three hours," finished Hammond.

"Not so amazing if McCarthy lived full time in Boston and had nowhere else to go. But we know he was treating Harold Fletcher in Los Angeles, also on twenty-four-hour call. We're faced with an interesting problem: how does this guy get around so fast?"

"And how does he walk through walls?" added Hammond.

Cohen grunted. "I leave that to you. Now, the best for last," he said, and yielded the floor to Slater, who held up McCarthy's cigarette lighter.

"Anyone need a light?" he asked. "Hope not, because this is not your garden variety Zippo. A light from this one will put you *out* like a light. Forever. It contains a lethal dose of a little-known gas distilled from tropical cone shells.

"There's nothing much new about the device itself," Slater continued. "It's just like any other butane lighter. The Russians have been using this little devil for years. But the gas—that's something else. Very new, very classified. It comes from a deadly species of cone shell called the textile cone, found in profusion from Polynesia all the way to the Red Sea. Its sting consists of a puncture wound delivered by a highly specialized venom apparatus. The mortality rate from such a wound is 20 percent, higher than from rattlers and cobras. Death can occur within several hours. Symptoms begin with a burning pain, followed by numbness and tingling throughout the body, centering primarily on the mouth and lips. If the sting is severe, it will induce paralysis and possibly death through cardiac failure. To manufacture a lethal dose, you catch yourself a few cone shells, extract the poison, and distill a concentrate strong enough to kill instantly. I wanted to try this one out on Cohen, but he talked me out of it—"

He stopped. Hammond was getting to his feet, his face white. An image was running through his mind: Harold Fletcher's body slumped over a coffee table in the apartment at the Watergate—the chain-smoker who would never question the offer of a light from his own *doctor*.

That's why the ashtray was empty: McCarthy had *cleaned it*.

Hammond turned to Slater. "Are you sure it leaves no trace? We've got a body that might have to be exhumed."

"Waste of time. Let the poor guy rest."

Yablonski stood up, staring first at Hammond, then at the ominous cigarette lighter. "Fletcher?" he asked.

"I'm almost sure," Hammond replied with disgust. He nodded at Slater. "What about fingerprints on that thing?"

"*Nada.* And none on his stolen car, either. Personally, I'd say the guy doesn't have fingerprints, or maybe he burns them off regularly."

Cohen and Slater spread their hands simultaneously and Slater said, "That's all, folks." They wrapped up, stacking all the originals, tapes and reports, on Hammond's second desk and chucking duplicates back into their suitcase. Hammond asked them to take the videotape and run it for Gault, and to keep going on their content analysis of Yablonski's Zethacide session.

As soon as they were gone, Hammond turned back to Yablonski. He was tense with anger. "How do you feel about McCarthy now?" Hammond asked.

"I'd like to settle up." He got to his feet. "Nobody runs my life for me."

They sent out for coffee and doughnuts, which arrived just ahead of a yeoman from the NIS Data Center with the results of investigating the names taken from Yablonski's tape.

Butler and Martin were both deceased. So was Terkel: he'd committed suicide in 1967. They were still checking on Rinehart. Of the handful of names checked through BUPERS, only one turned up alive and available: Olively, listed as a patient at the Navy Psychiatric Center, Bethesda, Maryland.

Hammond thanked the yeoman and looked at Yablonski. "Remember anything about Olively?"

"No. I'm sorry."

"Don't worry." Hammond reflected a moment, then said, "I think we should pay him a call. Feel up to it?"

"Okay."

They were just leaving the Pit when the receptionist motioned Hammond to the phone. It was Jan Fletcher, calling from Dulles Airport. She was going back to L.A. to straighten out her husband's affairs and get his will filed. Hammond barely listened—he still had images of her husband taking the light offered by Dr. McCarthy. But he couldn't tell her that. He asked for her home phone number.

"Why?"

"I want to keep in touch," he replied.

There was a silence from her end and Hammond found himself listening to the airport terminal sounds over the line, then a set of digits came across in a hurried voice: "Four-seven-three, seven-three-oh-four." She hesitated another second, then said, "Thanks for showing me you haven't changed at all."

She hung up and Hammond scowled with confusion. Was that a compliment or an insult?

An insult, he finally decided, as they drove up Wisconsin Avenue to the National Naval Medical Center. And she was right. He hadn't changed. His job still came first. But what was she supposed to be to him now? Friend? Sister? Conscience? He decided he would get in touch with her . . . someday . . . if only to get in the last word. But if he contacted her again, wouldn't he be obliged to tell her the truth about her husband?

Hammond parked the car and walked with Yablonski across to the Psychiatric Center. He had a twofold purpose in bringing Yablonski along. Perhaps the sight of an old shipmate might stir something in Olively—or vice versa. Hammond needed more information from Yablonski and he was hoping to get it without Cohen's and Slater's methods.

The Psychiatric Center was a three-story complex with one whole floor devoted to the care of permanent government wards. Hammond and Yablonski were met by a civilian resident and Hammond briefly outlined his purpose. They were sent along to the recreation ward in the company of an attendant named Hanson, who had a pale face and an egregious grin and looked more like an inmate than a guard.

The huge recreation hall resembled every nuthouse

Hammond had ever seen in the movies. These men really did exist on the fringes of humanity. They were pathetic shells. Hanson agreed: "These are the hard cases. None will ever get out of here. They're all victims of arrested development or regression. You won't find any gross errors in here: everyone belongs."

There were patients everywhere: on couches, at card tables, around the TV, dancing to records. Two of them were on a caged balcony, building castles in a sandbox. A few were grouped at the far end of the hall, attempting calisthenics under the supervision of another attendant. While most did their best with toe-touching exercises, one old fellow insisted on doing knee-bends instead.

"Now, let's see, you want George Olively. Right over there." Hanson guided them toward a table near the arts-and-crafts counter, at which was seated a small, fiftyish man resting his chin on his hands and staring into space.

Hammond heard labored breathing and realized after a moment that it was Yablonski. His face had become yellowish and he was sweating. He seemed to be fighting back nausea. He fell behind as they came up to George Olively. The little man gave them an empty look as they stepped into his line of sight. His hair stood up in disarray and his white pajamas were rumpled.

Hanson said, "We're making great progress with him. Watch." He went to the crafts locker and Olively immediately sat up, smiling eagerly. Hanson brought him a set of crayons and a big pad of paper and Olively fell happily to work, scrunched over his table like a little gnome . . . or a child. He drew in slow sweeps, then changed colors to fill in his people.

Then Olively paused, having difficulty with his drawing. He made little moaning sounds and picked at a sore on his cheek.

Hammond examined Olively's work—stick figures at the level of a first-grader. He looked closer. The drawing was a set of curved lines converging at a point in the background. In the foreground were the stick figures of men with their arms raised, a few of them holding hands, big smiles on their moon faces.

Olively would start to draw a figure then stop before it was complete, rock back in his chair, and growl to himself. Then he would dive in again, draw another figure . . .

Hanson let this go on for perhaps five minutes, then he said, "George? George, look at me. Look up." Olively was bouncing in his seat. He stopped and focused slitted eyes on Hanson, then laughed uproariously.

"George, how are you today?" asked Hanson, ignoring the laughter.

Olively stopped laughing and set his crayons down in a neat row. Then he rubbed his head, grinning foolishly, and said, "All gone."

He jumped out of his chair and ran to the wall, pressed his back hard against it and covered his face with his hands.

"It's a game," explained Hanson. "What's the game, George?"

"Nah-here! Nah-here!"

"Oh yes, you are here. I can *see* you, George!"

"NAH-HERE!" Olively insisted. He shook his head and clapped his hands. "All gone!"

Hammond had the chilling feeling he knew precisely what Olively was talking about. Yablonski moved around the table and stared at the stick-figure drawing.

"Hammond!" he croaked. He pointed at the sketch and now Hammond was certain. The converging lines were the forward section of a ship, the point of convergence obviously the bow. The figures were crewmen standing in a circle, arms outstretched, holding hands. And the incomplete figures were meant to be disembodied men in various stages of invisibility!

Olively leaped back to his work and stood in front of it, frantically pushing Yablonski away and making hand motions to indicate danger. Yablonski stumbled back and Olively calmed down.

"It's a classic case of childhood regression," Hanson explained, oblivious to what was really going on. "We're lucky we managed to stop him at age-level five. . . ."

Hammond did not contradict him. There was no reason to. He heard a groan beside him and turned to see Yablonski backing off, driven away by a silly grin that had come over Olively's face. Yablonski whirled suddenly and bolted across the room, crashing into a crowd of dancers and knocking them to the floor.

Instantly, the men in the room were on their feet, screeching and hurling epithets. Yablonski made a half-hearted attempt to help one of the men he'd knocked down, but the man kicked him and screamed and Yablonski backed away in revulsion, racing to the exit.

Hanson quickly became a forceful shepherd, screaming back at the men, wearing them down, then calming them. Hammond was left with Olively, who was supercharged with excitement. While patients rushed about in every direction, Olively dove at the table, snatched up his drawing and ripped it to shreds, howling with glee. Hammond moved to stop him, but he was too late. In the pandemonium around him, Hammond succumbed to a wave of frustration and slammed Olively up against the wall.

Olively screeched in fright. He threw his head back and forth and struggled to escape Hammond's grip.

"Olively, listen to me!" Hammond ordered him harshly. "Listen to me! The *Sturman*, Olively . . . *Sturman*!"

A flicker of recognition, then that silly grin again.

An alarm went off somewhere outside the hall and attendants came running in. One of them raced right up to Hammond and laid a hand on his shoulder. "Sorry, sir," he said, "you'll have to leave!"

Hammond held Olively a moment longer, then turned him loose. Olively dashed to his table and grabbed a crayon. Hammond shook free of the attendant and stared at the pad of paper as Olively drew three numbers in the unsure hand of a five-year-old child.

1 6 6.

Then he looked up at Hammond with that crazy smile. As the attendant whisked him to safety, Hammond heard Olively muttering, "All gone . . . all gone . . ."

10

Hammond found Yablonski outside, sitting on a bench in one of the Center's expansive parks.

"McCarthy had him committed in 1965," said Hammond. "Signed the papers himself, as a civilian psychiatrist."

Yablonski said nothing. His hands were motionless at his sides and his face was turned up into the warming sun. Slowly, his chin came down and he stared at the grass in front of him. Then he looked up and met Hammond's gaze. "We should have left it alone. McCarthy was doing us a service by burying this thing."

Hammond bristled. "Oh, no, he wasn't. He was killing you by inches. You can't purge a real experience from someone's mind. You can shove it into a closet and bolt the door, but it's still going to be there, waiting to get out. You might have gone another ten years with McCarthy, but some morning you'd wake up in terrible trouble and he wouldn't be there anymore . . . because I'd have nabbed the sonofabitch!"

Yablonski stared at him.

"You can't just think about yourself, Yablonski. There are still other people walking around with the same problem. We've got to find them—and McCarthy."

Yablonski was very still, then he got up and stuffed his hands in his pockets. "All like Olively . . . ?" he asked in a cracking, beseeching voice.

"No!" Hammond snapped. "He's one of McCarthy's failures! It could just as easily have been *you.*"

Yablonski nodded dumbly, then his body shook with a sudden tremor. He kicked the bench and stared at the psychiatric building. "It's so crazy . . . I almost think I belong here."

* * *

Hammond took him to Hogate's, a restaurant in southwest Washington. Yablonski had nothing to say on the drive to the restaurant, and once they were seated at a table, Hammond had to order for both of them. Hammond tried to draw him out, but Yablonski's conversation was restricted to monosyllabic grunts.

Their table overlooked the Potomac and finally that seemed to help. The placid river had a soothing effect: Yablonski could relate to it. He began to ramble about his love for the ocean. From boyhood he'd been involved with the sea, first as a poacher off private docks on the eastern seaboard, then in his teens as a crewman aboard deep-sea boats. He had enlisted in the Navy to keep out of Korea, thinking he could do a nice, easy tour as a yardbird.

"And then they got to me," he said. "Volunteer for this, volunteer for that. Come on, ya big Polack, what're you afraid of? There's a war on."

"You volunteered for this experiment?" asked Hammond.

"Must've," shrugged Yablonski. He screwed up his eyes and struggled to clear away the cobwebs. "Damnit, I still can't get it straight. I volunteered: I know I did."

Hammond guided the conversation back to fishing: the last thing Yablonski needed right now was more catharsis. Olively had been enough for one day. He got Yablonski to talk about the years after his Navy duty, land-locked because he had developed a psychological fear of the sea, always afraid to stray too far from Boston because of his need for McCarthy. He had taken a string of unfulfilling jobs. He'd been drunk a lot, too, and the center of several barroom brawls. It wasn't until he met Rosie that his life began to take shape.

"Who's Rosie?" asked Hammond.

"Momma," said Yablonski. "We got married in 1961. We were both a little old to have kids, so we didn't. I married her because she got me to talk. I'd been close-mouthed for years. She just dug into me, over and over: 'What do you love, Cas? What have you ever done with your life that meant something to you?' 'Fishing,' I said. 'Fishing it is, then,' she said."

He smiled proudly. "She got me back to the sea again."

"She's a great woman, Cas. And she loves you very

much," said Hammond, feeling a twinge of regret at his own emptiness.

"I know. She's put up with a lot . . ." He paused and then grew worried. "But if I become like Olively . . . I don't know."

Hammond excused himself and went to call his office for messages. There were none. He returned to find Yablonski working on his fifth cup of coffee. He drained it, squinted through the window at the line of black clouds rolling in from the east.

"We'd better beat it," he said. "We're in for a hell of a storm."

Dusk settled over Georgetown along with the first raindrops as Hammond looked for a parking place on Jefferson Street. He dashed up to his flat and dropped off his briefcase. As he hurried with Yablonski up the wet sidewalk toward the inn, a man in a tattered windbreaker crossed the street and fell into step behind them.

Walking with his head down to avoid the rain, Yablonski had finally gotten around to discussing McCarthy. "You know what I can't figure?" he said. "How I ever got suckered by that bastard."

"You weren't the only one," Hammond answered. "He fooled lots of people."

A car drove past them, scooted into an opening along the curb, and parked by a fire hydrant.

"But I always thought I had good judgment," said Yablonski. "I can read the weather, the ocean . . . and most men. Jesus! Talk about being wrong."

Hammond only half-heard him. He was distracted by movement in the parked car just ahead. A man got out of the passenger side, left the door open, and shambled toward them.

"Commander?" he said.

Hammond squinted at him. "Yes?"

"Help an old Navy man down on his luck?"

Oh, crap, he thought, the panhandlers are getting bolder. He stopped. Then he heard the footsteps coming up behind. He grabbed Yablonski's arm, muttered "Sorry," and made to pass on the inside.

The panhandler blocked their way and pulled something from his sleeve. Hammond heard a click and the switchblade snicked open.

"Guess we'll help ourselves," said a voice behind them.

Hammond whirled. Yablonski stopped in confusion. The man in the windbreaker stood about an arm's length away. They heard the click of *his* switchblade.

"Wallets," said the panhandler.

"Okay!" Yablonski shouted, startling everyone. Then softly, he repeated, "Okay . . . just take it easy . . . don't stick anybody."

Insanity, thought Hammond. He could see the rush-hour traffic on M Street less than a hundred feet away. The Dutch Inn was only yards—

"Now . . . I don't have a wallet," Yablonski said. "No wallet . . . just a money belt. . . ."

"Ain't that convenient," said Windbreaker.

"I'll wear it home," said Panhandler.

Hammond felt the movement as Yablonski fumbled with his buckle and started to draw the belt out of his pants. What money belt? wondered Hammond, then got the idea. . . .

"C'mon, Admiral. You, too!" said Panhandler.

Hammond reached into his back pocket slowly, careful not to let his fingers tangle in the cloth.

The knives flashed and both muggers lunged at once. Hammond sidestepped. Windbreaker shot by and Hammond's foot whipped a leg out from under him. He hit the wall.

Yablonski ripped his belt free and flailed away at Panhandler with the buckle end.

"Into the street!" shouted Hammond and pulled Cas with him, then yanked off his uniform jacket and wound it around his forearm.

They stood side by side for a second, Yablonski dangling the belt, scraping the buckle along the blacktop like a rattler threatening his prey. "Come on, you bastards," he muttered.

The muggers erupted at them. Windbreaker jabbed at Hammond and his blade went through the jacket, getting tangled as Hammond twisted his arm. Hammond kicked back and they went down in a heap.

Yablonski danced on the balls of his feet, goading Panhandler, who shifted the knife from hand to hand and edged in looking for an opening. Yablonski dodged to the right and, as Panhandler lunged, brought the buckle end of his belt around hard. He tore off a piece of cheek. Panhandler screeched, dropped his knife, and stumbled back.

Yablonski swung the belt like a whip, forcing Panhandler back until he stumbled, then Yablonski pounced on him, looped the leather around his neck, and dragged him down.

Hammond rolled on the street with Windbreaker. He still had the knife arm pinned, but felt punches raining down on his side.

Panhandler rammed his elbow into Yablonski's gut and knocked the breath out of him. Yablonski let go and fell back against a parked car. Panhandler dove to the ground, scooped up his knife, and, as Yablonski reached for him again, cut him in the leg.

Cas went down with a pained yell, then rolled under the car.

Panhandler swore and turned to see about Hammond.

They were bathed in light as a car turned off M Street and headed toward them. A squeal of tires. The car stopped. Windbreaker released his knife and jumped back, frightened. Hammond struggled to his feet. The driver flicked on his high beams and held down his horn.

Windbreaker stumbled out of the light. Hammond pulled the knife from his jacket and whirled to confront Panhandler.

Everyone froze, except the man on the horn. They stood there for an eternal second, bathed in light: Hammond hunched over in the street, Yablonski half-emerged from under the car, clutching his knee.

Panhandler whirled to his partner, shielding his face from the light. "Fuck it!" he yelled. "Let's go!"

He raced for their car. Hammond made a move to follow, knowing he couldn't catch up, but prompting the muggers to put on a burst of speed.

Both men jumped into the car. The motor roared to life and they drove off, fishtailing all the way up to M Street.

The horn stopped. The persistent driver got out and rushed over. "You need an ambulance?" he asked, determined to be helpful. The street started to fill with people.

Hammond ignored them and the rain. It was starting to pour. He bent over Yablonski. "How bad is it?"

Yablonski's teeth were clenched. He felt gingerly around his leg and examined the blood on his fingers. "I always bleed when I'm cut."

Hammond helped him up. "You fight dirty."

"Not dirty enough. Nice little city you've got here."

Yablonski put his weight on the bad leg and winced. "Jesus. Is it open season for muggers all year long, or just when it rains?"

"Those were not muggers."

Yablonski stared at him in disbelief. Hammond helped him through the crowd. "It's all over, folks," he said. "Give us an address, we'll mail you some blood."

Somebody laughed. The crowd broke up. The man from the car was still looking for recognition. He followed Hammond and Yablonski to the curb. "Thanks for the horn, friend," said Hammond, and shook his hand. The man beamed and walked away.

"What do you mean, they weren't muggers?" growled Yablonski, hobbling painfully.

"Muggers don't attack crowds. They like one victim at a time. For sure, not two big guys. This was a setup; they were pros and they blew it. They must have followed us from my place."

"Who—?" Yablonski stopped, catching on. "McCarthy?"

Hammond nodded.

Now Yablonski got the point. "My wife!" he said. He pushed away from Hammond and stumbled toward the inn entrance. Hammond followed. They ignored startled looks from the desk clerk and bellman. They rode up six floors with their eyes glued to the indicator.

Before the elevator doors were fully open, they burst into the hallway and raced to penthouse nine. Hammond banged on the door. "Mrs. Yablonski, open up!"

Not a sound.

"Outta the way!" snarled Yablonski and braced his shoulder for a charge. Hammond turned the handle and pushed in. The room was dark.

"What's the password, wise guy?" came Menninger's voice from within.

Hammond and Yablonski froze, then Hammond said meekly, "Don't shoot?"

"I'll think about it, sir. Jesus Christ, use your head next time, will ya—otherwise you'll lose it!" Menninger switched on the light and stuffed his .38 back into its shoulder holster. He closed the door behind them.

"Anybody come in?" asked Hammond. Yablonski was already heading for the stairs.

"ROSIE?" he called out.

"I'm okay, Cas." She appeared on the upper landing,

frightened but in perfect shape. Then she saw the blood. "Your leg!" She came down the stairs fast and took him to a chair.

Hammond explained what had happened, then asked Menninger to call a doctor. While he went to the phone, Hammond checked his arm for damage and discovered no cuts, only one large bruise. He smelled a roast cooking in the kitchen and wondered how any of them could eat after all this.

Hammond turned at the sound of a muffled sob. Mrs. Yablonski had sunk onto her husband's chest to stifle a burst of crying. Hammond felt awkward; Yablonski eyed him darkly.

"I hate to admit it," said Hammond, "but there's no way we can make a firm connection between what just happened and this Dr. McCarthy business. *We* know it, but nobody else will believe it."

Yablonski brooded a long moment, then nodded in resignation. His wife was looking from one to the other. "What are you talking about?" she said, getting to her feet and facing Hammond. "My God, you've been playing with his life! What are you going to do about it? *Write a report?!*"

"Momma—" said Cas, reaching for her hand.

She pulled away. "No! He's perfectly willing to put you through hell, but if somebody else tries, he should be willing to stop it!"

"Momma, he's doing his best."

"Cas . . . he's trying to tell you that they could kill you and get away with it!"

Yablonski stared at his wife, then looked at Hammond searchingly.

"Mrs. Yablonski," said Hammond. "They were after *me.*" Her anger subsided and she looked confused. Yablonski got hold of her hand and this time she didn't pull away. She was close to tears again. "You're right, though," added Hammond, "they could get rid of all of us. So we have to get you out of Washington, right now."

"Doctor's on his way," reported Menninger, returning from the phone. "How's the leg?" He bent over Yablonski and peered at the wound. He sent Mrs. Yablonski for cold water and a cloth.

Hammond went to the phone and called Jack Pohl at home. "Jack, I want that safe house and I want it tonight! Don't give me any more crap! Whoever's out there now, you tell them to make room or clear out! I'm putting my people in there now and that's that!"

He hung up immediately and smiled to himself. He hadn't told Jack Pohl where to reach him, which meant Pohl had no choice. He returned to the couch. Mrs. Yablonski was hovering in Menninger's way.

"He's going to be okay," said Hammond. "And he's going to be hungry."

She looked up from Cas and nodded. She forced herself back into the kitchen. Hammond sat down with Yablonski and watched Menninger cleanse the wound with cold water, then wrap a dry towel around it. "Didn't go too deep," he said. "Should be walking on it in a couple of days."

Menninger finished and went to call for transport. Hammond sat in silence until Yablonski voiced the question going through both their minds:

"Who the hell is behind all this?"

"I have no idea," said Hammond, "but they've just raised the stakes. I'm in to the finish."

Michaelson and Andrews came out in the NIS camouflage van with the doctor, picked up the Yablonskis and Menninger, and hauled them off to the safe house in Herndon. The last thing Yablonski said to Hammond as he was helped into the back of the van was, "Don't forget about me, buddy."

Hammond promised he wouldn't. He knew what Yablonski meant: he wanted to be included when Hammond got McCarthy cornered. He was fully committed now.

Hammond went home, daring the lone walk down the street to his flat, eagerly peering into empty cars and doorways, itching for another go, but no one showed. He arrived home safely, but he felt even less safe behind closed doors. The attackers must have known his address: they'd been lying in wait for him.

The hell with it, he decided, and plowed under the covers. Tomorrow the track-down would start in earnest. If they could get his address, then by God he could get theirs. His eyes were just locking shut when he saw the little calling card Jan Fletcher had left behind. A single scarf, dropped or placed under his easy chair by the bedroom window. Hammond snaked over the side of the bed and plucked it from the carpet. He brought it to his nose.

Her perfume. He wriggled back under the covers and played with the silk between his fingers. This time he let himself go, summoning up images that he had long ago forced deep into the recesses of memory: her body, her face soft and radiant, flesh warm and rippling, hair in his fingers . . .

He groaned and shoved the scarf under his pillow. He closed his eyes and forced himself to sleep, cursing her.

When he saw the envelope sitting on his desk, with Paul Mallory's return address, he knew immediately what it was: the list of government vendor companies insured by Tri-State. He skimmed the prestigious names while sipping black coffee. He was familiar with most, and there was no reason to assume any of them were illegitimate or fronts. Was he reaching? Maybe. Somebody from one of these companies could have written Paul Mallory an anonymous letter, somebody who knew Mallory and Fletcher—but the writer would have to have known of Hammond's involvement. McCarthy? There was no reason to assume McCarthy knew enough about the insurance business to feed on its hidden fears of rumor and innuendo. No, McCarthy must have gone to someone who knew the business—whom to write to and what to say. One of Tri-State's clients? An employee?

Hammond swore. It could be anyone. It was another goddamned blind alley. Just the same, he intended to hang onto this list. He stuffed it into his briefcase, which by now was bulging with papers on the whole Fletcher-McCarthy-Yablonski debacle. It was getting to be a pain to lug it around.

He called Slater at the lab and was not surprised to hear him weary and snappish. "We're not really making progress with any of these tapes, Hammond. We're going in circles. Why don't you come over and sniff around for a while?"

"Maybe I will."

The Naval Research Laboratory was in the southernmost corner of the District of Columbia. To get there, Hammond had to plow through a herd of traffic. But the worst part of the journey was the arrival. The Navy Lab buildings were situated right next to a huge sewage disposal plant at the edge of the Potomac. The aroma was all-pervading.

Hammond clumped through miles of corridor until he

found Cohen and Slater in the electronics workshop, a wide room littered with movable equipment. Cohen rose and stretched as Hammond slouched over.

"Sonofabitch, this place stinks," said Hammond.

"Goodness, he noticed," Cohen grinned. "We're recommending this site for the new opera house."

Slater was in a foul humor. His beard was sticky with the soup he was gulping from a can. He was hunched over a large piece of equipment, listening to an agonizingly slowed-down replay of their session with Yablonski. It was the voice-print analyzer, and Slater kept scanning reams of computer graph paper spilling out on the floor, looking for telltale signs of—

"What the hell *are* you looking for?" asked Hammond.

Slowly, Slater looked up and exchanged glances with Cohen. Both men shrugged in unison. "Damned if we know," they said.

"But we'll find something," added Cohen.

"Very funny. What part are you listening to now?"

"Oh, a good part. Real good." Slater stopped the machine, switched off the graph run, changed speed and ran the tape.

Hammond listened to his own voice asking Yablonski, *"Martin, Cas. Tell me what happened. Why does he scare you? Did he hurt you? Come on . . ."*

Hammond let them run the tape until they got to Yablonski's outburst of screaming: *"Zero . . . Gone! . . . Rinehart warned us . . . don't get locked out! . . . Terkel suicide . . . Olively and Butler . . . walking through walls . . . Rinehart . . . those bastards! . . . They knew—"*

Hammond reached over and shut it off. Cohen held up a sheet of paper. "Zero. Don't get locked out. For the life of me, I can't figure what he's talking about. Sounds like some sort of code. . . ." Cohen shook his head.

"Well, maybe it is," suggested Hammond. "Code for an action or a part of the experiment, whatever that was."

"Maybe," agreed Cohen, grinning at him. "But that's just another guess, isn't it?"

"Run it back," said Hammond. Slater replayed the section and Hammond slammed down the pause button after Yablonski's line, *"Walking through walls . . ."*

"Yablonski's wife said something about walking through walls. She thought she saw her husband do that."

Slater and Cohen stared at him—their silence loud in its intensity. "She thought she saw what?" asked Cohen.

Hammond didn't answer. He knew how strange it sounded, how impossible. He changed the subject. "Any more word from BUPERS on the name Rinehart?"

"No," said Cohen, still aghast. "That's the only one that doesn't check through."

"Maybe he wasn't in the Navy," suggested Slater offhandedly.

Hammond's eyes widened. "Of course!" he shouted. "Even if it was a Navy operation, they could have had a civilian running it!"

"Great!" exulted Slater. "Now if you can just figure out which of the ten zillion projects he might have been connected with in 1953, you're in clover."

"Have you guys looked into that at all?"

"Can't get anywhere without a name. ONR has all the records on classified as well as non-classified projects, but without the code name, you're up shit creek."

"Couldn't we just give them an idea what it was about?"

"Then you have to depend on memory," said Cohen, "and there's no one at ONR who goes back that far."

Hammond asked Slater to run some more of the tape.

"Who was Rinehart?"

"He . . . ran the project . . ."

"What project, Yablonski?"

A flurry of thumping sounds, then a louder one, a body smashing against a wall.

"THIN AIR! MARTIN JUST VANISHED! STEPPED OFF THE DECK AND WENT ZERO—!"

Abrupt silence, then the sound of a sack of potatoes hitting the floor. Long silence . . .

Hammond depressed the pause button again. Slater leaned back and let him take over the machine. Hammond replayed the section twice.

"Who was Rinehart?"

"He . . . ran the project . . ."

"What project, Yablonski?"

"THIN AIR! MARTIN JUST VANISHED—!"

Hammond looked up with an inscrutable smile. "That's it," he said.

"That's what?"

"Don't you get it?"

"Get what? He never answered the question," said Cohen.

"The hell he didn't."

"He changed the subject and told us how this guy Martin vanished into thin air—"

Hammond played the tape again, and stopped at the words *"THIN AIR!"* He looked at Cohen and Slater triumphantly and said, "That's the name of the project!"

He didn't give them time to recover. "Who do I see at ONR?" he asked.

"Commander Canazaro," replied Cohen.

Hammond barely acknowledged him with a nod—he was already marching toward the exit. "Call him. Tell him I'm on my way and I want him to be there!"

Slater sighed and ripped off the end of the graph paper, grabbed a hunk of it, and announced he was going to the can.

11

Commander Hector Canazaro, head of the archive section at the Office of Naval Research, turned out to be a short, dark Latin with a pencil-thin mustache. He waved Hammond to a seat facing his desk and smiled primly.

"Here's everything we have on Project Thin Air, Commander," he said, and presented Hammond with a bound file folder, stamped prominently with the words TOP SECRET.

"Have you had a chance to go through it?"

Canazaro nodded. "Briefly."

Hammond unwound the binding. "Was the start date 1953?"

"No, 1942."

Hammond looked up in surprise.

"The cover brief will give you the historical sequence of the project. Everything's listed in chronological order."

Hammond slipped out the cover brief and examined it. It was an index of names, dates, and places. Most of them meant nothing to him, but at the very top of the list was a name he was delighted to see: Rinehart!

He pulled a notepad from his pocket and laid it on the desk. "I'm going to make notes," he said, "but I'll want a Xerox of everything."

"No problem." Canazaro took the papers out of the file and bunched them so their edges were straight.

Hammond went back to the top of the brief and said, "First entry—12 March 1942. Security clearances for a Dr. Emil Kurtnauer and a Mr. Whitney Rinehart. Who are they?"

Canazaro scanned the first two memos. "Kurtnauer was a physicist—University of Chicago. Austrian citizen. Hired as chief scientist for the team. There's a note here—see letter of recommendation from Albert Einstein—"

Hammond's eyes widened in surprise. "Let me see," he

said, and took the clearances. After examining them and verifying the name he asked, "Have you got that letter?"

Canazaro fumbled with the papers, then shook his head. "No."

"Okay," Hammond said, and made a note. "Now what about Rinehart?"

Canazaro read aloud: "Hired away from Sperry Corporation and assigned as administrative chief of Thin Air."

"Anything else on that date?"

"Yes. Orders cut for a Captain Charles A. Sartog to become Navy liaison."

Hammond wrote down Sartog's name, then looked at the next entry. "4 May 1943?"

"Authorization for Sartog to requisition DE-166, USS *Sturman*. Lieutenant Commander Leslie Warrington appointed C.O."

Hammond reached for the two pieces of paper. Mimeographed orders, brittle with age—more connecting links. The skeleton was starting to grow flesh right before his eyes.

"27 October 1943 What's that about?"

"Seems to be a report on Warrington. He had a nervous breakdown and was relieved of command."

Hammond took the paper and scanned it. It was nearly as brief and cryptic as the covering entry, which simply gave the date and title of the document. There was no explanation for the C.O.'s breakdown.

"4 September 1944," said Hammond.

"Back up. You skipped something."

Hammond checked the cover brief. "That's the next entry."

Canazaro shook his head. "There's a set of orders here for a Captain Richard Steinaker to succeed Sartog as Navy liaison."

"Effective when?"

"10 April 1944."

Hammond tapped the cover brief and frowned. "What happened to Sartog?" he asked.

"Not covered in here."

Hammond felt the first twinges of annoyance. "Is there any other mention of him?"

Canazaro riffed through the diminishing pile of papers and finally said, "Nothing at all."

"Don't you find that a little strange? They bring in a

new man; there should be some indication of what happened to the old one."

"Well, there isn't."

"Seems like we have a few gaps in the chronology. What about September of '44?"

Canazaro scanned the next sheet of paper. "Pursuant to the directive of Presidential Order number . . ." He read on silently, then handed the paper to Hammond. "You'd better read this one yourself."

Hammond took it, conscious of Canazaro's agitation. Beneath the official jargon, the letter was ordering a drastic cutback on funding for Thin Air. It mentioned in clear language the importance of another top-secret effort called "The Manhattan Project" and how that was to take precedence over anything else.

Hammond looked up slowly and met Canazaro's grim stare. "In other words," Hammond said hoarsely, "Thin Air was in the same class as the building of the atomic bomb." He paused, incredulous. Today everybody knew what the Manhattan Project was. But who ever heard of Thin Air?

"How many inquiries have you processed on this?" he asked.

"I think yours is the first." Canazaro's brow furrowed. Two fingers curled one side of his mustache. "But there were hundreds of these wartime projects. If they were successful, fine. If not, no one over heard about them. I would guess Thin Air must have been one of the flops."

Hammond was not convinced. "I show four more entries," he said, resuming the work, "the last one in 1955."

Canazaro read from the remaining papers, summing up each of them in a sentence: "3 March 1945, Dr. Kurtnauer resigns and Dr. Edmond Traben is put in charge of the scientific team. 1 April 1948, a group of six Navy pilots are assigned to the project. No names given. 24 July 1949, Captain Steinaker dies in an air accident."

Hammond glanced over each document to be sure Canazaro was right. It was frustrating. Everything was so skimpy.

"Last entry?" said Canazaro.

"29 August 1955."

"Right. Dr. Traben recommends that the Navy drop Thin Air. The Navy agrees to do so."

Hammond read the documents. The way they were

phrased made one thing clear to him: a high security project that had been in development for thirteen years had abruptly been consigned to the graveyard of scientific abortions.

Then why was it still haunting Yablonski?

Canazaro scooped up the papers as Hammond closed his notepad and said, "There are holes in this file you could float a carrier through. In fact, if I were looking at this cold, I couldn't begin to tell you what Thin Air was all about. Yet I find it right up there in importance with the Manhattan Project. How do you explain that?"

Canazaro shrugged and reached for the cover brief. "I can't."

Hammond sprang to his feet and paced the small office. "And what the hell happened to those six years between 1949 and 1955? According to the official record, nothing! But I'm almost positive experiments were conducted in 1953 at the Philadelphia Navy Yard onboard the USS *Sturman*! The same ship Sartog requisitioned ten years earlier, yet there's not a single mention of it! Why is that, Commander?!"

Canazaro fumbled to retie the string around the file.

"It's as if everything pertinent has been systematically left out," said Hammond. "Or *removed*."

"Look, Hammond," Canazaro said quietly, "I've seen this happen before. Some Navy projects are still so sensitive that the files have been doctored just for guys like you. You come in, examine this, and after a minute you don't know what you're looking *at* or *for*."

"Then why keep these records at all?"

"To fulfill our function. We can say we have something on file. There's enough here to indicate the project did exist, but no more than that. There doesn't have to be."

"If the Chief of Naval Operations ordered you to produce the complete file on Thin Air, could you comply?"

"I'd hand him this," said Canazaro, waving the file.

The pattern was repeating. The file on Thin Air and the strange computer linkup at BUPERS that nobody could trace. The road went just so far, then hit a blank wall.

"Who would you suggest I ask?" Hammond said quietly.

A tight little smile creased Canazaro's face. "I'm just as much in the dark as you. The information is simply not available."

Hammond took a deep breath then blew it out. "What

about some of the names?" he sighed. "Kurtnauer, Rinehart, Traben? Ring any bells?"

Canazaro leaned back in his chair with a frown. "No," he said. "Sorry . . ."

Hammond thanked him. "If you have any more thoughts on this, I'd appreciate a call."

"Absolutely."

"And if anybody else gets in touch with you about Thin Air, let me know right away."

"You bet."

Hammond returned to the Pentagon, went straight to his office, and closed the door. He felt a lump rolling in his stomach as he telephoned the safe house in Herndon. Nerves. Excitement. The sense of getting closer.

"MAGIC," answered a low voice.

"Up your fairy godmother with a—"

"Okay, Hammond," breathed the voice. It was Ike Menninger. He scolded, "You could follow the rules once in a—"

"Just put our guest on the phone, Ike."

Yablonski took the line. "Hello?"

"How's it going, Cas? Treating you all right?"

"Just great. Momma loves it."

"How's your leg?"

"Better." There was an expectant silence.

"Feel up to answering some questions?"

"Fire away."

Hammond read from his notepad. Everything he'd written down. When he finished, he asked Yablonski if it meant anything to him.

Another silence.

"'You mentioned Rinehart before, Cas. We've got it on tape."

"I'm sorry . . . I just can't remember," Yablonski said, agitation creeping into his voice. "Is it that important?"

"Yes."

"Well, damnit, I'm sorry—"

Hammond cursed to himself. Things kept going in and out of Yablonski's memory: it had been tampered with so much.

"I'm going to send Cohen and Slater down to work with you again," said Hammond. "We've got to have the benefit of what you know. It's not going to be pleasant, but at least you won't be left with the residual effects you've had in the past. No more nightmares, Cas."

The pause got even longer, then Hammond heard him growl back, "Hammond, I don't want to end up like George Olively."

"You won't. Sure, there's a risk. But remember, these two men are on your side."

"Where are you going to be while all this is happening?"

"I don't know yet. I'll be with you if I can. Will you do it?"

There was an audible sigh, then: "Yes."

"Ten a.m. tomorrow, then. And thanks. My regards to Momma."

"You're a real politician, Hammond."

Hammond laughed and hung up. The rolling lump had become a knot in his stomach. This was the rotten part of his work: manipulating people. And for *what?* Jan Fletcher was right. He was a bastard who set himself no parameters. He hadn't the faintest idea how Yablonski's mind would react to further tinkering, yet he was prepared to go ahead and tinker.

And there *was* a risk. There most certainly was. Hammond could only hope it was minimal. He already felt responsible for Harold Fletcher: he didn't need a second helping of guilt.

Cohen agreed to work on Yablonski, but he wasn't happy about it. "I don't like it," he said flatly. "We're rushing him."

"Then do it without liking it," said Hammond, just as flatly. "We don't have time to cock around. There's a maniac on the loose: McCarthy. You and Slater handle this end of it, tomorrow morning at ten." Hammond slammed down the receiver.

His foul mood was interrupted by the arrival of a messenger from ONR. In the bulky envelope were Xerox copies of the Thin Air file, and something else: a worn book with a tattered dust jacket and a note from Canazaro clipped to the front. The note said simply, "Call me when you get this, H.C." Hammond lifted the paper and stared at the book cover. *A Station in Space,* it was titled . . . by Whitney Rinehart.

Hammond's throat started to pulse with excitement. His hand shook as he dialed Canazaro.

"Commander Canazaro?"

"Hammond? You got the book?"

"I got the book."

Canazaro took a deep breath. "It occurred to me after you left that the name Rinehart *was* familiar, but I couldn't place it. Had the feeling I'd seen it on a book cover. So I called my wife and asked if we had a book by a Whitney Rinehart. She laughed, said I should remember it. It was the one thing she had when we got married that I'd wanted to throw out."

"What's it about?"

"UFOs. It's old, written in the fifties. Tears the government apart. Tells how proof was being suppressed, the public kept in the dark, and *why*. That's just chapter one. It goes downhill from there. I don't think it's your cup of tea, Hammond. The guy who wrote it wasn't playing with a full deck."

"Canazaro—I owe you a steak."

"Hey, listen, I'm not saying this is the same guy, but it is the same name."

"Leave that to me. Thanks. And thank your wife."

"Just return the book someday or I'll never hear the end of it."

Hammond skimmed through *A Station in Space*. It was indeed the work of a crackpot—loaded with illustrations, gimmicked-up photos, and half-baked theories. Some of Hammond's wild burst of enthusiasm subsided while reading this stuff. From his own writings, Rinehart didn't sound too promising as a key figure in this case.

Hammond called the publishing house and inquired about contacting the author. He was directed to the publicity department, where a young man listened politely as he identified himself and stated his request. "We're unable to give out home addresses and phone numbers of authors," the man said, "but if you'll give me some time to verify your credentials, I'll see what I can do."

Hammond agreed grudgingly and hung up. Thirty minutes later, he was called back. "Commander Hammond?" the voice said.

"Yes," Hammond answered.

"Good. You're for real. I had to do some checking to track you down. Thanks for cooperating."

"No trouble. Would you like a job?"

The young man laughed, and then got serious. "I spoke with Mr. Rinehart at his home—"

"Where?" interrupted Hammond.

"One second, sir. He doesn't want to speak with anyone connected with the Navy, so I'm afraid I cannot give you his number."

Hammond ground his teeth silently. "Look," he said, "call him back and tell him I'm a Naval investigator working on a special case and there are lives at stake. Ask him to call me back, collect!"

"Okay, sir . . . I'll try."

Hammond sat for another hour, not daring to leave. Finally the phone rang. It was the receptionist with a collect call. He told her to have it traced, then waited eagerly to be connected.

The scratchy voice sounded like a cross between Gabby Hayes and Walter Huston. "This is Rinehart speaking."

"Mr. Rinehart, my name is Hammond. I appreciate your calling—"

"Make it quick, will ya?"

"Yes, sir." Hammond took a breath. "What can you tell me about Project Thin Air?"

There was a pronounced silence, then Rinehart snarled, "Why are you people still hounding me? After all this time?!"

Hammond winced. God, he was loud. "The government moves slowly, sir. I would like to hear your side."

"You're too late to change anything!"

"Change what, sir?"

Rinehart chuckled dryly. "Sonofabitch—why don't I just hang up?"

There was a significant silence, and Hammond suddenly knew why. "Because you'd like someone to find out what really happened."

"Oh? Would I?"

"For instance, how about the first head of the project—Dr. Emil Kurtnauer?"

"Never heard of him. Anything else?"

Hammond didn't know whether Rinehart was being cantankerous or cagey. Whichever, he had to play along. "Well then, how about—?"

"Back off, sonny!" Rinehart snapped. "Not over the phone!"

"Yes, sir. What if I brought you to Washington—at government expense?"

"There's not enough money in the world to get me back in that town, Hammond."

"Then I'll come out to see you."

"I might not be here."

"I'll take the chance, sir."

The line abruptly went dead.

Rinehart was obviously a kook of the highest order and Hammond had little hope about the sort of information he would get from the man. But it was still his first firm lead—and the only prospect who might talk with authority about Thin Air.

The receptionist called back with the results of the trace. She had gotten the phone number and area code from the operator and had pinpointed the area as Taos, New Mexico. Hammond contacted the FBI computer and in ten minutes had Rinehart's address.

He went down to the Pentagon Transit Center and picked up maps of New Mexico. It took him twenty minutes to plot his route from Kirtland Air Force Base to Rinehart's backwoods home outside Taos.

Five minutes after Hammond took off alone in another F4 from the MATS terminal, a Navy Lieutenant Commander walked into Base Ops and casually checked the status board. He was a big man and the uniform was a tight fit. He took off his cap and scratched his crewcut black hair. Probing eyes noted Hammond's departure time and destination: Kirtland AFB, Albuquerque, New Mexico.

The hand froze on his head for just a second, then he relaxed and leaned over the counter, winking at the Air Force dispatcher.

"That flight to Kirtland," he said. "That's a friend of mine. Guess I just missed him. Is that an RON?"

The dispatcher obligingly checked his papers, looking for "rest overnight" on Hammond's departure. He shook his head. "Didn't file a return flight plan, sir. Could be RON, could be anything. Hope he makes up his mind."

The Navy officer returned his smile. "Me, too," he said.

He left the building, walked to the parking lot, climbed

into a Navy staff car and drove to a pay phone on the base. He called a number in Los Angeles, California, waited for an answer, then spoke one short sentence:

"He's on his way to see the old man."

12

Taos was on a high flat plain at six thousand feet, under the massive red rims of the Sangre de Cristo Mountains. As he drove across the plateau toward town, Hammond passed rows of cottonwoods twinkling with fresh-fallen snow, illuminated by sunlight streaming through black clouds. Ancient adobe churches were dusty-pink and ranch spreads stretched across acres of sparse grazing land.

Hammond was delighted: he'd never seen this part of the country before. He could easily understand why an old recluse might choose to live out his life here.

He drove swiftly through the plaza, spotting one of Taos' Pueblo Indians standing in a doorway, wrapped in a blanket and clutching a shopping bag. He passed a young couple shuffling through mud at the side of the road, both dressed in ragged jeans and sporting long, stringy hair. The old and the new, living in harmonious proximity.

He stopped to ask directions at a broken-down gas station. He was sent about five miles out of town, then east up the lowlands into the Sangre de Cristos. Rinehart lived in a low adobe house on one of the back roads beside a stream lined with cottonwoods. In the yard was a battered '58 Ford. Smoke curled from his chimney. A light snow was still falling, piling up in the patches left over from the last fall.

Hammond parked his borrowed Air Force staff car and stepped out. He was struck by the intensity of the fresh air—and the chill. He zipped up his flight jacket. Clutching Slater's Uher tape deck under his arm and with cassette tapes stuffed in his pockets, Hammond jogged over to the house and banged on the door.

A long moment later, the old wooden door creaked open and warm air rushed out. He stared at the suspicious old man glaring at him from inside.

"Mr. Rinehart, I'm Hammond." He stuck out his free

hand. Immediately, a ball of fur between the old man's legs scooted back out of the way. Another cat strolled up and sniffed the threshold, trying not to seem too interested in the stranger. Rinehart regarded Hammond warily, then opened the door and motioned him in.

Hammond stepped into a long, low room cluttered with old books and periodicals. Bookshelves covered every available space on the walls. There were no pictures; everything seemed to overflow into piles on the floor and against the walls, even behind the few sagging pieces of furniture. . . .

Cats and dogs were everywhere, roosting in beds of magazines, moving quietly or ranged about the room in sleep. The place reeked of dog and old newsprint.

Hammond managed a wan smile at Rinehart, who still hadn't said a word, but stood at the closed door, studying him.

"Tea?" the old man finally croaked, and had to clear his throat with loud rasping hacks. Obviously, he did very little talking up here in his hideaway. But it was the first sign of civility and Hammond made delighted sounds.

"Beautiful country up here, Mr. Rinehart. Never seen anything like it." Hammond followed him out to the kitchen. Filthy, cracked dishes were all over the counter. Rinehart shuffled to the tap, filled his kettle and put it on the fire. He held up a box or crackers, which Hammond declined. He didn't know how he was going to drink that tea.

He strolled back into the living room followed by a dozen pairs of eyes. The cats and dogs quickly grew accustomed to him, except for one skinny Siamese who bolted every time Hammond moved. He watched Rinehart shuffling around in the kitchen—a thin, stooped old man with a patch of wispy white fur on his head, his skin parchment yellow and drawn tight over a skull face. His broad expression could be as easily mistaken for displeasure as a smile.

He returned with a pot of herb tea and poured it into chipped mugs. Hammond noticed his hands shook slightly. A couple of fingers were missing and a couple were stubbed. Rinehart sat down in a fluffy old chair and sipped his tea, quietly regarding his collection of garbage. Hammond also sat down and placed his tape recorder on a stool.

"Know anything about UFOs?" croaked Rinehart.

"A little."

"A little, huh? Won't do you much good. Makes you one of the great uninformed. Gotta know a lot. It's important."

"I'm sure it is, sir."

Rinehart grunted, agreeing with himself. Then his eye fell sharply on Hammond. "Never seen one myself. But I know they're around. How's that for faith, son?"

"Commendable."

"That's what it takes to accept things: faith. Knowledge through faith—the certainty that something *can* exist—against all odds." Rinehart spoke with a hurried tone and a chuckle at the end of every sage comment. He smiled—at least Hammond took it for a smile. "Sounds like religious hooey, don't it, son?"

"Remarkably." Hammond grinned back.

"Hah!" Rinehart hooted, then cackled to himself and regarded Hammond with less suspicion. "Time to time, maybe you'll get up and poke them logs, would you?" he asked.

Hammond glanced at the fire, then nodded. "You know why I'm here, Mr. Rinehart. It has nothing to do with UFOs."

"Oh, yes it does. Everything has to do with UFOs."

"Excuse me, sir, but according to your book, you were drummed out of government service because you believed that," Hammond said. "I would have thought . . ." He stopped.

"That my tune had changed? Hah! They booted me out all right—called me an embarrassment. And it *was* because of my theories on UFOs. At least, that was the excuse they used."

"There was another reason?"

Rinehart sipped his tea and looked at Hammond with shrouded eyes again. Hammond was still for a moment, then put down his tea and made a show of loading the Uher. "If you don't mind, sir, this conversation will be useless if I don't record it."

"It'll be useless either way, son, because you're not equipped to believe any of it."

"We'll see, sir."

Rinehart sniffed in contempt but added nothing. Hammond set up the mike and switched it on. "The fire, son," mumbled Rinehart. Hammond rose and poked the fire. He heard the question snapped at him from behind: "Why do you want to know about Thin Air?"

Hammond propped the poker against the wall. "I was brought into it by someone who claimed to have been involved," he said, "and who has since died under peculiar circumstances."

"What circumstances?"

"He was murdered."

There was a flicker of concern. "What was his name?"

"Harold Fletcher. He was one of the crewmen aboard the *Sturman* in 1953."

Rinehart shook his head. "Doesn't ring a bell." But he put down his tea and sank deeper into the chair, his parchment brow furrowed in worry. "Who murdered him?" he asked.

"His psychiatrist, a man who had been brainwashing him since 1955 to forget his involvement with Thin Air." Rinehart stared at him, expressionless. "And I have a second former crewman under wraps who tells the same story. Quite a coincidence. Same psychiatrist, too."

Rinehart's eyes lowered to a point across the room. When he spoke again, his Gabby Hayes accent was gone. "Brainwashing is not uncommon where security is concerned, Hammond. You should know that."

"Brainwashing, okay. But murder?"

"Perhaps as a . . . last resort . . ."

"Not in this country, Mr. Rinehart!" Hammond snapped.

"No . . . you're right . . ." He took a deep breath and closed his eyes. His head shook in sorrow or regret, Hammond wasn't sure which. "It's still going on," he mumbled.

"What is?"

He jumped up suddenly and bellowed an obscenity. "It was a stopgap measure," he growled. "Psychologically vital!"

"Are you talking about the brainwashing or the murder?"

"They're both *ugly terms,* Commander!"

"No, sir. Ugly acts."

"I'm well aware of that!" he shouted. "We called it *fear control.* It was a form of hypnosis. Without it, they would have gone insane and probably died or committed suicide! As some of them did. It was a necessary expedient!"

"Strange, isn't it?" Hammond pointed out, goading him on, "how after all these years expediency has degenerated into murder."

Rinehart stopped moving and turned an agonized gaze on Hammond. He rubbed a hand over his face and then flopped back into his chair. "You really know nothing about it, Commander . . . or you wouldn't say those things . . ." he mumbled.

"Then you better start filling me in," Hammond said quietly.

Rinehart closed his eyes again. A moment later, they flew open and he said, "Do you know what Thin Air was?"

"No. That's what I came to find out."

Rinehart snorted, then said, "It was the development of invisibility . . . as a weapon."

Hammond nodded carefully without reacting.

"It came about in 1941 as a secret project under wartime emergency. It was initiated by a man named Emil Kurtnauer, whose roots in it extend back to 1933." He paused a moment, scratching his eyebrows. "Do you know anything about him?"

"Just what was in the ONR file."

"Oh, that." Rinehart laughed. "What a joke." Rinehart settled himself into his chair and tapped his fingers on the arm, organizing his thoughts. "Emil Kurtnauer was an Austrian physicist much influenced by Albert Einstein's theories of relativity. He was studying in Düsseldorf in October of 1933 when Einstein and Niels Bohr met in conference at Brussels. Kurtnauer went there and pestered them until Einstein agreed to sit down with him. For two whole days they discussed an application of Einstein's Unified Field Theory that Kurtnauer wanted to work on. Einstein took great pains trying to talk him out of it, insisting that the theory, which he'd put forth in 1929, was desperately flawed and any applications of it could only compound the error. Kurtnauer insisted to the contrary: there was something to it and he intended to devote himself to his project. Einstein, sensing determination, encouraged him to send over his findings and he in turn would keep Kurtnauer advised of his own progress. So Kurtnauer happily went home.

"But 1933 was also the year Hitler rose to power. Kurtnauer, a Jew, fled Germany in 1935, emigrating to America. He got in touch with Einstein, who helped him secure a teaching post at the University of Chicago. Eventually, he was taken under the great man's wing as a part-time assistant. Einstein put him to work on the Unified Field Theory, giving him calculations to work out and problems to toy with."

Rinehart leaned forward, resting his elbows on his knees and gently moving his hands as he spoke. His guarded manner had vanished.

"You see, there was a marked difference in the way these two men approached science. Einstein was the great *reducer*. He believed certain physical phenomena had more than passing similarity to one another. Electrons moving around the atomic nucleus, planets revolving around the sun—Einstein concluded that space and the atom were different aspects of the same thing, and ought to be considered in relation to each other. His ideas about unification were aimed at distilling everything down to a few simple basics.

"Kurtnauer, on the other hand, was a great *applicator*. He wanted to put those simplified theories to work even before they were proved. It's as if the two men were clinging to the same tree, Einstein trying to find the roots and Kurtnauer climbing out on a limb."

He stopped. Hammond was mixing a smile with a distinctly puzzled look. "Am I going too fast for you, son?" asked Rinehart.

"A little."

"Well, let me see if I can clarify. You have any idea what relativity is all about?"

Hammond swallowed. "Vaguely," he said.

"Hah! Good answer." Rinehart's blue eyes twinkled. "First of all, let's take a few basic quantities." He ticked them off on his stub fingers. "Energy, matter, time, space, and gravitation all have something in common: they're effects we find operating inside both space *and* the atom. They're unifying forces, but in scientific observation we separate them into two groups, the two elemental forces in the universe: electromagnetism and gravitation.

"Electromagnetism comprises the basic units of matter and energy—concepts falling under what we call quantum theory—while all our ideas on space, time, and gravitation are described by relativity.

"The attempt to unify the two began with Einstein's Special Theory of Relativity, which says that for all systems moving in a uniform manner relative to each other, the natural laws governing them are the same.

"The sun sets up a gravitational field in space and the planets spin around it. Within the atom, the nucleus sets up an electromagnetic field which keeps charged particles spinning around it. But the sun also has an electromagnetic field, which we recognize as its poles . . . and the atom also possesses gravitation. So they're equivalent. Interchangeable concepts.

"Einstein wanted to show how gravitational attraction was interchangeable with electromagnetic field—to build a bridge between microcosm and macrocosm. That's the 1929 theory that Dr. Kurtnauer fell in love with. But Einstein always felt his own work on it was inadequate. He spent the rest of his life trying to revise it."

Rinehart studied Hammond, trying to gauge his comprehension. Hammond stared back like a first-year physics student who knew he would never make it to the second year.

Rinehart sighed and spoke very slowly. "In Special Relativity, Einstein's equation, $E=mc^2$, says that energy is equivalent to the mass of a body multiplied by the square of the speed of light." He held up the stubby forefinger of each hand and brought them together until they were side by side. "Matter converts into energy and back again depending on what you do with the velocity at which it moves.

"In General Relativity, gravitation is a field exerting a geometrical force on the bodies within its influence. When light, an electromagnetic force, enters a gravitational field, it *bends* . . ." Rinehart curved a hand in Hammond's face. "The angle at which it bends is relative to the mass and velocity of the gravitating body."

Hammond managed a look of intense interest, but Rinehart knew that only half of what he was saying was getting through.

"In simple language," he continued patiently, "what Kurtnauer saw in unifying these forces was the opportunity of altering the state of a single body by playing with the way we perceive it. If he could set up a gravitational field oscillating on an electromagnetic frequency, it should *contain* everything within that field, yet permit him to alter its state of being."

"Alter it in what way?" asked Hammond.

"Make it invisible."

Hammond stared at him. Of course that was what it

was all leading to, but he still found it hard to accept. "That's right out of Buck Rogers and Flash Gordon, Mr. Rinehart."

"Sure it is. But where do you think rocket travel came from? Laser beams? Space stations? They're all cases of reality mimicking art."

Hammond squinted at the rows of science-fiction magazines crowding the bookshelves over Rinehart's head: *Amazing Stories*, *Air Wonder Stories*, *Astounding*, *Galaxy*. . . . He wanted to laugh, but Rinehart was making it too painfully real for that.

"Make . . . make *what* invisible?" he finally asked.

"People."

Now he did laugh. Rinehart just watched him, devoid of feeling.

"It's an old concept," he conceded. "But it could work if the right approach was used. Since all relativistic effects depend on the presence of an observer separate from the uniform bodies in motion, the effect could only be measured by someone outside the field.

"In other words, I could stand here while you could be set to vibrating inside Kurtnauer's field at some incredible velocity. *I* would then perceive *you* becoming *invisible*."

Hammond took a deep breath and held it for a moment, his mind racing. Rinehart smiled and said, "Maybe you'd like to see it on paper."

Hammond nodded, so Rinehart got up and rummaged in a bookshelf, dragging out a battered notebook. He flung pages around until he located an old yellow sheet and pulled it out. He passed it to Hammond, saying, "That's all I've got left of Kurtnauer's original proposal to the Navy at the end of 1941."

Hammond studied the paper. It was marked with a little numeral 3 in the upper right corner and contained only a few typed lines:

> Matter could be restrained from total conversion
> into energy by the controlled application of
> a radiation field of sufficient gravitational
> intensity to contain a body or bodies moving
> uniformly near the velocity of light, thereby
> rendering them invisible to outside observers.

Rinehart smiled. "Kurtnauer believed that by employing a gravitational field generated from an electromagnetic source, he could control the loss of mass and prevent things within the field from turning to pure energy. He could simply make them move so fast that they couldn't be seen."

"What was it all for?" asked Hammond. He had to restrain himself from jumping in with a dozen questions at once.

"When the Japanese attacked Pearl Harbor, a lot of secret projects sprang up under military auspices. Kurtnauer went to the War Department with his proposal, a plan for developing invisibility as a weapon against the Japanese. The War Department was already swamped with similar ideas, but when Kurtnauer mentioned his association with Einstein, they sent him along to Frank Knox, who was then Secretary of the Navy. Knox approved the project, gave it its somewhat ironic name, Thin Air, and appointed a committee to administrate. Kurtnauer was to head the scientific team, I was made project director, and a Captain Sartog was appointed Naval liaison." Rinehart sipped his tea and thrust his skinny legs up on a worn footstool.

"I had been a consultant to the Sperry Corporation in California since the mid 1930s—involved in research programs with the Navy. I was a bug on things that nobody else wanted to touch, and I was well-known to Frank Knox. He brought me in, threw the project in my lap, and said, 'Don't let these boys get out of hand. You're the project director and they're answerable to you. . . .' "

Rinehart snorted bitterly. "Later on, I think he forgot that conversation. Anyway, Kurtnauer hand-picked a small group of physicists and engineers from across the country," he continued. "And I had them all moved to Philadelphia. We took over quarters in the Navy Yard there, windowless sheds with heavy security. We lived there day and night, meals and recreation. We were like prisoners, allowed to take long walks on the breakwater but no fraternization with other people on the base."

"Excuse me," said Hammond, "but was there a man named Traben among those scientists?"

Rinehart's eyes seemed to glaze over with coldness. "Yes," he said. "Kurtnauer made him his personal assistant. It was Traben's daring that really moved the project along. Kurtnauer was a theoretical physicist, and a genius at it. But he wanted everything to work on paper first. That's all he cared about. It was Traben who insisted that we requisition a ship, a new DE. He felt we needed something big, that if this process were ever to work as a weapon, we had to prove it on a grand scale. He intended that we would make the entire ship invisible and bring it back undamaged."

"Was that the *Sturman?*" asked Hammond.

"Yes. Captain Sartog requisitioned DE-166 even before she came off the ways, and had her modified before completion. They eliminated a three-inch cannon and the entire forward gun mount on the main deck, at Traben's direction. Sartog martialed a corps of engineers to construct our equipment, which consisted of the field generator and electromagnetic couplers producing enough power and range to affect the entire vessel. These were fitted into one of the *Sturman*'s engine rooms, completely replacing the port engine."

"Why did Traben have them remove the forward gun mount?" asked Hammond.

Rinehart leaned forward and spoke with distaste. "Because he had an ace up his sleeve. He knew that the goddamned ship, invisible or otherwise, was useless without a crew. He needed men to subject themselves to the field, and he needed a place for them to stand in plain view, where they could be observed by someone outside the field."

Rinehart bounced to his feet and the nervous Siamese shot across the room. He stuffed his hands into his pockets and scowled at Hammond. "It could have been the ultimate weapon of its time. We could have made the ship and its crew invisible, guided them to a destination by remote control, then turned off the field and let them attack! Imagine where they could have popped up! Guam, the Philippines, Tokyo Bay! In the blink of an eye! Suddenly, there's the *Sturman*, blazing away! If we had succeeded, Commander, they could have called off the Manhattan Project. There would have been no need for the atomic bomb!"

Hammond looked doubtful. "You were saying—if you had succeeded—?"

Rinehart blew out his breath. "It was Traben's fault.

The sonofabitch moved too fast. The experiment *was* a success, but the after-effects on the men were disastrous. It was nothing we could have foreseen, but we should have taken precautions. . . . Kurtnauer suffered personally. It nearly destroyed him . . ." He trailed off, lost in a painful memory.

"Well, what happened?" asked Hammond. But Rinehart wasn't listening. He shook a finger at Hammond, like a father lecturing his son.

"You have to understand Kurtnauer," he said. "He was a *humanitarian*. He shared that with Einstein, who disapproved of the bomb, and I'm sure he was not in favor of Kurtnauer's project either, once it became clear what it was going to be. And Kurtnauer, if he had suspected the side effects, would never have allowed the experiment to take place."

Hammond was impressed. Rinehart was sounding less and less like a crackpot. He paced the room and spoke about Sartog's appointment of Lieutenant Commander Leslie Warrington, a close and trusted friend, as commanding officer of the *Sturman* in 1943.

"She was commissioned on the fourth of July. Warrington had her from the beginning. They used a volunteer crew from the East Coast bases: Norfolk, Newport News, and Boston—mostly machinist's mates and engineers. The men were told only that the ship would be subjected to a kind of force field, making it impossible for them to be seen from outside it. The drills were repeated day after day for months to make the whole project seem ordinary. Warrington wanted his men relaxed and familiar with the routine when they were finally ready for the big moment."

Rinehart stopped pacing and threw another log on the fire. He warmed his hands over the flames and went on: "But Traben insisted time was at a premium and we had to proceed with the ultimate experiment as soon as possible. Kurtnauer, on the other hand, was cautious. Without further testing on lab animals, he felt it would be too dangerous to use men. Traben turned to me for arbitration and I took the matter to Frank Knox."

He fell back into his seat. The dog in the basket behind him yawned. "By this time, the Secretary had concluded invisibility was a desperately needed, vital weapon. So he told me to perfect it and do it fast.

"What about Kurtnauer's objection?" asked Hammond.

"I had to go back and convince him. It wasn't easy, but at that time, Emil was still willing to believe in his adopted government."

"He had doubts other than the use of men?"

"Later on, yes," Rinehart said, not looking at Hammond. He rubbed his knee-joint and grimaced. Hammond guessed arthritis.

"In October of 1943," Rinehart continued, "the *Sturman* received final preparations. And on the morning of the twenty-second, just before dawn, she was towed out of the yard, then south into Delaware Bay to a point well off the coast of New Jersey."

"This was with the full crew?"

"Full experimental crew, yes. At no time did she have a sailing crew, per se."

Hammond glanced at the tape. He was going to run out soon.

"From an observer ship stationed two thousand yards beyond the effective range of the field, I watched with Kurtnauer, Sartog, and Traben. We conducted rehearsals the rest of the day, then let everybody sleep until dawn the next morning. Then the experiment began. The *Sturman* was not anchored. Her engine was shut off and she was allowed to drift and roll. Warrington was positioned on her navigating bridge, his hand over a 'dead-man' switch which would allow him to shut off the field generator in the event something went wrong.

"Around four-thirty on the morning of October twenty-third, Sartog whispered instructions into the radio. Warrington pulled a switch on the *Sturman*'s bridge and the field generator went on below deck. It produced an incredible amount of power and set up a vibration aboard the ship that quickly accelerated to enormous velocity. The generator was tuned to a frequency that would ultimately vibrate at 90 percent the speed of light, nearly 168,000 miles per second."

Hammond whistled. "How could the ship withstand that kind of stress?"

Rinehart smiled patiently. "That's what I was trying to tell you before: the ship and the field vibrate together. Everything within the field is contained, kept intact in its original form. Uniform bodies in motion, Hammond, behave as if they are a world unto themselves. And actually, they are."

Hammond nodded, sure that he was never going to grasp all of it, but sufficiently convinced that whatever had happened was extraordinary.

"Even two thousand yards away, we could hear the high-pitched hum, could feel the initial vibrations as a rippling shock wave built up and rolled across the water. Then the hum got so high we couldn't hear it anymore.

"Warrington's voice came over the radio, curiously low-pitched and slowing down like a record player that had just been shut off.

" 'It's creeping up,' I remember he said, and then the radio fell silent. From the observer ship, we saw the effect spreading outwards: progressive fading, shimmering, then full transparency, then finally—the *Sturman* simply blinked out."

"Vanished?" asked Hammond.

Rinehart nodded. "In its place was a convex depression in the water and clear sky on the other side."

Hammond stared at him. He had been expecting this tale to end in failure. He should have known better—there had to have been some early success for this project to have continued as long as it did. The details were frighteningly similar to Fletcher's and Yablonski's nightmare, but the experiment Rinehart was describing had taken place ten years earlier!

"The field acceleration had leveled off to a constant velocity," Rinehart continued, "reaching an equilibrium that put it in another time/space framework.

"I checked my watch. The whole process had taken only two minutes. The acceleration had built up slowly then made a final rush toward the moment of complete invisibility. I looked over at Kurtnauer and was surprised to see his face covered with perspiration. He said something about communications . . . that Warrington's voice had slowed down because the field was approaching the speed of light. It meant we wouldn't be able to communicate. We wouldn't know what was happening to the men."

"You didn't expect that?" Hammond asked.

"No. Some things, I regret to say, slipped by us. We stared at the empty space in the water for almost fifteen minutes. The gain on our radio was wide open, but nothing came over. Not even static. Not even the hum of the field generator.

"Kurtnauer grabbed my arm and said, 'Bring them

back!' " Rinehart closed his eyes and frowned to himself. "Using remote radio control, I cut in the reversing generator, which automatically slowed the forward velocity. The field had to build up acceleration again to pull itself back the other way. In a few moments, the *Sturman* blinked back into view, at first a hazy transparency on the water, then gradually solidifying. . . ."

Rinehart rubbed both knees now and rocked slightly, back and forth, relating the story as though he had lived it over and over all these years. Hammond watched him and wondered how he could have survived all this and not come out twisted.

"Prior to the experiment, we had agreed on a procedure for allowing latent effects to wear off. So from two thousand yards away, we waited for three hours, observing through high-powered binoculars. We could see the crewmen on the forward deck, some standing, some sitting or lying down, a few wandering around aimlessly. But we couldn't raise anyone aboard by radio.

"When the three hours were up, we revved engines and plunged toward the *Sturman*. Kurtnauer, Traben, Sartog, and I boarded her. We climbed to the main deck and went forward, stopping to stare at the men.

"They were ranged around the forward deck, most of them in a dazed stupor, but some clutching their heads and sobbing.

"We found Warrington on the navigating bridge, slumped in a corner, glassy-eyed, his limbs gone rubbery. We tried to coax him back to consciousness. There was a crewman nearby who tried to tell us what had happened. He spoke in a kind of garbled drawl. There was something wrong with his speech: his tongue wouldn't work properly. He managed to tell us that Warrington had collapsed at the height of the effect. He'd been watching the men through the bridge window, had seen them going in and out of visibility. It seems the effect was somewhat erratic until it reached its ultimate velocity, then everything became uniform, transparent, and then a blackness settled outside the field—

"But the men were screaming and stumbling around. Everyone panicked when the decks started to vanish and they thought they were going to fall through into the sea. Seeing the men standing like islands in empty space, Warrington must have simply blacked out from fear.

"It was too much for Kurtnauer. He left the bridge. But Sartog—I'll never forget the look on his face—was whispering to his old friend Warrington, trying to reassure him." Rinehart shook his head. "We were all sick and scared just being on that ship. The overwhelming fear these men had experienced hung over the *Sturman* like an infectious disease . . . but there was worse to come."

"Worse?" echoed Hammond.

"The latent residual effects, incredible recurrences—"

"What do you mean?"

Rinehart stood up, reached for the teapot. He stood silently a moment, his hand resting on it, then he spoke as if he were reliving the worst horror of all.

"Within forty-eight hours, the men were suffering short periods of invisibility again . . . and without the triggering impulse of the force field."

Hammond stared at him. The man was piling one incredible incident on top of another.

"I saw it happen to Warrington myself. Kurtnauer was with me. Warrington was lying on a hospital cot right about where you are, talking about what had happened in as calm a voice as he could muster . . . when he just seemed to fade from view. We saw his outline under the sheet and when he realized he'd become invisible again—and that it was uncontrolled—he started screaming."

Rinehart looked at Hammond with remembered terror in his eyes. "It was horrible," he said. "This disembodied voice coming from an empty bed. He kept on screaming until Kurtnauer had the presence of mind to grab his body and hold on, to give him some contact. He felt Warrington's hands clutching at him, and gradually the man came back into sight.

"But that was the end of him," said Rinehart. "His mind was gone."

13

Rinehart threw another log on the fire and Hammond poked it for him while the old man went to brew another pot of tea. The Siamese had lost some of his skittishness and even leaped up on the mantel to watch Hammond work with the fire. It crackled noisily and spread warmth around the room. One of the dogs came off his bed of magazines and padded over to lie in front of it.

Hammond sat back in his chair and flipped the tape over in the Uher, reflecting on the volumes of information Rinehart was so freely supplying. He was full of questions, but he thought it would be better not to start badgering at this stage. Let the old man finish telling it his way.

Rinehart came back with a new pot of tea and the same box of crackers he had first offered Hammond. Gnawing hunger got the best of him; Hammond ate and drank eagerly. Rinehart sat down and resumed his story.

"We had to commit Warrington," he said. "And he wasn't the only one. At least four other crew members followed him into the asylum almost immediately."

"Did they ever get out?" asked Hammond.

Rinehart shook his head. "They all died there. Several other men committed suicide. They couldn't handle the recurring invisibility. Never knew when to expect it, how extensive it would be or how long it would last. . . . A couple of them manifested even stranger effects, first becoming invisible, then de-molecularized. . . ."

"De-what?"

"De-molecularized. Without the gravitational control of the field generator, the invisible molecules tended to drift apart. Basic structure was lost. And they were susceptible to molecular mixing."

Again Rinehart was going too fast for him. "What caused the recurring invisibility?" Hammond asked.

"My God, Hammond, if we knew that all our problems would have been solved. We never found out."

Hammond spread his hands. "Then what is this molecular mixing—?"

Rinehart fixed him with a cold stare. "It gave the men the occasional ability, if you could call it that, to walk through walls."

Hammond straightened. His mouth opened.

"In actual fact, it meant that the body could drift through solid substance driven only by residual forward velocity. The action even defied gravity. The de-materialized man would simply continue motion in the direction he had been traveling, uninhibited by solids in his path. If he was walking across a room, he would continue to move right through the walls. If he was coming downstairs, he could drift right through the floor. No control, no way of stopping it."

Hammond was aghast. "How did the men re-materialize?"

"The effect simply wore off after a while. It was like being in a trance. We had to let it run its course."

"Is it possible some of the men might still be going through this today?"

"Doubtful," said Rinehart, shaking his head, "although possible. We found that the rate of recurrence diminished with time. But for a year and a half, we had some terrible cases. Of the original crew, only five men were living when the war ended. One man died in the strangest manner. He was suffering repeated invisibility and molecular breakdown. Most of the time, he would drift out of his house and down the street until he re-materialized on a neighbor's lawn, shaking and screaming his head off. But one morning, his wife happened to be watching when he went sort of transparent, not completely invisible, and drifted through a wall. He didn't clear it in time. His body re-materialized . . . *fused into the wall.*"

Rinehart paused, then explained, "His molecules had mixed with the wood and plaster. Half of him was protruding, the other half . . ."

Hammond gaped. His stomach shriveled in disgust.

"His wife called—hysterical," Rinehart continued. "Traben and I rushed right over. We found him still alive, screaming with pain. His vital organs were still functioning but he'd lost his wits. The parts that protruded were blue and distended. He was struggling in vain to free himself—"

Rinehart's face sagged. "He died before we could help him, though God knows what we could have done." He lapsed into morbid silence for a long moment, then added, "His wife had to be committed. Just as well, because I don't know how else we could have kept the lid on."

Hammond was so shocked he could say nothing. This day would provide him with nightmares for the rest of his life.

"I'd rather not discuss the side effects anymore," said Rinehart. "I'm sure you can see they're nothing but gruesome."

"I understand. I don't particularly want to hear anymore. But what did Kurtnauer do about all this?"

"He protested. Vigorously. To me, to Traben, to Sartog, to Frank Knox. Traben felt we could get the bugs ironed out and resume experimenting within a few months. But at that time, the worst of the effects hadn't yet appeared. As things got worse, Kurtnauer intensified his pressure on us. He was screaming that we stop and reconsider while Traben was pushing for improvements and secretly working on them alone. When Traben came to tell me what he was doing and showed me on paper the changes he had in mind, I could only feel that Kurtnauer was being unproductive. Traben and I went to Sartog, who backed us up.

"Kurtnauer decided the only way he could help was to concentrate his efforts on minimizing the side effects. He left the field theory for Traben to pursue. You must understand what this meant: Kurtnauer was literally abandoning the work he had developed from scratch.

"By early '44, Traben was ready to resume experiments on the *Sturman*. Sartog personally took command of the ship. It was his penance for Warrington.

"By this time, we had coined terminology for the side effects. 'Going zero' meant becoming invisible. 'Getting locked out' meant staying invisible. The first time that happened was in March. The *Sturman* and her new crew went zero for thirty-five minutes—there was no communication with them whatsoever. We tried radar from the observer ship—the *Sturman* proved undetectable while invisible. It looked like a major success. When the ship was brought back, one man was missing: Sartog. He had gone zero and somehow become locked out.

"Traben and I searched the *Sturman* from top to bottom. We couldn't find a trace of him. The engineering officer, who had been standing with him on the navigating bridge, had seen him release the dead-man switch at the height of invisibility. No one ever knew why, but we thought he had probably been trying to recreate his friend Warrington's movements. He was last seen drifting backwards on the bridge, almost transparent, with this horrified expression . . . until he faded completely away."

Rinehart took a deep breath and sighed. "We brought the *Sturman* back to the Yard and put her under maximum security in a covered drydock. For days afterwards, teams of machinists explored every inch of her, looking for something out of place. They found nothing. Kurtnauer was with them . . . all the time. He never said a word to us.

"Then one of the volunteers of that experiment went zero in his hospital quarters and was locked out for three days. He was found when someone inadvertently stepped into a corner of the room . . . and touched his invisible body. The contact is what brought him back. The laying-on of hands. At first, only the part of him that was being touched came into view. The attending orderly grabbed more of him and gradually he returned to normal solidity.

"He wasn't aware three days had passed. He thought he'd been gone only a few seconds. He had been in a state of invisible suspension. Unfortunately, he died a week later. This new side effect was ironically termed 'deadlock.' "

"You never found Sartog?" asked Hammond.

Rinehart shook his head. Hammond grunted, then relaxed a little. His whole body ached from Rinehart's story. He felt weak, as if he had been through it all himself.

"There was a crewman named Martin," Hammond said. "Was he another case of deadlock?"

Rinehart smiled grimly. "That was later. Much later. We'll get to it." He sipped his tea, continuing his story with his free hand upraised, gesturing with the stub fingers. "The side effects mushroomed out of that one incident until we had as many as from the first experiment. Kurtnauer demanded we put a halt to everything."

"Forgive me," said Hammond, "but what took you so long to see his point?"

"The war, Commander. We were still at the height of it on both fronts. The tide had turned in our favor, but there was always that pressing urgency. I'll admit I was of half a mind to close up shop. But Frank Knox was still backing us and Traben was more insistent than ever that all we needed was more time and money. So I capitulated. But I insisted we bring in a fresh eye. We needed a replacement for Sartog, a new Naval coordinator. Traben recommended a man he knew very well: Captain Richard B. Steinaker. He was approved by Knox, and I saw no reason to look elsewhere, so Steinaker moved in. And he quickly determined that Kurtnauer was too close to the project and not daring enough.

"Then, in April, Frank Knox died and was replaced as Secretary of the Navy by Forrestal, who proceeded to cut our materiel acquisition fund virtually in half. Traben pointed out to Steinaker that if we didn't get back on the track soon, the Manhattan Project would suck up all our funding." Rinehart laughed. "The s.o.b. even stole one of Kurtnauer's favorite arguments from the early days, claiming that Project Thin Air was potentially a much more humane weapon than the atomic bomb. Steinaker fell for it. Kurtnauer, in the meantime, was still working on the side effects. He came up with a partial solution: hypnosis."

Hammond sat up again, struck with the realization that Kurtnauer in 1944 may himself have set the stage for Dr. McCarthy.

"He recommended tailored treatment for each man in what amounted to brainwashing the experiences out of them. He started with the few men from the second experiment who hadn't already committed suicide or gone to the loony bin. The method was primitive but effective on nearly all of them. What he managed to get under control was not the side effects, but the *fear* of latent effects. Several of these men continued to have zero experiences, even lockouts. Those who didn't lived in constant fear of them: these were the ones he was most able to help."

"Did that recharge everyone's enthusiasm?" asked Hammond.

"Hah! Kurtnauer wasn't about to drop the ball there!

He came straight to Steinaker and me and showed us what he'd accomplished. He insisted on more time to perfect this before we resumed experiments. Traben learned about it and turned it into a sort of war, playing both ends against the middle. He would tell Kurtnauer that there was a freeze on experiments, then he would run to Steinaker and tell him that Kurtnauer was interfering with the forward progress. He was out to strip Kurtnauer of his authority."

"Ambitious fellow," commented Hammond. "Was he like that when you hired him?"

"He grew with the job," Rinehart said dryly. "In January of 1945, another experiment was approved. Kurtnauer protested and threatened public disclosure. He was immediately asked to resign. He refused and endured pressure for months, forcing Thin Air to a standstill.

"Then the war in Europe ended and the Allies located the German concentration camps. The shock was too much for Kurtnauer. He realized that relatives he hadn't heard from in years must have been destroyed in those camps. When he learned of the ghastly experiments performed by Nazi camp doctors on Jewish prisoners, he saw a glaring parallel between their misdeeds and his own supposedly legitimate activities. . . .

"He threw in the towel. He resigned from Thin Air and returned to the University of Chicago and ultimately moved to Israel . . . where he probably still is, as far as I know."

"Why didn't you resign?" asked Hammond.

Rinehart tried to seem casual. "Morally, it was a sore point. Politically, we were justified. Besides, it soon became a lost cause. Thin Air was shelved as the Manhattan Project took precedence. And by August of 1945, when the first atomic bomb was dropped on Hiroshima, there no longer seemed to be any need for an invisible Navy.

"But Traben still saw a future in it, and somehow he convinced Steinaker. They kept it alive with the advent of the Cold War. I had my own problems. My office had expanded and I was handling other projects. 1947 was the first year of flying-saucer sightings. I was getting all the reports as a matter of course. And then I had an idea and went to the newly organized Department of Defense with it. In those days, everyone was speculating about what flying saucers really were: people in government circles were almost willing to believe they could be of Russian origin. I felt that whatever they were we should be developing something similar for ourselves. I felt it strongly enough to put everything else aside and lobby for it twenty-four hours a day.

"I left Thin Air in the hands of Steinaker and Traben. They couldn't have done better with a blank check. In 1948, they secured the cooperation of Naval Air to conduct invisibility experiments with aircraft. The first ones were done with radio-controlled, pilotless planes. And they were enormously successful. The next logical step was to employ manned aircraft."

Rinehart poured himself more tea. Hammond refused another cup: he was starting to feel water-logged and drowsy. It was too warm in Rinehart's house, almost like a sauna.

"I should have stopped it then," Rinehart was saying, "but I had lost control. Traben had set up the whole thing with Naval Air himself and they trusted him. And I . . . I was well on the way to becoming a laughingstock because of my stand on flying saucers.

"So it looked like it was going to be their greatest victory. They got a young pilot, Lt. Albert Sinclair, to go up in an F-80 Shooting Star in June of '48. He zeroed for twenty-five minutes. He was completely undetectable on radar and came down with no side effects. You can imagine Traben's excitement. They grounded Sinclair and the plane for one year and watched for repercussions. Nothing. Then in July of the following year, they sent him back up in the same plane—no field generator, no experiment —just a simple cross-country flight to see that nothing would go wrong. Steinaker went with him.

"The jet crashed. Steinaker's body was found in the wreckage, but there was no trace of Sinclair: he hadn't ejected. The pilot's seat was intact—the canopy hadn't been opened—so where was he?"

"Gone zero?" said Hammond.

Rinehart nodded. "Undoubtedly. And then he'd probably become deadlocked, unable to get back."

Hammond whistled. Rinehart rose and shuffled to the window, peering through dirty glass at the gentle snowfall outside. "That's how we got our first public exposure," he said.

"It made the newspapers?"

"Sinclair was a well-known figure, a war hero. Naturally, the papers never got the true story, but it shook everybody up." Rinehart chuckled bitterly. "Even Traben."

Hammond checked his tape, saw it was time to reload, and, while he broke out a new cassette, asked Rinehart to collect his thoughts about the 1953 experiment.

Rinehart turned a blank gaze on him for a long time, then sighed. "Traben wasn't finished after that incident," he said, "just slowed down again. He realized it was time to come up with a genuine attempt at defeating those side effects if he ever hoped to get another experiment under way, so he went back to the lab for the next five years—like a good little scientist.

"Frequency modulation, or FM as we know it, was not even in home use yet. It was still in the military and experimental stages. Traben got interested in that and saw it was possible to modulate the original frequency that was propagating the field. I doubt if this means anything to you, Commander, but it was a genius idea. Traben experimented on lab animals and inanimate objects with different modulations from different sources. Finally, he was making an effort to alleviate repercussions. And in a sense he took the same approach Kurtnauer had—fight the fears. The vibrations of the propagating field had been disturbing neural impulses in the brain, altering perceptions, heightening fears. . . . Kurtnauer had used hypnosis to combat this. Traben planned to use a modular source to control the amount of electromagnetism reaching the brain. He could do nothing about the vibrations of the field—the men would still have to withstand that—but no longer would their fears be increased by mental disturbance. That was supposed to be the result."

Rinehart left the window and ambled across the living room without saying a word for a long time. Hammond happened to look down between his legs and saw the Siamese curled up on his feet. He'd made a friend.

"October of 1953. Ten years from the first experiment, twenty years from Kurtnauer's first meeting with Einstein," said Rinehart.

He launched into it, describing in detail the same story Hammond had heard twice before, once from Harold Fletcher and again from Casimir Yablonski. It jibed remarkably. But Rinehart had more insight.

The hand-holding procedure was another Traben contribution. He had found that body contact was terribly important during the acceleration phase to stabilize mental states. It gave the men something tangible to cling to, the knowledge that friends were there; and, although they were invisible, there was the illusion that they could help each other.

Everything would have been all right if two unforeseen events hadn't taken place.

"The frequency modulation had never been tried out on such a scale before and it brought about an effect purely by accident," said Rinehart.

"You mean the movement from Philadelphia to Norfolk?" asked Hammond.

"Yes," Rinehart said slowly. "The *Sturman* disappeared in the usual manner. From our point of view on the observer ship, nothing seemed different. Then she reappeared a few moments later, much sooner than expected. It wasn't until we got aboard and calmed down the men that we learned what had happened. Traben was utterly astonished. He had no explanation for it at first. How could an entire ship with a crew of nearly twenty men move from one place to another in the blink of an eye when none of the forces in use could have led to that? It meant outside influence."

Hammond was puzzled. "Someone tampering with the field?"

"Nothing deliberate. An accident—or coincidence, if you will. Traben was able to determine that the only thing about this experiment differing from all the others was the use of frequency modulation. Something outside the field must have affected that modulation, causing what Traben termed an 'instantaneous spatial transference.' We nicknamed it IST. Such a transference could occur only if the entire field were *drawn* to a receiving station at another location. In order to convert a mass to energy and move it through space/time, there must be a pin-down point at the other end, or the mass will just dispel itself in sudden disintegration."

"My God," said Hammond, sitting up. "Is that what happened to Martin?"

"One thing at a time," growled Rinehart. "That was the second unforeseen event. For the *Sturman* to make an instantaneous transfer to Norfolk required an unwitting party in that area using a powerful receiver operating on the same frequency modulation as the experiment in Philadelphia.

"Traben checked with Norfolk officials and discovered they were operating a radio school out there, and, on the same day as our experiment, they had been conducting tests of their own equipment aboard a Navy lighter. And our men had seen it crossing the *Sturman*'s path."

Hammond was confused for a moment, then he remembered Yablonski's story, how he had shrunk back on the bed, reacting to something passing by. "That little boat just missed us!" he had said.

"It's the very nature of FM to be drawn to the most powerful receiver, like homing in on a beam." Rinehart smiled and then cackled. "You realize this is the classic mode of scientific discovery—set out to prove one thing and find something completely different." He laughed harder. "Thomas Edison holding the light bulb up to his ear and whispering, 'Hello? Hello?' "

Hammond laughed too, until the old man calmed down and said, "Instantaneous spatial transfer . . . you know what the lay term for that is, don't you? The science-fiction term? *Teleportation.* Traben stumbled on it, just like a goddamned prospector!"

He sat down again and gave his body a rest. He closed his eyes and mused in a soft voice. "The reactions . . . Traben's friends in the Pentagon . . . embarrassed. Despite all his assurances, every experiment seemed to go foul . . . one way or another. . . . Nobody seemed to appreciate this great discovery. . . . They just looked at the record of the man responsible and saw failure after failure. . . ." Rinehart's eyes popped open and he said with glee, "Invisibility became almost as big a laughingstock as my UFOs. The one time Traben came up with something viable, they scoffed. Of course, they were right, I suppose. The men . . ."

Hammond didn't have to ask what he meant. Fletcher and Yablonski and the rest of the 1953 crew had suffered as much as the others—after the experiment.

"The attempt to alleviate side effects was a bust," said Rinehart. "The modulation had no effect whatsoever on anybody's state of mind. Fortunately, the men had been prepared ahead of time, told what to expect before and after. So their fears were greatly reduced. But no one had told them they were going to vanish from Philadelphia and pop up in Norfolk. . . . And no one warned them what would happen to Martin . . ."

Hammond looked at him expectantly.

"Fear . . . fear caused him to break contact with the others. He jumped off the bow, apparently during the moment of highest return acceleration. Vibrating at nearly the speed of light and making a sudden exit from the field, his mass was completely converted into energy and dispelled into space."

Rinehart looked at the floor and said flatly, "He exploded. And every man on deck saw it happen. That's why later on so many of them went crazy and committed suicide. They were anticipating the same thing happening to *them*."

Rinehart sighed with the weight of it. "In ten years of work, we never got rid of the aftereffects, because we couldn't treat the most important one of all: *fear*. These men *suffered* from fear because their very existence was so unstable."

Rinehart went to the kitchen to heat up a can of soup. Hammond envied him his appetite but realized he was used to this story. Hammond looked down at the Siamese cat sleeping on his feet. He wanted desperately to stretch. He eased one foot out first, then the other. He left the cat in peace and rose on stiff limbs. He walked around the house a while, inspecting Rinehart's magazine collection, then he went into the kitchen.

Rinehart resumed talking as if on cue. "Traben quite suddenly acquired a case of guilt fever. He became very outspoken, urging the Navy to halt all experimentation in this field. He spoke to Pentagon officials, the chiefs of staff, Department of Defense— He went on a one-man crusade to show the error of his ways—"

"Quite a turnabout," said Hammond.

"Yes, wasn't it? But he was still working on his own, in secret, trying to duplicate what had happened with Norfolk. His concern for the men was a front."

"A front—are you sure?"

"You had to know the man. He was at his peak, in his mid-thirties. He had ten years of experience behind him, learning how to be shrewd and devious. And he had acquired a powerful friend with money."

"Who?"

"Ever heard the name Francis P. Bloch?"

"Maybe." Hammond's brain raced.

"Industrialist. Founded a small company in the early 1950s that has since grown to immense influence—Research Technology Industries."

Hammond recalled the company from articles in the *Navy Times*. They were a big private contractor for Naval weapons and electronic guidance systems.

"Bloch and Traben were very close even before RTI was formed," said Rinehart. "When Project Thin Air was finally closed down in 1955, Traben was appointed to RTI's Board of Directors and made head of Research and Development."

"Are you suggesting that Traben took his work on Thin Air over to RTI?"

"Isn't that obvious?" Rinehart smiled. "It's the only thing the man had worked on since 1942."

Rinehart brought his soup to the living room and Hammond made him repeat his last statements for the tape, then he asked, "You're saying that Bloch and RTI were capable of taking risks that the government had already written off?"

"You find that so hard to believe?" Rinehart asked almost casually.

Hammond regarded him with suspicion, realizing it was possible the old man's bitterness was making him fantasize plots and invent ulterior motives. What grounds had he presented to back up his accusations against Traben that couldn't be interpreted by a Board of Inquiry as plain old sour grapes?

"If you suspected he was acting purely in his own interest, why didn't you say something at the time?"

Rinehart waved a hand at his houseful of UFO literature and said, "Who would have listened to me? I told you before—I had literally cut my own throat in Washington."

"So? You had nothing to lose by exposing Traben." His calm eyes locked onto Rinehart's. The old man seemed to tremble, then threw up his arms in exasperation.

"All right!" he said. "They worked on *me!* Do you understand that? They tried to pull that brainwashing crap on me; they were brainwashing everyone by then—even those who didn't need fear control got it—but on me it didn't *take!* And I let them think it did. To this day, they still believe that on Project Thin Air, my mind is a *blank!*"

Hammond did his best not to appear shocked, but he felt a cold knife digging into his chest. "Were you afraid of Traben?" he asked.

"Of course I was! I spent a decade with him. I may not have had proof, but I had cause enough for suspicion!"

"You let them work on you—willingly?"

Rinehart sighed. "I wanted to get out, kiss off Washington for the rest of my life. And if they felt they had to insure my silence, I was prepared to give them anything, as long as I got peace of mind."

Hammond tapped his fingers together and watched the old man squirm. "I think you know, Mr. Rinehart, that the alternative was your *life*."

Rinehart shook his head in denial, but Hammond leaned forward and spoke with cold disdain.

"And you knew it was the same for every man who ever participated in that project. As long as their mouths could be kept shut, they were allowed to live. It would have drawn too much attention to just bump everybody off in one shot, wouldn't it? But gradually, over the years . . . You knew, didn't you? And you let them get away with it?"

Rinehart jumped up and snarled, "I could be making it all up, you know! Just a crazy old man! Ranting and raving, whether it's about this—or this—!" He slammed a hand down on a stack of UFO periodicals. Then he stalked across the room and leaned against the other window, his back to Hammond.

The interview was over. Rinehart put another log on the fire. Hammond got up, gathering his tapes and recorder and sending the Siamese in a mad dash for cover. The log burst into flame and Rinehart quickly poked it to the back of the grate, cursing and pulling the screen into place. He turned and scowled at Hammond.

"What will you do?"

"Think about it," said Hammond. Rinehart shrugged and Hammond asked, "How much money would you say the government might have invested in Thin Air—all told?"

"About a hundred million dollars," said Rinehart.

The figure jolted Hammond. If it had been that costly, and Traben had continued his work under the auspices of RTI, he would have required enormous funding, with costs spiraling to match the inflation rate over the years. . . . But RTI would have been under close scrutiny because of its substantial Federal contracts. Since 1955, how could they have spent millions of dollars on Thin Air and managed to conceal that from the world? The project had failed too many times before; it was unlikely they would have thrown good money after bad. And RTI was a business; they would not be playing Mayo Clinic to Fletcher and Yablonski unless there was still a need for secrecy.

Unless Thin Air was still alive.

It was too confusing. He would have to sort it out when he got home. From the perspective of distance and sanity.

Rinehart was shuffling to the door. Hammond watched the stooped figure and wondered how so much detailed memory could still be at this man's fingertips. Maybe the bitterness kept it alive. Certainly that and the UFOs were all he had to think about.

Hammond paused to look back at the collection of UFO literature. Rinehart noticed and said, "Still think I'm nuts, Commander?"

"Just eccentric."

"Everything is relative. Ask yourself: can you say for certain that flying saucers don't exist? No. Because they're no more fantastic than Project Thin Air, and that *did* exist."

With a smile of satisfaction, Rinehart opened the door and Hammond shook hands with him, then trudged outside. It was cold and the snowfall had made the yard slushy. He heard the door close and glanced back at the old house. He squished up to his car and stashed the Uher and the tapes in the back seat.

It was only as he opened the driver's side that he caught a glimpse of the battered pickup truck sitting up the road under a cottonwood.

14

The truck meant nothing to Hammond. His attention was drawn to the white-carpeted hills and the heavy clouds that covered them. The snow might return in force at any moment.

With a sigh, he walked around to the trunk, opened it, and strung a set of chains out behind the rear tires. Ten minutes later, with the car warmed, his flight jacket zipped tight, and his knees soaked through, Hammond drove cautiously out of Rinehart's yard.

His taillights reflected off the fogged windshield of the pickup truck. It was an old Ford half-ton with faded blue paint spattered with mud.

Inside the cab, two men sat quietly watching Hammond's car creep off into the descending dark. The driver picked up a rag and wiped the inside of the windshield, whistling an aimless tune.

"Are we going to sit here all night?" his companion asked.

The whistling stopped.

"We should have taken both of them . . . in the house."

The driver handed him the rag and in the darkness flashed him a hostile glare. "Bullshit," he said. "Get your corner—I can't reach it." Without waiting for an answer, he turned the ignition key. The motor roared to life. He switched on the parking lights, eased out from under the cottonwood, and drove slowly past Rinehart's house.

It started to snow again. Hammond kept the staff car in low gear. Even with the chains on, the winding road was slippery. He drove by instinct, with a light touch to keep the rear wheels from breaking loose. Little snow flurries danced in his headlights. Stands of cottonwood, their trunks and branches sheathed in sparkling white, shimmered briefly as the car passed by. Below the road, down by the stream, the ground was heavily drifted. Hammond remembered some of the large rocks he had seen on the way up; most of them were now blanketed with snow.

The pickup truck growled down the road in low gear. Equipped with snow tires, it had more traction than Hammond's car. The driver held his acceleration steady and charged through the dusk.

Hunched over to keep his head from hitting the top of the cab, he peered through the windshield to follow the tracks of Hammond's car, visible even in the dim reflection from his parking lights.

His companion stubbed out a cigarette in the ashtray, reached under the seat and grabbed an M-16 rifle. He held it loosely across his chest, the barrel up.

"What do we do if he makes it to the main road?" he asked.

The driver kept his eyes straight ahead and worked the wheel. "Let me worry about that, Doc. You just take care of your end."

"I still think we should have—"

"Don't start that again," the driver snarled. "If you hadn't screwed things up, we wouldn't be here in the first place. I figure we'll catch him on the last stretch, just before we hit the highway. It's straight there, so I can see if there's any other traffic coming. If it's all clear, he's yours. If not, there's still plenty of time before he gets back to Kirtland."

The driver increased his speed slightly. The heavy snow tires obliterated Hammond's track, leaving behind a distinctive herringbone pattern of their own.

Hammond's rear-view mirror picked up the glimmer of lights. They looked to be far away but coming up fast. He eased the staff car around a sweeping curve. The craggy hills rose sharply on his right; across the other side was a stretch of darkness he knew must be the stream bed. The slushy road stretched ribbon-straight before him. The highway to Taos was less than three miles away.

He glanced in the mirror again and saw the lights were still far behind. It never occurred to him they might be parking lights, and closer than he imagined.

* * *

An ungloved hand shoved a clip into the M-16 and cocked it. The driver switched off his lights as the truck slid around the end of the curve, its tires throwing up a plume of snow. Hammond's car was less than one hundred yards ahead.

He gunned the accelerator. The tires held. The man with the rifle rolled down his window and leaned out. His left foot reached for the hump in the middle of the floor, bracing against the bumpy acceleration.

Hammond sensed something behind him, but his attention was drawn to a shiny spot in the road that his headlights had picked up. Water running off the hill must have frozen. He tapped the brakes to slow down before he hit the ice. He felt the rear wheels start to go and corrected to keep from fishtailing. The rear end swung close to the rocks at the base of the hill.

The skid saved Hammond's life.

He didn't hear the crack of the rifle, but he flinched as the right side of his rear window shattered. Bullets chewed through the back of the passenger seat and smashed the windshield.

Hammond jammed his foot down on the gas and tried to get clear.

The rear wheels spun, then dug in. The car lurched forward. Hammond's ears filled with a metallic screeching sound as the passenger side slammed into the hill.

The next blast shredded his right rear tire. He spun across the road, shot off the shoulder, and plowed through loosely packed snow. A hidden rock bounced the car up in the air. It slid along on its right side, threatening to overturn, then dropped back and slammed down so hard that the left door flew open.

Hammond was catapulted out of the car through the snow-filled air and darkness. He crunched into a deep drift and was vaguely aware of sinking into wet snow.

Up on the road, the truck slid to a stop. The driver switched his headlights on full beam. They watched the car slide into the creek on its left side. A cloud of steam enveloped it as icy water flooded the hot engine.

The man with the M-16 got out, removed the empty clip, and inserted a fresh one. He walked to the edge of the road, looking for a place to climb down.

"Where do you think you're going?" the driver shouted.

"Make sure he's finished! Be with you when you get swung around!"

"You've got a clear shot at the gas tank from here, Doc. Torch it. We've got other things to do."

The man on the road hesitated, then brought the rifle up to his shoulder. He emptied the entire clip and the bullets smashed into the exposed underside of the car.

The roar of the gas tank exploding startled Hammond. The ball of flame shot up some yards below him and to the left, but the heat was so intense it melted the snow he was lying in. He forced himself to sit up, ignoring the agony of movement. Over the crackle of flames he heard a car door slam. Carefully, because he was between the fire and the road, he looked up. He couldn't focus: everything above him was just a blur. He blinked and in spite of the pain sucked in several deep breaths. As his vision returned, he glanced up at the road again. The headlights swung around and he glimpsed the truck. It looked like the one he'd seen at Rinehart's.

He watched it move off, heading back into the foothills. He wondered fleetingly why it didn't continue into town. He waited for it to disappear around the curve before he pulled himself out of the snow. Nothing seemed broken, but he felt light-headed. . . .

The tapes! He had to get the tapes. He floundered toward the burning car, getting as close as he could. The fire was consuming the interior. One look showed him that everything was beyond saving.

He sagged and cursed at the loss of his evidence. But he was lucky to be alive—it wasn't the tapes they were after. He took in more air and moved up toward the road, looking for a place to climb over the bank. When he had inched his way to the worn blacktop, he began to feel the effects of the cold. Wet clothing and no shelter in sight: he could still die, just from exposure.

Standing close to where the truck had turned around, he saw in the glow from the fire heavy tread marks in the snow. He noted the strange pattern. Something glinted by the roadside. He bent down painfully and his fingers closed over a brass cartridge case. He stuffed it into his pocket and, with a backward glance at the burning car, started up the road as fast as he could travel. He figured it was two or three miles back to Rinehart's house. But he knew he had to get there. He knew now why the truck had turned around and gone back.

The old man was a sitting duck.

Twenty minutes later, gasping for breath, he lost his footing and fell to the road. He was dizzy, cold, and winded. He struggled back to his feet and pulled up the collar of his flight jacket. As long as he kept moving, he would be all right. He broke into a slow trot, eyes downward, concentrating on his footing, trying to fight off the numbing effects of the cold. This is ridiculous, he thought. In Washington, it was still autumn. Birds, sunlight. He wasn't even wearing a winter uniform. He laughed at himself.

Smoke still curled darkly from the chimney as the pickup rolled back up the dirt road to a position behind the cottonwoods. The engine off, the door on the passenger side creaked open. Crepe-soled boots crunched through snow as the gunman walked to the back, reached into the open bed, and pulled out a five-gallon can of gasoline.

The driver kicked his door open and trudged through the mud toward Rinehart's house. One hand was stuffed in the belly pocket of his parka, clutching a blackjack. His ears perked up. He heard cats meowing for dinner.

It was going to be a snap.

Hammond's breath rasped out of his throat, giving no relief to his burning lungs. He plodded on, ignoring the pain. He kept between the tire tracks and tried to estimate how much farther he had to go. Maybe another mile, maybe more.

Voices off in the distance broke through the roaring of blood in Hammond's ears. A flickering red glow lit the underside of the clouds ahead of him. From deep within, Hammond summoned his last reserves of strength and forced himself on.

By the time he staggered into Rinehart's yard, the fire was well on its way to burning itself out. Several men stared at him curiously then went back to hosing down the final flames. Clouds of smoke and shreds of charred paper boiled up into the air, mingling with the snow.

Hammond stood by helplessly, shivering. Several dark objects lay in the slush around the doorstep. Rinehart's pets: dead.

What a setup. The perfect accident for this place—a fire constantly stoked in the living room, the house stuffed to the rafters with old magazines and papers. "Just an old firetrap," they'd be saying in the *cantinas* tomorrow. "Finally went up. Shoulda seen it, *amigos*. Barbecued cats and dogs all over the place and barbecued Rinehart inside. . . ."

Dazed and heartsick, Hammond stumbled along the dirt road, away from the fire. His eyes swept the flats and the banks of the stream, looking for that Ford pickup. . . .

Nowhere. He looked down at the snow on the road. Amid the jumble of footprints his eyes picked up the distinctive tread of the snow tires he'd been following for so long. They cut off the road, heading out into an open field.

Hammond followed them until they seemed to just stop. The light from the fire was so dim, he couldn't be sure at first. Then he saw two Mexicans running toward him across the field, waving flashlights. They were headed for the fire. He hailed one of them and the man stopped, planting his light on Hammond's face, studying him curiously.

"*Madre* . . ." he said, and blinked.

Hammond realized he must have looked like hell. "Can I borrow your light?" he said, pointing to the tire tracks. He hunkered down on his knees to indicate he wanted to examine something.

The Mexican and his companion both came over and shined their lights where Hammond wanted.

The tracks stopped. He felt his heart leap. One hundred feet from the road, the tire tracks simply vanished.

Just like McCarthy.

When he returned to Rinehart's yard with the two Mexicans, the old man's body had been brought out. Hammond felt nausea well up in his throat.

Because of him, another man was dead. This time there had been nothing subtle about the means. It had been an all-out effort to stop both of them. Hammond had sorely underestimated the opposition.

Black soot was still drifting over the snow like fine

ground pepper. They had underestimated him, too, he thought to himself. He was barely conscious of the approaching siren—he was so busy letting the anger build up. As a New Mexico State Police patrol car rolled to a stop, Hammond decided the killers had made a terrible mistake. It was no longer just his job or a favor for an old girl friend.

They had made it *personal.*

15

The State Police gave him a good going-over and Hammond was in no mood to cooperate. They were understandably upset about the bullet-riddled and burnt-out Air Force car they had found in the stream bed. They were suspicious about his presence at Rinehart's house, coincidentally also burnt-out, and annoyed by his untouchable attitude.

Hammond phoned Admiral Gault from the police station in Taos, in the presence of the police chief, Captain Montez. Gault listened to Hammond's brief explanation in utter silence, then asked to speak to Captain Montez. Gault assured the chief that the nation's security was at stake and Hammond was acting under the direct authority of the Pentagon. He never said *who* in the Pentagon, but that was enough.

Hammond got back on the line and Gault told him, "I want a better explanation from you as soon as you can get to a security line." The click-off came like an exclamation point.

Hammond was released from custody. He stayed in Taos overnight, licking his wounds and letting his uniform dry out.

He was in Captain Montez' office the next morning as the investigating officers reported in with their clues. The vanishing tire tracks in the field turned out to be the biggest single head-scratcher. And Hammond was not about to offer hints. As for footprints, they were too late. If there had been any at all, they had been obliterated by snowfall, soot, and the trampling feet of fire-fighting neighbors.

Hammond's story, although cloudy in its motivations, was borne out by the evidence. He told the police he had been attacked on the road while returning from his meeting with Rinehart on what he termed "government business." The police found expended shell casings on the road near his demolished car that matched the one Hammond had picked up. They were all 5.56 millimeter. Hammond told them he had heard automatic fire: from that they deduced it must have come from an M-16, but without the weapon in hand, the information was useless.

Neighbors verified that Hammond had shown up at Rinehart's house *after* the fire was under way and had appeared out of breath and in great concern.

Several officers were sent to canvass the local motels to see if any strangers had checked in or out recently. Aside from the usual tourists and their families, results were negative.

It seemed as though the men in the pickup and the pickup itself would never be found in Taos. And since Hammond hadn't seen the license plates, there was no way to trace them.

Before noon, he was driven back to Kirtland Air Force Base where the Motor Pool was even less overjoyed with him than the State Police had been. A Navy officer had lost an Air Force car—to them it was a major crime. After changing into a fresh uniform from his flight bag, Hammond was hustled over to the base commander's office where he sat cooling his heels. He got permission to use a security line to contact his commanding officer.

Admiral Gault wasted no time in tearing into Hammond. "You put an innocent man in jeopardy with your flagrant disregard for procedure, and now the man ends up killed! I don't know if it was an accident or murder, but I do know so far you've produced two dead bodies and no case!"

Hammond stayed calm and managed to get across in brief the substance of his interview with Rinehart and the fact that the trail now pointed toward a physicist named Traben and the head of a huge conglomerate named Bloch.

"F.P. Bloch?" Gault exploded.

"Yes, sir—"

"But that's insane! I know Bloch. He's a friend of Smitty's. He's a major figure in Washington. And he's no crook!" Gault paused and Hammond heard muffled swearing. "You're going to need more than the opinion of a dead man, Hammond. I hope this time you've got something on paper!"

"Uh . . ." Hammond could hardly bring himself to explain how he'd taken tapes of everything but the tapes had been lost when the car had been demolished. . . .

Silence from Gault. Then finally a resounding, "Swell. You should've gone to Okinawa. All right, here's what I'm going to do: I'll double security at the safe house and I'll send backup men out to help you."

Hammond protested. "I can move better alone."

"Really?"

"I know how it looks," said Hammond, "but I need more time and I can't waste it explaining things to a bunch of agents—"

"Hammond!" Gault's voice crackled over the phone. "If you blow it now, it's out of your hands! And you're out of a job!"

"That's encouraging," Hammond said to himself as he hung up. He stepped out of the office and a guard returned him to the base commander's waiting room.

Ten minutes later, Hammond was summoned quickly inside. He steeled himself for the expected tongue-lashing, but General Walter J. Pasko turned out to be a calm man who listened attentively to Hammond's explanations. He interrupted Hammond's apology for the loss of the Air Force staff car.

"It isn't every day we get a little Starsky and Hutch out here, Commander. It's clear what happened and the Air Force does have other cars. Of course, the Navy will have to pay for that one. . . ." Briefly, he flashed a sly smile. "Now, with that aside," he continued, "let's turn our attention to how you got into this little mess."

General Pasko was eager to play detective. But Hammond told him the absolute minimum, invoking the terms *classified, top secret,* and *need-to-know,* language the general clearly understood. Hammond revealed only that he had been on a high-level mission to interview Rinehart for NIS. He thought no one had known he was there, but obviously he was wrong. Someone had known enough to get one man and try to get the other.

Pasko asked about Hammond's movements prior to flying out of Washington. Hammond began to think along the lines the general was suggesting. He hadn't told anyone where he was going. He had kept security tight for once. But all along in this case he had been involved with Navy people. Only a Navy man, or an impersonator, could have penetrated BUPERS and set up that warning system in its computers. Dr. McCarthy used Navy facilities like they belonged to him. Wasn't it possible that he or someone else posing as a Navy man followed Hammond into the MATS terminal in Washington, examined the status board, and found out precisely where he was going?

That someone would have known that Rinehart lived in New Mexico and would have made the connection immediately.

They had let him go ahead and interview Rinehart, knowing damned well they were going to bump off both men—but in separate locations, so no one else could be sure of the connection.

Hammond shriveled inside. He was a marked man. These people evidently had tentacles all over the country. But who were they and what were they going to so much trouble to hide?

If Rinehart was right, then Edmond Traben was clearly at the center of it. Hammond's fist curled involuntarily. He wanted a neck to wring. He looked up and saw General Pasko staring back at him.

"Not angry at me, I hope," Pasko said.

"No," said Hammond. "Thanks for your help."

"Anytime. I'll let you know if we need any more cars wrecked."

Hammond went back to the ready room and recovered his flight bag and briefcase from a locker. From the briefcase, he fished out the list of companies he had received from Tri-State—government vendor firms for whom they were underwriting insurance.

His finger ran down the list; he was looking for Bloch's company, RTI. It wasn't there. But there had to be a connection between Fletcher and Traben. What other motive was there for Fletcher's murder?

He borrowed a phone and called collect to the NIS Data Center in Washington, where he asked for a listing on Research Technology Industries. He was given phone numbers and addresses for the Washington offices, New York offices, and the general plant in Pasadena, California.

Hammond figured he was closer to Pasadena, so he tried that first. He called and asked to speak to Edmond Traben.

"I'm sorry, sir, but Dr. Traben is not in this month."

This month? What kind of business was this? Hammond asked where Traben could be located.

"Sir, he spends most of his time with his own company, Micro-Tech."

Hammond bumbled on the phone while his eyes ran down the Tri-State list again. There it was: Micro-Technology Laboratories, Government Vendor Number 5600081, address and phone number in Manhattan Beach, California.

At last he had the direct connection. Harold Fletcher worked for Tri-State and Tri-State insured MTL and MTL was run by Edmond Traben.

He went back to the ready room and wrote out his flight plan. Destination: the military terminal at L.A. International. He changed into his G-suit and handed in his papers, instructing the dispatcher not to list him on the status board.

Hammond touched down at L.A. International shortly after noon. During the flight he had been thinking of the other good reason for coming to Los Angeles: Jan Fletcher. She lived somewhere in Brentwood. He still had the phone number she had given him when she'd left Washington: 472-7304.

Hammond went straight to the pay phones and called her.

"I promised to keep in touch," he said.

"I didn't quite believe you. Harold's dead: we don't need to worry about his records anymore."

"Look, I don't know how much we still have in common, but we do have things to talk about."

There was a long silence, then she asked, "What are you doing in Los Angeles?"

"Well, business, actually—"

"Look, Nicky," she interrupted, "I never was interested in your work and you wouldn't share it with me anyway, so don't bring it to me now. . . ." She hesitated. "Unless you've found out something . . . ?"

He hesitated, wanting to tell her, to take her into his confidence because he believed she could be trusted, but then she might become a target, too, and he didn't want that.

Then what did he want?

"How about dinner tonight?" he asked.

There was a long hesitation, then she said, "I don't feel like wearing black in public, so you'd better come here. Take pot luck."

"You're on." He copied down the address and hung up, not knowing whether to be elated or scared. He hurried over to the Motor Pool and checked out a car. He had no trouble; his reputation hadn't preceded him.

It was an impressive building half a block long, set among acres of undeveloped industrial land on the east side of Manhattan Beach. A huge marble sign identified the firm in gold letters a foot high: MICRO-TECHNOLOGY LABORATORIES.

Hammond parked and walked to the entrance. The olive drab building was cold and sterile with a polarized glass façade and manicured landscaping. The sky was overcast; the bleakness of it all gave him the willies.

He walked through electric-eye doors and found himself inside a narrow but tall lobby, fully three stories high. A security man guarded the inner entrance. There was a reception desk in the center of the foyer.

On the wall over the inner entrance was an enormous blowup, a photograph of the plant with some impressive copy set across it:

MTL CONTRIBUTIONS
TO PROJECT TRANSAT:

TranSat Integrating Contractor
Structural and Thermal Systems
Data Acquisition and Processing
Power Control and Distribution
Flight System Software
Aeroshell
Orbiter Communications
Computer Command System
Data Storage Memory
Communications Sequencing Computer
Attitude Control System

What in hell would a firm this solidly entrenched in multimillion-dollar space contracts want with something as weird as Thin Air?

It struck Hammond he might be barking up the wrong

tree with respect to Traben. But he had to see him first. He marched up to the reception desk, showed his ID, and explained he was here on government business.

"Ordinarily, Dr. Traben sees visitors only by appointment," the ex-CIA type said. "This may take a while."

"Enjoy yourself," said Hammond. They were going to check his credentials. Good. That saved him the problem of informing Gault of his whereabouts. And it minimized the risk that he might disappear while visiting Micro-Tech. He sat down calmly in the lobby and waited.

Forty minutes later, an enormous bull of a man banged through the lobby and lurched over to meet him. He was so big his shoulders preceded him; he walked on the balls of his feet. He was dressed in a plain gray suit with the coat open and flapping so that anyone could see he packed a gun—a little .38 stuffed into a hip holster. But he had a big friendly face.

"Commander Hammond, I'm Joe Coogan, Chief of Security for MTL," he said, and threw out a meaty paw. Hammond shook it. "We're in the same profession," Coogan said with a smile. "So, what can we do for you?"

"Well, I really came here to speak with Dr. Traben, if that's all right."

"Sure it's all right," Coogan reassured him. "It's just going to take some time. He's a very busy man."

"—And would I like to come back tomorrow, is that it?"

"Not at all," Coogan said absently, checking his watch. "Come on, we have time. Let me show you around."

Hammond followed him, surprised. He had thought they were going to brush him off, but instead they were going to romance him.

Coogan gave him a mini-tour of the plant, explaining some of the projects they were involved in and showing him some very impressive equipment. And along the way Coogan did a little pumping: "We do tremendous business with the Navy, designing the micro-electronics for some very sophisticated guidance systems and newfangled radar transponders. You ever get into any of that, Commander?"

"Not lately."

"I find it fascinating. I'm bananas for gadgets, buttons, and the like. MTL has an almost 99 percent success factor with their Naval applications. You aware of that?"

"No."

"Almost never have failures. We're conscientious—that's why we get contracts. I'm sure the NIS uses some of our equipment."

"No, not that I—" Suddenly Hammond recalled that no one had identified the most sophisticated of the little bugging chips that had been planted in his office. This one is for Gault, he said to himself, as he took a wild shot: "Oh, we *are* looking over a brand-new sort of listening device. It's about yea-big. . . ." He demonstrated with finger and thumb. Coogan didn't bat an eye. "Wouldn't have some of those around, would you? I could show you which one."

Coogan laughed. "I'm afraid not, Commander. That stuff is all top secret. I can't even admit we make those things. In order to show you anything like that I'd have to see clearance."

"Of course." Hammond smiled at the double-talk.

"But if the Navy's interested, I'm sure we'd like to be involved."

Cool. Very cool. Hammond moved to the next door.

"Oh, not that way. Back out the way we came."

Hammond continued smiling. He liked unsettling this big cheese. It was fun playing cat and mouse and being the cat for a change. Then he thought back to that cold road outside of Taos, the two tons of steel pursuing him. It would have to have been a big fellow maneuvering that truck. . . .

Coogan's bulk followed him through the door and they walked in silence down the hall until Hammond asked, "Job keep you close to home?"

"Sure does," Coogan replied. "We're very security-conscious. I hardly get a chance to travel even as far as San Diego. My wife's been complaining for years."

Hammond took another stab in the dark: "Not like being in the Navy, is it? All that travel . . . When did you get *your* discharge?"

Coogan didn't answer. He was already reaching for a door. His smile was automatic as he ushered Hammond through to Edmond Traben's outer office.

"Secretary's right over there, Commander. Emily, this is Commander Hammond. He's cleared to see the chief."

"Thank you, Joe," smiled Emily.

Coogan was gone before Hammond could thank him.

"Please have a seat, Commander. I'm afraid it's going to be a few minutes."

Hammond sat down, smugly contemplating the man in the inner sanctum, wondering if he was disappointed to learn this Naval bloodhound was still alive. So far, no one else seemed upset.

The few minutes became thirty before Hammond found himself face-to-face with Edmond Traben.

He turned out to be sixty-odd years old, balding, with piercing blue eyes and a thin, pinched face. He was sleek and trim and well-dressed, the epitome of a successful businessman. He was lighting a pipe as Hammond stepped in and used it to wave Hammond toward a bulging leather chair.

"Well, Commander," he said quickly, "I'm sure you have a reason for this visit."

Hammond smiled. "I'm here to inquire about Project Thin Air."

Traben was expressionless for a second, then blew out a cloud of smoke. "I didn't realize anybody was still interested in that." He looked back at Hammond and spread his hands expansively. "Great period in my life, you know."

"Maybe you could explain your involvement . . . in your own words."

Traben grunted and said, "I believe the project is still classified. I would need assurances that you're cleared to look into it."

"I'm sure your security chief has already verified me. But I'll add that I know what Thin Air was; I know the names of a lot of the people involved, and I'm on direct assignment from NIS."

Traben sat forward and rested his arms on the desk. He seemed alarmed. "I hope this doesn't mean the government is thinking of reactivating the project."

"Would that bother you?"

"Of course. I'd hate to see them waste the money."

"You wouldn't be . . . wasting money on it yourself, would you, Doctor?"

Traben shook his head so quickly he must have known the question was coming. "I find it hard enough to get financing for viable enterprises. I wouldn't *think* of wasting my own money on it."

"Yet you thoroughly believed in it—for about thirteen years."

"I believed in Santa Claus, too, once upon a time. But mass hypnosis and disorientation are passé in this day and age."

Hammond perked up. "What?"

Traben looked at him with suspicion. "Commander, if you really know about Thin Air, then you know that's what it was: a method of rendering the enemy impotent by leading him to believe he was disoriented, so he wouldn't be able to function or fight."

Hammond felt something clutch inside him. He smiled weakly and asked about the *Sturman.*

"Experimental vessel. We subjected her entire crew to our device and it succeeded. They were disoriented as hell."

"Why did you need a ship? Why not controlled lab facilities?"

"The *Sturman was* a controlled lab facility. We had to have the isolation of an expanse of sea in case the field spread too far."

"If it was successful, why was it never used in combat?"

"Unfortunately, there were aftereffects, psychological problems that lingered on."

"For how long?"

"I would imagine they are still extant if any of the crew are left alive. They would probably be under treatment, even today."

He seemed appropriately grim about that. Hammond asked if he knew personally of any crewmen under treatment. He shook his head.

"The War Department decided not to employ our device, afraid that the enemy powers would retaliate with something even more insidious. Possibly chemical warfare. So they opted for the big effect, the blow that would end everything: the atom bomb."

"But you and Rinehart stayed with the project until 1955."

Traben's eyes grew dark and cloudy. He was silent a moment, then began to speak about Rinehart as if he were describing an unpleasant relative. "He was a maniac who couldn't see the possibilities. He tried to get everything stopped. I had to fight him at every turn. He became convinced we were experimenting with something *preposterous* and doing unspeakable things to human beings!"

Quietly, Hammond asked, "Were you?"

"Good Lord, no!" Traben barked.

"Rinehart claimed the project dealt with invisibility," said Hammond. "If that's not true, then why was it called Thin Air?"

Traben was patient. "The thrust of the disorientation technique was to make the enemy *believe* he was confronting an invisible adversary. In that sense, the name was quite proper. Besides, the War Department had a pixie sense of humor. You recall Overlord, Torch, and Market-Garden?"

Traben smiled at his point, then his eyes narrowed. "I gather you've been talking to Rinehart. . . ."

"I've seen him, yes."

"He's a *totally unbalanced man!*" Traben exclaimed. "He ended up writing books about flying saucers!" He burst out laughing.

Hammond smiled thinly. "Yes, that is damaging to a reputation, isn't it?"

"What people do with their lives is their business, Commander," Traben lectured, "but when they invent stories about impossible plots against humanity and insist they are true, it's more than irresponsible. It's criminal!"

"What plots? The man wrote about the conceivable existence of flying saucers. He never insisted they were invaders."

Traben stared at him, then relaxed, tamping his pipe.

Hammond said, "I should probably have a talk with Dr. Kurtnauer."

"What for?"

"According to Rinehart, you went out of your way to get Kurtnauer kicked off the project."

Traben looked at him for a long moment, then said, "That's just what I mean. Rinehart is crazy. Dr. Kurtnauer is *working* for Micro-Tech!"

16

Hammond struggled to maintain his composure. "How long has he worked for you?"

"Since 1968." Traben observed Hammond coolly. "What's wrong, Commander? You seem upset."

"Just surprised. Can I see him?"

"Certainly, if you don't mind going to Israel."

Hammond's confusion deepened. "He doesn't work *here*?"

Traben shook his head. "I'm sure Rinehart told you that Kurtnauer went to Israel in the early fifties." Hammond nodded. "Well, at least he's told you one thing that's true. Kurtnauer is an Israeli citizen, highly respected, and at home in their scientific community. He's of great use to us there."

"Doing what?"

"Research."

"What is he working on?"

"Various projects. Classified."

"Kurtnauer is a physicist. Why would he be working for an electronics company?"

"Commander, *I'm* a physicist. And I'm Chairman of the Board. Sometimes we have to go the way the wind blows."

"I would still like to meet him. Does he ever come to the States?"

Traben hesitated. "Occasionally. In fact, Dr. Kurtnauer should be here in about three weeks for a meeting. It's probably just as well you wait till then. He would be difficult to reach right now. He's on a field trip for us. But if you're anxious, we can try to locate him for you."

Hammond thought about it for a moment, then said, "I'll wait. Does he commute here often?"

"Once or twice a year."

The intercom buzzed and Traben's secretary informed

him he had a meeting in five minutes. Hammond rose and said, "I guess that's it. Dr. Traben, thank you very much. I appreciate your time."

Traben escorted him to the door. "You're welcome. And please feel free to give me a call if you need further information."

Traben put out a perfunctory hand and Hammond held on to it longer than he should have, flashing Traben a thin smile that said, "I'm not as dumb as I look." Yet that was exactly how he felt: stupid.

The door closed and Hammond turned in the waiting room. The secretary said, "Mr. Coogan will be right with you, sir."

"Thanks." Hammond headed for the door, intending to do a little exploring on his own, but when he opened it, Coogan was already on his way up the hall.

"So! How'd it go?" he asked.

"Dandy."

"Great. Come on, I'll take you back to the lobby."

Hammond followed him down another corridor and a flight of stairs, aware they were taking the long way around.

Coogan led Hammond into a huge designing room, long and high and crowded with electronics and technicians in white lab coats. Hammond had no idea what he was looking at, but the miles of electrical wiring and exposed printed circuit boards looked real enough. There were computers everywhere, whirring or blinking away. If it was just a show, it was a damned good one, but Hammond couldn't allow himself to be that paranoid. He noted the international cast: Japanese, Chinese, Germanic types, even a few who were conversing in Russian.

They left through another door.

"Impressive," said Hammond. "What was it? An international prayer meeting?"

Coogan laughed. "Top-secret Navy project. So you can report to your people that MTL is on the job."

"I'm sure you are."

"I hope you enjoyed your visit, Commander. Was Dr. Traben helpful?"

"More than I expected."

"I'll bet you had a slanted view of things before you came in here."

Hammond shot him a glance. "What's that supposed to mean?"

"Commander," Coogan said in a hushed tone, "this fellow Rinehart has always been a pain in our ass. He's been trying to sic investigating committees on us for years. He was Traben's partner, but he got drunk with power. Thought he was a scientist himself. Couldn't stand the idea that Traben could do it and he couldn't."

"How do you know so much about Traben's past?"

Coogan smiled. "I'm head of security, Hammond."

Hammond nodded. That was all fine, but how did Coogan know that Hammond had seen Rinehart?

They parted company outside the front entrance. As Hammond walked back to his car, he felt overwhelmed by the whole performance.

Traben had been masterful. He had undoubtedly thought Hammond dead until he actually appeared in the lobby, at MTL's doorstep, so to speak. Yet in the short time Coogan had kept him occupied, Traben had managed to assemble his act.

Maybe Hammond would have a chance to see Kurtnauer in three weeks—if Traben couldn't invent an excuse. Was this a gigantic stall? If they were doing it to buy time, how much did they need and why?

He couldn't help himself: his instincts said Rinehart had told him the truth. And if he had, MTL would never be able to produce Kurtnauer. But that could be checked through State Department records.

And what about Coogan—the security chief—big and beefy with his black hair in that military crewcut? He had spoken of Rinehart without any prompting from Hammond. Did he know Rinehart was dead?

Hammond stopped at the car door, pulled the file out of his briefcase and checked the number that had been on all the flags at BUPERS. He was already sure.

9805CGN.

CGN. Coogan.

He stood back and stared at the olive drab building. Façades. All of them façades. He could tell tales to Gault from now till Christmas, but without cracking those façades and dredging up real evidence, he was, as Slater put it, up shit creek.

Was it possible Rinehart had been lying? That Traben

was as innocent as he portrayed himself? If so, why was Rinehart killed?

Because once Hammond had found him, he became too dangerous. So they had murdered him, tried to kill Hammond, failed, and now had thrown him a bone to gnaw on.

Until they could try again.

He shivered. Before he got into the car, he made a thorough search for a bomb.

Hammond drove straight to the Federal Building in Westwood. At the Navy Office of Information, he showed his credentials and commandeered a desk and a phone. He managed to reach Ensign Just-Ducky at home. She let out a great big sigh. "You know, Hammond," she said, "this is ridiculous. If you want a date, you don't have to fly all the way to Los Angeles to call me."

"Very funny. Have you got a pencil?" She grunted a reply. "Okay, get hold of the Data Center first thing in the morning. Have them run a check through BUPERS on one Joseph Coogan, possible former Navy officer. Have them check the State Department for current status on the passport and visas of one Dr. Emil Kurtnauer, Austrian-born, possible naturalized American with dual Israeli citizenship. I want to know whether Dr. Kurtnauer has returned from Israel at any time in the last ten years. If so, dates, port of entry, et cetera. Then I want a run-down on security clearances for Micro-Technology Laboratories in Manhattan Beach, California. Was Kurtnauer ever cleared by the FBI to work there? And I want a complete portfolio on the company itself teletyped to the Los Angeles Navy PIO. I'll be here at 0900 tomorrow morning—that's noon your time. Okay?"

There was a long silence punctuated by a groan, then she asked him to spell Kurtnauer.

"One other thing," he added, "get hold of Cohen or Slater through Jack Pohl. Have one of them call me here at 0930 tomorrow."

"Yes, sir."

"And get some rest, Ensign. You sound like someone's been pushing you too hard."

Jan Fletcher lived in a fashionable section of Brentwood, north of Sunset Boulevard on a street called

Homewood. The house was a one-story ranch-style home on a large tree-shaded lot. Hammond walked to the front door and rang the bell.

She opened the door and smiled tentatively as she let him in. She walked ahead of him and down a few steps to the living room. It was long, with huge glass doors that opened onto a patio and an enormous backyard. There was a novel overturned on an ottoman, and a half-empty cocktail glass on the coffee table.

"Can I get you a drink, Nicky?"

"Please." He nodded. She went to the bar and he looked around, impressed by the decor. It was very California, especially the fossil-stone and brass fireplace that jutted out into the center of the room.

"I wanted to get rid of that," said Jan, following his gaze, "but Harold loved it." She returned with Hammond's drink. "A big fireplace was his status symbol. Comes from living in too many apartments with radiators."

She met Hammond's gaze and let him search her face. Her eyes seemed cool and distant.

"I'm all right now," she said. "I've gotten used to being alone again." She picked up her drink and sipped at it.

"I'm glad," he said, and smiled.

"You're glad I'm alone?"

Hammond blinked. "I'm sorry. What a dumb thing to say."

She sat on the edge of the ottoman, her knees pressed together. "Hammond . . . why are you here?"

He sighed. "I think I acted like a rat before. I wish there were some way I could make it up to you."

She studied him objectively. "There is. Tell me what's on your mind."

He laughed. "I thought you said not to bring my work around."

"If it concerns me, then it's not just your work—it's an obligation."

He felt something move in his stomach. "I guess I do owe you . . ." he said and paced to the bar for another ice cube. He called back over his shoulder, "How much did Harold confide in you?"

"That's impossible to answer, isn't it? If half his life were a secret, how would I know it?"

"You always seemed to know when *I* was hiding something."

She smiled and crossed her legs, relaxing. Hammond walked back slowly, his eyes on her calves. She looked so good in a skirt. . . .

"You did look into his background, didn't you?" she said. "That's what you've been working on; that's why you're here."

He nodded. "Believe me, there's nothing in Harold's past that will ever change your opinion of him, whatever that is. But he knew things that he couldn't . . . that were buried inside." Her expression changed to puzzlement. He took a deep breath and said, "What if I told you that Harold's nightmare was *real?*"

She stared at him. "What—what do you mean?" she stammered.

"I mean real. All of it. Not just a dream: it happened. He really was in Philadelphia, there was an experiment, and he was part of it."

Her eyes were wide. "Is it true?" she breathed.

"Let me put it this way," he said. "I've found other men with the same dream." She stared back. "And the same *doctor.*"

Her eyes searched his, probing. "McCarthy—?"

"Yes."

He made her sit down, then briefly described what McCarthy had been doing to his patients for twenty years. He told her about Yablonski and Olively, but he held back on Harold's death. She would ask soon enough: it wouldn't take her long to put two and two together. She listened stonily as he described McCarthy's technique, then interrupted him to ask why.

He explained Project Thin Air quickly and calmly, and she sat there, growing incredulous. He had just finished telling about the 1953 experiment when she rose slowly and left the room.

Hammond followed her into the kitchen. He watched her move around like a zombie. She put lamb chops under the broiler, then turned to make a salad.

He caught her eye and said, "You don't want to believe it. I can't blame you."

"I'd rather believe Harold was crazy."

"So would I."

She glanced at him once, then wouldn't look again. She concentrated on the dinner. He wasn't surprised by her disbelief. It was an idiotic story. He'd known that as he was telling it. It would be a miracle if Gault accepted even one word of it.

Finally, Hammond sighed and said, "I'm feeling grubby. Would you mind if I had a bath?"

She put down a paring knife without a word and led him to a huge tiled bathroom, then walked out, closing the door.

While the tub filled, he stripped and examined his cuts and bruises in the mirror. He looked like a patchwork quilt of red, green, blue, and white. What a mess. He rummaged for Epsom salts to put in the tub and stopped to stare at the array of toiletries on the counter. She had not yet removed the traces of Harold Fletcher.

He eased into the hot water and relaxed. He could feel tension melting away. But the ache from head to toe was still there. He slid down until the water was up to his chin. It was soft, soothing, and quiet. He closed his eyes. . . .

The door was thrown open with a bang and his knees jerked up involuntarily. He saw Jan coming at him with a terrible look.

"You sonofabitch!" she screamed.

She banged the sliding door back. Her hand swiped downward and caught him across the cheek. She bent over and flailed at him, slapping from every direction. She was sobbing with rage.

"Jan!" he yelled. "Jan, for Christ's sake!"

He managed to grab one of her hands but couldn't get the other one.

She held his mouth shut with her fingers. He strained for leverage. "Don't say anything," she warned. "Ever again! Don't ever say anything to me again! *You killed Harold!*"

She was staring at him, her lips contorted into a snarl. Then her eyes swam with confusion. She weakened, realized what she was doing, then let go. . . .

Hammond clutched the side of the tub and pulled himself up, sucking in air.

"You killed Harold," she sobbed. "And I killed him, by sending him to you."

She broke into tears. Her hands fluttered and he grabbed one of them. Her head sank onto his shoulder and she knelt at the side of the tub, sobbing herself quiet.

"We didn't kill him," Hammond whispered.

"But if he hadn't come to you—if you hadn't looked into his past—"

Oh God, he thought. She's blaming us both for Harold's heart attack. She still doesn't understand that it was McCarthy.

But maybe . . . maybe it *was* my fault, he thought.

Her coldness had vanished. She helped him out of the bath, paying no attention to his nudity. She was solicitous of his bruises and, as she rubbed them with ointment, demanded to know how he had got them. There was no point in holding back anymore, so he told her about MTL and Traben, about Rinehart's death and his own close call. She still found Thin Air hard to believe, but he'd made her understand the danger. Now all she had to do was connect murder to her husband's death.

By the time they sat down to dinner, the lamb chops were cold, but they ate voraciously. Flickering candlelight warmed their faces with a yellow glow. Hammond sipped wine and wallowed in one of Harold Fletcher's terrycloth robes.

"You don't have anyone staying with you?" he asked.

"No."

"What about your mother?"

"She never travels. She won't leave New York."

"Girl friends?"

"I don't really want anybody. Harold's boss calls once a day."

"How long are you going to stay in retreat?"

She didn't answer for a long time, then she said, "I'm glad you're here."

"I know. That's why you tried to drown me."

She choked out a laugh, then smiled: it was pleasant seeing her happy again. He got up on impulse and came around the table to stand over her. She looked up at him with amused interest. He leaned over and kissed her lightly on the lips. She wasn't surprised at all. Her amusement turned to trembling fascination. She closed her eyes and he kissed her again. Her hand closed over his.

They made love long into the night, then fell apart on the sheets in a sprawl and let the cool air from the open window dry their bodies. They touched hands and lay quietly in the dark until they were asleep.

Jan woke Hammond at around four in the morning and complained of being cold. Hammond pulled up the sheet and arranged the blanket and she huddled with him. He peered through the dimness and saw her studying his face. Her eyes were warm now.

"Nicky?"

"Umm . . ."

"Why did we do this?"

He said nothing and she didn't press him for an answer. They both lay there and thought about it.

"Are we going to be a thing again?" she asked.

After a moment, he said, "I feel like a football. You can grab me and run for the goal or kick me back to the visiting team."

She smiled. "I don't like football."

"Good," he said. "Then you name the game."

"I can't . . . yet."

"Just as well."

She was silent again, for a long time, then she said, "I guess I should wait until all of Harold's affairs are settled before thinking of myself. God, I'm so tired of answering questions. Accountants, lawyers, insurance men . . . Can you believe one of the companies that insured Harold sent an investigator around the other day?"

"Really?"

"He was very pleasant, but he was asking all sorts of questions."

"What questions?"

"About what Harold was doing in Washington, where he'd been, who he'd seen. I didn't tell him we had met with you. I said only that he'd gone on business."

Good girl, Hammond breathed to himself.

"He asked if Harold had seen a doctor while he was in Washington. I said I didn't know. Then he asked something really nervy—if Harold was open with me about his personal problems."

Hammond managed to stay calm. "What did he look like?"

"The investigator? He was big, very big, with black hair, a crewcut. . . ."

Hammond tensed. Coogan.

"Has anyone else been around asking questions?"

"No. Who would be?"

Hammond forced himself to keep his mouth shut. He didn't want her to feel she was in any danger.

"Listen, the insurance companies have no business harassing you. Don't let any more of those guys in. And if that one comes back, call *me*."

"Where?"

"In Washington. And maybe it would be a good idea if you came back with me."

She looked at him seriously. "I can handle myself."

Oh, no you can't, he thought, not against *this* type of insurance.

"I'll come to Washington," she said, "if I just can't keep away—from you."

Comforting. He was suddenly very frightened. By coming here, had he put her life on the line? Was Coogan watching, even now?

17

Hammond went to the Federal Building in Westwood and stopped off at the FBI offices first. He requested round-the-clock surveillance for Jan Fletcher. He was introduced to Special Agent Morrow. "I can't tell you anything about the case I'm working on," he explained. "Just keep a close eye on the lady and don't let her see you."

"What are we looking out for?" asked Morrow.

"Strangers. Possible attempt on her life. I don't know yet. She's recently widowed. Shouldn't be any men going in or out and she's discouraging visitors. I suggest you bug the front door and monitor conversations."

"But that's illegal," said Morrow with a big smile.

"So?" Hammond watched him scribble a few notes absently, then leaned over the desk and covered the paper with his hand. "Hey," he said, "I'm not fooling. This is not routine. Two people are already dead, and I don't want *anything* to happen to her."

His voice had risen, attracting attention from other agents. Morrow looked at him tightly, then smiled. "Don't worry," he said quietly.

"Okay." Hammond nodded and left.

He walked into the Navy Office of Information at three minutes to nine. He was taken back to the chief's desk and handed papers that had just arrived via long-distance photo-copier. They were copies of the MTL portfolio and several pieces of information.

The top sheet was a memo on Coogan. It read:

> BUPERS reports a COOGAN, JOSEPH K.,
> Lieutenant Commander, U.S. Naval Reserve,
> Social Security No. 028-49-7721
> USN Serial No. 1389805
> Released from active duty August, 1955.
> Limited annual service to present.

Hammond glanced through the information several times before he caught the telltale clue in the middle of the page:

9805—the last four digits of Coogan's serial number and the final link in the code: 9805CGN-166.

The red flags in the files at BUPERS were set up to notify Joe Coogan of any inquiry into the *Sturman*'s former crewmen. Coogan, still on limited duty in the Navy, had instituted this procedure himself, but how?

The second memo contained a report on the status of Dr. Kurtnauer. Records showed that he had gone to Israel in 1950, had taken Israeli citizenship, and had never returned to the United States.

The next memo was from the FBI. No security clearance for any Emil Kurtnauer at MTL, now or ever.

Hammond's heart was pounding. So Traben *had* thrown him a curve. What a stupid move to pretend Kurtnauer was coming over from Israel. He should have known that Hammond would find out the truth and his suspicions about all of Traben's operations would only be heightened.

They had to be stalling for time.

Hammond turned to the MTL portfolio. Micro-Tech was a subsidiary of RTI, whose principal stockholder and Chairman of the Board was Francis P. Bloch. Bloch had founded RTI in 1955 and Edmond Traben's name appeared on the first Board of Directors. When Micro-Tech was formed in 1962, Edmond Traben became that company's principal stockholder and chairman. Joseph Coogan, Chief of Security, had held his post since the founding and, prior to that, had been head of security at RTI from the time he left the Navy in 1955.

The key date was 1955, when all the plots were hatched, the conclaves met, and the umbrella of secrecy was drawn over everything.

At exactly 0930 the phone rang and Hammond was buzzed. He got on the line with Slater.

"Hiya, Hammond, what's on your mind?"

"Where are you calling from, Tom?"

"MAGIC."

"Is Yablonski listening?"

"He's exercising in the backyard. I can see him from my loft window."

"How's it progressing?"

"Like squeezing toothpaste. It all came to the top yesterday afternoon. He's remembering names and dates like a repentant mobster up before a Congressional committee. We can't shut him up."

"Any side effects?"

"No. I think we've blown all that away. He's still got some anxiety about McCarthy, but I think that's mostly his need for revenge. A nice murder should cleanse his soul."

"I'd love to give him the chance."

"Better make it soon, Nick. He's talking about going home. So's Momma."

"They don't like the hospitality?"

"They don't see the danger."

"Nobody ever does. I'll see them when I get back. I think I can scare the daylights out of them."

"How about you, *señor?* Anything on Thin Air?"

"Plenty, but I'll tell you later. Do me a favor—ask Yablonski if he ever knew a man named Coogan. Navy. Lieutenant Commander Joseph K."

"Just a minute. Larry's got the notes. . . ." Slater was gone for a moment, then Cohen got on the phone.

"Here we are," he said. "Lieutenant Commander Joe Coogan, head of security for Thin Air. Yablonski met him once, probably in 1954."

Hammond whistled. 1954? "Was Yablonski involved with Thin Air after 1953?"

"Yes. He now recalls spending a great deal of time under special care. He's beginning to realize he never did go back to his original assignment. His records are absolutely false. He was discharged through a special processing station in '55."

"Anything else on Coogan?"

"Yes. He said Coogan left Thin Air sometime in mid '54 to move to Washington. The rumor was he got assigned to BUPERS."

Hammond nearly crushed the receiver. So that's how it was done. As far back as 1954, Joe Coogan had infiltrated BUPERS and set up his coded alarm system. So the cover-up began even before the project went private. Traben must have been plotting with Bloch ever since the abortive experiment of 1953.

Hammond told Cohen to make a transcript of his notes and send it to Admiral Gault along with a note that Hammond would be back to meet with the admiral and Smitty later that day.

Hammond hung up and called Ensign Cokeland at BUPERS in Washington. He was asking her to run down Lieutenant Commander Coogan's association with BUPERS when she interrupted him.

"No need," she said. "I know Lieutenant Commander Coogan. He's Naval Reserve. He works here two weeks every summer."

"He still does?" cried Hammond. Then he realized he should have known there would be an inside man to update those files. And two weeks a year would be sufficient.

Before leaving for the airport, he tried calling Jan. She was out. He hoped Morrow was on her tail. He didn't like depending on the FBI. But once he laid his information in Smitty's lap, he felt sure there would be action on all fronts.

Hammond was back in Washington by mid-afternoon. He went straight home to shower and change and prepare briefs for his meeting with Smitty and Gault. The admiral's aide called him at 1700 and said, "Come down to the Pentagon at 1745. The meeting will be in Mr. Smith's office. The admiral says to tell you you're putting your head on the block."

"Tell him to sharpen the knife."

Hammond arrived at John Allen Smith's office ten minutes early, to be told that Admiral Gault was already in conference with him. While he waited, he tried to guess what he'd be walking into once he passed through the door.

The civilian Director of Naval Intelligence was a big, courtly, bearded fifty-year-old Mormon. He dressed in baggy tweeds, had a secret weakness for iced tea, and always struck Hammond as being slightly out of place amidst the sleek brass of the Pentagon. But it was Smitty's temper Hammond was thinking about. Whoever crossed swords with John Allen Smith was invariably carried out on his own shield—belly-up and bleeding.

Smitty himself ushered Hammond in, waving him to a chair next to Admiral Gault. "Glad to have you back with us, Nick," he said. "That New Mexico business sounded very ugly."

"It could have been worse, sir," Hammond said.

Smitty nodded. "The admiral and I have been reviewing the case. What did you find in Los Angeles?"

Hammond opened his briefcase and handed over Xeroxed copies of a handwritten report he had hastily prepared: his conclusions that Traben and Coogan were responsible for the brainwashing activities in order to cover up their involvement in further applications of Thin Air. The paper also explained in brief what Thin Air was.

For the next hour they sifted through details. Hammond answered every question thrown at him, patiently and thoroughly. They were openly doubtful of Rinehart, as he had expected them to be, but in the face of Traben's attempt to send Hammond chasing after Kurtnauer, Rinehart's story smacked more of truth.

Gault was particularly annoyed by Coogan's dual role. "Could we be looking at a *mole operation?*" he asked.

Moles were deep-planted enemy agents who burrow in, go underground, and stay dormant until activated by the control that planted them. "Doesn't look that way, sir," Hammond said. "I don't get any feeling of foreign involvement."

Smitty agreed. "This is a domestic affair. I'm convinced of that. What I find hard to accept is *why?* We're not dealing with any nickel-and-dime outfit. MTL and RTI are big corporations. What are they working on? Why should they go to such extremes? There's more to this than just the fact the Navy's been compromised."

"Compromised?" Gault snorted. "Let's face it, since some time around 1953, the Navy's been *had!* You know what would happen if certain senators got wind of this. They'd turn it into a three-ring circus! We don't need that kind of media coverage."

"No, but we do need a full-scale investigation," Smitty said. "We have to establish a clear link between MTL and Thin Air."

Hammond took a chance. "I think it would be a serious mistake to involve more people right now. We would just be warning the opposition of our intent—"

"They must know your intent!" growled Smitty in rebuttal. "What do they think the NIS is—National Innocent Society?"

"Sir, I'm sure they know what we'd like to do to them.

But they're acting cocky because they know we don't have hard evidence yet."

Smitty studied him through hooded eyes. "Go on."

Hammond wondered if he would end up tossed out on his ear. "I think everything that's happened points to one conclusion: a major effort by a private company to perfect the mistakes that cropped up in a former Navy project. Nothing really illegal in that, except that their security methods indicate it is probably not in the public interest to let them continue. We could nail them right now on the little stunts they've pulled, particularly that business at BUPERS. But we can't just look under the rug and expect to discover what the secrecy's all about. We've got to know *what* we're looking for and *where* to look!" He paused and shifted in his seat. "I think they're close to having what they want. That's why they're stalling for time. If we start throwing agents at them right and left, they'll just put a cork on the operation and stand there laughing at us. We're only effective if they don't know where we're coming from next."

Smitty stroked his beard with absentminded distraction.

Gault was unruffled. "If they're so close to finishing," he asked, "why are they acting like maniacs? They could just shore up their patents and announce them to the world."

"The matter of money, Admiral," said Smitty. "Enormous amounts of it. Where is it coming from? If Thin Air as a Navy project cost a hundred million dollars, and MTL has been working on it in secret for over twenty years, think what that figure would be at today's prices."

"Astronomic . . ." rumbled Gault.

"Right. And even F.P. Bloch hasn't got that much to toss around. Obviously, they're not finished yet: they can't risk a cutoff of funds. That means it's coming from outside."

"Foreign investment?" suggested Gault.

Smitty shook his head. "That only adds unwanted partners. I'll tell you the way I would do it. I'm MTL. I'm a government vendor. My largest source of development money comes from military appropriations. So I just divert funds from legitimate contracts to feed my own private research."

Gault's mouth opened. "You mean Uncle Sam is their partner?"

"Silent and unwitting."

Hammond glanced from one to the other, eagerly twitching in his seat, excited by this revelation. Thank God for businessmen in government, he thought, then he said, "Sir, I'd like to forego the full investigation for right now and concentrate instead on their accounting."

"You mean a cost run," said Smitty. Hammond nodded. "How far back?"

"Nineteen sixty-two, the year they were founded." Smitty's eyes slid to Gault and Hammond quickly added, "Sir, I'm sure you see it yourself: if we catch them with their hand in the fiscal cracker barrel, we can simply chop it off. For a start."

Smitty shook his head. "A logical next step, Nick, but not wise, for two reasons. One, it would require Department of Defense approval, and that means an uproar. Two, the GAO belongs to Congress. Before you know it, every mouth in the capital will be flapping. And as you say, Dr. Traben will simply put the cork on. And worse than that, if we're *wrong* . . ." He shrugged, then glanced at Gault. "What do you think, Admiral?"

"I think half-measures are too risky. We should find out more, then throw everything we've got." He stood up. "There's something else we can do without blowing the whistle. Retired admiral I know represents RTI here in Washington. Let me see what I can get out of him."

"Do it," said Smitty. "Anything else from you, Nick?"

"I'd like to get some background on Bloch."

Smitty chuckled. "I can do better than that. How would you like to meet him? He's throwing a party Friday night at his Georgetown home. I'll see that you're both invited."

Homewood Drive, along with most of the western part of Los Angeles, was shrouded in a thick blanket of fog. The street lights glimmered weakly.

Special Agent Morrow sat in the back of an old camper and poured himself coffee from a thermos. He'd been parked across the street from Jan Fletcher's house since seven p.m., peering blearily through a one-way window into the lady's front yard. His only consolation was warmth. He thought with sympathy of his partner, Putnam, freezing his butt off in the Fletcher backyard. He checked his watch: it was nearing five a.m.

A slow-moving car rolled to a stop in the dark area

halfway up the street and snapped Morrow to attention. He set down his cup and grabbed the radio mike. "Stand by. Got a possible."

Even as Putnam acknowledged, Morrow realized he'd been hasty. The man who emerged from the car was carrying a stack of newspapers. He walked to the far end of the street in boots that clumped on the pavement. He began tossing papers onto the front lawns.

Morrow depressed the mike button. "Relax, Putnam. Guy's delivering papers." He watched the man work his way back up the street. When he returned to his car to replenish his stock, Morrow sat back and drained his cup.

The next time he looked, the paper man was approaching the Fletcher house. But instead of tossing the paper, he walked up the drive. Morrow watched him drop it at the front door then cut across the grass and disappear through a hedge. Morrow looked for him to emerge on the next front lawn.

It took him a few vital seconds to realize something was wrong. He stabbed the mike button. "We've been snookered. He's going around the right side!"

Putnam shot out from behind a tree in the back garden and raced down the path, catching just a glimpse of feet slipping through an open window.

Morrow heard three clicks from Putnam's set, the prearranged signal that meant unlawful entry. He switched to the police frequency and requested a back-up unit to make a silent approach. As soon as the dispatcher acknowledged, Morrow bolted from the back of the camper and charged across the street fumbling for his master key. He opened the front door and slipped inside the house.

It was dark and he moved hesitantly.

Putnam forced himself to wait a few seconds before following the intruder through the window. Once inside, he eased silently along a wall. But he bumped into a little Pembroke table and knocked a lamp to the floor—

Morrow heard the crash and ran for the hallway. He saw a softly glowing panel of light switches and jumped to it, flipping them all on at once.

"FBI!" he shouted. "Stay where you are!"

Jan heard the lamp crash in her sleep. The warning shout woke her up. Groggily, she raised her head from the pillow and peered at her open bedroom door. The hall light blinded her. She could hardly see the silhouette in the doorway, but she sensed something and screamed. Then she saw the glint as the pistol came up, and she froze in disbelief.

Putnam and Morrow spotted the big man in the hallway at the same time. Putnam fired a warning shot as he saw the man's right arm stiffen.

The echo cannonaded down the narrow hall. The intruder whirled, red hair bristling, his beefy face contorted with anger. His arm swung around and his silencer muffled two shots. The second one got the hall light.

Both FBI agents froze in the sudden darkness. The faint sound of a door clicking closed set them in motion again. A quick glance into Jan's bedroom assured Morrow that she was all right. She shrieked when she saw him, but Putnam grabbed his arm: there wasn't time to explain.

Putnam pointed to another bedroom. Morrow pulled out his flashlight while Putnam gently pushed open the door. Morrow played the beam over the room. With a nod to his partner, he dove through the doorway, rolled on the carpet, and came up with his revolver aimed one way, while Putnam rushed in and spread his legs to brace himself the other way.

But they were alone in an empty room.

They stood immobile, eyes flicking around at the walls, the locked windows, the closet. . . . Cautiously, Putnam approached it and slid open the doors from either side. Except for clothes, nothing.

The would-be assassin had vanished.

When Morrow's heart stopped thumping in his throat, he went to confront Jan. But he had no idea how he was going to calm her down.

18

Hammond waited in the terminal at Dulles International. He was tense and angry—had been ever since he received the call from Special Agent Morrow.

He checked the arrival board. The plane was late. He couldn't relax until Jan was safely with him.

It had to have been McCarthy. Was this the great secret MTL had been keeping all these years? Had they created a league of disappearing assassins?

McCarthy had vanished from Jan's house the same way he had vanished from the detention cell at the Boston Navy Hospital. And the way Coogan—if it was Coogan—had vanished along with his truck from the field outside Rinehart's home in New Mexico.

But why would a respectable electronics firm be involved in something so penny-ante? Unless it was a sideline, a by-product, an outgrowth of self-protection covering something far more sinister.

That still left Hammond with the same unanswered question: what were they up to?

The jet came in and he watched Jan walk up the ramp, dressed in jeans, a sweater, and dark glasses. She was carrying a stuffed overnight bag, and she was escorted by Morrow.

She walked right past Hammond and waited for him by the escalator, giving him the cold shoulder. He couldn't really blame her: he should have told her what could happen. But he hadn't expected such a bold attack.

"Have any trouble getting her out of L.A.?" he asked Morrow.

"No. She got on the plane as Mrs. Morrow, a blonde." He held up a flight bag. "Always wondered what it was like to be married," he said, then added wryly, "Christ, Hammond, I hope you're wearing cast-iron jockey shorts. She's out for blood."

They picked up her baggage and then separated in the parking lot. Morrow went off with Michaelson to FBI Headquarters in Washington, while Hammond drove Jan to the safe house in Herndon. The trip was anything but enjoyable.

She took off the dark glasses and he saw how red her eyes were. Her chin jutted out and she hissed, "You didn't tell me. You didn't have the decency to let me know my life was in danger. What was I supposed to do—figure it out for myself?"

"Jan, I'm sorry. I tried to tell you—"

"You *did not!* And why are they after me? What have I done? What am I supposed to know? Is it because *you* came to me?"

He had no answer. She swore as loud as she could. He glanced over: her mouth was trembling.

"Harold was murdered, wasn't he?"

Hammond nodded.

"Because he came to you! You've got the *touch,* haven't you?"

"Now, wait a minute—"

"I *won't wait*! I'm going to—" She stopped, trailing off.

"You're going to Herndon," Hammond said, "to a safe house with two other very fine people. And you're going to sit down and hear me—"

"Who broke into my house?" she interrupted.

"McCarthy."

She stared at him. "Harold's *psychiatrist?*"

Hammond raised his voice. "Damnit, McCarthy killed your husband! I'm sure of it! And I don't know *why* you're acting like *I* did it!"

He finished at a shout. She stared at the road ahead. He fell silent and neither spoke again.

He turned off Monroe Park Avenue to Worchester, then looked for Merlin's Way. The house nicknamed MAGIC was halfway up the block. He parked the car on the street and blinked the lights twice. A moment later, Ike Menninger stepped out on the verandah of the two-story brick house and waved.

Hammond got out of the car and walked around to open the door for Jan. She sat there pouting.

"Jan?"

"Go to hell."

His teeth tightened and he shook with anger. He grabbed

her arm and yanked her out of the car. She stumbled in surprise. He spoke fast and thinly. "They've made two attempts on my life and one on yours. There's a man inside that house who's been through the same hell as your late husband for more than twenty years. They tried to kill him, too! I would like to nail them before they nail us, Mrs. Fletcher!"

He was conscious of another warning lurking inside: it was a race against time, not only for their own lives, but to prevent the murder of all the remaining Fletchers and Olivelys and Yablonskis.

Jan met his angry look with a cold scowl. She needed someone to be upset with. Hammond released her and she walked to the house alone.

Mrs. Yablonski was happy to have feminine company and took Jan upstairs to a bedroom to get settled.

Hammond joined Yablonski and Menninger in the den. Cas looked better. He was dressed in jeans and sweatshirt and seemed eager to hear about Thin Air. Hammond set up Menninger's tape recorder and sat down to relate as much as he could recall. He planned to use the tape as his report to Gault.

Hammond kept nothing from Yablonski. He explained that Rinehart had confirmed the nightmares. He told the history of the project, then described the gunplay, the chase, the fire, Rinehart's death, and his own visit to MTL.

Yablonski paced, growing angry, more than once interrupting to have something repeated, then cursing what he heard.

Hammond explained about the attack on Jan and that seemed to trigger something inside Yablonski. He went to the window and gazed out grimly. Hammond knew what he was thinking: at last he was taking the danger seriously. There would be no more talk of going home. If they were prepared to bump off *wives* . . .

Yablonski watched his wife come down the stairs and enter the kitchen. Then he whirled and said, "What are you going to do?"

Hammond explained about the party at Bloch's tomorrow night and how he hoped to confront the man and rattle his confidence.

"I want to go," said Cas.

"No. Too dangerous." Hammond didn't explain what

he really felt was dangerous about it, that Yablonski might lose control and blow the case.

"Hammond, when are you going to stop protecting me long enough to let me be useful?"

"You've been put through enough . . . but I may need you later."

"When?"

Hammond didn't reply. They both knew it was a brush-off.

Yablonski sat down opposite Hammond and caught his eye. "For what they did to Olively and all those other guys, I want to be there when you close in. I've been in plenty of bar fights and I know how to knock heads. Gimme the chance," he said through his teeth.

"We're not ready yet."

"When you are . . . ?"

"Front-row seat, Cas."

She laughed. "You want me to play femme fatale?"

"No. Just be decorative. You can divert attention from what I'm doing."

"What will you be doing?"

They were sitting in Jan's room, far apart. She was on the bed; Hammond was in a chair by the window.

"My investigating act," he said. "Look, I could use you as a decoy. It'll be like flaunting failure in their faces. Should be fun to see them squirm. And at the worst, you'll have a good time. I hear Bloch's parties are sensational."

"What about safety?"

"You'll be surrounded by Navy brass."

She sighed. "Oh, Hammond . . ."

"What?"

"You're going to have to buy me a dress. I just haven't got a thing to wear."

She batted her eyes at him.

They convened at Smitty's flat on 29th Street, less than half a mile from Hammond's. There were Hammond and Jan, Gault and Smitty, and their wives. The two Navy men were in dress blues, the ladies wore gowns, and Smitty effectively hid his bulk inside a tentlike tux.

Jan was open and charming, much to Hammond's relief, even sweeping aside the muttered condolences offered by Smitty and Gault and captivating them with a warm and radiant smile.

As he strolled past Hammond to get the ladies a drink, Gault mumbled, "That's a widow?"

Certainly Jan was not behaving like a widow, nor did she even resemble one. Her gown was a pale green silk off-the-shoulder, with a sash draped across her breasts. Her brown hair gleamed, pulled back tight to fall around her neck in Grecian curls. Hammond could hardly take his eyes off her.

Smitty excused himself to the ladies and led the men into his den, a dark oak-paneled cave lined with books. He poured them Scotch and plain soda water for himself from his private bar, then he sat down and faced Gault.

"Okay, Admiral, let's have it," he said.

"I spent all of yesterday morning with Admiral Larry Corso," Gault began. "He's Bloch's Washington rep. Retired six years ago as chief liaison for Naval Air Systems Command and he collects a fat pension. But he's a double dipper, because he also takes a fat paycheck as a lobbyist for some of the big defense contractors. And he's got a direct line into the Navy Chief of Staff, close ties with the Armed Forces Appropriations Committee, and the cooperation, if he needs it, of the White House.

"He made it clear that he resents us sticking our noses into Bloch's business if only for one reason: both RTI and MTL are prime contractors on a super-sensitive, top-secret Navy project, the most advanced orbiting weapons guidance system of its kind. They've been developing it for years and they're very near completion. Admiral Corso, 'in the interests of the Navy' as he puts it, will take any steps necessary to see that this project is not jeopardized."

Hammond snorted. "Did you drop any hints about the steps Traben and his people have been taking?"

"I did. And he looked at me like I was crazy. In fact, he got furious. He seemed to be aware of you, Hammond, and was quite upset. He accused us of cooking all this stuff up and he demanded to know why."

Hammond looked to Smitty for comment, but the big man sat silently behind his desk. He didn't even appear to be listening.

Gault resumed. "I checked with the CNO. The business

about the guidance project is true. Very hush-hush. It's Micro-Tech's biggest contract, and RTI is a major subcontractor."

At last Smitty let out a grunt. He shifted in his seat, picked up a pencil, and began to doodle. "You know, it's very interesting," he said. "I've had the Government Accounting Office do a preliminary audit on both companies going back some five years, just a check of in-house records. RTI is clean as a whistle. But on some of MTL's larger deals, contracts in the range of half a billion dollars, they've frequently requested enormous increases in funding. If, for example, they've got three big projects going and one of them falls into trouble, they have no compunction about running immediately to Defense for more money. You would think they'd want to uphold their sound image and simply rob Peter to pay Paul—fall back on company profits. But no way." He stopped, then looked at Gault.

"You were right," said Gault. "They're kiting funds."

"Sure they are," Smitty agreed. "And if they've been doing it for twenty years, it could amount to millions—certainly enough to finance Thin Air."

"And without absolute proof, we can't touch them," Gault sighed.

There was a long silence. Gault tossed down his Scotch.

"It would be nice," began Hammond, "to sort of hint to F.P. Bloch that we know what he's doing."

"Wouldn't it?" said Smitty thinly. "They're making a bona fide threat. Corso wants us to lay off."

"But we're not getting anything in return," growled Gault. "That's a helluva one-sided bargain."

"At least he's giving us a little time," said Smitty. "He could have charged right over to his 'friends in high places' and had us hog-tied."

"But he didn't," said Hammond, putting down his drink, "because he doesn't want to attract attention. That means he *knows* what's really going on in there!"

"Possibly," Smitty grunted. "In any case, we can continue to pursue this discreetly, as long as we don't antagonize Admiral Corso. I too have the ears of the Navy Chief of Staff and the Appropriations Committee." Smitty flashed a wry smile.

Gault shifted uncomfortably. "I'm afraid Corso is a little better connected. The present Navy Chief served under him for ten years, and the head of the Appropriations Committee is a cousin."

Smitty's face grew dark. "If there's one thing I hate, it's pushy admirals," he snarled.

Gault's eyes widened.

"Present company excluded," Smitty added.

Bloch's house was a four-story Victorian mansion in the most fashionable section of Georgetown. The palace occupied a corner lot and dominated everything around it. Floodlights blazed against the façade. The circular drive was awash with Cadillacs; diplomatic license plates abounded. It was obvious that Bloch moved in very high circles. Hammond adjusted his uncomfortable dress uniform and followed the others into the house. Gault stopped Smitty and pointed to a flock of Lincolns with Arab plates.

"Does Bloch deal with the oil cartel?"

Smitty shrugged. "Nowadays, the Arabs show up at every party."

The foyer was enormous, with stairs opening onto two landings above. The floor was marble, the walls pale blue and hung with priceless oil paintings. Carved oak doors opened onto a ballroom on the left, where most of the party seemed to be gathering.

As servants appeared to take their coats, Hammond swept the room with a searching gaze. He spotted a small knot of Arabs watching a group of Americans move down a side hallway. Smitty nudged him and indicated the men disappearing down the hall.

"Big-shots from the oil companies," he said.

The door was gently closed by a butler. Hammond glanced back at the Arabs—their eyes were riveted on that closed door.

"That's a hell of an odd tableau," he whispered to Smitty.

Hammond led Jan into the mass of people who made up the Washington social scene, pointing out several senators and congressmen. He was enjoying her excitement when he caught sight of a beefy face regarding him coldly from across the room.

It was Joe Coogan.

Hammond introduced Jan to a senator from Iowa and left with a promise to return with drinks. He walked directly over to Coogan, who greeted him with a big smile.

"Thought you never traveled," chided Hammond.

"Special occasion. I got called."

"Really? I don't see your boss anywhere."

Coogan laid a hand on Hammond's shoulder, then hurried off to someone else he knew.

Hammond let out his breath, surprised to find how nervous he was. He didn't really believe Coogan would try to kill him here.

He wandered back to the open oak doors, first checking to see that Jan was occupied in conversation. No problem: she was flirting with *two* senators now.

He positioned himself in the foyer, covered by a group of new arrivals, and glued his eye to that side hallway and the closed door. Smitty came over and Hammond asked if he would get Jan a drink and keep an eye on her.

"Naturally," said Smitty. "And what will you be doing?"

"Waiting for Mr. Bloch. You might point him out to me."

"He's not here yet."

Hammond shrugged but remained where he was. After five minutes of waiting, he glanced around and noticed that most of the Arabs had moved into the party, but two of them had stationed themselves near a potted fern.

Suddenly, the door swung open and the oil men emerged in twos and threes, looking casual as hell. The Arabs stared intently at each face, as if trying to sense what was going on.

The last man out was tall, cadaverous, and sixtyish, with a jaundiced complexion. He had an imperial manner and a fast smile for the dozens of guests who immediately descended on him.

It had to be Bloch. Hammond was sure long before Smitty returned with the Gaults and Jan, picking him up to take him over to where the host was holding court.

"Francis!" Smitty boomed, cutting through a knot of well-wishers. The way opened for him the instant Bloch responded with a big, warm smile. The smile stayed there, fixed and generous, until Smitty introduced Hammond.

Then it clicked down about four notches.

Dinner was sumptuous, luxurious, and stately, but Hammond was perturbed to find that last-minute seating arrangements placed him and Jan opposite Coogan, at a table far from Bloch, and even farther from his companions.

The dining room was as enormous as the ballroom, draped with heavy curtains over French windows. The chandeliers seemed to enhance the gleam of pleasure in Jan's eyes. The room was arranged in a succession of small round tables, each seating six. Coogan, Hammond, and Jan were at a table with three Arabs, directly in front of a window. Hammond was uncomfortably aware of being the perfect target for an assassin waiting on the street outside. Coogan seemed to relish his discomfort.

During dinner, Hammond stole glances at Bloch, sitting across the room with several grim-looking businessmen. He was animated; they were listless. Hammond recognized two of them as oil men he had seen coming out of that hallway earlier.

He continued watching Bloch, but his attention was drawn back to his own table by Coogan's deep, raspy voice telling Jan how lovely she was. Hammond smiled to himself.

Jan handled Coogan expertly, encouraging the compliments and casually flirting. But when one of the Arabs inquired as to Hammond's job in the Navy, Coogan got down to brass tacks:

"Commander Hammond is a super-secret agent of the Naval Investigative Service," he said, "sort of a waterlogged James Bond."

The Arabs nodded and laughed. "Is this true?" one of them asked Hammond. He shrugged flatly.

"Of course it's true," said Coogan. "And who are you investigating tonight, Commander?"

"Nobody."

"Oh, I can hardly believe that. I can't think of any other reason why an agent of the NIS would be invited to a Washington soiree. Perhaps you're investigating these gentlemen!"

He waved at the Arabs. Hammond looked up at them. Their smiles vanished.

"Come on, Hammond," laughed Coogan. "Tell all!"

Hammond smiled at the Arabs. "You can relax, boys, I'm here to investigate Mr. Bloch's chopped liver."

Coogan roared and the Arabs joined him, relieved.

Hammond gazed out the window intently.

* * *

After dinner, Jan went off to the powder room and Hammond got up to follow Coogan, who turned back with a grin. "I'm not going anywhere special, Hammond. You really don't have to tag along."

"I like dogging your footsteps. Maybe you'll trip and I can catch you."

"Your girl friend is a knockout, Hammond."

"You know who she is: Harold Fletcher's wife."

Coogan smiled broadly. "You mean widow," he said.

Hammond stopped in his tracks, his brow darkening. Coogan turned back to him, hands stuffed in his trouser pockets. "If I had a girl friend like that," he added, "I wouldn't keep her in Washington. The dangers of mugging."

"How would you know that since you spend all your time in California?"

"I've been told."

Hammond stepped away, knowing Coogan would follow him now, eager to continue the taunts. And Coogan did without hesitating a moment, not realizing until too late that Hammond was maneuvering them toward Bloch.

At the last moment, Coogan reached for Hammond's arm but found it jerked from his grasp. Hammond walked right up to Bloch among a group of businessmen and Arabs.

"Mr. Bloch," he said, "I'd like to compliment you on your Chief of Security." Hammond slurred a bit, playing tipsy.

Bloch's eyes flicked to Coogan, who stood anxiously a few feet away. "Mr. Coogan works for MTL," he said quietly.

"Yes, I know. I visited your plant out in Manhattan Beach. I was very impressed; I'm impressed by everything I learn about Micro-Tech."

"Are you doing research on us, Commander?" The cold smile edged into place. The Arabs looked on with interest.

"Research?" repeated Hammond. "Yes, you might say that. For instance, I've discovered that MTL handles a lot of government contracts—a few small jobs and a lot of big impressive ones." The Arabs looked away, but their ears became antennae. "I find it curious that a certain Navy project requires astonishing amounts of government funding while the others seem so damned self-sufficient. Why is that?"

"The Navy project involves more experimentation. Especially since it's not into production yet—"

"What's the nature of it?"

"Really, Commander. If you don't already know, then it's none of your affair."

Hammond smiled and said, "Oh, I know what it's supposed to be, but I've been wondering if it's really something else."

Bloch gave him a wintry smile and a muttered excuse, then moved off with his Arab guests. Hammond found himself the object of curious study by those around him who had overheard the conversation. He looked for Coogan, but the big man was gone. He spotted Jan outside the powder room in discussion with Mrs. Gault. Smitty and the admiral were occupied with several friends.

Hammond decided to do some exploring. He slipped out to the foyer and snatched a brandy from a passing waiter. He loosened the collar of his uniform and waited until none of the suspicious types were watching him, then casually wandered up the winding staircase. He held his breath all the way to the first landing, knowing that if he made it that far, it was unlikely he would be spotted by anyone below.

He stepped onto the landing and looked both ways. Then he glanced down at the foyer. No one had seen him. With his pronounced shuffle and the brandy held loosely in his hand, he looked like a drunk in search of the bathroom.

He wandered down the second-floor hallway and peered into every open room, finding little of interest—except for the sitting room in which he discovered a glittering couple staring at each other with smoky eyes; they didn't see him.

Back to the landing again, then up the next flight of stairs. On the third floor, Hammond was a bit more cautious. It would be tougher to explain if he were caught up here.

Most of the doors were closed. And the goddamned floor creaked. Hammond cursed the old house, but he began letting himself through the doors, one by one. They were all expansive bedrooms, superbly decorated. Even the slim shaft of light thrown from the hall made clear their opulence. Fortunately, none of the rooms were occupied.

In the third bedroom he entered there was a light on across the room, a silvery beam coming from what looked to be a bathroom door, slightly ajar. Hammond hesitated a long moment at the bedroom door, his ears straining to catch any hint of breathing.

There was none.

He entered the bedroom and closed the door behind him. He waited with his back to the door, softly whistling to himself and playing his drunk act, while his eyes became accustomed to the gloom. There didn't appear to be anyone waiting for him. It was a room fit for a king, with a bed the size of a swimming pool, enormous fluffy pillows, mirrors on the ceiling. . . .

He walked slowly across to the bathroom.

Pausing at the door, he peered cautiously inside. As bathrooms go, this was particularly spacious—and gilt, tiled, and carpeted. It was also a mess, with face towels and washcloths flung about, traces of hair, soap, and powder on the counter . . . and an open shaving kit on the sink, alligator leather with the initials "FPB" in gold script.

So there was no doubt that this was Bloch's bathroom. He went in and set his brandy down on the counter. Spanish tile, he noted, beautifully fitted, too. He moved to the toilet. As long as he was here . . .

Then he noticed the groove worn in the carpet in front of the shower, as if something had been dragged across it in an arc. Hammond stared at it a moment; it was a curious imperfection in such a lavish house. His eyes traveled up to the large shower stall standing against the wall. Against it, not set into it; it had the obvious appearance of an afterthought. The door was one one side and the shower faucets against the opposite wall. Peculiar.

Hammond opened the shower door and peered inside. It was dry as a bone. Not a drop of moisture, not even the odor of recent use. Hammond reached for the hot-water tap and turned it. Nothing happened. The flow was turned off.

He stepped back out of the shower, puzzled. He glanced at the bathtub. It was a large sunken affair, and halfway up the wall were shower taps. If Bloch took showers in that, what did he need this stall for?

Hammond hunkered down and examined the groove in the carpet, which lined up with one corner of the stall. It looked as if the entire stall could swing out on that arc.

He got up and braced his hands against two corners of the stall and tried to move it in the direction of the groove. It didn't budge. There had to be an operating mechanism, a release trigger. He looked around for a lever, a switch—anything. There was a panel of wall switches by the bathroom door. He moved to it and tried them individually. There was one for the heater, one for the fan, one for the light. The fourth didn't appear to operate anything. He left it in the "on" position, then again tried to move the shower stall.

This time it came away and swung across the carpet, scraping into the groove—and exposing a small vault behind it.

As the stall swung fully open, a light blinked on in the vault, a low-wattage darkroom safety light. Hammond could see that in the center of a six-foot-square space stood a low metallic pedestal, apparently containing some sort of instrumentation.

Cautiously, he stepped into the vault.

19

The walls were bare and painted with a dull black finish. Hammond stood over the pedestal for a full minute, leaning first one way then the other, scrutinizing it. The pedestal stood three feet high. It was circular and about fifteen inches in diameter. It resembled a surround-speaker system and appeared to be an anodized aluminum sheath with vents. Hammond squatted and peered through the blades. The sheath was packed inside with conduits and copper coils wrapped tightly around a long piece of white metal.

He sat down on the floor and in the feeble light peered upward through the vent. There were two coils, one behind the other, connected at the top by a thick metal core that curved in an arc between them. The core was bisected by a rod that ran down between the coils and permitted them to spin on an axis. Hammond guessed the apparatus was some sort of powerful electromagnet that could whirl on a fulcrum and radiate its power outwards, probably to the limits of the vault.

He knew immediately what it was: a refinement of Emil Kurtnauer's field generator, the electromagnetic couplers that Rinehart had described. The power generator was probably located lower in the pedestal. He tried to get a look at it but the blades were slanted down and outward, making it impossible. He wondered if there were a way to open the apparatus. He duck-walked around it and found that it was anchored to the floor by three bolts—and he didn't have a wrench.

No matter. He knew what was there. The specifics weren't important. It was what the machine *did* . . .

It made people invisible.

The realization caught up with him in a surge of ugly black fright. He wanted out. What if someone was waiting for him in the bedroom, invisible . . . ? What if they closed the vault door on him, turned the thing on and made him disappear . . . ?

He backed toward the entrance, dreading the telltale click that would indicate the generator was starting. . . .

He stepped out safely and only then let out his breath. He stood with his back to the open shower stall and looked around the empty bathroom. There wasn't a sound. Nothing moved. He couldn't even hear the party sounds three floors below. He tried to convince himself not to be frightened. Then he gazed back into the vault at the pedestal standing on that black floor like a futuristic barstool.

Somewhere in this room there had to be controls. Not in the vault: he was certain those walls were solid. He began to search the bathroom, pulling out drawers, rummaging in the linen closet. . . .

He opened the medicine chest and found only the usual array of pills and grooming aids. He slid the door closed and was about to move on when he noticed the hinges. . . .

Peculiar. The doors were sliding mirrors, but there were hinges on either side of the chest. He felt under the extended lip and tugged. One side of the chest swung away from the wall, exposing a panel of instruments. It seemed to be a computer, with a coded programming keyboard and a black glass panel that Hammond took to be a light display for digital readout. Numerical touchplates were grouped in the center with keys to one side marked VERB and NOUN. Other keys were marked CLR, PRO, KEY REL, ENTR, and RSET.

Hammond tried to think where he had seen something like this before, something almost exactly the same: NASA. This was a goddamned DSKY! A Display Keyboard like the ones used aboard the Apollo spacecraft.

VERBs and NOUNs could be programmed to key numbers and fed into the board, instituting a predetermined activity. But what activity? Why something so sophisticated if all that was required was to turn on a machine that would generate a force field? Unless it did something else—

He thought he heard a sound.

He froze and waited, his hand on the open panel. Nothing more. Imagination. But he'd seen enough. He closed the panel until it made a soft click. Then he turned and shoved the shower stall back into place. He went to the wall switches and flipped the fourth one to off.

He took a deep breath and opened the door to the bedroom, whistling softly.

Coogan was silhouetted in the bedroom doorway.

Hammond snapped his fingers and said, "Oops, forgot something." He ducked back into the bathroom and flushed the toilet. He snatched his brandy glass from the counter and strolled out, weaving a little drunkenly. He grinned at Coogan and slurred, "Wouldn't want to leave any telltale signs, would I?"

Coogan stayed in the doorway and growled, "You had to come all the way up to the third floor to do that?"

"No, gorgeous. I was looking for you."

"You've found me."

"Want to step out of the way?"

Coogan just glared at him.

"Okay," said Hammond. "All gloves off. You're not going to like it, bub, but I've been doing some shitting other than on the master's pot." He watched Coogan blink. "That sweet little deal you've had going over at BUPERS for the last twenty years, that's 'all gone,' to quote a friend of ours named Olively."

Coogan flinched.

"Not only that, but *if* you ever have another tour of duty with the Navy, I'll see that you're assigned to something constructive: like the alligator census in Georgia. The secret is to count their feet and divide by four."

Coogan shifted and Hammond scooted through the opening. In the hallway, he twirled his brandy glass and rocked back on his feet, returning Coogan's scowl.

"And if you think I don't know everything about Project Thin Air, you're right. The rest of it you're going to tell me in front of a Naval Board of Inquiry. You and Traben and even Mr. Big-Shot Bloch!"

Coogan stepped out in the hall, his threatening bulk poised on the balls of his feet. Hammond tensed, convinced the man was about to charge. Then Coogan got himself under control and managed a smile that came off as more of a grimace.

"You're going to look damned foolish without any proof," he said.

"Just give me time."

Coogan laughed wickedly. "I'm not going to give you anything, Commander, *especially time!*"

They glared at each other. Hammond carefully put his

brandy glass down on a side table and confronted Coogan, balling his fists. Coogan laughed throatily.

"Relax," he said. "We're not going to do anything to embarrass the host now, are we?"

"Certainly not," Hammond muttered.

"Not while you're still inside this house," Coogan finished, his eyes practically gleaming with anticipation.

Hammond shook his head sadly. "Coogan," he said, "it's going to make me so unhappy to put you behind bars. You deserve something better, like a cyanide suppository."

Coogan just continued to smile—stiffly, as if he knew he had the upper hand. Hammond waved him away in disgust, picked up his glass, and walked back to the landing, not bothering with the drunk act anymore. He tried to whistle but discovered that his lips were quivering too much. He made the landing and scurried downstairs.

Coogan was right. He hadn't enough proof—or time.

What had he really stumbled on in that bathroom vault? An invisibility generator? Or something even more insidious? And what did any of it have to do with F.P. Bloch's oil dealings?

He paused on the landing atop the broad foyer staircase. People below were laughing and enjoying themselves. Hammond wondered if the spider's web was closing around them, too. An aura of power seemed to ripple through the house and touch everyone.

Did it?

He found Jan Fletcher sitting on a small couch in the ballroom, her legs tucked under her bottom, sipping brandy and listening to two ancient congressmen trying to impress her with their Washington gossip. She glanced up at Hammond's approach and visibly brightened. The two old bores looked up at Hammond, then back at her, then fell silent.

Hammond held out a hand. She accepted it and he pulled her up. She came into his arms for a lingering embrace, then wheeled back to hook her arm through his. She said nothing as he led her on a slow saunter around the room.

"More brandy?" he asked.

"No thanks." She leaned over and took a quick nibble from his ear, whispering, "More *you*."

"Forward little lass, aren't you?"

"Forward thinking. Forward doing."

"Right here? On the ballroom floor?"

She wrinkled her nose. "Too crowded. How about your apartment?"

Before he could reply, Admiral Gault loomed in front of them. He caught Hammond's eye and waved.

"Enjoying the party?" asked Gault.

"Apart from a little run-in with Joe Coogan, yes," said Hammond. Jan suddenly looked concerned.

"What kind of run-in?" asked Gault.

"I found something in a bathroom . . . that you wouldn't normally find in a bathroom." Gault arched an eyebrow and opened his mouth to demand an explanation. Hammond winked at him. "We can discuss it tomorrow. It'll suffice to say that our host is in this up to his teeth."

Gault scowled openly and rumbled something to himself. "I think you better get out of here," he said. "Back to MAGIC."

"Okay." Hammond nodded. "Have to pick up my car first." He nodded to Gault and escorted Jan away.

Forty minutes later, a cab swung down Thomas Jefferson Street and stopped at the canal. Hammond helped Jan out and paid the driver. The cab turned around and drove off while Hammond walked to his car. He stopped, cursed, and turned back to Jan. "I better call MAGIC," he said, "and tell them we're coming, or we're liable to get blown right off the porch."

She stood on the tow path, watching him with her wrap held tightly about her shoulders. Hammond looked into her eyes. Her lips parted. A cold wind was blowing along the canal, scattering leaves and rustling branches. She shivered. He offered his arm and gratefully she slipped a hand through it. He wanted to hurry to the apartment, make his call, get going to safety. She wanted to take a casual stroll down the tow path.

What could he do? He had to oblige and, when he thought about it, it was nice having her here again. She felt warm and soft next to him and she leaned her head on his shoulder peacefully.

They were across from the entrance to his building when she stopped and turned into him. Her hand went to the back of his neck and gently began to stroke. Hammond shivered, and not from the chilly night air. Her lips met his and he felt himself sinking into them. Her other hand climbed his chest and caressed his cheek. He was surprised and giddy from excitement.

"I think we're putting on a show out here."

"Nobody watches," she said. "We used to do this, remember?"

He remembered. He pulled her with him, heading for his front door. The lamp along the tow-path threw a weak light as he fished for his keys. Jan moved to one side while he fumbled at the lock. The key turned and he swung the door open, standing aside to let her pass. It was dark inside and she hesitated, testing for the staircase with her foot.

Dark. What happened to the hall light? It struck him, almost too late—

Jan was already on the first step when Hammond grabbed her and pulled her back roughly. He slammed the door then lunged sideways off the stoop, ignoring Jan's surprise.

Something chunked into the door twice.

Hammond stared at twin holes. Jagged, splintered wood canted up at a crazy angle. He heard the thump of heavy footsteps charging down the stairs. He looked up. Could they chance a run for it? Risk a bullet in the back? Make the canal? Jan's face was chalk-white. She was fumbling with a spiked heel—

Hammond shoved her into a crouch in the dark, then flattened himself next to the door. It flew open. A burly figure in a black trenchcoat stepped out, gun first, and Hammond struck, tackling low and sending him sprawling.

They scrambled for position on the grass. The gun came up and Hammond lashed out at the exposed wrist. The gun flew away and Hammond caught a glimpse of the silencer. A heavy fist came down hard on his back.

Jan screamed. Hammond went down. The attacker jumped up and aimed a vicious kick at his head. Hammond grabbed the foot and twisted. The man screamed in pain and Hammond saw his face. Crewcut red hair, a huge drinker's nose with nostrils flared.

McCarthy landed hard. Hammond swung his leg without getting up and planted a shoe in McCarthy's ribs. Then he whirled and dove for the gun.

The barrel was still hot and McCarthy winced when Hammond jammed it under his chin. "Do something stupid," Hammond snarled. "Give me an excuse!"

McCarthy tried to edge away, but Hammond kept the gun at his throat. McCarthy was gasping, his face flushed redder than usual. His hands were thrown back clutching grass.

Hammond glanced around quickly. Jan was crouched in the bushes, one hand over her mouth, eyes wide in horror and fear.

"It's okay now," he said.

She stared from him to the assailant. "Wh-who is he?" she stammered.

"Mrs. Fletcher, meet Dr. Lester J. McCarthy."

Her breath caught. She made an inarticulate sound and sank to her knees. Hammond heard quavering sobs and they made him angrier. He prodded McCarthy.

"Up, you sonofabitch!" he said.

McCarthy carefully got to his feet, breathing hard, guarding against another blow from Hammond. Hammond grabbed his arm and jerked him off-balance, thrusting the gun into his ear.

"Any more surprises in my apartment?" he said.

McCarthy didn't reply. Hammond flipped him around and made him raise his hands and clasp them behind his head; then he searched the trenchcoat. McCarthy had no other weapons.

Hammond faced him. For some reason known only to him, the doctor was smiling. "I'm glad you're so happy," said Hammond. "Now you can explain to me in very plain English just how you got out of that cell in Boston."

McCarthy gave him a contemptuous look. The wrinkling movement must have affected something in his huge nose. He sneezed twice, pulling one hand down to cover it, then very obligingly putting his hand back behind his head.

A light went on several houses down and somebody appeared at the window. They were attracting attention. Hammond motioned McCarthy toward the apartment entrance. He wiggled a hand at Jan and she stumbled to join them, keeping well back.

"Hold it," said Hammond as soon as McCarthy crossed the threshold. "What'd you do with the lights?"

"Switch," said McCarthy. He sat down on the steps and rubbed the back of what Hammond hoped was a very sore neck. Hammond's eyes were away only a few seconds as he fumbled for the light switch. The moment it went on, Jan shrieked. Hammond whipped around.

McCarthy's hand had descended to the base of his neck, where he held it tightly in place, pressing against the flesh—while his entire body faded from sight.

Hammond stood rooted in place while the figure vanished from the steps. Within agonizing seconds, Hammond was alone again with Jan, whose screams echoed up the stairwell.

20

For the longest time, Hammond couldn't move. He heard Jan fall away from him and sag against the wall, her screams diminished to terrified weeping.

McCarthy had disappeared like a will-o'-the-wisp. There was no sign of him, not at the top of the stairs or out on the grass. He was gone, as if he had never been there, but Hammond had his gun, a murderous-looking .45 with a silencer. It dangled from his hand as he stumbled back to Jan and pulled her close. She shook in his arms.

He led her over the threshold and listened at the door of the first-floor apartment. No sound, no lights—they must have gone away for the weekend. Thank God.

Hammond's grip on the gun tightened. He raised it as a feeler and led Jan upstairs. He pulled the key to his apartment and opened the door. It was dark inside. He flipped on the light by the door and explored the living room with his eyes and the gun.

Jan breathed shakily beside him, clutching his shoulder. He drew her inside, slammed the door, and locked it. He paused, listening. Nothing. He switched on a light.

The door to his office was slightly ajar. He pushed it open slowly, peering into the darkness and listening before he turned on the light. There seemed to be no one inside, but there certainly had been. Books, papers, and bills were strewn all over the floor. In the center of his desk, held together with a strap, were his briefcase and all his files on Thin Air, ready to go like a stuffed picnic basket. Hammond managed a smile: McCarthy had failed to get away with them.

He heard Jan gasp behind him and turned. She was peering over his shoulder, wide-eyed at the mess.

"Why don't you go fix your face?" he said softly. "Your mascara's running." She was hesitant to go alone, so he led her to the bedroom, checking the bathroom for her.

He left her, went to the kitchen window, and looked down at his front yard. His mind raced until he began to see the pattern. A device, worn at the base of the neck or implanted there, allowed McCarthy to remove himself at will by dematerializing from anywhere he wished and rematerializing. . . .

Where?

Instantaneous spatial transference. IST. Teleportation. They had stumbled on it in the Philadelphia experiment of 1953. *Stumbled on it.* Two years later, Project Thin Air had been shut down and the principals involved had moved into private industry. And more than twenty years later, those principals were murdering people to keep their secret. . . .

They had failed with invisibility, so they had turned instead to teleportation.

It was far more useful and apparently less dangerous. McCarthy didn't seem to suffer from chronic aftereffects. And he used the process regularly. He was able to beam himself in and out of the cities where he conducted his "treatment" of the surviving project participants. Very commendable: they were willing to keep these men alive and under control as long as they didn't get nosy, like Fletcher, or start to talk, like Rinehart.

Or investigate, like Hammond.

Now it all hung together, he realized, but still it was nothing more than a defensive operation. It had to cover something bigger. *What?*

He returned to the living room and inspected the front door, trying to determine how McCarthy got into the apartment. Was he able to teleport himself *into* a place as well as out of it? Hammond felt around the lock and found scratches left by a burglar's pick, or what he took to be a burglar's pick. McCarthy had entered by conventional means. Hammond wasn't sure if he should feel relieved.

He brought brandy into the bedroom for Jan. He heard the water in the sink go off, then the bathroom door opened, and then he saw her drying her face. She glanced at him across the room.

But he wasn't watching her. He was staring at his bathroom and the open door of his shower stall. If McCarthy could make himself vanish from one place, he had to reappear at another. Somewhere there was a receiving station, a pre-set instrument that acted like a homing beacon to bring him to a safe location. The landing place was probably a small, enclosed room . . . like a vault.

Hammond put down the brandy, whirled, and charged into his office. He grabbed the phone and froze. Bloch's number. He didn't have Bloch's unlisted number. And then he remembered: Smitty would have it.

After ten rings, he got Smitty's butler, who was sleepy and very slow. The wait was interminable, but finally Hammond had Francis P. Bloch's home number.

The call was answered by one of the servants. Hammond could hear the party still going on in the background. He breathed easier and asked to speak with Admiral Gault. The servant left the phone for what must have been only a minute. To Hammond it was forever.

He glanced at his desk clock and calculated that McCarthy had vanished less than ten minutes ago. Bloch's home wasn't too far away. If McCarthy had walked it, he could be there in twenty minutes.

But he hadn't walked.

"Hullo?"

It was Gault, a little sloshed.

"It's Hammond, sir."

"You left too soon, Nick. They just broke out the twelve-year-old Scotch."

"Admiral, I want you to look around. Tell me if you see a man with red hair, a tall Irishman with a drinker's nose."

Gault hesitated. "Christ, Hammond, if this is a joke—"

"No joke. It's important. Where are you?"

"In the goddamned foyer. What am I supposed to do? Search the house?"

"No, sir. Wait a minute. Has anybody come through the front door in the last ten minutes?"

"No."

"How long have you been there?"

"Hammond, what is—?"

He broke off. Hammond listened.

"Just a second," Gault said, his gaze distracted by something he saw on the second-floor landing. Two figures were descending from the third floor. He recognized the big fellow named Coogan; he was talking to another man in a plain blue suit, carrying a black trenchcoat over his arm. He had a bloated face and red hair. . . .

"I think I've found the nose you want," Hammond heard him say.

"Where?" Hammond said anxiously.

"Upstairs with your friend Coogan—"

"*Upstairs?*"

"That's what I said. Who is he?"

"McCarthy."

Hammond heard him suck in his breath then swear out loud. "Shit," he said, "want me to nab him?"

"No, sir—please! And don't say anything to him."

"Then what the hell do you want me to do?"

"Sir, he tried to kill me about fifteen minutes ago."

Gault fell silent again, then his voice dropped two octaves. "Where are you?"

"My apartment."

"How did he get back here so fast?"

Hammond started to explain, but Gault interrupted him. There was silence and he felt his heart begin to thump.

"He's coming downstairs," Gault whispered. He gazed furtively upstairs at the two men who had finally parted. Coogan remained on the landing while the red-headed man clumped downstairs, keeping his eyes locked straight ahead so he wouldn't attract attention.

McCarthy stepped off the stairs, and his crepe-soled shoes squished across the marble as he headed for the front door.

"He's leaving!" hissed Gault. "Hammond, I can't let him go—"

"You've got to!" Hammond shouted back.

It was too late anyway. McCarthy passed Gault without even seeing him. He was out the door and gone.

The admiral made a move to follow and stopped. He stood poised to leave the party with the host's telephone as a souvenir. He made a foul face, then brought the receiver up. His gaze automatically swept up with it and he found himself locking eyes with Joe Coogan, standing stiffly on the landing overhead.

"Uh-oh," Hammond heard him say. "Coogan caught me looking. Hammond, I don't know where your doctor friend is going, but I suggest you avoid another house call."

"On my way."

"Where?"

"MAGIC."

* * *

Hammond threw on plain clothes and a jacket, wondering whether he finally had some concrete evidence against these characters. Jan was a witness: McCarthy had tried to kill them. *I have the gun,* he remembered, and ran to the living room to get it. He stuffed it into his briefcase along with all his papers on Thin Air. Gault could vouch for the fact that McCarthy got back to Bloch's house in better than Olympic time. And that device on Bloch's third floor, that was his Grand Central Station. Hammond smiled neatly—they would never be able to get rid of it fast enough. Tomorrow he could go in there with a Federal search warrant and an army of FBI agents, drag the CNO along by the scruff of his neck, and—

"Shit!" he yelled, and punched the wall. It wasn't enough. It might be enough to start an investigation, but if there was a secret project somewhere that these people were trying to protect, Intelligence could never move fast enough to keep them from hiding it.

He had to catch them red-handed, actually standing there up to their hips in misappropriated funds—

"Nicky?"

Jan stood in his office doorway in his jeans and sweater, staring quizzically at him. She looked tired.

"I'm sorry, honey," he said. "We'll go now."

He grabbed the case and turned out the lights, then guided her to the door. She stopped as he opened it, too frightened to go out.

"It's okay, Jan." She wouldn't move. He had to pull the gun out of his briefcase and start down the stairs. She came out on the landing, frowning at him.

"What good is that against an invisible man?" she demanded.

"He's not invisible," said Hammond. "He's just great on fast getaways."

He took another two steps and looked back.

"How do you know?" she said.

He felt a shiver of discomfort and looked out into the night. He swore under his breath. How *did* he know?

The drive back to Virginia was long and dark. It was sixteen miles north on the Dulles Access Highway to Herndon. Jan sat curled up at Hammond's side, staring uneasily at the road ahead. It started to rain. Thunder and a few forks of lightning. Her eyes grew heavy with exhaustion and, against her will, she went to sleep.

Hammond watched the wipers slap back and forth and thought of that night on the back road in Taos. He began watching the cross streets and checking his rear-view mirror, anxiously gripping the wheel every time a speedster zoomed up behind and passed him.

He looked at Jan. Was she strong enough to take all this? Could he keep her protected? For how long? And when it was over, would it be over for them, too? They'd had one night together, an emotional collision, but it didn't mean their relationship had resurfaced. Hammond was too confused and nervous to know what he felt. He didn't want Jan to get hurt, not physically or emotionally. But did he want to get involved again?

He pulled up to the house on Merlin Street just after two a.m. A security man stepped out of the bushes while Hammond was gently waking Jan and helping her out of the car. The security guard flashed a light on them and Hammond barked the password. They were covered all the way up to the door. Before Hammond could knock, it opened and Ike Menninger smiled sleepily at them. He was in pajamas and robe.

Jan was asleep again. Menninger helped Hammond carry her upstairs. They put her on the bed and drew a quilt over her, then slipped out of the room and closed the door.

Yablonski was in the hallway waiting for them. "How'd it go?" he said, tying his bathrobe.

"Downstairs," whispered Hammond.

Menninger stood guard on the landing while Hammond and Cas went down to the den. Cas was anxious to hear all about the party, so Hammond recounted the evening in detail. When he finished describing McCarthy's attack, Yablonski was wearing a dark scowl and clutching the arm of his chair so hard his knuckles were white.

"I wish you'd let me go," he said. "I could have stopped that sonofabitch from following you."

"He didn't follow us. He was there waiting. Spent the whole evening ransacking my office. Besides, how can you stop a man who can teleport himself out of your hands?"

"How did he know you'd come back to the apartment?"

"I don't think they know about the safe house. Oh, they

might guess, but they don't know where it is. I'm sort of glad we did go back: now at least we know their trump card. But I still haven't figured a way to arrest anybody."

"And hang onto them," Yablonski added.

"That's not what I mean. Grounds. Except for McCarthy, I haven't got grounds."

Yablonski got up and motioned Hammond to follow. They went to the kitchen and he offered Hammond a piece of the pie his wife had baked. They ate in silence, Yablonski busy thinking.

"I see Menninger's put on some pounds," said Hammond.

"Like a bird. Eats twice his own weight in a day." Yablonski smiled, then grew serious. "You need hard evidence against these people, right?"

"Lost without it."

"What about the equipment that was aboard the *Sturman*? The ship may have been scrapped, but I guarantee you they wouldn't have junked all that stuff. Too much of it and very expensive. There must be records of where it went, who got it, and when. And if it ended up in the hands of your buddies at Micro-Tech, then I'd say you've got them by the balls. You could probably bring in a whole Congressional investigation. Am I right?"

Hammond stared at him. "Want to come with me tomorrow?"

Yablonski concealed his excitement. "Where?"

"Operational Archives."

Yablonski smiled.

At 0900, while Jan was still asleep, Hammond phoned Ensign Just-Ducky at the Pentagon and asked her to arrange a meeting that afternoon with somebody in Naval Archives. She called back twenty minutes later and informed him that a Lieutenant Gordon McWilliams would meet him at the Historical Display Center in the Washington Navy Yard at 1330.

The phone rang again and it was Gault's secretary. "You're wanted for a meeting in Mr. Smith's office at 1100, Commander."

Hammond decided they wanted a report on his activities last night. Fine. He would take Yablonski along and hit the Navy Yard afterwards.

Hammond didn't wait around for Jan to wake up. He

and Yablonski had to get rolling fast. It was Saturday morning and the traffic on the Dulles Access Highway would be heavy. At the door, Mrs. Yablonski straightened her husband's bomber jacket, took his face in both her hands, and kissed him warmly on the lips before she let him go.

Hammond followed him to the car and took the wheel. As they pulled out of Merlin's Way, Yablonski seemed uncommonly determined.

"What is this, Cas, *Commandoes Die at Dawn*? Why are you and your wife so solemn?"

Yablonski was silent a moment, then he said, "I had a dream last night. . . ."

Hammond stiffened. "About the *Sturman*?" Yablonski nodded. "Same dream as always?"

"No. Some of it was. Becoming invisible, being frightened, the blackness. . . ."

"What was different about it?"

"I kept seeing McCarthy everywhere I looked." He shivered convulsively.

"That sounds like a normal paranoid nightmare."

"We're going to meet them today, Hammond," Yablonski said quickly. "We're going to be right in the middle, just you and me."

"Part of your dream?"

Yablonski shook his head. "It's going to happen. I don't know how, but it's going to be today."

Hammond drove silently, then asked, "How many of them do you figure there are?"

"I don't know."

"Take a guess. I'd like to know how many bad guys we'll be fighting off."

Yablonski's mouth clamped shut and he looked away. "Bloch could have minions by the carload. What do you think?" Hammond persisted.

Yablonski shrugged.

"Personally, I think it's a small organization. Bloch, Traben, Coogan, McCarthy, and a handful of others—maybe a dozen at most in on the whole plot. Everybody else, including Admiral Corso and that international gang of scientists at MTL, knows only what they need to know."

He glanced over and saw Yablonski looking at him again. "Engineers work on projects in bits and pieces, like at an automobile assembly plant. Except at MTL I doubt if they get to see the final product. It's just a matter of Traben telling his crew they're developing a top-secret project for the Navy, so secret they can't even be told what it is."

"Are you telling me everybody out there is innocent except the top dogs?"

"Probably."

"What makes you so sure?"

Hammond concentrated on passing a truck, then said, "From 1955 on, these guys have been very busy trying to limit the number of people who knew what was going on. I can't see them risking that knowledge today in the hands of a large, far-flung organization. These are not super-villains with a thousand men at their command, all wearing neatly pressed space-age uniforms and carrying advanced laser weapons. That's comic-book time. This is a close-knit band of very determined, very vicious, and, I suspect, very greedy human beings. Why else did they send McCarthy out to get me? Your fucking *psychiatrist*, for God's sake! Why was *he* the hatchet man?"

Yablonski swallowed. "Because they couldn't risk sending anybody else?"

"Exactly. With their unique mode of transportation, they can minimize the risk of exposure by having their key people do everything. Since they can teleport anywhere there's a receiving station, they only need one or two assassins—at the most."

"What about the two creeps who tried to get us?"

"Paid muscle. Those two and a few others make up the inner circle."

"Paid and ignorant, Hammond? Good guess, but—"

"Damned right it's a good guess. But do you see the implication? If we flush those four key people out in the open, force them to tip their hand—!" He calmed down. "You're right," he said quietly. "We will be in the middle—very soon. But it might not be today."

Yablonski gazed out the window at the traffic whizzing by.

"Yes, it will," he said.

When they arrived at the Pentagon, it became clear that the conference with Smitty wasn't going to be any ordinary staff meeting. Ensign Just-Ducky came right to the point: "Admiral Corso, Admiral Gault, and Mr. Smith are waiting for you."

Hammond hurried back to his cubicle with Yablonski. He closed the door and uneasily changed into a fresh uniform.

Yablonski watched him from his chair. "Are they gonna bite your head off?"

"Funny," grumbled Hammond. "That's the feeling I always get when I'm called to a meeting with no agenda." He grabbed his tie and fumbled with it, heading for the door.

"Knock 'em dead, kid," Yablonski said casually.

Hammond threw him some papers from a stack on his file cabinet. "Reading matter. Enjoy yourself."

"What is this?"

"Re-enlistment forms."

Yablonski was tearing them in half as Hammond banged out the door. He found Andrews in the coffee room and asked him to watch Yablonski. "And don't let anyone near him," he added.

Two minutes later, Hammond was standing in Smitty's waiting room, pacing in apprehension. The door opened and Admiral Gault stepped out, closing it partially behind him.

"Nicky," he whispered, "we may have to act for a while as if you're on the spot, okay?"

Hammond blinked. "*Act?*"

Gault smiled, then set his face into a properly somber expression and propelled Hammond into the office.

Smitty didn't rise. He sat behind his desk walruslike, benign and inscrutable. But Admiral Lawrence J. Corso, USN Retired, bounced up from the leather sofa and stood at parade rest. Hammond looked at him carefully. He was an older man, well dressed in a tweed suit and brown bow tie. He seemed powerful. His head was shorn to an iron-gray crewcut. His eyes were blue and piercing, set in a face of uncompromising strength; the tight flesh seemed to stretch back to his ears, giving him a stern, masklike expression. He was an Airedale: a tiny set of Naval Aviator's wings were pinned to his lapel. His eyes flicked to Hammond's wings in a moment of silent reproach. If the Navy permitted, undoubtedly he would have worn his uniform.

The introductions were carried out by Gault, who quickly took the chair on Smitty's left, consigning Hammond to the one in the center of the room, allowing Corso to circle him like a prosecutor stalking his witness.

"All right, Admiral, it's your show," said Smitty.

Corso wasted no time getting to the point. "Commander Hammond," he said, "I made what I felt was a legitimate request of Admiral Gault with respect to your investigations into MTL. Yesterday, your superior assured me you would comply with my request. Now, to my dismay, I find that you are continuing to badger and accuse innocent parties without cause. Mr. Bloch was quite upset about the direction your conversation took last night, and very much so by the fact that you searched his house without permission. He resents your intrusions and, I must say, so do I."

"Admiral—" Hammond cleared his throat. "I resent the attempts on my life."

Gault said nothing. He was watching Corso. Smitty made a low, noncommittal noise in his throat but sat with his hands pyramided.

Corso stopped pacing and stood in front of Hammond, his back to Smitty. "Let's get one thing straight, mister, the people I represent have no connection whatsoever with any attempts at foul play. They simply would not use those methods! Why in the world do you think *I'm* here?"

"Because *they* failed three times."

Corso went off like a skyrocket. "How dare you make such unsupported accusations? How dare you!"

Hammond was quiet for a moment. Then, in as calm a voice as he could muster, he listed his reasons: "I have the assassin's .45 in my possession. I have his phony ID. There's an Air Force staff car in New Mexico filled with bullet holes. A former associate of Dr. Traben got himself charcoal-broiled because he talked to me. There's a man in my office who was attacked along with me by two goons in a phony mugging. The FBI stopped a housebreaking in Los Angeles before *it* became a murder. And the person responsible for most of this was seen at Bloch's house last night, fifteen minutes after he tried to kill me!"

Hammond looked to Gault for support, but the admiral was motionless. Hammond stiffened. Was this going to be the final head-chopping party? Had he gone too far?

"That's impossible!" bellowed Corso, beginning to circle Hammond. "You're paranoid, Commander. Where is your proof? This assassin—can you prove he works for Mr. Bloch or Dr. Traben?"

Hammond quietly informed him about Coogan and his secret warning system at BUPERS.

Corso laughed at him. "Are Joe Coogan's fingerprints on those files?"

Hammond hesitated.

"Did you fingerprint the files?"

Hammond shook his head. Corso clucked with contempt. "You fail to employ ordinary police methods in your investigation. You would rather depend on your own leaps in judgment!"

"It doesn't take much leaping to know when you're being shot at," said Hammond.

"Or unfairly accused of doing the shooting!" Corso shouted in Hammond's face. Then he walked around behind the chair. "On the face of it, Commander, I think you're the worst investigator I've ever met in my life," Corso concluded, flinging sympathetic looks at Smitty and Gault.

Neither of them denied his statement.

"Commander Hammond," he said, circling again, "the people you are so bent on persecuting are developing something for the Navy that you will one day be extremely grateful for—"

"That may be, sir, but what I think they're developing isn't what *you* think they're developing."

"It's vital!" Corso yelled. "And you're a damned fool for trying to jeopardize it!" He whirled to Smitty. "This whole discussion is of course unofficial. I don't want to have to carry it any higher." He glanced at Hammond. "Don't make me."

The next move was Smitty's. He didn't budge from his chair. He simply turned a bit to face Corso. His voice rolled out quiet and relaxed. "Larry," he said, "I'm afraid I don't share your assessment of Commander Hammond's capabilities. All told, I think he's handled himself fairly well. As for the persecution of innocent parties, Commander Hammond entered this case on a perfectly legitimate basis and, whether or not the attempts on his life really occurred in the manner he says, the fact remains that several people have died in the course of his investigation—"

"All the more reason—!"

"May I finish?"

Corso turned red, then nodded.

"Now, Larry," said Smitty, "you were in the Navy long enough to know that we don't take kindly to threats, real or implied. If anything should happen to my good friend Nicky here—if he should fall up a flight of stairs or step in front of a bullet—I'll know the first place to look. And you know how embarrassing it can get to be hauled up in front of your peers to explain yourself. By the way, my contribution to this discussion is *strictly* official. And I don't *have* to carry it any higher."

Corso stared at him, paralyzed with disbelief. "I see," he said finally. With a dirty glance at Gault, he walked out.

The door closed and Hammond sagged in relief. "Thanks for the support," he said to Smitty.

"He's not entirely out of order, Nick. You haven't any proof that Bloch and Traben are behind these murder attempts."

Hammond stood up. "Well, sir, am I supposed to get killed before we . . . ?" He spread his hands.

"Nick," said Gault, "they *are* working on a top-secret Navy project. If we blow them wide open before they finish it, it will throw a cloud over everything and it certainly won't advance our careers."

Hammond frowned. "Has it occurred to either of you that Bloch and Traben may have sold the Navy a bill of goods? Has anybody seen this secret guidance system?"

"Not yet," said Smitty.

"And I'll bet you never will. They need the time and the money to complete something else!"

Smitty grunted and got to his feet. "They are scheduled to deliver a satellite package containing the guidance system to Vandenburg Air Force Base in exactly four weeks. If we disrupt their forward momentum, they'll flush it down the toilet along with whatever hanky-panky they're up to."

"Well, what are we going to do?" asked Hammond. "Sit back and let them have their way?"

"We'll do what's best for the Navy," said Smitty.

"Sir, they've got assassins capable of disappearing at

will! Is that good for the Navy? Last night, Dr. McCarthy attacked me at home. He got away by pressing something on the back of his neck and vanishing right in front of my eyes! You want to talk about weapons systems? This guy is a one-man task force! All he has to do is get into a place—he's got a built-in getaway! Do you want *that* in private hands?"

Smitty slid his gaze down to some papers on his desk. "If you can prove any of this with rock-hard, indisputable connections—believe me, it won't stay in private hands. But we cannot ignore the importance of that weapons system."

Hammond swore aloud. "That's what they're counting on! That nobody will make a move against them because the U.S. Navy has its greedy little eye on one tree while there's a forest growing under its feet!"

Smitty said nothing. Hammond walked over to Gault and said, "How about it, Admiral?"

Gault studied the floor. "Do your best, Nick."

He left the meeting feeling that he had been supported, but with empty words. He suspected, in fact, that if he failed or even got himself killed, the whole matter would be swept under the rug because it would be "what's best for the Navy." By making counter-threats to Corso, all Smitty had done was buy Hammond some time. Corso would go running back to his boss and make noises about his own credibility being at stake and couldn't they lay off Hammond for a few days . . . ?

But that's about all that threat was worth. Hammond was on his own. So he and Yablonski had better move now. As Yablonski had said, today was the day.

Hammond stormed into his office and found Yablonski nodding, half-asleep.

"How'd it go?"

"I've just been promoted . . . to resident football."

"Congratulations."

Hammond paced behind his desk, plotting revenge against Corso, Coogan, Traben, Bloch—all of them. He stopped when he realized they were probably doing the same for him—and there were more of them.

He pulled off his uniform jacket and threw it over the chair. Yablonski watched silently as he unlocked the bottom drawer of his desk. He shrugged into the shoulder holster, rolled his arms several times to make sure the straps weren't binding, then unzipped the leather case that held his personal weapon: a Browning 9mm pistol. It was non-regulation, and so were the hollow-point rounds that nestled in the clip—thirteen of them. Hammond shoved the clip into the butt, pulled back on the receiver, and jacked a round into the chamber. He flipped on the thumb safety and slid the pistol into his holster.

As he patted down his jacket, Yablonski got up sternly. "It's our turn, isn't it?" he said.

Hammond nodded.

The Washington Navy Yard was on the southern tip of Capitol Hill, facing the Anacostia River. In the southeast corner of the yard, just back of the riverfront, was the Naval Historical Display Center. Hammond and Yablonski met Lieutenant Gordon McWilliams in the lobby at 1330. Hammond estimated him at six-foot-six and still growing.

McWilliams escorted them to Classified Operational Archives in Building 210 and led them into his office.

McWilliams' desk was flanked by heavily sagging bookshelves. "We inherited most of this stuff when they broke up the old reference group in BUSHIPS," he explained. "Guess we were doing the same work. You know how it is with rampant bureaucracy. What can I do for you fellows?"

"Lieutenant," said Hammond, "we're trying to establish the disposition of certain special equipment that was once aboard a destroyer-escort, back in the 1950s."

"Which one?"

"DE-166, the *Sturman*."

McWilliams threw a long arm over the back of his chair and pulled down a copy of the Naval Vessel Register from about three shelves up.

"We've already checked the NVR. She was struck in late 1957."

"That's okay, sir. Just like to look for myself." He flipped pages and stopped on one, ran his finger down a list and then across. Then he nodded. "December to be exact."

"The people at NAVSEACOM were of the opinion she might have been sunk for target practice."

"Very possible. I don't know why you went to them. That information would be here."

"Can you give us the disposition of that ship from about October of 1953 to her demise?"

"Sure." McWilliams reached back again and pulled down Volume 2 of the Directory of Naval Fighting Ships. He prowled through it in silence for a few minutes while Yablonski borrowed his NVR.

"Okay," said McWilliams. "USS *Sturman*, DE-166, on Special Status until July of 1955, then reclassified AGTR, Technical Research Ship, and placed under the Admiral's Reserve Fleet at Norfolk. Stayed there until June of 1957, then placed on DAR, scheduled for disposal—out of commission—Atlantic. She was returned to Philadelphia in October of that year, stayed there until she was sunk as a target on December 8." He looked up.

Hammond glanced at Yablonski, who was deep in thought, then paced the office and stared at the volumes of Naval records around him.

"She was at Norfolk from 1955 to 1957?" he asked.

McWilliams nodded.

"Any way to determine what she was doing in the Admiral's Reserve Fleet?"

McWilliams thought for a moment, then wheeled around in his chair and scanned his books. He got up and stretched to reach the top shelf and a thick ledger filled with yellowed papers. "These are the Fleet Transfer Records of the Commander, Naval Base, Norfolk, from 1950 through 1960. All the records on East Coast bases are kept in this office."

It took some twenty minutes of skimming through memos and reports of 1955 before he landed on the right one. It was a memo signed by Rear Admiral Costigan, the base C.O. at Norfolk. As of September, 1955, the *Sturman* was placed on loan as a research vessel . . . to RTI.

He found return papers dated February, 1957.

Hammond and Yablonski exchanged looks. For almost a year and a half, DE-166 was in F.P. Bloch's hands—more than enough time for them to have removed all the special equipment.

Hammond pored through the memos relating to that transfer and found not one mention of any equipment disposition. To Admiral Costigan, it had apparently been just another DE taken out of commission. Hammond saw the pattern: Traben must have connived to have the ship moved to Norfolk immediately upon shutting down Project Thin Air. A new home, new yard workers, a new base C.O. unaware of her history . . .

McWilliams produced the final memo signed by the same Admiral Costigan releasing DE-166 to be towed out to the Atlantic and used for target practice in late 1957.

Hammond sat back and clasped his hands behind his head. "That's that," he said to Yablonski. "Twenty years ago. We'll never be able to track down that stuff now."

Yablonski didn't hide his unhappiness. Then Hammond caught a puzzled expression on McWilliams' face.

"What's wrong, Lieutenant?"

McWilliams was comparing entries in the Fighting Ships Directory. He skimmed the list of DEs struck or sunk and then checked it against the list of surviving ships. "That's really weird," he said.

"What is?"

He put the book in front of Hammond and Yablonski and pointed. "Here's an escort of the same class still carried by MARAD, the mothball fleet. DE-161, the *Cooper.*"

"So?"

"That's impossible. My father was gunnery officer aboard the cruiser that sank her for target practice."

Hammond snorted. "Another error committed by the U.S. Navy."

"You miss the point," said McWilliams. "That was around 1957."

Hammond looked up. Yablonski straightened in his chair. "Are you sure?" Hammond asked. "You were a little kid."

"I remember the name! My dad made up a poem for my little brother: *The Cooper was a trooper, we fired till we tired, it took us half a day till we sank her like an anchor!*"

"Where does it say she is now?" asked Yablonski.

"Philadelphia."

Hammond stared at the list, his excitement growing. Someone could have been playing musical ships. Maybe it was nothing more than a paper foul-up—and maybe the

Sturman was still in existence, although disguised. It was worth finding out. Fleetingly, he wondered if Joe Coogan had ever worked for Operational Archives. He stood up.

"Let's go have a look at her," he said.

21

McWilliams gave Hammond the registry for the Fourth Naval District. Hammond quickly found what he was looking for: Naval Inactive Ship Maintenance Facility, Philadelphia.

He called the number. The chief on duty told him that DE-161, the *Cooper,* was indeed berthed at the Navy Yard but that he couldn't go aboard without proper authorization.

"How do you want to handle this?" Hammond sighed affably. "If I go through the Commandant, Fourth Naval District, I'll be forced to tell him you were uncooperative and knowingly interfered with an official investigation. Is that what you want?"

"Uh, no, sir," mumbled the chief, thoroughly cowed. "When would you care to look her over?"

"This afternoon will be fine."

"She's rigged with interior lights. I'll have them turned on."

"Do nothing of the sort. All I want from you is a map showing her location. Leave that at the main gate, along with two flashlights. No activity around her— Hold on just a minute."

McWilliams was dancing around like an agitated scarecrow, waving his long arms in the air.

Hammond covered the mouthpiece and stared at him. "What the hell is wrong, Lieutenant?"

"I've got a sudden urge to see Philadelphia, sir."

Hammond glanced at Yablonski. He shrugged his shoulders and looked away. "I don't think so," Hammond said and took his hand away from the phone.

"Commander!" McWilliams whooped. "Sir, if it wasn't for me, you wouldn't even know about the *Cooper*. Please."

Hammond chewed on it for a few seconds, then barked into the phone, "Chief, make that three flashlights."

* * *

The Philadelphia Navy Yard was at the south end of Broad Street. From the main gate, Hammond could see red brick buildings and huge sheds stretching off into the gloom, down towards the Delaware River. The Marine guard gave him a box of flashlights and stuck out a clipboard.

"Chief Mills wants you to sign for this, sir."

Hammond scrawled his signature and walked back to the car, fishing out an envelope resting on top of the flashlights. In the car, all three men studied the map. The *Cooper* was three-quarters of the way down N Wharf, across from the Supply Center, the outboard vessel in a five-ship side-tie.

Hammond drove slowly along the wharf, his car bumping over uneven asphalt. Gray dampness hung in the air, a dank, depressing soddenness. Fog rolled off the water and crept across the tops of ships, obscuring everything higher than twenty-five feet. The old warships gave Hammond a feeling of sadness. Once filled with men and purpose, now they sat quietly at their last moorings—like tawdry ladies dressed in faded paint—sealed up to protect them from the further ravages of time.

Yablonski had the map and pointed out, "That's the hospital ship. Should be some submarines behind her, then ours."

Hammond grunted and parked the car behind a shed. The three men got out. He passed around the flashlights and said, "I don't want any lights topside. Wait till we get below."

They moved away from the shed, heading for the first gangplank, shivering in the chilly darkness. It was late afternoon, but the fog made it nearly as dark as night. They stopped and stood for a moment, gazing up at the enormous hulks with their multiple decks and threatening guns, tied one next to the other, side by side, parallel to the wharf, and connected by individual gangplanks.

Hammond went up first and the others followed, tramping aboard the deck of the first ship. They crossed four destroyers in silence, passing between the base of the superstructure and the back of the forward-deck gun emplacement. River smells, mixed with the oily odor of Cosmoline, wafted over them. Their faces became slick with mist.

They stopped at the starboard gangplank of the fourth DE. Yablonski wandered forward and stood for a moment, hands on his hips, studying the features of the *Cooper*. When he rejoined Hammond and McWilliams, his face was a mask of despair.

"What's wrong?" asked Hammond.

"That's not the *Sturman*."

Hammond felt his excitement drain away, replaced by heaviness. "You sure?"

Yablonski pointed. "Don't you remember? The *Sturman* had no forward gun mount. It was removed to allow us more space on the main deck." His finger was leveled at an enormous three-inch cannon. "What the hell do you call that? A popcorn machine?"

Hammond studied it. It was definitely a cannon, and definitely the one that belonged there. He glanced back at the other DEs. Same cannon in the same place—on all of them.

He got a feeling of uneasiness and asked Yablonski, "Is there anything else?"

Yablonski looked at him in disbelief. "Isn't that enough?"

Hammond was mulling. "According to McWilliams' records, RTI had the *Sturman* for about a year and a half. Plenty of time to replace that gun mount. Just a simple piece of cosmetic surgery and *voilà!* Convincing disguise."

Yablonski regarded him darkly.

"But let's not jump to any conclusions," said Hammond, "until we've been through her."

McWilliams hadn't the faintest idea what Hammond was talking about. His eyes slid over to Yablonski, catching the slight nod of agreement. He followed them across the connecting gangplank.

The *Cooper*, like her sisters alongside, was sheathed in moisture, condensation running off the bridge superstructure into puddles on the wooden main deck. Lines attached to fairleads secured a yellow tarp wrapped like a cummerbund around the navigating bridge. Hammond turned around, looking at the ship they had just left: no such covering arrangement there. Nor had there been on any of the other DEs. And it looked strangely out of place here—too new.

Yablonski and McWilliams had passed under the blast shield, heading for the access hatch on the starboard side, directly under the smokestack. Hammond hurried to join them. He stepped over the lip of the hatch and swung it closed behind him, then switched on his flashlight. Yablonski and McWilliams followed suit.

Three beams played down an empty passageway, picking out a network of rubber-coated electric wiring that stretched fore and aft.

"Dockside power for the dehumidifiers," Hammond said.

As dank and gloomy as it was outside, it was dry as a bone inside. To reinforce the impression, a motor switched on somewhere forward and they felt a flow of air against their cheeks as the dehumidifiers sucked up the moisture they had let in upon entering.

Yablonski took the lead, guiding them down the passageway from memory, passing several staterooms with their doors open. Inside, there were bed frames bare of mattresses, hanging lockers with their doors secured to hooks on gray-painted bulkheads.

"Officers' wardroom should be coming up," Yablonski said in a throaty whisper.

They stepped into a large room, then stopped, aware of a drumming sound overhead. It took a moment for them to realize it was raining. They looked warily around the wardroom. The long table was still in place, but everything else had been stripped out.

McWilliams played his light over the forward bulkhead, stopping midway across, about a foot below the ceiling.

"What are you looking for?" asked Hammond.

"See those four holes? That's where the identification plate was. Someone's taken it, screws and all."

"Souvenir hunter?"

McWilliams shook his head. "I'd say yes if she was going to be cut up for scrap. But she's still carried on MARAD's permanent list. You just don't do that."

Hammond spent several minutes rummaging around, his light probing into the open, empty cabinets that lined the bulkhead. The end result was a big fat zero. Exasperated, he straightened and realized that only he and McWilliams were in the wardroom.

"Where's Yablonski?"

McWilliams shrugged. "Out in the passageway."

Hammond darted out of the wardroom and saw the rays of Yablonski's flashlight forward of him. He hurried down the corridor to where Yablonski was standing and warned, "Let's keep together, Cas."

Yablonski didn't answer. He shined his light on a closed cabin door. Hammond reached for the knob.

"I've already tried it. It's locked." Yablonski's light slid down to the deck. "Take a look at that."

At first, Hammond didn't see what Yablonski was pointing out, so he circled it with his light: a cut-out portion at the bottom edge of the wood where it fitted against the doorjamb. Gray wire was neatly spliced into the thicker wire that ran along the base of the bulkhead.

"Now, that's interesting," said Hammond.

McWilliams joined them and the three men stared at the closed door. Hammond put his shoulder to it, but it wouldn't budge. Yablonski moved him aside, braced his back against the opposite wall, and lashed out with his foot. The toe of his shoe slammed into the doorknob and snapped it off. Hammond slowly pushed the door open.

Yablonski hung back. Hammond heard him beginning to breathe shakily. In the eerie light, his face looked dangerously grim. Hammond stepped into the cabin with McWilliams ducking behind him. Their eyes took in a made-up cot, a small electric heater, and a hot plate. Several books were piled neatly in a corner next to a closed locker. Hammond opened it and stared at the clothing hanging inside.

He pulled out a set of yardbird's coveralls and tossed them on the bed. It was the officer's rig that interested him. He held the dark blue jacket out in front of him, his light picking up a nameplate over the breast pocket:

McCARTHY, L.

"Cas!" Hammond barked.

Yablonski stepped in, his face already pale. He stared at the uniform jacket, emotions playing over his features.

"Jackpot," said Hammond, smiling.

McWilliams reacted only to what he saw. "Someone's been *living* down here!" he announced, like Papa Bear discovering Goldilocks.

"Living, eating, sleeping, and sneaking around," agreed Hammond, giving the uniform a shake. "With this, he can get on or off the base at will, and with that"—he threw the jacket on the cot with the coveralls—"dressed as a yardbird, he can move around anywhere on these ships."

He was interrupted by the whine of a generator starting up. It jolted all of them. Yablonski listened briefly, then groaned and sagged against the wall, his eyes bulging. Hammond could almost taste his fear.

"Yablonski!" he snapped.

Cas struggled for control. McWilliams shifted his gaze from one to the other in confusion. "That's coming from somewhere aft," he said.

Hammond unholstered the Browning and said quietly, "This time it won't be so one-sided." He eyed Yablonski. "We better have a look at the engine room."

Yablonski sucked in a deep breath and lurched out of the cabin. He waited uneasily while Hammond and McWilliams put the cabin back in order. They stepped into the passageway and Hammond closed the door, then led them toward the stern.

They dropped down one deck level, ducked through a hatch, and stepped out on a platform. The engine room lay below them.

Four hooded lights, evenly spaced along the overhead, threw weak cones of illumination over the entire compartment. The whine was louder, coming from a generator at the far end, between the engines. As Hammond scanned the compartment, checking for movement, he wondered who had switched all this on. Hadn't he specifically told Chief Mills over the phone, *no interior lights?*

Hammond snapped off his flashlight. The room seemed out of balance to him: everything shifted to the starboard side, and there was too much open space to port. Yablonski went down the ladder and stood in the center of that empty space.

Hammond and McWilliams descended and joined him. "Is this where the force-field machinery was?" Hammond asked.

"Yes, all the way up to the bulkhead behind you."

Hammond glanced around. There was nothing there now, nor any sign that anything had ever been there, yet what about the open space? Yablonski pointed to open stud-holes bored into the deck. And marks in the steel decking where machinery once must have been. The herringbone pattern was not as thoroughly scuffed there as elsewhere.

Yablonski said quietly, with full confidence, "This *is* the *Sturman.*"

McWilliams had moved to the center of the engine room,

gaping at the enormous diesels that sank below deck and rose through the overhead. He stopped by the generator and noticed something odd. "Hey, look at this," he called.

He was pointing to a digital timer set on the deck beside the generator. Hammond and Yablonski came over to examine it, but Hammond was more intrigued by the cables running from the generator into the mass of tanks and pump casings on the starboard side. He followed the cables into a dark corner to a wooden crate.

The crate looked solid enough, but when Hammond lifted it he realized it was a very light wood, probably balsa, like a movie prop. And when he held it away, he found himself looking down at a duplicate of the pedestal he had seen at Bloch's house.

His breath constricted in his chest for a moment, until he was aware of the other two peering over his shoulder.

"Now we know what the generator's for," he said thickly.

Yablonski backed away, bumping into McWilliams, whose curiosity had set him to bouncing on his heels. "Would somebody like to tell me what's going on?" he asked.

Hammond set the crate down on a pump casing, stared at the pedestal, wondering where the computer controls might be, then he turned to McWilliams. "I want you in the next compartment. If you hear anyone coming, let us know—quietly."

McWilliams looked hurt.

"*Now*, Lieutenant!" Hammond snapped.

McWilliams' mouth clapped shut; he bobbed his head and left.

Hammond knelt down by the pedestal, tempted to yank out the cables. Just another station along the network, he thought. He'd give odds they would find the brother of this one buried somewhere in the Boston Navy Yard—and more of them God knew where else.

Hammond rose, brushed past Yablonski, and stared at the numbers glowing on the face of the timer. They changed. New time-ticks appeared. The sequence was meaningless to him, but the implications were obvious.

"This clock is programmed to switch on the generator at assigned intervals," he explained. "The power drain is minimal, so it doesn't attract any attention. Late afternoon, too. Quitting time at the yard. Not a chance in the world anybody would be aboard to hear this thing." He shook his head. "The bastards think of everything."

Yablonski shifted behind him, his shoes scraping on the deck plates, his face rigid with fear. "Can we get out of here?" he croaked. His voice echoed in the emptiness and Hammond had a sudden crazy impression that all the talking they had been doing was echoing throughout the ship and at any moment McCarthy would come through a hatch—shooting.

Hammond straightened, tightening his sweaty grip on the Browning. "I don't want to leave," he said. "We've finally nailed a spot where McCarthy hangs his hat. Wouldn't you like to get your hands on him?"

Yablonski nodded, but his eyes rolled toward the pedestal. "But let's get away from that fucking machine."

Hammond desperately wanted to find the computers to try to put them out of commission. But Yablonski was far too edgy to stand still for a systematic search.

Hammond turned on his heel and led the way out, not bothering to cover the pedestal with the crate. They picked up McWilliams and spent the next thirty minutes combing through the below-deck compartments, moving carefully, Hammond covering them with the Browning. They were all jittery now, like little boys exploring a haunted house. McWilliams had a dozen questions to ask, but his companions' grim faces were discouraging.

By the time they returned to the main deck, Yablonski's fear had settled into a general uneasiness. It was still raining, but after the dry confines of the ship's interior, the moisture was refreshing. Hammond looked up at the superstructure, noting that he couldn't hear the generator from where they were standing.

He slipped the Browning back into his holster and moved to the ladder. "Let's check the bridge," he said. "Then we can leave."

They climbed, wet rungs slippery under their hands and feet. Yablonski forced open a hatch and they entered the navigating bridge, ducking under the lines securing the yellow tarp.

Yablonski's light settled on a square glass window forward of the helm. It ran from knee level almost to the overhead; it was triple thickness, bedded into a metal frame. The covering tarp had completely concealed it from the outside. Yablonski moaned. "That's the clincher . . ."

"What is?" asked Hammond.

"The window. It was built specially, for observation, so the captain could keep an eye on us during the experiments."

"He's right," said McWilliams. "That's not standard. Ships of this class had round ports across the bridge."

Hammond studied the glass. He jumped when he heard Yablonski gasp. "The compass—look at it!" Hammond glanced down.

The binnacle light was on; shining softly, it bathed the compass in a red glow. The compass card was moving. It swung steadily until magnetic north had been pulled through a 180-degree arc.

Yablonski's eyes bulged, darting around the compartment.

"What the hell could do that?" Hammond asked. "The generator?"

Yablonski shook his head. He was backing away, forcing McWilliams back behind him. McWilliams froze, sure that he had bumped into something. But nothing was there. His fingers stretched into the darkness and felt around. He touched something at about shoulder level and three feet away, but he couldn't see what.

"Jesus!" he sputtered. "What the hell is this?"

Hammond swung his light around to McWilliams' shaking fingers. They appeared to be meeting resistance. In the light beam, he and Yablonski watched with rising astonishment as an apparition began to take shape. Under the lieutenant's groping fingers, a sallow face materialized, bobbing slightly in mid-air. Sunken pale-green eyes gazed at the light. Then shoulders appeared, covered by a watch-jacket and an open shirt with gold oak leaves pinned to the collars. The image spread downward; the uniform was Navy, but decidedly out-of-date.

McWilliams was moaning, his words jumbled.

Hammond wrenched his eyes from the apparition's face. There, on the jacket over the breast pocket, was a name stenciled in black letters . . .

SARTOG.

McWilliams tried to pull away, but a ghostly hand locked onto his wrist and he shrieked. The head turned slowly and the eyes swung past Hammond to rest on the compass stand. Thin lips struggled to form a word, but there was no sound.

Hammond followed Sartog's gaze and saw the binnacle light on the compass wink out. Then the compass card spun rapidly back the other way, the degree indicators blurring in the dim light.

McWilliams threw up his hands violently, breaking the grip on his wrist. He crashed to the deck and rolled backwards.

As soon as contact was broken, the body started to fade from view. Hammond couldn't move: he was mesmerized by the pain and suffering etched into that tormented face. The vanishing hand stretched out toward him and the eyes pleaded for him to take it. . . .

Yablonski shouted, "Grab him!" and lunged forward, tripping over McWilliams and sprawling to the deck.

Hammond tried to take the hand and missed. He watched the phantom disintegrate, fading to a dim pulse of light, then out, leaving no trace.

Yablonski crawled across the deck and jabbed at the air, trying to make contact again. Too late. The thing was gone. They were frozen in silence, listening to their own labored breathing. Hammond recalled Rinehart's chilling words: "Sartog went zero and got locked out." The phrase drummed at his mind again and again, finally blending with the rain beating overhead. And he remembered Warrington and the other crewmen getting locked out in their hospital rooms, the laying-on of hands the only thing that saved them. But this was something else. What had Rinehart called it? "Deadlock. A state of invisible suspension." The victim was trapped in another dimension. Scattered atoms, confined to a certain area, waiting to be brought back into a cohesive whole by human touch and something else. . . . Residual velocity of the force field? After thirty-odd years? It didn't seem possible . . . or likely. He gazed again at the compass. There were magnets built into it to act as dampers, to keep it accurate. Only a magnetic field stronger than the one in the compass could have caused the shift they had witnessed.

And the reappearance of Sartog.

But what magnetic field? Where?

Yablonski stood up, shoulders sagging in despair. He took it as a personal failure. "He went zero on us, Hammond—"

McWilliams also rose. "Mother of God," he groaned.

"What the hell was that?" He stumbled to the hatch, avoiding the area where the figure had materialized.

Hammond edged toward the spot and felt around slowly, carefully, for Sartog's body. Nothing. Not even a trace of body heat.

"Come on, Hammond. We've had enough." Yablonski was standing at the hatch with McWilliams.

"What do you mean, enough?" Hammond controlled his own shaking. "I thought you were hot to get these people. Christ, we've got more evidence than we can handle—"

"No heroics, damnit!" Yablonski snarled. "Let's be smart and get reinforcements." McWilliams nodded vigorously.

Hammond stared at them. Of course Cas was right. Hammond was himself feeling giddy, spaced-out. Events were moving too fast. Sartog—what an astonishing find! He felt daring, but he couldn't risk the lives of these two men.

He stepped out and looked fore and aft, but the rain obscured his vision. He swung his leg over the lip of the bridge and one-handed himself down the ladder, followed by the others.

On the main deck, he drew the Browning again, and released the safety. Now it was getting to him too. The silence seemed ominous. Even the rain thudded louder than usual. He motioned for Yablonski and McWilliams to go ahead to the gangplank.

Then they all heard a hatch slam open somewhere aft.

They stood like granite statues just behind the starboard breakwater, each one ready to urge the others to run, each so petrified he couldn't move.

A figure appeared on the main deck, and they fumbled with their flashlights. The figure froze, caught in the triple beam.

"McCarthy!"

It was Yablonski who yelled. Hammond peered through the rain at the figure backing away toward the lifeboat mounting.

Yablonski swore and charged after him.

Dr. McCarthy stumbled backward and almost fell through the open hatch.

"Yablonski!" Hammond yelled, cocking the Browning. He broke into a run, McWilliams following, and they caught up with Cas a moment after he had jumped into the passageway. A noise from aft drew all three flashlight beams. For an instant, they saw McCarthy again; then he shot down a ladder and disappeared from view.

"The engine room!" yelled Hammond, wondering even as he said it why McCarthy would go there, allowing himself to be trapped.

Then Yablonski bolted down the corridor and Hammond stopped thinking. He just ran, with McWilliams at his heels. They stormed down the ladder, stumbled through two other compartments, then stopped just short of the engine room.

The overhead lights were off.

Hammond stuck his head through the hatch and looked down. "McCarthy!" he yelled. "You've had it! Come on out!"

No answer. Hammond beamed his flashlight down, taking cover behind the hatch. No one fired back at him, so he eased out onto the platform and swept the engine room with his light. McCarthy was nowhere to be seen.

Yablonski heard it first—a low whirring sound. He stiffened in alarm.

Hammond listened. The whirring sound grew.

On impulse, Hammond swung his light over to the pump casings. Fear shot through him as he realized how wrong all this was. McCarthy could escape just by punching the back of his neck and disappearing. Why run down here, back to the pedestal?

Unless it was a trap.

The balsa crate was lying where he'd placed it, and he could just make out the top of the pedestal. He swung the light away and realized the pedestal was glowing—horizontal shafts of orange-yellow, stacked one on top of the other like light through venetian blinds . . . or through a vent.

And then he understood why Sartog had reappeared. The magnetic field generated by that thing when McCarthy had used it to come aboard—

"He's started the force field!" Yablonski shouted and yanked on Hammond's arm, making him drop the gun. It fell off the platform and smacked to the deck, going off with a loud crack!

Hammond whirled, stunned immobile. Of course! He watched Yablonski's eyes widen in terror as the pitch began to build. Like lambs to the slaughter, they had been *led* down here.

Hammond shoved McWilliams out of the hatch. "We've got to get off!"

McWilliams needed no further urging. He shot down the corridor, knocking the flashlight against a hatch and losing it. The beam whipped around before hitting the deck and going out.

By the time they made the ladder, the midsection was fading out in concentric radiation. McWilliams heaved himself up, then helped Yablonski and Hammond. He whirled to charge up the next corridor. Yablonski grabbed him.

"Grab hands!" he shouted, locking onto both of them. They careened along the corridor, trying to ignore the plates fading beneath their feet.

McWilliams got a glimpse of what was happening and slammed himself against the bulkhead. Yablonski kicked him and shouted, "Don't look! Run!"

The access hatch was only a faint outline when they stumbled through it, bashing their limbs against already invisible metal.

The main deck was completely invisible. Shadowy outlines shimmered below, then faded away. Machinery beneath their feet gave way to open water.

They sprawled on the solidity of the deck, afraid to move, yet they could see the next destroyer, whole and unaffected, only yards away. They scrambled toward it.

A wall of energy rolled over them as, with hands still linked, they struggled to their feet. They raced around the base of the bridge and crashed into the invisible deck gun.

"We're not going to make it!" Hammond yelled.

"We've got to!" Yablonski snapped back, and felt the way for them with his leg extended, around the open end of the steel wall.

Hammond felt himself falling. Yablonski tightened his grip and suddenly threw McWilliams forward like a discus, over the rail and onto the next ship. The effort was too much. He lost his own balance, staggered backwards, and sprawled on top of Hammond.

Then everything began to darken around them. Hammond tried to scoot toward the rail, but Yablonski held him down, warning, "Too late! Don't leave the field!"

Hammond remembered what had happened to Martin and stared with growing terror at McWilliams on the other DE.

McWilliams had landed in a heap and looked back, horrified to see Hammond, Yablonski, and the *Sturman* completely disappear from sight.

Mooring lines that secured the four remaining ships went slack. The ships slipped into the trough left by the *Sturman*. McWilliams was thrown across the deck.

His yell of surprise was drowned out by the sound of snapping lines and grinding metal as the remaining DEs compensated for the outboard loss.

22

Sprawled on the deck on his hands and knees, Hammond watched with horror the destroyer vanishing underneath him.

In the misty grayness, with the generator screaming to a high pitch around him, he saw his own flesh fade to a vague shadow. Fingers closed about his arm; vibrations coursed through the contact. His body became light and airy; his muscles relaxed; limbs turned to rubber. Forces built up around him, surging from beneath to totally engulf him. Pressure in his head became a rhythmic ache, pounding like surf on a rocky shore. The light waned to feeble, and the last thing he saw was the terror-stricken expression on Yablonski's nearly vanished face.

Then he slipped through a veil of blackness and lost all feeling, all sensation. He was numb even to the overwhelming sense of dread within him.

He drifted in space for an endless time, then consciousness rolled back and he felt a reassuring touch on his arm, a grip that rooted him to something.

Seconds later, he revived to the echo of turbines winding down in some vast expanse of enclosed emptiness. He thought he was in a tomb. Murky blackness, then a thunderous clap of water smashed against hull plates, and his eyes pierced a rapidly clearing fog. In the gloom, he felt his body and the deck beneath it return to solid wholeness.

He couldn't move. There was serenity and peace in not moving. He was afraid if he did move it would start all over again. His head weighed a ton and sagged between his stiffened arms; he still crouched on hands and knees. The grip on his arm had become viselike. He glued his eyes to the wooden deck and thought he could see molecules swarming back to inert stability.

After a moment, the pressure drained from his head

and he was able to raise it a few inches, expanding his range of vision. It was still dark, though not as black as a moment before. Again he was sensitive to an echo and had the impression he was indoors. But it was still the deck of the *Sturman* under his touch. Through the darkness he saw shapes high overhead and immense wooden beams on either side.

Rafters. And the intersection of a catwalk.

He and Yablonski and the *Sturman* had all moved into some sort of huge enclosure. Not a tomb at all, but a old wooden shed.

Hammond glanced to his right to see what was gripping him. Yablonski's knuckles were bone-white, wrapped around Hammond's upper arm.

Hammond wobbled to his feet and helped Yablonski up. They heard shouting and tried to focus on the sound, somewhere off the starboard bow. They saw men with flashlights hurrying along a narrow platform that ran toward the hull of the *Sturman*.

Suddenly, Hammond knew where they were. This enormous shed was a floating indoor drydock.

More shouts—from hefty men wearing gray jumpsuits, with automatic weapons slung over their shoulders. The platform inclined to an elevated ramp off the starboard side from which the men grabbed the *Sturman*'s mooring lines and attached them to stanchions.

Hammond had just taken a hesitant step forward when a voice boomed over a loudspeaker: "Commander Hammond, Mr. Yablonski, stay where you are. We'll come for you in just a moment."

Lights came on overhead, worklights among the rafters, casting eerie shadows across the *Sturman*'s foredeck. Patches of illumination spread down the walls of the shed, lined with big squares of insulating fabric.

The *Sturman* sat in shallow water with her bow nosed in like a car in a garage. There was enough room on the port side to park a second ship of the same size. And along that opposite wall was an enormous movable derrick with a twenty-ton swinging crane, on a set of tracks sunk into a concrete abutment.

Off the stern, at the open-sea end, were huge doors that looked as if they were meant to swing outward on underwater rails. Some thirty yards beyond the bow was a broad loading platform that jutted from the back wall, then continued around the right side as a narrow ramp until it rose and spread into a wide dock; that was where the armed men were milling.

Built into the wall behind the loading platform was a glassed-in control room. In the half-light emanating through the window, Hammond could make out shadowy figures working at instrument panels.

A diminishing glow from somewhere on the left wall of the shed drew his attention. Then he caught another one fading out overhead.

Pedestals. They were larger models of the ones he had seen in Bloch's vault and the *Sturman*'s engine room. There were four of them, one centered on each of the three insulated walls and one on the ceiling.

Hammond touched Yablonski's arm and pointed them out. "This shed is a colossal receiving station," he said. "The granddaddy of them all."

They were startled by a loud ratcheting sound from the dock to starboard. A gangplank swung out from the wall and was lowered on chains until it landed on the *Sturman*'s deck with a reverberating crash. More lights came up on that side, and they saw the dockworkers coming aboard with their weapons at the ready.

Hammond counted only five of them. And he recognized two as the muggers he and Yablonski had fought outside the inn in Georgetown. He had the vague satisfaction of confirming his earlier guess: the gang was indeed small.

Then Joe Coogan walked up the gangplank and stepped aboard, dressed in a plain suit and a turtleneck sweater. His coat flap was open, exposing a pistol in a hip holster. Coogan stood beside the starboard ammunition box for a moment, then spoke to one of the armed dockworkers. The man nodded and went up the ladder to the bridge.

Coogan smiled benignly across the forward deck at Hammond and Yablonski, who were standing next to the port breakwater.

"Well . . . did you have a nice *flight*?" he asked with a small laugh.

Yablonski took a step forward, but Hammond touched his shoulder in restraint. Coogan approached them and peered at their faces.

"You don't look too bad, just a little shopworn. Will you accompany me to the captain's cabin?"

Hammond gave Yablonski a small nod, indicating they

had no choice but to cooperate. Coogan sent them up the ladder to the bridge and then along the starboard side. The armed guard was waiting for them, posted outside the captain's door. Hammond wondered if Coogan knew about Sartog, the ghost of the navigating bridge. What if he appeared again? The guard opened the door and they entered a small, box-sized stateroom.

Sitting in the captain's chair was Dr. McCarthy.

He met Yablonski's stare with cold hostility. When Yablonski advanced on him, Coogan stepped between them.

"Sit down, gentlemen," he said. "No one's going to harm you. We're businessmen, not murderers." He smiled, expecting a retort, but Hammond said nothing. He sat on the bunk and Yablonski joined him. Coogan closed the door and said, "Well, Commander, were you impressed by your journey?"

"Possibly. Tell me where we are."

"Micro-Technology Laboratories, Plant Number Two, San Pedro, California."

"Okay, I'm impressed."

"Three thousand miles, Commander. We brought you clear across the country in less than ten seconds, though it may have seemed longer to you. Actually, it took more time to tie this ship to the dock than it did to get it here."

Hammond denied him the satisfaction of astonishment. "Those things on the walls outside," he said, "on the ceiling, in the engine room below, and in Bloch's bathroom—that's your mechanism?"

"Of course. And this . . . well, let me show you." He took off his jacket, rolled down the neck of his sweater and exposed a small button device strapped around his neck with insulated leads running down his back and across his shoulders. The harness traced a line down either side of his body. He turned so they could see it.

"If I want to move from here to the house in Georgetown, I call there and have the receiver coordinates set, then press this button whenever I'm ready to move, and poof! I'm there almost instantly. I can go anywhere I want if a receiver is pre-set to accommodate me."

"Sure cuts down on air fare."

"Doesn't it? Now, this adjustment is really interesting." He pulled up the bottom of his sweater to expose a small computer strapped to his side, a flat pancake of metal with a tiny keyboard. "I can move only myself or expand the field by punching out a diameter. I can teleport everything contained in the field with which I am in direct contact. This capability allows me to move objects of considerable size, such as—"

"A truck?" suggested Hammond. "Like the one you chased me with in New Mexico?"

"Like a truck, certainly. Or a destroyer . . ." He smiled and spread his hands to encompass the *Sturman.* "Except moving this ship required a modification of her special apparatus, which has been aboard for . . . oh, a couple of decades or so. Actually, this is the first time we've ever moved anything this size such a great distance. You've made history with us, Commander."

Hammond stared at his smile. He wanted to tear at it with his bare hands, but he couldn't move. He felt himself getting weak and woozy. Coogan came close enough to be grabbed, but Hammond could hardly lift a finger. Coogan peered into his eyes.

"Electro-narcosis," muttered McCarthy.

"Ah, yes," Coogan grunted. "This happens occasionally, Commander, to people who don't regularly travel by this method. It'll wear off in a while. Tell you what: why don't you and Mr. Yablonski ponder the implications of your status while the doctor and I go get you something to eat?"

Hammond saw Coogan's hand come out and approach his shoulder. For a second, he thought Coogan was going to strangle him; then he felt a finger poke him lightly on the collarbone. He fell backward, conscious but helpless.

Coogan laughed and opened the door. He went out with McCarthy, who slammed the door shut.

From his angle on the bunk, Hammond could see the shed lights reflected in the captain's porthole—a soft, comforting glow. He concentrated on it.

A few minutes later, he was able to sit up. The weakness faded and he glanced at Yablonski, who had apparently suffered the same reaction: he was breathing in short bursts, his hands clutching the bunk. They sat and observed each other for a long time, then Hammond said, "I hope McWilliams follows through."

"What good will that do?" grumbled Yablonski. "We vanished. As far as they're concerned, we're gone. How are they ever going to find us?"

Yablonski bent over and rubbed his head in his hands.

Hammond tried to reassure him: "Look, if they intended bumping us off, they would have done it already. Let's just sit back and see what comes."

"It's not that," moaned Yablonski. "It's the aftereffects. I can't go through all that again!"

"It won't happen. They seem to have gotten the bugs out. Coogan and McCarthy use the process all the time."

Yablonski made an attempt to believe it, but he was still not buying. "I'm telling you, they're messing with something that can backfire. It happened before."

Yablonski had nearly thirty years of horror associated with this business: he couldn't be expected to accept it.

The food arrived a half hour later, and with it, F.P. Bloch.

The guard entered first with a tray of sandwiches and beer. Another guard could be seen outside the door. Yablonski had been seated in the captain's chair when the door opened. He got up and backed away from the guard. Hammond lay on the bunk and didn't move, just watched. He had removed his useless shoulder holster.

He didn't even react with surprise when Bloch stepped in and closed the door. Bloch too used teleportation. And why not? His tall, cadaverous form was outlined in the half-light from the single desk lamp as he surveyed his prisoners. Hammond took a long look at him, noting the face shaped like an inverted triangle, the blue Pierre Cardin suit, black alligator loafers, and dark burgundy tie. Bloch smelled of expensive cologne.

He swung the captain's chair back to front and straddled it, resting one arm across the back. With the other he reached for a sandwich and took a healthy bite. He looked up at Yablonski's strained face.

"Not bad. Can I interest you fellows—?" He held the tray out with the thinnest of smiles. Yablonski took it and offered a sandwich to Hammond, who accepted one without a word. Yablonski returned the tray and Bloch tossed them each a beer. He took one himself. When his guests were eating and he felt caution had been dropped, Bloch said, "I know all about your meeting in Washington this morning, Hammond. While I'm not inclined to do anything nasty to you, if I'm forced to, I will. Understand?"

"I think Mr. Yablonski would like to know who's feeding him."

"My apologies." Bloch extended a hand to Yablonski. "Francis Bloch," he said.

Yablonski hesitantly shook hands. Bloch's smile flashed on like a warning light, and off just as quickly. He turned back to Hammond.

"I've come to the conclusion," he said, "that it's dangerous to have you on the wrong side. You've seen our demonstration: have you any idea of the potential?"

"I think so," said Hammond, watching Yablonski retreat into a corner.

"In any case, let me point out a few things." Bloch sipped his beer, thought for a moment, then chose his words carefully. "Look at the turmoil this country is in today. Because of an energy crisis, foreign nations are holding a sword at our throats. Transportation costs are rising, manufacturing costs and taxes"—he shook his head and announced with disgust—"incredible!"

Hammond's eyes probed him, reading an unexpected sincerity in the way he sat, the gestures he made.

"Government bureaucracy," continued Bloch, "a hopelessly stupid entanglement through which nobody can move with expediency. Who suffers? The people. Correct?"

Hammond nodded. "So far."

"I can rectify this, Commander." Bloch gestured with one hand. "I can change things. Use your imagination. Can you see how?" He waited for Hammond to comment.

"You tell me."

Bloch stood up, thrust one hand into a pocket, and began pacing. "What do you think would happen if overnight we could do away with the normal means of transporting freight and replace it with something far more efficient and infinitely less expensive? I mean do away with trains, ships, planes, trucks. Not only would we cut down on the unit cost of a product, but we would do away with the need for transportation fuel, for *oil*. We would break the stranglehold these foreigners now have on our commerce!"

He stopped for a moment and eyed Hammond with interest.

Hammond was motionless, then he said, "You want to put the Arabs out of business?"

"A marginal benefit."

"Then why invite them to your parties?"

"In any endeavor, there are winners and losers, Hammond. I enjoy observing their distress."

Probably enjoys pulling the wings off butterflies, too, thought Hammond, but he said nothing.

"Perhaps you don't realize what we've accomplished," Bloch resumed. "We moved the *Sturman* clear across the country in seconds. And this is not the only receiving station of this size. In the last two years, we have been quietly planting them around the world. We buy a shipping yard or warehouse in a city like Tokyo or Bangkok or London, three technicians go over to install the equipment, and we're operational within several months. We have already located ourselves at eleven sites around the world, and that includes a half-dozen stations in this country. If need be, Commander, I can move you and the *Sturman* to New Zealand or Alaska in an instant! I can move anything: enormous quantities of food, clothing, prefabricated shelter for starving nations. In a matter of hours, I can relieve people who are suffering the effects of a natural disaster—"

Hammond interrupted, "And move armies? Tanks, weapons, bombs?"

Bloch stopped again and smiled. "Coming from a military man, I should have expected that. You may not believe me, but I have no interest in using it that way." His eyes grew cold and he leaned closer to Hammond. "However, if it falls into the hands of the U.S. Government, that's exactly what it will be used for."

The silence was deadly. Hammond regarded Bloch with stony suspicion, but he couldn't get the man to falter or even look away. He believed what he had just said, believed it wholeheartedly.

Hammond came back cruelly. "You siphoned off government money to develop it. I think they'll insist on ownership."

"First they must get hold of it. And until now, I've been too careful to let that happen." He sat down again.

"Once they find out you've been kiting funds for twenty years, there won't be a thing you can do to stop it."

Bloch smiled slightly. "Consider yourself apart from the Navy for a moment, out of the service, simply a voting American." He tilted forward on his chair and said simply, *"What makes you think the government will make better use of this than I will?"*

The question caught Hammond completely off guard. He glanced at Yablonski, who still stood in the corner, his face hidden in shadow.

Bloch untangled himself from the chair and stood up, unbuttoning his coat and putting his free hand on one hip. "Twenty-odd years ago," he said, "the Navy gave up developing this because its future as a weapon was dubious. That was as far as they could see. I took it over because I saw the real potential. I was involved with Traben before 1953, before the so-called accidental experiment that sent the *Sturman* from Philadelphia to Norfolk. And let me tell you something, Commander Hammond, it was no accident."

Bloch looked sharply at Yablonski and continued, "The whole business with frequency modulation was carefully engineered to accomplish precisely what it did. It was *my idea then*—and it's mine *now*."

He looked back at Hammond. "My interests lie in economics and world commerce, Commander. I'm a businessman, not a murderer."

Hammond smiled. Coogan's line. But it wasn't hard to tell which one was the mimic. "That depends on the scale," he said. "To you, a few lives lost in the line of business are like casualties in a war. You don't consider yourself responsible."

"You have to see the whole picture," Bloch shrugged.

"I'd like to tell you how many admirals I've heard that from. In case you haven't heard, Mr. Bloch, the ends don't justify the means."

"How do you think the people would react if they found out we had something that could help relieve massive suffering and the government was going to take it over and use it only as they saw fit?"

Hammond swung his legs over the bunk and swooped to his feet in a move that startled Bloch. "You think they're going to trust *you* instead? You're as transparent as glass! You're not doing this for the starving children in Asia. You're a businessman out for profit. You're playing a power game and you've got a price! You'll sell to the highest bidder, whether it's the U.S. Government or the richest American oil company, and you've been courting *them* like a lovesick suitor!"

Bloch bore the attack in silence, his face at dead calm. When Hammond was through, he rebuttoned his coat, saying, "You're contaminated, Hammond. You've been in government too long. You can't see through them the way I can."

"Maybe so, but I'd like to know how you intend to retain control of your great discovery."

At that, Bloch's smile became almost obscene. "I will set up a network of teleporting devices around the world, in every nation that will buy them—and they all will, even the Arabs, because they won't be able to compete in the world market without them—and that network will be serviced strictly by my own personnel. If anyone tries to tamper with our operation, the machines will be removed the same way we removed the *Sturman*. Instantly." His voice rose: "When teleportation arrives on the market, no country or business will afford to be without it. Otherwise, they will simply cease to exist."

The implications were staggering. If Bloch was right, he was going to be the world's next biggest monopoly and, after a few years of successful business, perhaps the only game in town. Economic control was the only possible way to dominate in this world, and Bloch had the means to make it work.

"Even our way of life will change," Bloch was saying, expounding on his dream. "The daily routine we depend on will be different. And it's all going to happen quickly. It's taken us years to perfect this, but now it's only a matter of putting it into production and acquiring locations. You're at the age, Commander, when you're still flexible enough to accept the changes, to roll with them. I admire your tenacity and intelligence. You have pursued us with consummate skill and a lot of ingenuity. I do not share Admiral Corso's opinion of you. Do you understand what I'm saying?"

Hammond shook his head.

"I'm offering you your life," said Bloch. "I want you to join me, immediately."

Hammond stared at him, hardly believing his ears. He asked simply, "What about Yablonski?"

Bloch held Hammond's gaze long enough to communicate an unspoken answer. Then he swung his eyes around and settled on Yablonski's pale features. Yablonski's eyes were slitted coals of defiance.

Bloch became silky smooth. "Of course there's a place for you as well," he said, without specifying. He turned back to Hammond pointedly. "Think it over. Both of you."

He turned and rapped twice on the door. It swung open and he stepped out. Hammond heard his steps fading away.

The guard remained poised outside the door. A second man came in to remove the lunch tray. When he went out, Hammond heard a bolt slide. He jumped quickly to the door and pressed his ear against the wood.

He listened until the jiggling sound of the tray had completely faded, then he heard a scuffling sound just outside the door: the guard had remained.

"So there's a place for me, too," he heard Yablonski snort, and turned to see him step into the light, his cheek quivering with rage. "Sure there is," he continued. "Underwater inspector without air."

"Probably," Hammond agreed.

Yablonski pulled off his jacket and tossed it aside, then sank down on the bunk and ran a hand through his hair.

Hammond looked at his own hands; they were quivering. Nerves. Was it Bloch's confidence or this ship and its ghosts? Sartog—Hammond shivered. He felt he hadn't seen the last of Sartog.

What to do about now?

Maybe if Bloch was serious about wanting Hammond on his side, Yablonski's life could be bartered into the deal. But the idea of negotiating with these horrors on any terms filled Hammond with nausea. There was no choice.

They had to escape.

23

The silence in the cabin was broken by a series of thuds from somewhere forward. Hammond looked out a porthole. Three dockworkers were struggling to fold the yellow tarp that had been wrapped around the bridge superstructure. He watched as they lowered the huge canvas down the ladder, then left the ship with it, clumping down the loading ramp.

The sound of a heavy door closing reverberated throughout the shed. The soft illumination outside faded to darkness as the worklights were dimmed.

"What's going on?" Yablonski asked, his voice flat, unemotional.

"They took down the tarp that was covering the bridge."

"Oh, Christ," said Yablonski, "they're going to send the ship somewhere else. . . ."

Hammond suspected he was right. Whether one or both of them would be going with it, he didn't even want to guess, but the *Sturman* was probably due for a quick trip to some out-of-the-way port, where it could not be traced and they could take their time about destroying it.

"You know," said Hammond, "unless my count is wrong, there's only one guard left in this whole shed—the clown right outside our door." Hammond saw a glimmer of hope shoot across Yablonski's face. "That doesn't mean we can get out of this," he continued, "but it does cut the odds."

"To what?" Yablonski mumbled. "To only one of us getting killed?"

"Look, why do you suppose we're still alive?"

Yablonski shrugged. "They're slow."

"No, I think something's holding them back. If Bloch really wants me to throw in with him, then he won't dare mess around with you: he knows I'd never cooperate."

He watched Yablonski carefully, not believing his own

words for a second, but hoping they would have the right effect. It was so preposterous, Bloch's trying to hire him. What for? Unless Bloch was planning to do away with some other member of the team, such as that renowned fumble-foot, McCarthy. Yes, that made at least a bit of sense.

Yablonski slid to the edge of the bunk and said, "Suppose you're wrong. Suppose it's all lies and he does intend to get rid of us, and he's just stringing us along until . . . until there's some reaction in Philadelphia! If they come knocking at his door, asking for the *Sturman*, then he'll get rid of us!"

Hammond silently mouthed a curse. Yablonski hadn't been fooled by his optimism. It didn't take much imagination to picture what was going on in Philadelphia and Washington right now. The Navy might occasionally misplace a ship, but if they got an eyewitness report of one *disappearing*, it would shake up an awful lot of people. McWilliams had escaped by a hair's-breadth and could tell quite a story. But could he? How sure was Hammond that he had escaped? How sure was Bloch? McCarthy would tell him there had been three men aboard, but only two had been captured. Where was the third? At large in Philadelphia? Bloch would picture the same sequence of events as Hammond: the third man going to the authorities, probably the higher-ups at NIS; Smitty immediately suspecting who was responsible, then descending on MTL's Manhattan Beach plant like lightning. That would tip off Bloch to get rid of the *Sturman*. And Hammond. And Yablonski. Not in a million years would Smitty think to check MTL's San Pedro plant first.

Bloch had run a risk snatching the *Sturman* from Philadelphia. He had given Hammond the hard evidence he needed. If the NIS could walk into this shed and catch him with the ship, that would be all they'd need to lock him away forever.

But time was clearly on Bloch's side, and one minute was all he needed to dispose of the evidence.

Only if Hammond and Yablonski could escape and let somebody know where they were, and how they arrived here, could they hope to nail Bloch. Then, even if he disposed of the destroyer, the presence of these two men, three thousand miles from where they had been seen only an hour before, would be enough to clinch the case.

Briefly, he explained it all to Yablonski. "What the hell do we do about it?" Cas asked.

"Wait for the next guy who comes through that door. Then make our own opportunity. Until then, try to get some sleep."

Yablonski frowned deeply, then sighed and stretched out on the bunk.

Hammond eased into the captain's chair and closed his eyes, forcing his mind to slow down. He was confident now that he had a handle on what had to be done.

The cabin door slammed open and woke him. Out of the corner of his eye, he saw Yablonski shrink against the bulkhead. The guard stepped in, carrying a compact submachine gun. Then Dr. McCarthy's bulk filled the doorway, a brown leather case clutched loosely in his hand.

"Thought I'd drop in and see how you're doing," McCarthy boomed.

"Is this an authorized visit?" Hammond asked, rubbing sleep from his eyes.

McCarthy put the case down on the captain's desk, opened it, and pulled out a bottle of brandy and two snifters. "Compliments of F.P. Bloch," he said. "Old and good." He filled both glasses and, with a sweeping gesture, indicated they should help themselves.

Yablonski stayed rooted against the bulkhead, his face ashen. McCarthy's eyes swung to Hammond. "What are you waiting for?" he demanded. "Oh, I get it! You think it's drugged! Well—" He snatched up the bottle and took a healthy swallow.

He lowered the bottle, blew out a gust of air to cool his mouth, and, with great solemnity, handed a glass to Yablonski.

Cas reached for it gingerly. His eyes never left McCarthy.

McCarthy turned with a crooked smile. "You too, Commander. We're gonna drink a toast—to your future."

Hammond reached for the remaining glass and nodded at the guard. "How about your friend?"

"He's still on duty. Wouldn't do to have us all in the bag now, would it?"

Hammond took a sip. McCarthy was right: the brandy was good. "Are you really a doctor?" he asked.

"Sure I am!" McCarthy laughed, raised the bottle, and

took another pull, waving his free hand at Hammond. "Bloch wants you, Hammond. Wants to add you to the family."

Hammond snorted.

"What the old man wants, he gets. Always." He rocked back on his heels and chuckled throatily, enjoying a private joke.

The bottle clinked as he set it down on the desk. "Too bad that doesn't include Yablonski."

Hammond measured the distance to the guard. The submachine gun was pointed at his midsection.

McCarthy wagged a finger at him and warned, "Don't try it." He smiled at Hammond, then turned and reached into the brown case. He pulled out a duplicate of the tape recorder and microphone he'd used on Yablonski in Boston.

Yablonski saw it and moaned. Hammond felt his stomach roil. "Does Bloch think I'll work for him if you do this to Cas?"

McCarthy wrapped the mike cord around his wrist and glared. He pointed the mike at Hammond, who flinched instinctively. "Get used to this little gadget," he said. "Because after I've taken care of your friend, I'll start on you."

McCarthy made a final adjustment on the tape recorder, then slung the strap over his shoulder and let the instrument hang at his side.

"In case nobody mentioned it before, Hammond," he said, "we know where Mrs. Fletcher is . . . and Mrs. Yablonski."

Hammond felt himself stiffen. He opened his mouth but couldn't get his breath. He made a move to rise and the guard pushed him down with the barrel of the submachine gun. He glanced at Cas—who was staring at McCarthy, quivering with rage.

"So everybody's going to cooperate, right?" McCarthy continued smoothly. "Drink up, Yablonski. Might as well go happy."

Helpless, Hammond watched Yablonski slowly drain his glass, then drop it on the bunk. Cas drew up his legs and huddled against the bulkhead, his mouth closed, cheeks puffed out, looking as if his face were about to explode.

Satisfied that there was going to be no trouble, McCarthy punched the record button and a low hum started.

Yablonski covered his ears, trying to block out the sound. Two steps and McCarthy was at the bunk, holding the mike in front of him like a magic wand.

"Come on, Cas," he crooned. "It's just a little sixty-cycle hum, a soothing tone. It can't hurt you; it never has before. You've always liked it, Cas. It brings relief, remember? The nightmares—you don't like the nightmares. You don't want them anymore, do you? Want to get rid of them once and for all? Come on, Cas—"

He had an amazing, hypnotic tone, once he got going, but the drinking had made him impatient. And when he realized Yablonski wasn't responding, he grew irritated. Yablonski was clutching his ears so tightly, his fingers had turned white. McCarthy rapped on his knuckles with the mike—gently at first then with increasing vigor, all the while keeping up his patter.

Hammond watched, seething. All he could think of was Jan at the safe house, Jan curled up by a fire, waiting for him to come back, by a fire . . . like Rinehart . . . a sitting duck.

"Come on, Cas, quit playing with me. It's not getting you anywhere. This is what you've wanted all your life: relief from the torment, from those endless dreams of men vanishing, crewmates slipping through walls, drifting to their deaths, exploding into infinity. . . . Come on. . . . Come on!"

McCarthy was shouting now and Hammond shook watching him slap Yablonski's wrists with the mike, torturing the man until Hammond didn't even realize he was on his feet, snarling, "You sonofabitch!"

The guard's machine gun appeared under his nose and he stopped.

Yablonski's head rolled from side to side as he slid lower in the bunk, trying to avoid the blows and shut out that voice. Strange animal-like sounds came from his throat. McCarthy leaned over, still coaxing him. He tried to pry one of Cas's hands loose.

That's what Yablonski had been waiting for.

Both his hands shot out. He pulled McCarthy's face down and spit the brandy he'd been holding in his mouth right into the doctor's widening eyes. Then he shoved with flexed legs, caught McCarthy in the pelvis and sent him hurtling into the startled guard. Both went down in a jumbled heap.

Hammond grabbed the back of the chair and swung it over his head, aiming for the two men at his feet. McCarthy managed to roll away a split second before the chair hit. The guard caught a blow in the ribs. Hammond dropped on him instantly and got him in a neck lock.

Yablonski came off the bunk with a bellow. McCarthy was pawing for the door. Yablonski clamped a hand over his open mouth and pulled him back. McCarthy's hands groped for Yablonski's throat, trying to wrap the mike cord around it.

The guard's fingers quivered from Hammond's pressure on his carotid artery, but he still clawed for the trigger of the submachine gun. Suddenly, he shook violently, and Hammond felt something give in his neck.

The guard slumped and Hammond ripped the weapon from his lifeless fingers, reversed the barrel and clubbed McCarthy across the back of his skull.

McCarthy moaned once, then Yablonski let him slip to the deck where he was still.

Yablonski's breath came in shuddering gasps. He reached for the submachine gun.

"Give me that, Hammond," he muttered, a wild look on his face.

"Don't be a fool, Cas. One shot and they'll be all over us."

Yablonski raised his foot to kick McCarthy's face in.

"We've bought some time!" Hammond warned. "Now let's use it!"

Yablonski's foot hovered. Slowly, he lowered it to the deck, his terrible rage subsiding.

Hammond used his own shoulder holster to tie McCarthy, and a piece of the dead guard's shirt to gag him. Hammond checked the passageway, then the two men slipped out together. Hammond closed and bolted the cabin door.

They were outside, on the starboard edge of the navigating bridge. Silently, they made their way aft.

They went down the ladder, then kept low to the deck, which was still wet from the Philadelphia rains, and headed for the stern. In the semi-darkness under dimmed work-lights, Hammond could see that a heavy net covered the shed doors. Steel mesh vanished into murky water, cable strands glistening dully in the thin reflections.

"We're not going to make it out that way," Hammond whispered. Yablonski nodded.

Both men moved cautiously back to the starboard side and peered down the length of the shed. The platform and ramp beyond were deserted. The only sound they heard was the gentle lapping of water against the *Sturman*'s hull.

They crept across the gangplank and down to the loading dock in silence. Hammond still carried the submachine gun.

Double steel doors were recessed into the back wall, a safety light glimmering over them. Hammond peered through the long window of the control room. It was empty. There were phones inside. If they could just get in there, call Smitty, get him to warn MAGIC. . . .

He scanned the edges of the doors for any trace of wiring that would indicate a security system. Finding none, he slowly depressed the bar and pushed one door open.

Hammond went through first. Yablonski followed quickly, easing the door shut until it closed with a soft click, the echo swallowed up in a long, windowless hallway that stretched off to their right.

Hammond tried the door to the control room. It was locked. He was tempted to shoot it open, but that would be the end. They'd never complete the phone call. He gave up.

A faint light illuminated the far end of the corridor. Cautiously, they made for that light, past steel doors closed and numbered. Their feet scraped on a concrete floor.

They rounded the distant corner to face an open locker room some twenty yards ahead. They padded toward it, hugging the wall, every sense alert.

At the entrance, Hammond peered in. The room widened five feet on either side of the open entryway; there were green metal lockers on either wall and a pair of wooden benches down the center. And no one around.

They walked in and Yablonski sank down on one of the benches, his eyes scanning the lockers. Hammond went to the far exit, a pair of double wooden doors with a glass port in each. He looked through and saw another light where the next corridor made a bend to the left. Hammond propped the submachine gun up against one of the lockers. He jiggled a few of the doors. They were all locked.

"You want to open them?" murmured Yablonski.

Hammond nodded. "We could use some more appropriate duds—and this seems to be the nearest haberdashery."

Yablonski rose and grabbed one of the door handles. "Put your hands up here," he said, "one above the other below mine. It'll cut down the noise."

"You've done this before?"

"The terror of P.S. 146."

Hammond braced his hands across the locker door. Yablonski squeezed, then twisted suddenly, snapping the handle off. Hammond's palms had absorbed most of the sound. He opened the locker and found a white lab coat with a name across the breast pocket. He grabbed a hard hat sitting on the shelf and slipped it on his head. A little big, but all the better. It would conceal his eyes. He ripped the nameplate off the coat and shrugged into it.

Cas broke into another locker and got a similar outfit for himself. Just before he swung the second door shut, Hammond reached in and snagged an aluminum clipboard. "Good prop," he said.

Yablonski shrugged. "What about the gun?"

"A little conspicuous," Hammond said, and deposited the submachine gun in the locker, then closed it. "Let's see how far we get with just the disguise."

Yablonski smiled grimly. "Fine, but if we run into trouble don't shoot anybody with that clipboard."

They went through the double doors, eased down the next corridor and around the bend. They ignored an elevator and took a stairway to the next floor.

Muffled sounds of activity floated down the corridor. Moving briskly, they headed for the noise, looking for all the world as if they owned the place.

The room they entered was two hundred feet long and two levels high. The ceiling was networked with catwalks, tracks, and overhead gantries. The floor was flat concrete and around the walls were electronic monitoring stations to which various projects were hooked up. A forklift zipped by on electric motors, carrying a large square piece of machinery to another side of the room. Men moved about, dressed exactly like Hammond and Yablonski, in white lab coats, even carrying clipboards. And in a central area, technicians were clustered around a low scaffold surrounding the silver shell of something Hammond recognized immediately.

He looked for cover and spotted several rows of metal

bins along the near wall, supply stations for wiring and parts. He nudged Yablonski and they moved behind the bins. Hammond set his clipboard on the edge of one. Yablonski pulled out two boxes of wiring and they made a show of taking inventory while they watched what was going on.

Hammond pointed out the scaffold and the silver shell and whispered to Yablonski, "That's satellite casing for an orbital instrument package. This must be the assembly station for the Vandenberg project they're working on."

"Nice to know something around here is legitimate."

Three men in lab coats and hard hats were placing a panel inside the casing. They slipped it through the opening and hooked it up. Hammond wondered if that casing already contained the weapons guidance system everybody was fussing over. A supervisor on the floor watched a computer readout. One of the men on the scaffold shouted down, "Third module in place!" The supervisor nodded, picked up a phone and dialed.

Gradually, Hammond became aware that all work had stopped. Everybody was standing quietly, waiting.

Hammond and Yablonski stood uneasily by the bins, continuing to list parts on the clipboard, wondering if the sudden quiet meant their escape had been discovered.

A door at the opposite end of the room opened to admit a small group of technicians, who moved quickly toward the scaffolding. Dr. Edmond Traben, President of MTL, was in the center of them. Two men followed, pushing a flatbed dolly on which was a three-foot-high piece of machinery covered with a tarp.

They stopped at the scaffold and Traben climbed a short ladder to join the technicians crouched around the silver casing. He stuck his head in for a personal inspection. Satisfied, he withdrew and motioned to a man on the catwalk above.

The hook of a chain hoist was lowered from the ceiling by a hydraulic motor. One of the men nearest the flatbed grabbed the descending hook while the other gently pulled the covering off the concealed device.

Hammond sucked in his breath: it was another teleporting pedestal.

Stunned, he watched them guide it off the dolly. It rose slowly toward Traben and the waiting technicians, and Hammond followed its arcing path, mesmerized.

"That's it!" He snapped out of it. "They're going to put one of those up in space! There *is* no goddamned weapons guidance system," he hissed, "or if there is, these technicians believe that pedestal is part of it!"

The pieces fell into place. With a receiving station in orbit, Bloch could virtually eliminate the enormous expense and materiel required to launch space stations and orbiting satellites. He could send up a vault like the one in his Georgetown bathroom as well as an army of men in spacesuits, supplies, prefabricated and pressurized sections for living quarters, weapons systems. . . . Hell, the guidance device was small potatoes. What if he sent up a couple of homemade ICBMs with nuclear warheads? He could beam anything he wanted up to this little station . . . *anything.*

The possibilities were staggering . . . and endless.

The pedestal had stopped moving. One of the technicians stood on the edge of the scaffold platform and guided it into place, the overhead chain following on its wheeled track.

Hammond shuddered. Smitty had said that MTL was supposed to deliver the satellite package to Vandenberg Air Force Base in four weeks. Some package, he thought. It was about to be stuffed with the Cracker Jack prize of all time.

He turned to Yablonski and muttered, "We've got to stop them."

"With what? Your clipboard?"

Hammond looked at the men clustered around the scaffolding. It would be suicidal to barge through and start ripping out wires and gear. How much could they accomplish before they were dragged down and battered senseless? They had to try something that was as much a diversion as an assault.

"Why don't we just go out the far door and get to a phone?" Yablonski suggested, angry that Hammond was willing to chance everything when they were so close to safety. "They're not ready to launch that thing."

Hammond shook his head. "I can't risk another Navy snafu." He glanced back at Traben coldly. "Besides, I owe them a few."

His eyes scanned the room, stopping when he spotted a fire hose in a glass case on the side wall. He pointed it out to Cas.

They left the clipboard at the bins and sauntered toward the wall, Hammond muttering instructions and Yablonski nodding as they approached the hose case.

"It's wired to an alarm system," Yablonski whispered, his face fixed in a forced smile.

Hammond didn't care about the alarm; in fact, it would probably help create the confusion they wanted. But he was trying to estimate the hose length. What if he couldn't get close enough to the scaffold? It would be too late to turn back. Still, it was their only chance.

He took a deep breath and yanked open the door.

For the first few seconds, Hammond was the only one in motion. Everyone else in the huge room froze, riveted by the clanging bell, then Yablonski cupped his hands and yelled:

"FIRE!"

There was pandemonium.

The lab coat flying behind him, Hammond sprinted through the work force, holding the nozzle firmly in his hands while Yablonski reeled out hose from the drum and continued to yell "Fire!" every couple of seconds.

Men scattered, some looking for the source of the fire, others rushing to exits or running to help Hammond, most thankfully ignoring Yablonski, who fed hose and tried to read the instructions on the water valve at the same time.

Hammond plunged through the knot of milling technicians as Yablonski hit the valve. Hammond stood for what seemed an eternity, waiting for the water, then his eyes locked with Traben's. The doctor was still standing on the platform. His mouth flew open.

"Stop that man!" Traben spluttered.

The nozzle jumped in Hammond's hands and the water tore out of the hose, the sound drowning out the warning. Hammond directed a powerful stream at four men moving toward him. The force blew them back and gave Hammond room to maneuver.

He dodged between the men pressing around him and kept them at bay. He heard Traben's thin screeching behind and above him, and he whirled to blast the white-faced scientist square in the chest. Traben shot backwards off the scaffold and landed in a knot of men.

Hammond swung the nozzle and watched with satisfaction as water ripped into the opening of the satellite casing, rocking it on the platform. The other technicians scattered, jumping to the floor. Ruptured equipment cascaded after them.

Hammond ducked a pair of clutching hands and spun away, lowered the nozzle, and played water over the circle of men closing in on him. Thundering pressure forced them to retreat.

Then Hammond heard Yablonski screaming for him somewhere to the rear. He aimed the stream back into the satellite and glanced back to see what was happening.

Yablonski was trying to fend off the men crowding around him at the water valve. Hammond whirled the hose and blasted them from ninety feet away. But he was too late. Yablonski went down under a tangle of arms and legs.

Hammond raced toward him, but the hose went limp: someone had shut off his water. He heard voices rise in a shout behind him, then he was buffeted from all sides, swarmed over by a mass of excited men, all trying to take their anger out on him with their fists.

The punishment finally stopped. Hammond was hauled up, his arms firmly pinned behind his back. He faced panting, furious faces. Then the circle parted.

Edmond Traben, his clothing soaked and his face twisted into a mask of hatred, stopped only a foot away, his eyes boring into Hammond's.

"Do you know what you've done?" he asked hoarsely.

Hammond returned the stare, then nodded slowly.

24

Coogan walked briskly across the assembly room. He glanced down at the pool of water spreading over the concrete floor, then waded through the crowd of scientists to inspect their drenched satellite.

Several technicians with rags were already vigorously trying to wipe the instruments clear. But it was a hopeless mess. Delicate wiring had been blown apart by the high-pressure spray. Exposed printed circuit boards that hadn't yet been sealed behind protector panels were bent out of shape. Transistors had popped free. Micro-circuitry was already clogging with lubricants blown down from parts that hadn't been degreased yet.

The pedestal had been knocked over, crushing part of the satellite's computer system. Coogan bent down and stared into the pedestal casing. It was a quarter full of water. The coils were soaked.

Behind him, Traben was growling curses. Coogan turned to push through the technicians and found himself facing Hammond, who greeted him with a smug grin. Yablonski was a few feet away, firmly gripped by two engineers.

When he saw Coogan, Traben was livid. He screamed, "You're head of security! How the hell did they get out?"

Coogan's arm snaked out and seemed to rest on Traben's back. No one saw his fingers pinch the nerve. Traben's mouth opened and his face went pale. Coogan relaxed his grip but his eyes silently warned Traben to shut up. That part of it Hammond saw, and wondered how Coogan had the nerve to do this to his boss.

Coogan's gaze flicked for an instant to Hammond, then he turned to the milling technicians and gave them an authoritative smile. "Everybody back to work. We're under control here now. Nothing to worry about."

He clasped a couple of men on the back and urged them along. One of the Chinese scientists who had been wiping down the flooded instruments turned a particularly anguished face on Coogan as he was being herded away.

"Terrible," the man said. "Just terrible . . ."

He twisted away from Coogan and marched up to Hammond and Yablonski, berating them with a string of Chinese invective rising in pitch to near-hysteria. The other scientists permitted the Chinese to handle it for a moment, then suddenly they were all yelling.

Coogan muscled through and held up his arms for silence. He shouted above the din, "Quiet! Everybody quiet! Leave this to me!"

Hammond was sure that he had guessed right about MTL: most of the scientists were quite unaware of what they were really working on.

The Chinese was only two feet away from him, staring at him now with tear-filled eyes. "Why?" Hammond heard him ask, barely comprehensible in the shouting. "Why you do this?"

"I'm a Naval investigative officer," Hammond explained. "What you're working on here is illegal—"

He shouldn't have spoken. Several men surged forward, wanting blood. Coogan had to shove them back like rowdies from a street gang. Traben shrank back to the satellite and watched, horrified.

"Get back!" yelled Coogan. "Every goddamned one of you! Get a grip on yourselves! It's under control!" He grabbed the Chinese and pushed him back with the others. The shouting died down and Hammond seized his opportunity.

"I'm a Naval investigative officer!" His voice rang out in the abrupt silence, loud enough for everyone to hear. "These men are—!"

Coogan whirled and belted him in the jaw, cutting him off. Hammond fell back, sprawling. Two more security men came bounding in, uniformed company cops. Coogan shouted at them to take Hammond and Yablonski out.

Hammond hovered between pain and consciousness and wasn't aware where he had been moved until he found himself in a bare corridor with a security man gripping his arms in a classic wrestling hold. Yablonski was held the same way, knees down to the floor. Their lab coats and hard hats had been removed and tossed on the floor.

Coogan charged through the door, followed by Traben, who continued to berate him. "Where were you, Coogan?

I thought these men were under heavy guard. Do you have any idea what they've done?"

Coogan whirled on him. "Look, you run your end and I'll run mine!"

"But they've set me back months!"

"That's enough!"

Traben gaped at him, incredulous but silent.

"Report to Bloch and have him meet us back aboard the *Sturman*."

Traben seemed to shrink again. Hammond began to have a clearer idea of who was running things around here. Traben cast a sidelong look at Hammond and Yablonski, then muttered, "I want them out of the way."

Coogan said nothing.

Traben headed for the elevator and called back at the last second, "And do it yourself. McCarthy is hopeless!"

The elevator doors closed on him and Coogan turned back to Hammond, coldly assessing him.

Hammond still managed a pained grin. "Dissension in the ranks?"

Coogan let loose with a balled fist to his gut. Hammond's eyes flew open in shock. He gagged once, then slumped to the floor.

Yablonski's right hand instinctively curled; his whole body quivered with rage. He scowled at the pistol Coogan was leveling on his head.

"Pick up your friend," Coogan said.

The guard released his hold and Yablonski's hands dropped to the floor to break his fall. Anger rippled through him again and he stared at the waving pistol only a yard away. He could make it in one leap, but he knew the bastard was just aching to shoot him.

He dragged Hammond halfway to his feet and looked right into Coogan's eyes.

Coogan smiled and prodded him with the pistol. They began to walk back through the plant, one security man in the lead and the other in the rear. Hammond was a dead weight, but Yablonski didn't mind. He was contemplating revenge.

They re-entered the shed. Coogan threw on the work lights and marched Hammond and Yablonski back aboard the *Sturman*. He took them up to the bridge and opened the door, sending them in with the two armed guards.

He picked up Hammond's head by grabbing a tuft of hair and asked coldly, "Where's McCarthy?"

Hammond blinked, his jaw slack and throbbing. "I ate him," he said thickly.

Coogan flung him aside and marched out.

Hammond had a fleeting image of Coogan doing the same thing to Jan, flinging her away like a rag doll after doing other things to her, unspeakable, unthinkable things. Hammond went on thinking about it. It kept him mad—and that would keep him alive.

Coogan returned a few minutes later with McCarthy, who had a tennis-ball-sized lump on his head. Coogan's jaw worked, but he said nothing about the dead guard in the captain's cabin.

They were silent for nearly ten minutes, eyeing each other across the bridge—Hammond and Yablonski forced to sit in a corner of the deck, while Coogan leaned against the engine room telegraph stand. McCarthy paced impatiently.

Footsteps echoed along the main deck below, then clanged on the ladder up to the bridge. The hatch opened and Traben looked in uneasily. He entered carrying a doctor's bag, which he set with conspicuous significance at Coogan's feet.

Francis Bloch stepped in after him, gazed impassively at his prisoners, and shook his head in regret. "I had hoped we would work out our differences amicably," he said. "But your actions have made that impossible."

Hammond sighed. "I hope we're not going to get another lecture."

"Hardly." Bloch smiled. "What would be the point?"

"As long as we both realize that you're not in this to relieve the world of anything but dollars."

"I never said I was different, Commander. It's my way of going about it that's unique."

"No, it isn't." Hammond groaned. It hurt to speak. "You're like any other thief. It's just the scale of it that's frightening."

"I'd like to know something," Yablonski said, then waited for complete attention. "What were you intending to use that device in the satellite for?"

Bloch continued to smile as he replied, "A hole card, Mr. Yablonski. I've spent years perfecting something I believe I can handle better than anyone else. When it's brought out in the open, there's going to be uproar about how it was financed. If anyone tries to come in and take it away from me, I want the ability to protect myself—and I want it immediately apparent *how*."

There was silence, then Yablonski continued, playing dumb, "I don't get it. So you've got a receiving station in space. So what?"

Hammond gave a cracked laugh, then said dryly, "It's simple. He's going to put his satellite into orbit, then teleport some kind of nuclear device up to it. Probably got little gnomes building it in some back room right now."

Bloch shook his head sympathetically. "It pains me, Commander, to see such a bright man throw away a promising future. You've added up one and one too many times."

"I just did it again," said Hammond. "You'll have to build another satellite. The present one is a *wash*. Forgive the pun."

Bloch shrugged. "It'll take some time to fix."

"Rebuild," Hammond corrected.

"You've actually set the Navy back, not us. We just won't be able to deliver their satellite on time. But in any case, what have you accomplished? You're not going to be around when it's launched."

He turned to Coogan. "They're all yours."

Bloch moved to the door, held it open for Traben, who shook his head and said, "I want to be sure."

Bloch nodded and went out. Hammond listened for the footsteps retreating down the ladder and across the deck.

"Okay, boys," Coogan said. "Up against the wall."

The security men hoisted Hammond and Yablonski up and threw them face first against the aft bulkhead.

"Take off your shirts," Coogan ordered. "Come on!"

Slowly they complied, stripping down to the waist. Hammond looked at his belly. It was bruised and aching.

"Okay, turn around."

They turned and Coogan studied them, his eyes glinting in the weak light. He pushed himself away from the engine stand and reached down for the black bag.

"You first, wise guy," Coogan said, and came over to Hammond. One of the security men grabbed Hammond's arms and pinned them behind his back. Coogan opened the bag and drew out a teleporting harness, like the one he had shown them attached to his body. He held it up for Hammond to inspect and smiled.

"This is going to be an interesting experience for you, Hammond." Coogan strapped the neck-piece under Hammond's jaw. He ran the extension wires down each arm and fastened them with little squares of masking tape which he tore from a roll.

"See how simple it is? We'll have you all dressed up and ready to go in just a moment. McCarthy! You take care of the other one."

McCarthy stepped forward, snatched another harness from the bag, and strapped it to Yablonski, while the second guard held him fast.

Coogan finished running the last wire down from the neck strap to the pancake computer he was taping to Hammond's side.

"Where are you sending us?" Hammond asked.

"Where?" Coogan laughed.

There was something about the force of that laugh that sent a chill up Hammond's back.

McCarthy laughed, too.

"He wants to know where!" Coogan roared. "Why, bless me for a fool, Hammond. I really don't *know* where you're going! You see"—he pushed his face close to Hammond's—"we didn't bother pre-setting a station for you. You're just not going to land! You're going to *disappear*, Commander, into *thin air*!"

He looked into Hammond's eyes, eagerly anticipating a terrified plea. But Hammond was sizing up his chances of getting to the hatch before the guards could raise their weapons.

McCarthy was chuckling. Yablonski's lips curled in an animal snarl. McCarthy poked him in the Adam's apple and his head snapped back. He recovered, his jaw quivering as he glared at the doctor. He muttered, "Come on, come on . . ." goading McCarthy.

But McCarthy didn't fall for it. He finished taping the harness and stood back. "I'm not about to blow this," he said.

"You better not," Coogan said, then ordered Hammond to turn around. When Hammond didn't comply right away, the guards whipped him into position and again shoved his face against the bulkhead. They did the same to Yablonski, who got just a glimpse of the binnacle light starting to glow and wondered why . . .

Coogan bent over Hammond's side and punched a code into the computer. He stood back, waiting for McCarthy to do the same with Yablonski. Then he snapped, "Put your shirts back on. We wouldn't want you to catch cold."

The guards handed them their shirts and Coogan waited patiently until they were buttoned up. Then he said, "I'd like to say this is going to be painless, gentlemen, but I just don't know."

"You said you were businessmen," Hammond reminded him, "not murderers."

"We're flexible."

Hammond stared at the bulkhead in front of him. He closed his eyes, anticipating the slight pressure at the back of his neck that would send him whirling into oblivion. *Jan, Christ, I'm sorry*. Then he heard Coogan's voice:

"Dr. Traben, would you do the honors?"

Hammond sensed excitement next to him as he listened to Traben coming closer. He slid a look at Yablonski, who met his gaze and mouthed something. His face wrinkled frantically, and he cast furtive glances at the ship's compass behind them.

The guards released them and stepped out of the way as Traben stopped behind Hammond.

Yablonski tensed to make his move.

Hammond threw a quick look at the ship's compass and saw the binnacle light glowing brightly. The generator for the engine room pedestal?

He heard someone grunt.

Traben cursed, "Christ Almighty!"

Hammond looked at them. They were all staring at him. Had Traben pressed the button? Was he already on his way? He became aware of a strange feeling creeping up his legs, a vibration, at first gentle then increasing, mounting steadily. Then Yablonski grabbed his arm and Hammond followed his eyes to the bulkhead they were braced against.

A hole was opening up in the steel plates.

They could see molecules jumping and swirling away from a widening edge, and on the deck near their feet a second hole opened up and spread outward, radiating up toward their faces.

They whirled and saw more of the bridge beginning to dissolve in similar spreading patches. A portion of the starboard bulkhead had already evaporated.

The two armed guards panicked. They stepped backwards, flattening against the port side, raising their weapons as if to ward off evil.

Traben leaped back to the huge square window, his face convulsed with alarm.

Coogan stood petrified, gaping as the deck disintegrated beneath his feet.

Traben yelled, "Something's wrong! She's recycling! We've got to get off!"

Hammond sprang at Coogan, who reached for his gun but was too late. Hammond brought him down hard. Under their bodies, wood melted like a spreading pool of ink, forming a translucent hole. The ship's machinery was exposed below.

Hammond wrestled Coogan for the gun. He felt claw-like fingers grabbing his side.

McCarthy bolted for the door. Yablonski plunged after him, crashing through the swinging steel hatch. It clanged back against the bulkhead. He saw McCarthy fleeing down the ladder and rushed to catch him, shuddered to a stop as invisibility seeped up to consume the bridge deck.

The ladder had disappeared. He knew it was there, but he couldn't see it—

McCarthy was already below on the super deck. He had jumped off the ladder when it began to dissolve in his hands. He stumbled forward, groping along the three-inch cannon for support. Yablonski forced himself to step across the vanishing gun deck as he prepared to leap over the shield—

At the bridge port, Traben saw Yablonski hesitate, then make that leap into space. The shield forward of the gun deck eroded suddenly to a small patch of metal, giving him a glimpse of Yablonski scrambling after McCarthy. Traben gaped as more of the ship dwindled to shreds of steel and rivets.

Behind him, Coogan was still wrapped in a struggle with Hammond, trying to reach pressure points—

One of the two guards glanced at the bulkhead he was flattened against and saw it yawn open. A convulsive shudder tore through his body and he screamed. He screamed again as another hole opened in the deck directly beneath his partner's feet, then expanded to devour the man's legs.

The second guard shrieked in abject fear.

The forward section of the bridge shimmered and evaporated. Traben flung himself out of the way.

The first guard bolted for the new opening and tried to dive to the deck below through what he presumed to be empty space. The window shattered around him and he crashed to the gun deck, his body splintered by invisible shards of glass.

The second guard remained rooted where he stood, his cries becoming insane laughter as the emptiness shot up his body, until he was reduced to nothing more than a gaping mouth echoing a maddened howl throughout the compartment. . . .

Hammond kicked with all his strength and worked Coogan's body away from his, shoving until he trapped that grasping hand under his ribs. With both hands free, he bent Coogan's gun arm back at the elbow, the wrong way. Coogan grunted and released the gun. Hammond rolled away quickly and came to a crouch with the gun leveled. He stopped to see what was going on and froze, paralyzed with awe.

Coogan frantically clamped himself to the small patch of deck that was still visible.

For a costly moment, Hammond was blind to Traben, standing directly behind him, staring at the gun. Hammond was looking at the glowing binnacle light and the gyrating compass. The ship was being overcome by a wildly fluctuating field.

Traben reached out and grabbed Hammond in a bear hug, pinning his arms to his sides. With the strength of desperation, Traben hauled him toward the open space that had been the bridge window. One visible piece of glass hung in the emptiness; Traben was determined to impale Hammond on it. Hammond tried to get the gun around—

Coogan saw his chance and lurched toward him. Hammond fired from the hip. Coogan took the bullet just under his collarbone and toppled forward like a falling wall. He landed in a push-up position on the invisible deck and saw his hands become transparent shadows. Strength and fear kept him from succumbing to the shock of his wound. He looked up painfully at Hammond, his teeth clenched and his face contorted.

Hammond gathered his waning strength and hurled himself backwards, smashing Traben against the disappearing helm stand. As soon as he broke Traben's grip, Hammond stumbled away. Then he felt himself pressed up against something soft, yielding, yet invisible. He dropped the gun in the nightmare that followed. He touched soft, giving flesh, and a form spread into visibility outward from his hand, the molecules swirling into vague shape.

Traben flung himself at Hammond again, trying to regain his hold, yelling for Coogan to do something. Hammond ignored him and clutched the flesh-form: it unfolded from his touch both upwards and downwards at the same time.

"The button!" yelled Coogan.

Hammond felt Traben's fingers clawing up his back, inching toward the device strapped to his neck— He groped with his free hand to push Traben's face away.

He glanced down and saw Coogan crawling painfully across the transparent deck. Coogan stared up at Hammond, but his hatred gave way to bloodcurdling horror when he realized there were not two men struggling above him—there were three.

The new face was unfamiliar to him: pallid and ghostly, the eyes staring out of another world. Coogan saw Hammond's fingers clutching the third man's chest and the molecules settling into place. He gave an involuntary gasp as he realized the third man was *becoming visible.*

"Traben!" Coogan screamed.

Traben's fingers still fumbled to reach the button that would send Hammond to oblivion. At Coogan's scream, his eyes flew to the man looming only a foot away, the face an overpowering shock to his memory. He released Hammond with a shout of disbelief:

"SARTOG!"

On the loading platform, Francis Bloch sensed something wrong, something in the way the lights and shadows were flickering. But by the time he turned back to see, the *Sturman* was dissolving—in great, expanding patches, like paper consumed by fire.

Bloch broke into a run, charging back up the narrow platform to the deck, not knowing what he could do to stop the horror, realizing once he reached the flat level that there was no hope.

* * *

McCarthy fell to the main deck, into the forward gun mount enclosure. He scrambled to his feet and limped toward something still visible, a piece of the enclosure on the starboard side. If he could feel along the edges till he was out, he could find the side and jump to the dock.

But Yablonski was after him in a headlong rush, jumping from the blast shield to the deck, then scurrying monkey-like, his hands flung ahead to keep him from crashing into anything. The light began to go dim and things that had faded completely now swam back into view as transparent, outlined shadows.

McCarthy heard Yablonski behind him and whirled. Yablonski hurled himself at McCarthy and they landed in a tangle of flailing arms and legs. Yablonski got a leg-lock on McCarthy's middle and held him down, then pounded his face into the deck, hard.

McCarthy continued to flounder, but the strength had gone out of him.

Yablonski looked up at the bridge and his heart pounded with dread at the incredible sight of decking, bulkheads, machinery, instrumentation, guns—everything—rapidly sinking into a vague, shadowy outline.

The overhead work lights were fading; everything outside the ship was darkening to black. The ship itself seemed to be gathering for a final jump across space.

Through the shattered port on the bridge, Yablonski could see Hammond and Traben in a standoff and, between them—Sartog!

"Hang onto them!" Yablonski yelled. "We're going zero!"

He threw his arms over McCarthy and held him down, flattening both their bodies firmly to the deck.

Hammond heard the command and hesitated, undecided which of these villains to grab hold of. Traben was just a couple of yards away, shaking catatonically at Sartog's presence.

Then he saw Coogan edging toward where the gun had fallen. It was invisible now. But Coogan groped with trembling fingers. Hammond dove to the deck and grabbed him. Coogan snapped around with a snarl of frustration and pain, blood oozing from the wound high in his chest.

"Traben!" Hammond shouted. "Here!"

But Traben raised his hands and with a madman's force drove himself forward, intending to shove Sartog off into the black space beyond the open port. He never expected Sartog's hand to come up in a hideous gesture of welcome.

Traben's Cossack yell turned into a howl of terror as he ran right into the arm, felt it encircle his body, grasping for the contact that would bring its owner back among the living—

Traben back-pedaled, trying to escape the monster, but Sartog's grip was too firm. He had been hanging in limbo too long to be left there again. Traben's momentum was enough to carry them backwards until they plunged off the bridge together into black space, out of the force field.

For a fleeting second, they hung in mid-air, having lost contact with the deck. Then a convulsion of energy from within tore their molecules apart! Both bodies twisted into impossible shapes, then became wisps of matter dissipating into space.

Coogan and Hammond saw it all just as the ship made a final rush into blackness. Coogan thrust himself to his feet and backed away, terrified, pulling Hammond with him, going deeper into the compartment—

"Hang onto him!" Hammond heard Yablonski shout from below, and then all the vague outlines, even his own, went black once again.

Bloch shrank back, aghast, until he was flat against the wall of the shed. He watched the destroyer fade from sight, his dreams disappearing with it.

25

He could see nothing, but Hammond still shut his eyes and tried to tune out the sensations that swarmed around him. Motion buffeted his body and a retreating wave of pressure dropped into his center of gravity like surf pulling back from the shore, leaving him at peace. The ringing in his ears faded, to be replaced by crashing sounds, water surging around metal and metal straining rivets with ear-splitting creaks.

His eyes sprang open and he found himself flattened against transparent wood, his right arm up in the air, clutching what must have been Coogan's wrist; he didn't look to be sure.

The deck, regaining definition, seemed to pitch and plunge under him. He lay transfixed, palming the wood with his left hand, pressing his cheek hard against it to assure himself of solidity.

Then he swung his head the other way and looked out at where the square window should have been. Glass, broken and sharded, jutted up outlined in the frame, and beyond he could make out darkness. He shuddered with fear. Had they passed into oblivion? Had he and the *Sturman* by some fluke of an already monstrous process been hurled into a different dimension, a limbo from which there was no return?

No. The darkness wasn't as black, wasn't as nightlike as what they had just been through. It was broken by great rounded, drifting lumps . . . clouds.

They were outdoors. It was night and those were rain clouds, thunderheads, the kind he had seen that afternoon —in Philadelphia.

Dimly, Hammond became conscious of a ghastly screaming, which, for a moment, he mistook for an echo in his mind. But it was real and close by. His mind was still fuzzy and the ship wasn't quite solid yet, but somebody was gurgling horrible sounds practically in his ear.

Who? The guard who had gone mad? No, Hammond could see his unconscious form slumped in a corner. Hammond tried to raise himself and found he needed both hands to do it, but he couldn't pull his right hand free from whatever it was holding. He became aware of a tingling in those fingers, a weight pressing down on his wrist, stiffening his hand, and there was still that awful rasping shriek in his ear.

His head snapped up and he took in the whole hideous picture in one movement.

Coogan's mouth was open in a scream, his face blue and bulging as if about to burst, and the howling that tore from his throat was enough to appall the dead. His body wriggled pitifully as it blended in with the aft bulkhead of the bridge. He had stepped back too far and come through the spatial transfer to be embedded in the steel wall.

Hammond had to force his fingers to release their grip on Coogan. He couldn't understand why it required so much effort, until he looked at his arm: it seemed to be swallowed up where molecules of steel swirled into place around it.

He couldn't control himself. His head and shoulders were gripped by convulsions of terror as he pulled with all his might to free that hand. Suction tore at his skin and rubbed the top layer right off, until it was raw and welling up blood. But he had the wrist and the meat of the hand free. He gathered his courage for one final pull. It was like trying to pop his hand out of a milk bottle.

Finally it came, with hardly a sound. He fell back and saw the hole close into place after it. He lay sprawled on the deck, breathless, still quivering from the overpowering pressure—but it was nothing compared to what Coogan was suffering.

He couldn't tear his eyes away from that huge, bull-like figure protruding from a solid wall, sputtering, coughing blood, his eyes pleading for help, his body convulsing in paroxysms of strain, concentrating every effort into raising one arm—pushing, thrusting it out of solid steel. Constricted, blackened fingers poked through, wiggling.

Coogan's mouth gaped open, a tortured maw. His lips

were distended back into his cheeks, his teeth had clenched so hard he had bitten through the tip of his tongue; his eyes were angled painfully downward at those tiny twitching fingers, as if just getting the hand out would be enough.

The next scream was his last. It began deep in his throat and rolled upwards to snarl rage and defeat.

Coogan's protruding belly, one knee, both shoulders, and his head all seemed to jerk upwards in a final frenzied spasm, then the steel closed tightly about his muscles and he sagged.

His head drooped, the eyes stayed open and staring, reflecting the shock of death.

Quiet now.

Except for the distant sounds of water, and metal rubbing against metal.

And men shouting. Feet trampling on a deck somewhere outside.

The *Sturman*'s motion subsided as she settled back into her place at the end of the group of destroyer escorts.

She had come home.

Hammond stared once more up at Coogan's body, imprisoned permanently into the bulkhead like a gruesome whim of decor.

Then he rose to his feet. A warning nagged at him, something that cried to be done. His mind raced, trying to think what it was. He dragged himself to the shattered window and looked out, relieved to feel slick mist and cold air sweep across his tortured features once again.

It was Philadelphia. There were the other DEs. And there was McWilliams.

The lieutenant leaped across the space from the next DE even before the yardbirds got the *Sturman* secured once again. He stood warily on the main deck and glanced back at the crowd of men he had brought out; prominent among them were the enormous man with the beard, and the pacing admiral.

McWilliams gasped as Yablonski rose out of the darkness and hauled McCarthy to his feet. The doctor stared around at the ship, the clouds, the droplets of rain, and the gawking men with spotlights jabbing into his eyes.

"My God," he said. "My God . . ."

Yablonski flung him to the first Marine who jumped

across, then sagged to the deck and sat down, exhausted. A huge pair of legs loomed in front of him; he looked up into the bewildered face of John Allen Smith.

They had never met before. Smitty's eyelids closed in suspicion and he asked, "You're . . . Yablonski?"

Cas nodded.

"Where's Hammond?"

He pointed up at the bridge and they all saw Hammond standing in the open window. Then they heard him shout a curse, turn on his heel and lunge for the hatch.

He had remembered it. He had glanced down at the compass and had seen the binnacle light still glowing, the magnetic card deflecting.

He piled down the ladder and ignored the men up forward, ignored the lights and the commotion, his entire being bent on one final, absolutely essential purpose. He threw himself through the aft hatch and raced down the passageway in total darkness, crashing into bulkheads and open hatchways. He nearly fell down the companionway while fumbling for the ladder; then he dropped down the rungs three at a time. His feet rang on the steel platform as he burst through the last hatch.

There were no lights. His pupils widened but he could see nothing. He should have called to the men on deck, warned them to get off because the teleporting generator had become erratic and could start itself going any second again and send them all careening forever through time and space.

His hand throbbed painfully as he fumbled down the last ladder and groped his way between the engines, trying to find the generator. How was he going to turn it off in complete darkness? Where was it? *Oh, Christ, where the hell is it?*

Footsteps above, running along the corridors. He hadn't identified himself. What if they thought he was part of McCarthy's gang? What if they didn't stop to ask questions? What if McWilliams hadn't seen it was he who jumped off the bridge and shot aft to that hatch? What if they came in here brandishing M-16s with infrared sights?

The thousand terrifying fears racing through his brain multiplied the moment he caught sight of that weak red glow up ahead.

Oh, God, no! It's still on! Where was the generator? He had to find it—

The hell with it. He made for the glow. There was enough light to see the pedestal dimly. And the footsteps were coming closer, ringing on the metal behind him.

An ax—he needed an ax. He remembered an emergency cabinet somewhere on this side, behind the pedestal, in the open space between the pump tanks and the oil-drainage sumps. He tripped over the cables in front of the pedestal and reached down. He pulled at them, tugged with all the strength he had remaining. They wouldn't budge. He stumbled a few more steps and groped along the bulkhead. The cabinet—he had it. He ripped the door open and the alarm went off, a great deafening bell which he knew would draw those Marines with their weapons.

He fumbled past the extinguisher and felt his fingers close about a handle. He yanked and whirled around. The glow was growing brighter. Was it activating itself or was Bloch activating it from San Pedro? Hammond held the ax in front of his body and felt his way for a full agonizing minute. He reached it; he groped for the cables, then raised the ax and swung with all his might.

He missed. The blade bit into steel decking. He felt again with the edge, pinpointing the rubber insulation. The glow brightened and suddenly he could see what he was doing, but the humming had started again and vibrations were coursing through his feet.

He swung once more and this time the blade took a healthy bite out of the cables.

The lights snapped on abruptly and he was paralyzed in a back-swing, blinded by the glare.

"Freeze!" someone yelled, and Hammond froze, but only long enough to recover his vision. He glanced around and saw a Marine standing by the generator with a flashlight in one hand and an M-16 in the other; more Marines were piling onto the platform above.

Hammond pointed the ax at the pedestal to show the Marine. It was glowing fiercely. The Marine was suddenly conscious of the vibration shaking his legs. In his confusion, he dropped his light, made a grab for it with his other hand, and lost the rifle.

Hammond swung again. Again and again and again, he chopped through those cables until they split open and a hundred strands of wire protruded from each wound.

The vibrations stopped, the glow diminished, and silence fell.

"Motherfucker," Hammond whispered, and dropped the ax.

Hammond arrived back on the main deck flanked by two Marines, who had no idea who they were hustling around, and didn't care. But Hammond didn't give a damn, either. He wasn't about to waste what little remained of his energy in useless explanations. On the way up the corridor, he had ripped at the tapes holding the wires attached to his arms, pulled the pancake computer off his side, and unstrapped the neck harness. He gave the device to one of the Marines, again without explanation.

Yablonski was sitting on the deck. McCarthy stood forlornly in the grip of another Marine.

Smitty and Gault descended from the bridge and came to Hammond, their faces dazed and ashen. McWilliams remained above, staring at the body embedded in the wall.

"That's the most gruesome thing I've ever seen," said Gault, glancing back as two more Marines lowered the limp form of the guard who had lost his mind. His eyes were glazed; he was muttering gibberish and a line of drool bubbled from the corner of his mouth.

Hammond shivered.

"There was another one in the captain's cabin—with a broken neck," said Smitty, looking at Hammond for an explanation.

"Terminal bad luck." Hammond shrugged.

Yablonski stripped off his shirt and yanked at the wires taped to his body. When he had unbuckled the neck strap, he tossed the whole thing to Gault.

"Here's a clever little toy for you," he said.

"What is it?" Gault asked, turning it over in his hands.

"It's the device they used to teleport themselves from one place to another," Hammond explained. "And it's manufactured by our friend Mr. F.P. Bloch and the late Dr. Edmond Traben."

"Late?"

"Very. I would suggest that you do something right away about pinning down Bloch. We left him at MTL in San Pedro, but if he's wearing one of those goodies, he could be anywhere now—Boston, Tokyo, even his own bathroom in Georgetown."

Smitty smiled grimly. "It's all right. We're closing in."

Hammond looked over at McCarthy and said to Gault, "What about Jan and Mrs. Yablonski?"

McCarthy didn't even flinch.

"They're all right," said Gault.

Hammond relaxed. "Hear that, Doctor?" he said. Then he waved his arm at the *Sturman*. "Traben never got the bugs out, did he? She wasn't supposed to come back to Philadelphia. You're not as close to success as you thought you were."

McCarthy eyed him sullenly. "There are still the aftereffects, Hammond. How do you know they won't catch up with you?"

Hammond glanced at Yablonski, who stiffened, then glared at McCarthy with unconcealed hatred. They were squared off, eyes flicking at each other.

With a sudden lunge, McCarthy made his bid for freedom, yanking his arm away from one Marine, knocking down another, preparing to spring across to the next deck.

Yablonski kicked the legs out from under him and pounced. McCarthy sprawled on the deck. Yablonski pressed his face down by squeezing the back of his neck.

McCarthy screamed a reverberating, "NO!" but his plea trailed off into an echo as Yablonski's thumb pressed down on the button and activated the teleporting harness.

McCarthy blinked out.

Smitty and Gault shrank back, staring at the empty spot on the deck where McCarthy had been. Yablonski was left clutching at thin air, staring down at his hand.

There was a long, stunned silence before the Marines began muttering among themselves. Admiral Gault recovered from the shock and whirled to yell instructions about security, warning everybody to keep his mouth shut.

Hammond pulled Yablonski to his feet and muttered, "You did that deliberately."

After a moment of grim consideration, Yablonski's eyes met Hammond's. He said softly, "Prove it."

McWilliams appeared holding Yablonski's jacket and Hammond's holster, which he had retrieved from the captain's cabin. He rocked on his heels between the two of them.

Hammond gave him a look of genuine gratitude, and said, "Thanks." McWilliams grinned broadly.

The last thing Hammond would remember about that

night would be glancing over to starboard and seeing Smitty and Gault huddled in conference. From then on, during the helicopter ride to Bethesda Naval Hospital and afterwards, Gault did not meet his gaze again. The admiral was avoiding him.

By the time he was safely tucked into a private room in the security ward, Hammond was positive that another shoe was waiting to drop.

26

"Nicky? Are you all right?"

"Sure. I'm just stuck here in Bethesda for a few days. And I mean stuck. I feel like a pincushion. Yablonski and I have two needle-happy doctors. They visit us six times daily; other than that, we're in isolation."

"Why?"

He hesitated on the phone, wanting to keep the conversation light. "What have they told you?"

"Just that you're both in hospital."

Hammond shook his head and silently cursed Smitty and Gault. But at least they had assured him that Jan and Mrs. Yablonski were all right, that despite McCarthy's threat, no attempt had been made to penetrate MAGIC. Relieved, Hammond and Yablonski had decided it was all a bluff and, as long as Bloch's organization was being rounded up, no further danger existed.

Except the danger to themselves from possible after-effects.

"Nicky?" said Jan again, tentatively.

"Yeah, I'm here. Listen, I'll probably be out in a couple of days and I'll want to see you . . . before you go home."

There was a long silence. Hammond twisted the telephone cord.

"Don't chase me away so fast."

He wanted to feel relief, but he was too concerned about something else. "Jan," he said, "I want you to understand why I feel hesitant . . . about us. I've just been through the same thing that happened to your husband in 1953. There may be residual effects. . . . That's why we're here . . . under observation."

He paused for a reply. There was nothing.

"Jan, I can't saddle you with another Harold Fletcher."

"What are you talking about?" she said quietly, very much under control.

"Well, I'm not going to have nightmares, mental problems, but I might have other things . . . hard to cope with."

"Like what?"

"That's what we're trying to find out."

"Hammond, is this a brush-off?"

"No!" he protested. "No. I want to see you. I don't want you to go home until I see you."

"What makes you think I'm so anxious to go home?"

She was calmer than he was. And more determined, he sensed.

"You sound like Admiral Gault," she said. "He's been trying to get rid of me, too."

"What?"

"He came to us and said you were both at Bethesda, you were okay, but you couldn't be disturbed; and we should wait until you contact us. He wanted to send Mrs. Yablonski back to Cotuit and me back to Los Angeles." Now her voice broke. "Can you imagine what it was like—the two of us sitting here for three days going crazy wondering about you?"

"I'm sorry," he said. But he was more angry than sorry. Why should Gault deliberately try to put three thousand miles between Hammond and Jan? Only one possible explanation: he didn't want them together.

"How did you talk him out of it?" he asked.

"We threatened to yell our heads off." Hammond smiled to himself. "There's something else," she added. "They've brought in another guest. I just got a brief glimpse when he came in; he's been locked up ever since."

"Who is it?"

"You remember our host at the party Friday night?"

Hammond was stunned. "Bloch? Are you sure?"

"Yes," she said, and her voice dropped. "There's been a parade of strange people going in and out, along with your Admiral Gault and Mr. Smith."

It was puzzling. Why hadn't they handed Bloch over to the FBI? Certainly, they had enough on him now.

"Jan, can you sit tight for a few more days? We have a lot to talk about."

"Yes," she said. "We do."

When they weren't being tested for after-effects or jabbed full of needles, Hammond and Yablonski made elaborate plans for a fishing trip, to include two cases of beer, Mrs. Yablonski, and Jan. Hammond was in good spirits except at night, when he and Cas both lay awake anticipating the possibility of drifting through a wall or vanishing in their beds. . . .

On the afternoon following his conversation with Jan, Hammond got a call from Cohen. He had attempted to trace Dr. Kurtnauer in Israel, and until three days ago had been totally unsuccessful. Then Smitty stepped in, brought his full authority to bear. As Cohen explained it, the Navy Department was wildly anxious to speak with Kurtnauer.

"But he died in 1973," said Cohen. Hammond was silent a moment, feeling sorry for the old Austrian whose scientific idealism had wreaked so much havoc.

Hammond thanked Cohen for all his help, then hung up and mulled over the government's sudden revival of interest in Dr. Kurtnauer. Was it just to tie up loose ends?

He shook his head suspiciously. You're a detective, Hammond, he told himself. So detect.

By Monday, nothing had developed: no uncontrolled vanishing or disorientation, no residual effects at all. Hammond concluded that Traben and company had developed a cleaner process over the years.

Hammond and Yablonski were discharged from the hospital on Tuesday morning and flown by helicopter back to the Pentagon. They were taken directly to Smitty's office. They were alone, just the three of them, no Admiral Gault. Hammond realized he hadn't seen or heard from Gault in over a week.

"We have a task force out locating the rest of McCarthy's patients. Cohen and Slater will be handling the treatment from now on," said Smitty.

Yablonski nodded gratefully.

"We're questioning all the people at MTL. Except for a few inner-circle types, generally they didn't know what they were working on. And we don't want them to find out."

"What are you going to do with them?" asked Hammond.

Smitty fingered some papers. "Don't quite know yet. MTL still has a lot of legitimate contracts to fulfill. We'd like to keep their organization intact. . . ."

"*You* would?" Hammond said. "That's a private company."

Smitty smiled. "MTL is so far in the hole to the U.S. Government for misappropriated funds that they might as well enlist in the Navy."

Hammond didn't find it funny. "And Bloch?" he asked.

"I'm sure he'll be very repentant."

Hammond's eyes narrowed. Smitty was playing a game. "Don't tell me you haven't nailed him yet."

Smitty's eyes flicked to Yablonski. He said nothing.

Hammond bounced out of his chair. "Come on, Smitty! He's staying at a well-known sanctuary in Herndon, and Father Gault is hearing his confession every three hours! Now what are you doing about all those stations Bloch set up around the world?"

Smitty's gaze traveled to Yablonski again, and he sighed. "We're trying to set up a deal with him."

"Deal?" barked Yablonski.

"What the hell does that mean?" Hammond asked.

"You don't think we're going to let it slip out of our hands, do you? For the time being, it's in everyone's best interests that none of this be made public, so I will of course expect you both to uphold our policy of no discussion on this matter—with anyone. For Nick, it's an order, Mr. Yablonski; as for you, I'll have to depend on your good judgment."

There was dark silence for a moment, then Hammond spoke. "What sort of deal are you setting up with that sonofabitch?"

"We might give him a little more time to perfect it, under our supervision."

Yablonski was very still.

"What part of it?" asked Hammond. "The teleportation business? The weapons guidance system? The little pedestal in space?"

"All of it," Smitty said quietly.

Hammond stared at him, then exploded: "That bastard's going free! And you're going to be partners with him!"

Smitty shook his head and flashed a confident smile. "No, we're not."

Hammond had heard him more convincing.

"Look," Smitty continued, "I grant you that Mr. Bloch has proven to be a colossal villain, but some of the things he had in the works are eminently practical. Think of it this way: we've put a stop to his lust for power. That's all over and done with. He'll be working on this for only one reward: his freedom."

"What about the murders!" Hammond shouted. "Fletcher, Rinehart—"

"Can't prove he had anything to do with them. He'll maintain that was Traben's end."

"You know it's not!"

"Nick," Smitty began patiently, "this is more than one man's bid for supremacy. It directly affects the economic and military structure of the entire nation. We can't just padlock the doors and forget about it!"

"But it doesn't work!" snarled Hammond. "That ship was not supposed to return to Philadelphia! After all these years, they still couldn't control the process! It's too unstable! If Kurtnauer were alive, he would tell you the same thing!" He leaned over Smitty's desk, seething with anger. "Do you want another generation of Fletchers and Olivelys?"

Smitty was silent. His gaze shifted to Yablonski, who looked back at him sternly. "We're willing to take the risk," Smitty said casually.

Hammond sank back into his chair, weighing those words, reflecting on how strange it was that Bloch had been right in his suspicions of the government and what they would do with Thin Air if they ever gained control. In truth, they were not so far removed from Bloch himself. Given the potential of the process, should it fall under the control of *any* one person or nation?

Hammond crossed looks with Yablonski and sensed something more primitive in his reaction: cynical acceptance of betrayal.

Yablonski got up quietly and moved to the door. Hammond stared at Smitty, not quite knowing what was expected of him. Smitty saved him the trouble, accompanying him to the door and once more admonishing them both to be discreet.

"Do you really think you're going to keep this quiet?" Hammond asked. "With all the people who've been involved?"

"We hope so," said Smitty.

On the way down the hall, Yablonski muttered to Hammond, "Too bad Dr. McCarthy is unavailable. They'd probably have made a deal for his services, too."

They stopped into the NIS office and Ensign Just-Ducky informed them there was a staff car waiting at the Mall Entrance to take Yablonski back to Herndon so he could pick up his wife; they would be put on a plane at Dulles and flown back to Cape Cod.

Hammond accompanied Yablonski down to the Mall Entrance, his bitterness growing. "They want to do exactly what Bloch would have done. Use this thing like a political baseball bat—whip everyone into line! Some country gives us trouble, the Secretary of State merely says, 'You want teleportation? Get in step!' For God's sake, Cas, even if they never perfect it, the *potential* is always there. They can drop *hints*."

Yablonski grunted. "Let 'em. All I want is to get my wife away from them. Back where we belong."

Yablonski slipped into the car and stuck out a hand. Hammond shook it.

"Call me for fishing?"

"You bet."

"Soon?"

Hammond nodded.

"Want me to give Jan a message?"

"No." Hammond paused. "I'll call her before you get there."

Yablonski didn't know quite how to say goodbye. "Hammond," he finally managed, "thanks."

He slumped back in the seat and the car drove off. Hammond stood alone outside the Pentagon. Tuesday. He checked his watch. 11:20. He wondered if he should go back to work. His eyes moved up to the sprawling complex and he wondered about his future, about everyone's future.

A Navy limousine rolled up behind him and several men emerged. Hammond recognized civilian agents from the Headquarters Division of NIS, along with Admiral Gault. They were escorting retired Admiral Corso in for questioning. Corso still looked dapper, but he moved like the stuffing had been knocked out of him.

Hammond saluted as they passed. Gault returned the gesture automatically, but Corso just looked at Hammond with a mixture of uncertainty and fear.

Gault put Corso in the hands of another officer at the door, then came back to speak with Hammond. "I'd like you to get back on that Okinawa business. Lee Miller called. He's having trouble. Maybe you could fly out there tomorrow—in a few days."

Gault looked at the ground and shuffled, wanting to escape. Finally, he shook his head and apologized, "I'm sorry, Nick. I knew what the Navy had in mind. That night after Bloch's party, Smitty took me into his confidence. Naval Intelligence figured out what Bloch was up to based on your information and the death of Rinehart. They got hold of his book, *A Station in Space*. It's all there, chapter and verse, a whole section on the possible applications of teleportation with orbiting satellites."

Hammond looked up in surprise.

"He wasn't such an impossible old kook after all," said Gault. "It was *his* idea, only he never knew they were using it."

Hammond choked. "You mean *you knew?* And you just let me blunder around?"

"Intelligence figured it out Saturday morning. We had the information just before that meeting with Corso. We were going to conduct our own raid. You simply beat us to it."

"Good for me."

"Look, Nick . . . what the hell am I apologizing for? I'm the fucking admiral around here."

"Just can't get used to it, can you?"

Gault glared at him. "I'll see you tomorrow."

"No, sir. If it's all the same to you, I've got sixty days' leave coming and I'd like some of it now."

Gault said nothing for a moment, then spoke softly, "You've got it. By the way, Jan Fletcher left MAGIC."

Hammond stiffened.

"This morning. Didn't see any need for protection any longer, so . . ."

"Did she say where she was going?"

"Mentioned that there was a hotel here in Washington more to her liking. Besides, she still had the key. . . . Sorry she didn't work out, Nick."

Gault laid a sympathetic hand on his shoulder, then realized Hammond was smiling. He couldn't understand why.

He parked the Maverick on Thomas Jefferson Street and walked around to the park fronting the canal. A chilly breeze rustled the branches outside his second-story flat and stirred the curtains, her curtains, the ones she had put up more than two years ago. He heard the radio playing soft classical music, her favorite station. It was as if she had never been gone.

He walked across the grass and his shoes crunched on dead leaves. He thought to himself that of all the mistakes one could make with a woman, shutting her out of any portion of one's life was the most serious, especially if she wanted in.

So he tramped up the stairs, realizing that he was going to tell her the rest of the story, everything that had just happened, everything that Smitty wanted him to keep under his hat.

Maybe it wouldn't stop there. Maybe he would go to the *Washington Post* and speak to a couple of hotshot reporters.

There were always other careers.

Keep it under your hat, my ass. He opened the door to his flat. He heard her humming in the kitchen.

He walked right over to the open window and with a loud whoop tore the officer's cap from his head and sailed it out into the canal.

He heard a glass crash to the floor behind him and her voice cursing in surprise, then he walked in and kissed her.